The past is written by the living;
the future, by the dead.

Trigger Warning:

Death

My Name Was Nigel

Memoirs of a Killer Zombie

David O. Zeus

This Edition 1.0 Published by DOZ
ISBN: 978-0-9955917-4-5

Cover illustration (and on inside page) by Michael Hensley, reproduced
here with his kind permission.
Illustration Copyright © Michael Hensley. All Rights Reserved.
See Acknowledgements for further details.
Cover design by Liliana Resende.

For Me

and all who follow me

CONTENTS

Foreword & Introductions

Hello. My name was Nigel. I know that now. I didn't for a while, but it came back to me eventually. As we approach the end or, as I like to say, 'the beginning', I felt I ought to relate my experiences of this last solar cycle. Mine has been a journey experienced by many since my own rising ('birthday', so to speak) so what I will describe will not necessarily be news (or of interest) to many, but there might yet be a select few who would welcome this record. At the very least, this journal will lie as a testament to death by one who rose in the early light-darks. Whether you yourself be Bean or Muter, this is your journey.

At the time of writing this, I don't fully recall how I passed from Bean to Has-Bean to Muter, but I believe it will come back to me before I finish these pages – memories are restored, as I have witnessed in the journey of my colleagues. Not that it matters for I have reached the promised land and shall never return.

My name now shouldn't be 'Nigel', but as no one (Bean or Muter) was there to witness the circumstances of my parentage I am unable to give myself a proper name – a name, in what Beans call, 'death'. Therefore, with a degree of reluctance, I have resorted to my Bean name for the purposes of this document. A name I know only because it was written on a partly-destroyed label attached to my ankle when I rose from that city dump south of the liquid Black Road running through the larger dump, the metropolis of "London".

You should note that at times in this journal I struggle with some of the vocabulary, but I hope this record is understandable to

Bean (or the 'undead' as we like to call them) and Muter alike. Within these pages, I shall use the Bean vocabulary as far as possible. I realise that words mean so much to the Bean and, as you shall see, confusion is embedded in the Bean experience as a whole. They understand so little about their existence ('living' is a falsehood – it is merely 'existing').

My thesis is that it is the Beans who are yet to be born, to rise. Their 'life' is but nothing. The irony is, they know, deep down, the fruitlessness, the meaninglessness, of their existence. So, while I struggle to describe their failings in these pages please forgive me my inconsistencies. If you, reader, are a Bean you might care; for us Muters (the risen) the whole point is, we don't.

As I have said, the events described herein chart my journey of (and to) enlightenment. After all, it would be good to have a record of this next stage in evolution, but if any undead out there come across this memoir before their moment of reckoning, perhaps it will help them too. Know this – we share a destiny. We, the Muters, shall be generous in our welcome. Should you and I meet in death ourselves, please introduce yourself.

With regard to the structure of this journal I would start at the beginning, my 'birthday', but it is still hazy. As you will soon learn, Muters need to give these things a little o'clock. I was alone when I rose, not like today when any Muter usually has others around him or her helping them with their first steps in those early light-darks. I am pleased to say that we now have an extensive community and I have made it my mission to welcome all Muters into eternity. I think it is especially necessary now that there is a war coming. But Death shall prevail. It is our destiny after all.

There are too many kisses and bites to list them all here, but I have included a selection that were typical and illustrate the journey, questions, challenges and lessons of eternal life. If you don't know who you really are, read on. Learn how I lived it and how you can (or rather, *will*) too when I, or one of my Muter colleagues, come knocking.

And so I shall begin.

Having risen, the formative experiences for any Muter are their first feeds. Broadly speaking, the experience of feeding can be broken down into two types: the lovers and the fighters. Fortunately, I was exposed to both in my early light-darks, so my learning was broad and pleasing.

Thank you.

The author, Nigel

1. Rising

My first feed was a strange affair. I say 'strange', it felt strange at the time, but it is, of course, quite routine now. I had risen from the pile of Has-Beans along with a few other Muters in what appeared to be an enclosed city waste-dump south of the Black Road. In hindsight I think it was part of a disposal unit for Has-Beans that had been partly abandoned. Other Has-Beans (those yet to rise) littered the area. A number of us rose together. My head felt peculiar, but there was in my mind a form of clarity, there were no shades of grey. It was the first spark of an illumination, I suppose, an enlightenment of the senses. My senses were sharp, but an understanding of what I had become was blurred. This would change. During the events that light-dark it was as if I was in the middle of something momentous yet, in terms of my comprehension, several paces behind it (whatever 'it' was). Yet, there was no doubt, I was 'alive', re-born, fresh, a traveller in an undiscovered country.

My colleagues and I scaled the concrete and barbed wire fence surrounding the enclosure. A small part of me noticed that I was not experiencing pain as I scaled the wire and dropped down to the far side. The barbs were puncturing my pale, grey-green flesh but there was no discomfort. I landed hard on the ground, but again experienced no pain. We ran as a group of strangers across the wasteland not knowing where we were headed. As I ran my body too felt different. I was not out of breath. Nor did my thighs burn with the exertion.

We reached what seemed to be long, wide roads in a not-so-residential area of the metropolis, the lights of which twinkled in all directions. Dark block shapes of the Beans' buildings stood hard against the sickly orange glow of the Bean world. Looking at each other one last time in our confused state of mind, we handful of Muters, parted ways and ran off in separate directions. There was no flock instinct, no sense of competition or fear of the unknown. There was no feeling of insecurity or need for companionship. Nothing. Just me.

I ran through darkness. The clarity was both liberating and unsettling, yet I had a desire to seek solitude to gather the thoughts of my addled brain.

I passed through some run-down Bean residential areas and slowed to a walk. I remained strong, energised. Reaching a corner at the dark end of the street I suddenly found myself opposite two young, female Beans chatting nonchalantly as they rounded a corner. They stopped no more than two yards away from me and froze, staring at me in total disbelief.

They took a couple steps back panting in fear. I stepped towards them and tried to vocalise, but, wait, what was the problem? I was unable to articulate the consonants. There was no agility in my tongue and lips. I couldn't push air in a controlled manner past by vocal chords. My attempts probably emerged as breathless grunts, or breathy gasps, but, trust me, words were in there somewhere.

First, one scream, then another. The fat one screamed again and raced back around the corner. My instinct was to follow them, but as I took a step or two forward I was suddenly hit by a massive wave of the Bean's breathy moisture hanging in the air like a cloud of perfume. As I inhaled, I found my whole fleshy form soaked and washed in pleasure. I stood intoxicated. Stunned. For how long I don't know. 'Time o'clock' ceases to become an element, a concept in death. As I later understood, in eternity, units of o'clock literally 'mean' nothing.

The spell of the moment was broken by the sound of heavy footsteps returning towards me from around the corner. A moment later two young, medium-sized male Beans appeared. I don't know what they were expecting or intending to do. Perhaps they were wishing to exhibit a certain Bean masculinity in the expectation that they would be rewarded with mating with the female Beans. Whatever their expectation, the aggression in their brows and intentions exhibited in their pursed lips, fleshy facial muscles and limbs painted in swirls of ink, melted like a candy floss in a fiery furnace when it met a 'dead' Bean with rotting brows and no lips looking straight back at them.

They too took a few steps back. (Beans are forever stepping back.) The street experience on which they built their identity and projected through their stares regressed to Beanling expressions of confusion, fear and bewilderment. I couldn't help but feel sorry for them. In fact, I myself was thrown by the power of my own presence. Whatever the physical changes I had undergone, there seemed to be a distinct advantage. All things being equal, I knew I was the fitter and more predisposed to survive any confrontation, yet it seemed at odds with my hazy recollections of my Bean existence when I would have found myself unnerved in such a potentially aggressive encounter. I felt no fear, curiosity perhaps, but not the fear that oozes out of their little Bean pores.

The two Beans also turned and raced away around the corner, again leaving the perfume of their sweet breath lingering in the air. What was that? What had they been eating or drinking?

I moved on. I needed to think. The smells were new. My desires had evolved. My powers had evolved. I wasn't used to it. I walked onwards into the darkness welcoming it as it welcomed me, like a mother smothering me in loving kisses. The darkness was soft on my rotting tissue, its coolness soothed my evolving nature. I found an empty, boarded-up house at the end of a run-down terrace. I made my way upstairs to a bedroom and sank down in a corner to rest and think.

2. First Feeds: the Fighters

I remained undisturbed in that empty residence for...., as I say I struggle with o'clock, but I estimate it was a few cycles of light-darks.

I rested.

On one level I was aware I was not a Bean. This I knew because I was not conflicted. The 'Nigel' I had been, was a dream. A bad, broken, incoherent dream. I had now awoken. Much like a Bean can hazily recall snatches of dreams and images when they slumbered, so I could recall images and a fractured story of an existence once experienced. Now that I had risen and was alert, I did not miss the frailties of the dream-state. The vividness of 'death', enlightenment, call it what you will, was much preferred. That is not to say I was not aware of the conflicts in Bean thought-processes, but in my newborn condition, I could see it for what it was, and dismiss it. At the time I felt no disgust at the Bean state, in fact, I rather pitied it. Why did Beans revere 'life'? I'll tell you why, because they haven't been touched by the bliss of death.

As I reflected during these few light-darks, my eye sockets were opened. In due course the pity for the way the Beans lived their 'lives' turned to contempt. Bean life – the pursuit of material things (and the desire to preserve all such in the vain hope of keeping their destiny at bay) and the development of belief systems in order to maintain their world view – were of no consequence in eternity. Why wait until the body is weak and decayed before evolving? Couldn't they see that Nature had organised itself with disease to enable the Bean to expire? In truth, my contempt was probably prompted by a new sensation – hunger.

With darkness spreading across the sky I was feeling restless. I needed to explore. I was also still haunted by the lingering sweet smell of those four Beans which was accompanied by a raw desire for....I don't know what. It was a new sensation and I needed to explore it, to surrender to it.

Voices and noises drifted into the empty dwelling from somewhere near the rear of the property. Making my way to the bedroom at the back of the residence I put my eye socket to the holes of the protective metal grate fastened across the bedroom window. I saw a small garden enclosure lost to blackness and beyond that an almost circular space of wasteland around which the gardens of other residences were backed. The edges of the wasteland were bathed in the Bean sickly colours of street illumination, but the centre of the wasteland was also lost to the blackness of the dark-cycle.

The voices belonged to perhaps five male Beanteens sitting around in a group on park furniture smoking and talking. They drank the drink that loosens foolishness and ineptitude.

Not only did the sound of their nonsense carry, but so did their perfume drift across the cold, dark ground up the side of the house and through the holes punched into the metal. The aroma was ever so slightly cooled by the shadow of the night. How wonderful it must be to be up close to their bodies, I thought. The swirl and mix of five different Beans as they heaved, breathed and oozed their vapour was intoxicating.

It was clear that I must let my nature dictate my next movements and thereby their fate. As Beans, I felt nothing for them, but as creatures I ached for them. Such freshness. Within moments I had exited the house and crossed the darkness of the garden wall overlooking the wasteland. Their voices were louder, clearer; their freshness undeniable. Once again, I found myself torn between two contradictory sensations. I was feeling both confused yet never more clear. Clarity in Muterdom, bewilderment at Beanhood. I understood nothing of the Beenteens' animated sharing, not because I was unable to hear the words being uttered, but because there appeared to be a wholesale absence of meaning, no substance to their existence. It was, quite literally, all noise (but for their flesh which shouted meaning). Each exhalation was an exclamation of potential pleasure.

I felt pulled towards them.

I dropped off the wall and landed quietly on to the grass of the wasteland and took a tentative step towards the young Beans. Although sure in purpose, this was my first time. Was there a protocol?

I paused to process the events about to happen. With only an open and empty playing field behind them, there was no obvious route to safety should they take flight. I suspected they would not reach the gardens on the other side of the wasteland in time. I felt lean and fast and, judging by my lack of muscle fatigue when I first rose, I suspected I would not tire in any chase. There was no cool orb hanging in the dark cycle's sky, just the spill of artificial illumination falling onto green and grey urban surfaces.

It was an ideal environment for a conference with Bean. I was later to wonder whether the invention of artificial illumination devices had been the Bean subconscious preparing the way for enlightenment. A subconscious desire to invite the onset of eternal rest.

It is not that Muters don't like sunlight (although in fresh-borns there can be a period of adjustment for the skin tissue and eyes), it is really because the effectiveness of numbers and approaches to fresh Beans are easier in the cloaking of darkness. I later speculated on the congregation of the undead in metropolises being a similar unconscious desire to reach a destiny by making it easier for Muters to develop.

I stood there surveying five Beanteens on the verge of Beanhood before I noticed that they had fallen silent and were looking at me. Still unsure of protocol and still coping with my urges, I paused. Again, for how long, I did not know. I needn't have worried. Presumably reassured by the inaction of the creature in front of them, they played it cool. Ah, Bean youth.

The Beanteens then started to laugh at me, even perhaps to goad me to step forward. Perhaps this was the protocol, I didn't know. I drank in their aroma swaying from foot to foot until the moment was violently broken.

An empty drinks bottle bounced off me. Then another. I detected laughter which just pushed more heavenly aromas into the night. I drank it all in. Ironically the Beans' greatest pull (their perfume) was also possibly their greatest defence mechanism – for their aromas could almost lull a Muter into a state of reverie and inaction.

Otherwise, the Beans' actions did not alarm me, nor raise any other reaction in me. Nor did it prompt what I did next. No, it was my awareness of a fellow Muter (and perhaps a third) fifty yards off to my left on the edge of the playing field. They too had been drawn to this place by the pleasant aromas. We Muters are not competitive in the Bean sense, yet it is true that we are pulled towards our prey before it can be denied. I took one, then two quick paces towards the Beanteens, feeling I would appear to be smiling if only I had lips.

The Beans panicked suddenly. Their levity dissolved in their scramble to escape, no doubt in the hope to 'live'. But Muters move quickly when Beans are on the menu. I reached the larger, more appealing, Bean carrying more flesh, the other Muter and, as I suspected, a third, reached two of the leaner escaping Beans. I brought my Bean to the ground and in the briefest moment (of his brief seventeen summers of existence) I saw the power of my presence I had on him etched onto his face. An etching of the purest, unadulterated terror contorted into pretty patterns in his fleshy facial features. I could have spent hours just gazing into the turning, whirling white musculature. Such sweetness, such fight.

The Bean's chest heaved up and down rapidly with the breath of panic. I ripped back his upper garments and saw the flesh of his abdomen. My first. So smooth, so ripe. I ran my finger-bones across the pale softness of his pert flesh from which yet more aromas rose through heavenly pores. Coupled with his heavy panting, it was truly a cocktail of earthly, heavenly delights.

I could resist no longer. I drove my hand deep into his abdomen, puncturing the meat like a Beanling would plunge a warm spoon into soft ice-cream and opened up to view the treasures contained therein.

Oh, the delight.

Never in my wildest visions had I anticipated such living, breathing riches. The aromas unleashed ripped into my senses throwing my whole being into convulsions. I had no idea of the treasures contained within a Bean. How could I have not known? I could not recollect experiencing such all-consuming desire in my Bean-life. It was as if warm, freshly-baked bread was being presented to me amidst the sweetest juices of a carefully prepared salad of rich exotic fruits all pulsating with the warmth and succulence of juice and flesh. Despite the disregard that I might have had for the Beans, this was something with which I could not find fault. In truth, flawless delight. Pleasure on a cosmic scale and a beauty on a timeless scale. Not only could the treasures be drunk in by my eye sockets, but they could be tasted, ingested.

All the rainbow of colours were curled up and nestled like cushions amidst cushions. It was an art form which could be devoured. The secret of 'life' – the insides of a Bean, the flower of the cosmos. The Bean's juices were distilled, concentrated and fermented into the finest of wines. I now understood how the universe worked. This was indeed heaven. The kingdom of heaven was to be found in the Bean's breast.

I knew not which plum-like internal organ I lifted to my half-lips first, but when I punctured its soft membrane with my exposed teeth, the organ ruptured with a pleasing pop. The red juice splashed over my pale green skin like the coolest of soothing balms after a burning hot summer's light cycle. A basket of riches exploded in my mouth and zapped my once-flat palette with the force of a thousand suns before it slipped tingling down my throat like the richest cream from a virgin udder. And the fleshy forms of the organs were like a happy communion of the freshest of tropical fruits and the crispest of breads baked to soft perfection on the sharpest of spring mornings.

As I drank and swallowed I knew the essence of Bean – Death.

For tens of thousands of solar cycles, Beans had wandered the land and sailed the seas looking for 'meaning' never for a moment knowing that all meaning the universe had to offer lay tucked up nice and warm inside them. I'm sure if I had known in my own Beanhood that I myself could have been the source of such pleasure, I would have lived a life of fullest contentment. The Beans had nothing to fear. For no Bean, creature or thing should fear its destiny.

I looked down and into the pulsating open abdomen of this Beanteen with its warm steam gently rising into the cool night. The remaining shapes of different colours, different nutritious delights rested in service to me. Where and how does one begin?

A howling, raging hunger burned inside me and, like a beast, it knew it was about to be rewarded. It had awoken. I had awoken. I pushed my head downwards into the riches before me, biting, chewing, pulling the treasures from their resting places. Juices from one punctured organ oozed into the nest of cushions and mingled with the juices of others. I don't know how long I gorged.

I raised my head on occasion and saw my two fellow Muters feeding on the other Beans.

Was this their first as well? Or was this now routine for them? How could such a revelation become routine?

After a period, I sensed company. I looked up and saw two figures standing in the dim illumination of the wasteland in front of one of my Muter colleagues still kneeling at his open treasure chest. There was a flash and a bang and my Muter friend's head exploded in a flash of grey, green and red. He slumped to the ground.

One of the figures (a Bean of many summers) turned and strode towards me, his double-barrelled shooting device levelled at my own head. Once again, this was a first, and I was behind the curve. His half-illuminated face had no expression as he pulled the switch. There was a click, but no flash, no noise. By this time, I understood the scene in front of me. Smiling as best I could, knowing o'clock was short, I rose from my kneeling position and stepped over my feed as the many-summered Bean's composure slipped and he started to grapple with his shooting device.

I don't know what he saw of the remaining seconds of his existence as a Bean or how he interpreted it. He didn't stand a chance. His light-darks as a Bean had come to an end. Replenished and strengthened by my feeding, I covered the five yards to him in a flash. I suspect he drank in the smell of my flesh as the guts and juice of my first feed mingled with my second – the leathery loosened skin of the Bean twenty-five summers older.

I sensed the third and remaining Muter colleague approach the other Bean from the darkness behind and found the exposed flesh of the Bean's neck. I heard the Bean sigh his last as the Muter opened up the rich flesh. It was a member of the young gang of Beanteens who had presumably run for help only to return to offer himself up to destiny. Such thoughtfulness, such kindness. I didn't resent my colleague picking the sweet young thing, for I was finding a particular richness in my own find. The many-summered Bean was a fine vintage.

And so it was that in the darkness of a little piece of illuminated wasteland, I fed for the first time.

I knew now who I was.

Moments before was now a lifetime away. I had seen five young Beans and had been at a loss to describe their purpose on this earth. I could see now that four of the five had met their destiny (along with one gate-crasher), but one remained loose and was undoubtedly seeking assistance from other Beans. It was time to withdraw and find a safe place away from illumination and any other gate-crashers to our party.

I walked slowly to the exit, past Beanling swings and roundabouts that stirred distant memories of an empty existence. I was now fully born. I had arrived. Nobody had witnessed it except one young Bean. But I knew his face, I knew his perfume. It would be only right for us to meet again and for me to introduce myself properly – 'Hello, my name was Nigel'.

I slipped into the darkness and into a new world. Everything made sense. There were no questions, only answers. I pitied the Bean who endured an existence of Questions. Perhaps I could help them. They too should learn how to simplify their summers and understand earth's pleasures – feed and rejoice and, at the last, find peace and rest.

3. First Feeds: the Lovers

Over the following light-cycles I encountered others in quiet places. They would fight and struggle. I understood why, but on one occasion shortly afterwards I had an altogether un-confrontational experience with two Beans.

I was wandering home in the middle of the dark-cycle when I detected a slight aroma of Bean in the air. I wasn't particularly hungry, but the more I thought about not feeding, the more I realised that feeling hungry and feeding are two entirely different things.

With this in mind, I moved further into the shadows and followed the aroma until I heard quiet voices – the exchange of gentle words interlocking and dancing around each other in a hushed aria. The male Bean was sweetened by the higher octave of the female Bean. It was an invitation for me to dine. The sounds dripped from the cool night like cream into my body melting my insides at the prospect of receiving fresh juices.

Surviving as a Muter in a metropolis is relatively easy. The self-interestedness and self-preserve of the average Bean means that poverty and homelessness abound, so not many Beans take notice of a tall, slim, pale-skinned figure padding along pavements on bare skin and bone. I suppose that, in the darkness, my flesh merely gave the impression of unwashed feet. This being the metropolis, Beans make a concerted effort to ignore each other, but there is no doubt my own perfume also helped keep passers-by away. For sure, Death can thrive in a metropolis.

I followed the lover-Beans along the empty walkways and turned south with them as they headed towards their home base. I could easily keep my distance, the cool, still night kept the aroma fresh at a hundred paces. I was in no rush.

Eventually in the middle of the dark-cycle they entered a closed residential area. I watched as they stood opposite each other whispering nonsense about the 'present' and the 'future' – as I say, nonsense.

Muters carry no weapons, so we do not have to be selective about how, where and with what Beans to engage. I would soon have to make a decision about which lover-Bean to engage with and when. I crept quietly into a wooded grove and watched. The Beans had not touched each other properly, but there was an unspoken intensity between them which anticipated the touch of the other. The mood created between them seemed familiar to me. I had seen this scene before, I thought as I watched the would-be lovers alone together perhaps for the first time. I felt I had lived (or rather 'existed') this moment before myself.

And so I had – a hazy memory of the existence of Nigel-Bean returned. Nigel-Bean too had walked a young lady Bean home. I recalled that he 'Bean-cared' for her (in a vomit-inducing way as opposed to a digestible way). They were friends, but Nigel-Bean had wanted more. It made Nigel-Bean unhappy and he had wanted to communicate weakness to her, yet there was trouble between them. The street in which I was now standing reminded me of that Nigel-Bean moment. The scene had been a closed residential street just like this – simple modern houses with automobilic vehicles parked in front of them and wooded groves on corners.

I watched the young couple in front of me and, in the depths of my rotted memory, I knew I would never experience such 'feelings' again – antenatal pangs, I suppose. Yet I remained intrigued. I recalled Nigel-Bean embracing the female companion at the point of separation and noting that her hands had been pressed tightly into his back during the embrace. It had confused Nigel-Bean at the time. Why had the embrace been so warm? As Nigel-Bean and the lady Bean pulled themselves apart, Nigel-Bean had detected a wetness in her eye, but he had not reacted.

Before my own moment of enlightenment, Nigel-Bean had reflected on that moment. Nigel-Bean and the female parted that night and they were never together again. So, here I was, all Muter, watching a similar event unfold in front of me. Male Beans tend to have more muscle and bigger organs (making for a fuller feeding experience) and lady Beans tend to be slighter and delicate, yet, in this instance, I was drawn to the female. I did not need volume. I needed flavour. So, yes, it was clear, I would kiss the female tonight – but Muter-kiss not Bean-kiss. The act would also close and seal that memory of Nigel-Bean's. Or so I hoped.

I strode forward emerging from the blackness straight towards the couple. They turned towards me. Their shared moment of Bean-kiss, their memory-moment, nearly fully constructed was cruelly interrupted by their destiny walking towards them. What they had hoped to be a lasting memory (to be followed by many thousands more) was in fact their last memory. And it did not feature two bodies, but three.

Aghast, their mouths fell open in anticipation of their imminent passing. Before the lady Bean could raise the breath to scream, I had kissed her deeply in her neck. My arms wrapped around her waist to take her weight as she sank to the ground. I opened my throat to receive the fountain of liquid youth that burst into my mouth and rushed down to warm my cold, dry throat and insides. A true lovers' embrace.

Our lovers' moment passed before I felt the arm of her Bean companion around my neck trying to pull me from his dying would-be lover. I took the proffered bicep and kissed deeply into the muscle tearing the flesh away. He yelped and stepped back. Releasing one arm from my fallen lover I gripped his throat and

David O. Zeus

threw him hard away. He stumbled back, tripping on the kerb and collapsed in a quiet heap to be fed upon later. Alone again with my love, I lifted her and carried her into the darkness of the wooded grove from where I had come. I laid her down on the cool grass and moved my mouth close to hers to inhale her last sweet breaths. I was alive. Running my hands over the fully fleshed, toned form, ripened over twenty-five summers, I thanked not only the Beans who had procreated to produce such a delight but also her own destiny for leading her to my table.

Removing the juice-soaked clothing from her abdomen I viewed the pale smooth vistas of unblemished flesh. And with a quiet sigh of kneeling appreciation lowered my head to my warm prey and gorged. Indeed, she tasted of the lover-Bean. The recent happiness and excitement that had coursed through her veins now washed down and gargled in my throat before swirling about my insides.

16

4. My First Colleague – RooftopSuicide

Not many light-darks later I found myself on a secluded rooftop in the Bean metropolis where I intended to stay quiet and away from the hullabaloo created by my latest feed. The silence, as the darkness enveloped the metropolis, was calming; I could rest undisturbed. Silence is a great beauty. It is the sound of paradise. The darkness and stillness was cleansing. Beans will rise from their slumber, leave their tombstones built high in the sky, fatten themselves, tone themselves, procreate, busy themselves with 'existence', all in ignorance of their ultimate destination – at my table. The breathy perfume of millions of resting Beans seeped out of windows and doors and hung over the metropolis like an invisible fog of honey. It is a special moment to look out over the concrete fields of vanity and know that contained therein is an endless supply of nourishment.

My musings were disturbed by a noise from somewhere on the rooftop. A Bean? Yes. I slunk back into the shadows behind a skylight structure. It's true, a Muter can smell fear. In fact, a Muter can detect a myriad of chemical concoctions be they anger, love, joy or a thousand others. This Bean reeked of agitation. He was not violently exhaling perfume as if he had been undertaking vigorous exercise, no, his odour hung about him lightly.

From my vantage point behind the skylight contraption, I watched a many-summered, blond-haired Bean exit a door onto the roof, walk slowly to the roof's edge and gaze down at the street a few storeys below. I couldn't quite place the odour. He was not a Muter, but he had an air of death about him. Or rather he didn't have the air of the fight-for-(Bean)-life about him. He was muttering to himself as many self-absorbed Beans do. I watched as he, with beverage in hand, stood motionless on the roof's edge.

I felt a slight breeze run up my back, rise over my head and swirl and twist in the air towards him. His nose twitched. My cover was blown. He turned suddenly towards me and saw me standing a dozen yards away illuminated in the half cool light.

He didn't run. He just breathed. Transfixed.

I felt his pain. I stepped forward slowly revealing my form. I was aware that I looked different from him. Perhaps he had not seen a Muter up close. The skin of a Bean makes them look smooth, rounded, fleshy. That is part of their appeal after all. Plump and ripe. But my appearance is pitted with cavities and chasms into which the orange glow of the city cannot reach. Beans fear what they do not know and they do not know what they cannot see. He could not marvel at the sinews and tendons and muscle groups on display to him – the art of the humanoid form.

'RooftopSuicide' (as I later christened him) remained stationary. He did not run which in a way disappointed me. I enjoyed the hunt, the chase, but I rebuked myself. Here was a Bean who knew what he wanted. He was happy, enlightened enough to embrace his destiny.

I took another step towards him and, in an attempt to reassure him, tried to smile, but, without fleshy lips, I know that all I can display are a wall of broken teeth.

The problem with Beans is that they equate my look as undesirable as if I am in discomfort. I suppose I should not be surprised. My appearance is only usually associated with an automobilic vehicle crash, violence, pain or much-maligned death. Beans don't know that in fact I am not in pain, I am not a victim of violence and I don't drive. Drive where? Everything I needed was right here in the metropolis. On every street. In every home.

'I don't know who you are...,' RooftopSuicide-elect suddenly said. 'Or were... I don't care. Fuck, I don't care. Fuck you.'

I stopped. This was the first time I had been addressed by the undead. My sockets, mind and heart were opened. (Something I now endeavour to do for others.) I didn't feel as if I needed to reply. What was there to say? I waited and watched him (I had o'clock) and treated the moment as foreplay.

'You have no fucking idea,' he muttered, disconsolately.

'Work, life, women. It's all shit. Total shit. You and your little dim-shit brains have no idea. You just wander around...just fucking existing. Haunting the living. Terrorising those trying to carve out a living. There is no fucking point to your existence.'

RooftopSuicide-elect sighed. He seemed tired, but not fearful as Beans tended to be in these situations. He stood there, lost. Alone. There was no rush.

'Fuck, but what is the point of my own fucking existence?' he muttered, raising his eyes to my sockets. 'You and I are brothers of sorts. But, shit, I look a whole lot better.'

He took a few steps towards me trying to get a closer look at my features. I didn't mind; no harm in letting him have a few moments to gaze into the future.

'Do you remember what it was like?' he whispered. 'Did you have relationships? Do you remember what it was like to trust someone? Do you? You sack of stinking shit. God, if I had one wish, I wish I could turn her into a fucking zombie to spend the rest of eternity walking this sorry planet. Then she would know what space and time was. "Space and time. I need space and time." Makes her sound like a fucking Einstein. When she probably couldn't spell it. Dim bitch.'

He turned to face me. It would appear he was far from finished.

'You don't know, do you? You don't understand what I'm saying, do you? Jesus. And this is where it leads me, to a rooftop with a fucking zombie for company.'

RooftopSuicide-elect paused, turned and gazed over the roof's edge.

'What should I do? Make a final statement to the world?' he said nodding to the black abyss below.

'You're not going to remember my last words are you? You're not going to report my final thoughts to my family? Or to her? What should I say? What message should I give her? Words that would make her feel like shit, I hope. But how long would that last? Before long she'd be out being dined and 'comforted' by the fucker. Shit. He's welcome to her.'

RooftopSuicide-elect turned away and took a few steps towards the very edge of the roof bordered from the darkness by a knee-high parapet of brick. Suddenly, my new friend turned to me.

'Could you visit her?' he asked earnestly. 'Pay her a visit and pass on my final words to her? If I give you her address? In fact, if you could do it in front of witnesses that would be great. You could feast on her all you like. Not sure what she'd taste like, though. A bit podgy you see. Too much white wine in those first ten years of her working life. It's the way of them all now. But perhaps you know that?'

I watched him wallow in self-pity. I liked the word "feast" though. Yes, I suppose it is a 'feast' rather than 'feed'. Yet, I felt uncertain. Why should I be the one who feasts? Why couldn't he be the one who feasted on her? Why should I deprive him of that feast?

The Bean was wearing a purple open-necked shirt, a light-coloured jacket and crème-coloured trousers. I liked the colours and choice of fabric. I had learnt that fresh, oxygenated juice soaks into most fabrics beautifully and the rich redness stands out strongly against a pale background colour. There is something remarkably alluring about the sight of a Bean drenched in juice, like a soiled napkin at the end of a filling feed. The garment then takes on a history, it tells a story – a journey from a bland cleanliness to a rich destiny. I am not suggesting that Muters consciously select feasts based on the garments worn, but I do wonder whether clothing might have a subliminal effect not only on the feeder but the 'feedee'. By which I mean, was the Bean's choice of garment a subconscious cry for help? An appeal to be rescued from a monotonous existence – three score years and ten of utter despair?

'And then there is my work,' the undead continued. 'You have no idea how lucky you are to have left that all behind. I spend the waking day looking at screens and trying to get the best for people – people for whom I have nothing but contempt. My existence is a form of death. Then the stuff and people you do think you are living for, treat you like shit. What's the fucking point? At least you don't worry about mortgages and debts and status. Nothing like that in zombieland is there?'

He turned away and looked down again into the abyss.

'You must have had a job,' he said after a pause, before turning and approaching me all curious, looking into my sockets. 'What are you mid-thirties? Forty? What did it all lead to? To what end? All this shit,' he spat waving his arm at the horizon of twinkling lights.

'Do you understand anything that I am saying, dipshit?'

I said nothing out of respect for his final moments.

'Who are you? What's your name? Do you know your name? What did you do? I bet you never guessed you'd end up here? Spoil your plan did it? What happened? Bitten when you were alive or did you catch it afterwards? How does it work?'

My friend, RooftopSuicide-elect, stepped towards me. He was bold and curious. He thought he was looking death in the face.

'Did you dream? Have dreams? I wonder what they were. Nothing going on now in there is there?' he muttered tapping my forehead and shaking his own head. 'Trust me, you don't know how lucky you are.'

I was getting bored now. Self-pity is not a spectator sport.

I thought for a moment. I wasn't hungry, but perhaps I could grant this Bean a new lease of life. Perhaps I could grant him his wishes. I could be his god. Answer his prayers. I smiled as best I could. He looked curious.

I slowly lifted my hand from my side and moved it towards his hand. He saw the movement and perceived it as a non-threatening move.

'What is it? You want to shake hands?' he laughed.

I didn't. I reached forward and gently took his right forearm in my left hand.

'OK, now what?' he said now laughing somewhat nervously.

I turned it over to reveal the soft underside of his arm. Soft, pure, white and ripe. A peach.

'Nothing like your manky skin. Fuck, that's disgusting.'

He gently tried to pull his hand away in a Bean-polite way. Although I didn't forcefully hold on to his hand, I did not let go.

'Okay, thanks. Playtime over.'

I reached out with my right hand and brushed it slowly up his chest and clasped his neck.

'What the...'

This move of mine alarmed him and he started to back away, but not before I had kissed his peachy soft right inner forearm tearing out a mouthful of fresh flesh. I looked at him with dripping juice from my gums. RooftopSuicide-elect now just looked confused and aghast. Beans, such simpletons.

He looked at his arm and the mouthful-sized missing portion that I was now chewing slowly, then looked again confused at me as if he had been betrayed by an ally. Then, and as they all do, he started to man-scream. No sooner had the air been expelled from his lungs in a cry, I closed my fingers around his neck. As he gurgled like a new-born, I lifted him by his throat and walked him backwards towards the rear of the rooftop. I was not going to send him over the front of the house to meet his end on the pavement. It would break too many bones and would be too much of a spectacle, which, I grant you, is what he wanted. Such vanity. Suicide by one's own hand is such a self-interested way to go. No, I realised that this dead Bean just a few summers younger than me had unfinished business with his fellow Beans. Death would provide the answers. He needed to be a working corpse.

So, I carried him to the edge of the roof overlooking the back of the property. There was no street illumination or hard landing down there. No, just trees, vegetation, gardens and the abyss of the darkness. A soft landing and a cushion to be reborn. With one final kiss from his arm and one for good measure from his fleshy neck I lifted him high and threw him over the roof's edge into the blackness below. I glimpsed his expression as he fell. He still seemed confused. Why? I thought. I had given him what he wanted. He was planning it anyway. If anything, I provided the encouragement to compensate for his fear and Bean-doubt.

He made no sound as he fell to his destiny crashing through branches and fences landing with a muffled thud. I waited to see if there was movement in the shadowy black-green world below. But nothing. Just the rustle of the wind in the trees and the sound of branches scratching and clawing at each other. A fine place to rest. I shall see you soon, my new colleague, I thought.

5. Rooftop's Birthday & DogSmells

I was aware that a Muter should not hunt and rest in one place. I had not returned to the house I had spent my first few light-darks and had retreated to an area of the metropolis that was largely derelict. Other desirable places were wasteland and industrial parks – both were quieter and any Bean incursions were easily spotted.

A few light-darks had passed since my conversation with RooftopSuicide and I suspected his moment was near so I returned to his part of town. When not making a way through parks and shaded avenues, I moved slowly through the residential streets. I passed some young Beans walking, but I did not bother them. I had taken to wearing a long overcoat and a hat when travelling about the metropolis. A learning instinct returns in death.

I hopped over a metal railing near Rooftop's (former) residence and headed deep into the vegetation. I could detect his odour – ever so slight, but unmistakable. I heard small rodents and animals in the undergrowth scurrying away as I made my way through the greenery blackened by the night. I found RooftopSuicide curled up in the pile of flesh and bone crushing a flower bush. He had succumbed to a few skeletal injuries on his way down from the rooftop. A leg was probably broken. His neck was twisted, but functional. The rigor mortis of the musculature of the neck should be able to maintain a partially functional head and, in due course, he might regain full use of it. Pain would not prevent movement.

He had lost a lot of juice from a severe head injury. A real shame. A waste. Fortunately the deep gash on the side of the head had not punctured the brain. I reckoned he would have retained some memory function and his learning skills should return relatively swiftly. I could tell he was not ready yet, but I decided to wait – again, I had the o'clock. (In fact that's all I had.)

I made myself comfortable in the undergrowth under the growth of a large tree and rested. The great orb of the sky rose but its illumination could not penetrate deep into our seclusion. Early morning brought the sound of Beans rising to fill their light cycles with nothingness in the terraced houses running alongside the park. In mid-morning I heard the click and hushed swing of a nearby residence's door opening onto its garden. A dog came scampering up to the end of the garden twenty yards away and sniffed fiercely at the bottom of the fence. No doubt, both my and Rooftop's odours weaved their way through the thick wall of bushes and trees to the canine's nose. The barking started. Once again the door opened and the delightful odour of a young lady Bean drifted down the garden working its way back to me through the wall of vegetation. In a sweet, evenly pitched voice I imagined her pert lips and tongue clearly enunciating the consonants and vowels as she chastised the dog for making all the noise, and, for some reason, asking the dumb animal for its motivation in barking.

'What is that?' I heard her ask herself.

I was unsure whether she had detected me or my new recruit who lay in a heap in the bushes a few yards from her garden fence. Like most senses (and reasoning), Muters have a developed sense of smell. Post-rising there is a particular odour, but it recedes as the rotting of the Muter's flesh slows and halts. Our metabolism processes feedstuff differently and does not generate the continual perfume of the inferior Bean. Beans have learnt to wash themselves, a practice which enabled them to procreate more effectively leading them to be an infinite resource for death.

25

'Personal hygiene' has probably been the more effective ingredient of their success (in terms of population growth) rather than technology, language, law and ethics which they so foolishly pursue. However, washing and the use of artificial odours to deny the reminders of their decomposing state and destiny is in vain.

The young lady Bean muttered more to the dog and I soon determined that she was indeed curious and increasingly fearful. She led the dog back into her residence and locked the door. I looked at my slumped, twisted friend who I sensed was close to revelation. When a Bean enters the death zone, there is a journey to be made. A gestation. Each and every journey is personal. It cannot be rushed.

I returned to my shaded lair of vegetation to wait, but a short while later I was aroused once more by the smell of the same canine and the young lady Bean. This time, however, they were not on the other side of the fence in the safety of their own garden. No, they were approaching us from the parkland area behind us. I rose to my feet and stepped back further into the shadows. The dog, at the end of a lead, pushed its way through the bushes and low-hanging trees and emerged at the body of my resting friend, RooftopSuicide. The fragrance of the young Bean bloomed as she neared and arrived at the body of the Has-Bean. Hidden amidst the greenery I heard her mutter in surprise and shock.

Once the Has-Bean had been discovered, the dog became distracted and began to explore the immediate vicinity whilst still attached to its owner's extendable lead. Sniffing, it took a few steps into the undergrowth towards me. On finding me, it growled. I suspect I was the first of my kind it had come across. As I stepped forward, it stepped back, continuing to growl quietly in what I thought was a fearful state. As it retreated, its lead was caught on a piece of vegetation. Picking it up I yanked the lead hard pulling the creature towards me.

Beans are not the only creatures to be blessed with revelation, this I knew. I sunk by teeth into its neck. It was not a wholly desirable taste, but it was the least I could do for the animal that had brought yet another Bean offering. Within the whimper of a breath, the job was done and I discarded the creature into the bushes to let it find its own way on to the other side.

I quietly stepped through the bushes and found myself behind the young lady Bean as she rose to her feet having examined Rooftop. She began to punch the screen of her telephonic communication device. I remember them. Toys that preached enhanced communication between Beans, but ultimately kept them apart. True communication is tender and found only in the flesh. I don't know what she felt in those last moments. A slight twist of the neck and she went the way of her dog. I did not feast. I granted her a kiss and a future. We would wait together.

Blues then dark blues crept across the sky pushing the orange over the horizon. Blackness slunk after the darkening blues until it owned the whole sky. Coolness and silence reigned. The time was coming, but I waited with the cooling corpse of DogSmells-elect waiting for Rooftop's moment. There were a few false alarms – small rodents stirring in the undergrowth. Then in the dead of the dark cycle I was privileged to bear witness to my first Muter rising.

First, there was the gentle rustle of limbs stirring in the grass and twisting against the bushes, which was then followed by the occasional crack of broken bones and vertebrae. In death, nervous systems do not have a part to play. The body has learnt how to function as the musculature permits. I rose to my feet and stepped towards the twitching form as its eternity was revealed. I wanted my new protégé to see me for the first time. The birth is an important moment, I wanted to be there for him. His last Bean thoughts would have been me as he fell backwards crashing through branches and trees looking only at me, a black sky and stars. It might help his re-emergence if he laid eyes on me once again.

The Muter spread his legs and rose onto his arms. His neck was broken, but with some adjustment to its position he managed to place it in a relatively straight position. He pulled himself to his knees and then slowly lifted his torso allowing him to stand upright. I stood facing him like a proud father. He stood looking into my eye sockets. He had the same somewhat confused expression on his face as he had when he had been falling from the roof. I did not move. I smiled as best I could.

I knew what would be going through his mind. He would be adjusting to the new world. A world without fear. A world without self-consciousness. It is a disconcerting experience for a creature that had seen over thirty summers, but it was to be a sensation that would last for many thousands of summers.

RooftopSuicide looked down at the corpse of the Has-Bean hanging down by my side. I would offer her as his first feast, but he appeared not to be interested. He reached up to the large gash in his head. Blood from the wound had coursed over his head and down his neck. It had dried and matted his hair. The shirt was now purple with asymmetric blacker stains. Otherwise he looked relatively intact, though deathly pale. His mind was working. It is a slow process. I suspect he was swirling through the thoughts and words of his last memories. And there we stood, two Muters, in the dead of night ignorant of the world around us.

We might have stood there until the dawn, but our moment was broken by the shrill knell of the Has-Bean's communication device lying in the undergrowth. Rooftop bent down and picked it up and looked at it. It looked familiar, no doubt. He touched the buttons on the illuminated pad and the ringing stopped to be followed by the tinny distant sound of a Bean voice 'Darling, darling, are you there? Where are you?' Rooftop tried to speak into the device, but rotting vocal chords and speed of thought resulted in a few non-descript grunts. It would improve with o'clock, he would learn the limited vocabulary used by his fellow Muters. He broke off conversation with the Has-Bean's friend and looked at the body by my side then at me again, but, no, he had other ideas. He turned away and walked through the undergrowth towards the open park space bathed in cool light hanging high in the sky.

The electronic device's knell sounded again, but Rooftop had no use for such things and threw it away only for it to land in a large pool of liquid and sink silently. I lifted DogSmells-elect high and threw the body into a high-fenced compost container. I would return for her in the light-darks to come, but right now, I was keen to follow my first Muter-kiss (rather than feast) to wherever his fancy took in. It might be a bumpy first night's adventure, but I was there to help and mentor.

6. Rooftop's Birthday Party & ColourSplash

Even in my new eternal state I try to understand the Bean world. Not in an effort to empathise with them, but to facilitate the realisation of their destiny. A contradiction lies at the heart of the Bean. They have an impulse to survive, but to survive one must, in Bean terms, 'die'.

I had walked with Rooftop from the park through the dark streets until we reached a smart residential area of the metropolis. He was familiar with the streets, that was clear. He climbed the half-dozen steps up to a property's doorway and banged on the door. Nothing. Rooftop banged again. I stood patiently behind him in shadow on a lower step. Illumination appeared in the hallway and the door opened.

Now framed by full hallway illumination stood an attractive thirty-summered lady Bean in full blonde Bean bloom. Nicely presented in a white blouse (which almost cried out for a splash of colour) and a figure hugging skirt (ending with a couple of peachy calves), the Bean had about her neck a string of white balls. For a moment the sight of the white balls transported me back to another time, another place, but I was soon shaken back in the moment when ColourSplash-elect opened her mouth.

'Richie?'

Judging by the reaction of the blonde Bean, opening the door to a Muter in the dead of night was still an uncommon experience for a Bean.

'My God, Richie?' she repeated.

RooftopSuicide stood semi-silhouetted in the porch light, his head lolling from one side to another as his damaged neck was struggling to remain upright. His facial skin was largely unbroken nor had his flesh deteriorated much, but I suspect his features were unusually sallow.

Rooftop grunted something. (Again, ability to 'Bean-speak' is impaired at death.)

The lady Bean leaned toward him to get a closer look into Rooftop's eyes.

'What are you doing here? Are you okay? I thought we had spoken about this.'

A noise behind her made her glance back into the hall.

'Peter is here,' she whispered, turning back to Rooftop. 'With his step-daughter. I can't do this now.'

'Who is it, honey?' a male Bean voice echoed from within the house. A shiver of anticipation went down my spine.

'Who's your friend?' the lady Bean asked, trying to look over Rooftop's shoulder. I obliged and leaned into view.

In Bean o'clock, the following happened very quickly. In Muter o'clock it was leisurely. Rooftop stumbled forward towards the lady Bean which allowed his own sallow features to fall into the illumination falling from the hallway. The whole truth dawned on the Bean – 'Richie' had reached the eternal paradise ahead of her, but she needn't have worried because her time was near.

The hall suddenly echoed with the voice of the Bean Peter who, within a few strides, would be by the woman's side. Perhaps, by catching sight of me behind Rooftop, Peter immediately understood the nature of the visit. Allowing Rooftop to have his first bite undisturbed, I strode briskly past him into the hall and towards the neck of the Peter Bean. It was quick and clean. Rooftop's friend began to scream and stepped back. 'Richie' followed her into the hall and, with his heel, kicked the front door (almost) shut.

As I tucked into the fine form of Peter Bean breathing his last – all muscle and healthy organs, a true delight – Rooftop's Bean began an onset of pleas of mercy and forgiveness. Muters, all-knowing that we are, we are not in a position to forgive past life choices and actions. Furthermore, regardless of what Richie Rooftop might have felt for this woman as he squirmed for thirty summers as an undead was not relevant. Whether his intention was to bestow upon her the gift of eternal life or merely to feast on her one last time, I did not know. It was his call.

I later learned that a fresh Muter would not necessarily be so aware of the deep desire to engage Beans of past acquaintance. Normally, the addressing of so-called 'unfinished business' would emerge in due course, but as a result of Rooftop's first night endeavours I was keenly aware that new-risens' unfinished business had to be managed, ideally a dozen light-darks at least into their eternal life. I can only conclude that Rooftop's clarity was because his mind and attention had been immersed in the subject of his lady Bean at the moment he fell to his salvation from the roof a handful of light-darks earlier.

The o'clock was of the essence. All credit to Rooftop (it being his first bite), but he was making a meal of it. The lady-Bean was making far too much noise. I had been able to subdue the male Peter Bean relatively quickly and he slumped to the floor in respect and awe. As I gulped down as much juice as I could, I became aware that her wailing might attract the attention of other Beans late in the night. Although Rooftop's instincts in feasting were sound, I suspected his awareness and abilities in engaging in a struggle with yet more aggressively-defensive Beans might be challenging. Such things need practice.

The door to the property had now swung open so the Bean screams were echoing to some degree down the street and if, my senses were correct, the light breeze was touched by the perfume of approaching Beans. I therefore stepped in and assisted Rooftop with the juice-letting and the body-positioning.

But it was too late.

I heard the shouts of the approaching Beans. Male Beans – the more aggressive, 'problem-solving' Bean. I listened to determine numbers and age. I suspected from the sound of the footsteps, the shouts of 'Oi', 'what yer' (or similar) that they were intending to be confrontational. However, Beans are full of bluster and oftentimes ignorant of their bluster. The appearance of a Muter can sometimes clarify the problems to be solved.

Their desire to impose a solution soon waned once they saw me step out from the doorway. My features illuminated by the lamp hanging above me from the porch probably threw long shadows over my face. Such a sight was still an unusual sight for Beans. (I could thank a few rodents for that aspect of my appearance.) Death did not impact the facial features of many of my own fresh-borns as a result of me hiding them away while they managed their transition.

The three Beans who had noisily made their way down the street, stopped and stared for a few seconds before sheepishly scuttling off into the darkness, no doubt grateful that other Beans were not present to witness their pitiful retreat. I knew that they would not be gone for long. They would return, perhaps with uniformed Cloth-Head Beans in attendance, so I too retreated back into the house and closed the front door.

Rooftop was enjoying his past too much. Her blouse was, as I had predicted, now re-imagined in splashes of rich juice. Aware that he might wish to see her rise again and be functional, I indicated that we should make good our exit. I decided to leave ColourSplash-elect's male companion, Peter Bean, for the Cloth-Heads. Having tasted and drunk in his perfume, I suspected I would be able to track him down later if so desired.

I guided Rooftop (carrying ColourSplash-elect) up the first flight of stairs and then the second. I intended to exit a window on one of the upper storeys and head to the roof after which we could travel along the terraced rooftops to a secure location where we could leave a slumbering ColourSplash-elect until she was fit to rise in glory. However, as I reached the third floor of the residence, my nasal cavities were filled with the lightest and sweetest of perfumes. I stopped and turned towards a doorway. There was a gasp and a whimper. I stepped carefully towards the darkness of the doorway unsure what the perfume denoted. More danger? Was there another Bean in the house? With the confidence of death I pushed open the door to see a small female Beanling standing in the illumination from the landing lamp.

The Beanling of about seven summers stood motionless in a long white dress. Shoulder-length curly blonde hair fell around the big eyes and chubby pale pink cheeks of her round face. A form of angel. Even if I had not already feasted there was not enough meat or juice to make her an appetising prospect. Furthermore, I knew that her Bean skill set would not be developed enough to allow her to survive as a Muter. (Or so I thought at the time.)

That said, I believed I was looking at a Beanling who might open the door to Cloth-Head Beans and, in so doing, limit the effectiveness of our escape. Or the Beanling might watch our exit and inform the Cloth-Head Beans of ColourSplash-elect's resting place. With that in mind, I concluded the best option was to throw the Beanling off the roof.

I stepped forward and grabbed the Beanling's arm and dragged her up the final flight of stairs where I found Rooftop exiting a skylight after pulling his juicing lady Bean behind him. The Beanling with the chubby cheeks was light enough for me to carry in one hand. Having exited the skylight myself I soon found the four of us standing on a flat rooftop illuminated by nothing but the starlight (the great cool orb of the black sky itself obscured by cloud).

RooftopSuicide was looking a little confused. (He was still developing.) I needed to assist him in storing ColourSplash in a quiet place. Although he probably did not fully understand it himself, I could see that he was keen to find a companion in Splash. There was no harm in my niblings acquiring niblings of their own, I concluded, but, first things first, I determined to rid myself of the Beanling with the cheeks, so with an almighty swing I launched her off the roof down to the dark garden area ground below. Or rather, I tried to. Gripped by Beanling fear, she gripped onto my arm. So, I tried again. Once again fear clamped her little hands onto my forearm.

Just as I was preparing to swing her off the roof once more, I felt a slight impression in my forearm. Looking down I saw her jaws clamped on to my forearm. Instinctively I grabbed her forearm, a small twig of boney flesh, and bit into it puncturing its pale softness. Startled, the Beanling released her own grip, struggled free and darted off across the roof into the darkness. Still suspecting the Beanling might still alert others to our presence, I went after her. Rooftop followed me dragging Splash. I had come to the conclusion that the unpopulated rooftop would be a good place to hide Splash's flesh – any aromas would be open to the air. Furthermore, being littered with chimneys and crevices, the roof would be difficult for the Beans to reach and search.

After a short period of hunting I found the little Beanling tucked into a tiny crevice between chimneys. She was whimpering and hardly visible. I tried to pull her out, but the crevice was too narrow (or I was too big) preventing me from reaching her. It was only when Rooftop, who did not understand my actions, tried to place ColourSplash into the small space that the answer came in a flash, I could use the Has-Bean as a cork to block the chubby-faced Beanling's escape and ability to alert other Beans.

So, with much pushing and twisting, Rooftop and I pushed the Has-Bean, ColourSplash, into the space jamming her up against the Beanling. Pleased with our work for the dark cycle and relieved that Rooftop's first bite had coincided with his first nibling, we departed the rooftops determined to return at intervals to see how ColourSplash's awakening was going.

7. Making Friends

During one dark cycle shortly afterwards, and feeling replenished from a Bean feast, I decided to drop by the grassy bank near some railway lines where I had left a female Has-Bean a few light-darks before. Being fully aware of the confusion I myself had first felt when my sockets had been illumined, I felt an increasing responsibility to be available to assist at an awakening. Sometimes awakenings can be swift, other times the great orb must work its way across the sky many times.

The cool wind of the darkness carried the voices of passing Beans; it was often followed by the sweet smell of moist, perspiring flesh. I had no doubt the same wind carried my own sweet aroma to any nearby Beans prompting them to take a detour away from me as I sat and watched the cold corpse of the Has-Bean.

Imagine my surprise when my nasal cavities detected the strengthening sweet aroma of perhaps three of the undead. My ears pricked up as I heard the whisper and nervous pant of the three young Beans approaching – two males and one female. I stepped away from the resting Has-Bean and into trees and shrubberies thirty yards away from the railway line. They continued walking, but, rather than keeping to their path, they seemed to slow as they approached my area then, with urgent whispers, the three Beans began to work their way through the trees and shrubberies towards me hidden on the fringe of a wood clearing.

For a moment I had thought they might be hunting for other Beans to hurt, rob, maim, assault, but their whisperings suggested that it was me, a Muter, they were looking for. I was flattered. Memories of young male Bean machismo washed over me. I wondered if the two male Beans were seeking to impress the female Bean. Perhaps the female Bean was pleased to inspire competition in the two male Beans and was intending to watch them compete. I felt warmed and encouraged by their desire to 'wreak revenge' while simultaneously demonstrating their prowess by engaging with their enemy. But I wasn't their enemy, I was their liberator.

Once I understood what was going on I stepped forward out of the bushy vegetation into the cool light falling on the small clearing itself further illuminated by the artificial light falling from lamps overlooking the nearby track sidings and railway yard. The three Beans loitered, then began to circle me. I knew this because one of them said 'let's circle it'. The female Bean was an active participant; her behaviour suggested she intended not to be just an observer.

Assuming the first mistake they had made was looking for me that light-dark, this was the second mistake they made – assuming Muters have no comprehension of Bean-speak. Muters verbalise little. Partly because we do not feel the need to seek reassurance nor have a need to excuse embarrassment, but as I pondered this, it occurred to me that perhaps Beans are hard-wired to acknowledge their destiny. They know their destiny and so they feel drawn to it. Perhaps it is not a mistake, but an act of grace. A small act of self-revelation. And because Beans have not understood this deep impulse they dress it up in their writings as: courage, adventure, living life to the full, on the edge, when in fact the urge to offer themselves up to their destiny is buried deep in their psyche.

Even so, their fear stank. As they moved closer I assessed each one and considered their potential effectiveness as a Muter. There was a tall, thin one with long hair. There was a fat one. Finally, there was the female – cloaked (and hooded), strong, lean and focused. (In fact, somewhat curiously, there was the making of something abhorrent about her. Each of these nearly thirty-summered (or more) Beans carried a weapon. I deduced by the choice of weapon and the manner of their movement that they aspired to be Warriors-Beans.

The tall bean had a long pole, which he began swinging around his body in pretty circles. The fat one carried a metal sword. The female Bean carried a two-sticks-on-a-chain device that she too kept swinging about her body while staring intently towards me. I concluded that each was engaging in a form of warrior dance designed to instil fear in their opponent. But fear of what exactly? Death? Or was it an attempt to raise their own spirits? A communing of self-denial? Whatever it was, it was not working judging by the aromas now swirling about the small clearing.

Even though there were three of them, they didn't really seem committed to the activity. Each Bean would step forward and swing their weapon at me before stepping back and panting heavily. Until one of them committed to an attack I was happy to just watch in a bemused fashion and say nothing. I suppose I came across as a typical non-expressive Muter. But what is the point of 'expressing' something when I do not care for the expression nor the response?

The chain-and-sticks carrying Bean was more vocal in her dance (snarling aggressively), but did little else. They then helpfully communicated to each other their coordinated 'plan of attack'. (I suspected that it would not help me that much, because they would no doubt struggle to execute the plan.)

'Step in and whack it on the head then on the body,' said Chain-and-Stiks-elect to BeanPole-elect. 'I'll follow with a strike to the head and knees. This should bring it down. Then you,' Chain-and-Stiks-elect continued, turning to the fat man with the sword, 'swing down and strike it on the neck.'

BeanPole-elect and BroadBean-elect agreed, nodding vigorously, swinging their weapons around, shouting things like: 'yeah, fucker. You're gonna die motherfucker. Yeah.'

I was becoming bored. If I had been interested in attacking them they would be resting by now.

After more shouts of encouragement BeanPole finally stepped forward announcing his manoeuvre with an Arrhh! sound swinging the wooden pole-stick down at my head. I lifted my arm and grabbed its end inches from my head. A look of confusion fell over BeanPole-elect's face – first the brow, then the eyes, then his mouth. Still holding on to the end of the stick, I grabbed the middle of the pole (between his two hands), stepped towards him and twisted the weapon in a circular motion breaking his grip entirely.

Bean-ignorance is to be expected, but sometimes there are moments when it is profound. BeanPole-elect was confused to find himself without a weapon. I jabbed the end of the stick forward hitting him hard in the middle of the face. He staggered back as I heard Chain-and-Stiks-elect shout as she stepped towards me (as my back was turned). Feeling the rush of the displaced air as the sticks on a chain came rushing towards my head, I lifted the end of the stick I was now holding as I turned towards her. Her little stick hit my big stick hard and the chain wrapped itself around my pole. Once again I was met by that look of Bean confusion.

I lifted the lowered end of my stick in a circular motion up to her face and under her chin. With the end of my stick under her chin I stepped forwards pushing her back and exposing a nicely defined neck. Normally such a sight would be very tempting, but I prided myself in a certain amount of control. I took a second step forward and jabbed the pole into her neck. She staggered back clutching her throat gasping for breath. I followed up with two strikes to each side of her abdomen in quick succession. Before I could admire her finely tuned torso underneath her black cloak I sensed BroadBean-elect move towards me swinging his metal sword. Being fat, he was slow. He too helpfully alerted me to his arrival with a shout as he stepped in. (Do they ever learn?)

I turned, stepped forwards towards him, but away from the downward swinging blade, so that even if he were successful in completing the swing, the blade might only catch my ankle. But before the sword had passed the midpoint of the swing, I had the tip of my pole-stick behind his neck. A combination of his forward momentum and a circular flick of my stick threw him head over heels into the dirt. He landed square on his back wheezing. I looked at BroadBean-elect trying to think what was it about his life, his skill set, his diet that he was trying to achieve?

It all proved too easy, but why did they move slowly, so ponderously? Or was I able to move quicker now that I was in a physical form devoid of fear and reflection?

But it was not over. The tall (pole-stick-less) BeanPole-elect had picked up the sword from the ground and was now waving it around and shouting.

'Don't even think about it, motherfucker,' he shouted, protecting his prone friend as if BroadBean-elect – fat, flat and wheezing on the ground – was a more appealing bite than anyone else.

'You're going to die,' BeanPole-elect snarled, which was ironic because, as far as he was concerned, I was already dead, and, as far as I was concerned, so was he.

Chain-and-Stiks-elect was now also on her feet, but a little less sure of herself. Her weapon had been lost to the undergrowth, she was now dependent on her empty hands in which she appeared, yet again, confident. She crouched side on and looked at me fiercely. Obviously not feeling it was enough, she ripped off her hooded cloak in a sudden violent move and threw it in the darkness. Perhaps she thought the display of her well-toned and muscled upper body would scare me. Quite the opposite, the sight of a perspiring and gently steaming torso to a Muter was quite enough.

'What do we do?' asked BeanPole-elect.

I decided to make it easy for them and threw down the pole leaving me empty-handed and 'defenceless'.

'Here,' said BeanPole-elect seeing my action. He threw the sword towards Chain-and-Stiks-elect. 'You're better with weapons than me. Take the sword,' he said as it landed yards from his accomplice.

As BroadBean crawled away, the other attackers both started jumping and skipping back and forth, like some kind of dating ritual, making sounds and expelling the sweetest of aromas. Chain-and-Stiks managed to pick up the sword while BeanPole-elect skipped in with his fists held in a guard in front of him and tried a roundhouse kick to my head. There was no chance of the kick connecting, so I didn't flinch. He tried again. Again he was far from making contact so he sped in with a jumping kick aimed towards my abdomen followed up with a couple of punches. I shuffled back. A couple of his fist strikes hit my abdomen. I both felt it and felt nothing. BeanPole-elect skipped back. Emboldened, he shouted at his mate.

'I'll charge and attack him pushing him towards you. When I attack and the thing is focused on me, step in and kill the fucking motherfucker with the sword.'

Such aggression, I thought, and wrought with such emotion. So Bean. They attacked almost simultaneously. This time BeanPole-elect, with the few steps, had the correct distance and delivered a flurry of kicks to the stomach and my head. I (intentionally) took a step backwards (and towards) Chain-and-Stiks-elect who stepped in swinging the sword in a downward motion.

As previously mentioned, Muters do not suffer from the insolence of vanity but, if we did, I imagine the timing of my evasive manoeuvre would have made me proud. I caught BeanPole-elect's last kick to the head in my hand and, holding it firmly in place and aloft, stepped sideways thereby pulling the kicker's leg around perpendicular to Chain-and-Stiks-elect's downward swing of the sword.

The sword connected with BeanPole-elect's leg and the motion was powerful enough to sever the leg at the knee. He fell to the ground screaming in agony leaving me holding high his severed leg. Chain-and-Stiks-elect was stunned.

Seeing the juice beginning to ebb from the severed limb was too much for me and I bit and chewed into its red, raw, muscled end. Now it was too much for Chain-and-Stiks-elect, she panicked, swinging wildly at me for a few moments, before grabbing her hooded cloak and running towards the exit from the clearing, leading to the railway lines. I thought she would be lost to me that dark cycle, but she stopped at the fringes of the wood clearing. I watched as her shoulders heaved with panic and breathing. She slowly put on her hooded cloak. Did she think I would not see her now? But no, she took a step backwards. What had she seen?

She stumbled backwards further, revealing the figure who was blocking her exit – TrainTracks. She had risen! And I had missed it! I was both disappointed and proud. She looked well (pale, haggard) albeit confused.

Keen to make her acquaintance, I dispatched Chain-and-Stiks-elect and then found BroadBean-elect cowering in the undergrowth. I offered the kiss of BroadBean-elect to TrainTracks. She obliged and drank deeply. BeanPole tried to drag himself away, whimpering, but soon collapsed in a quivering heap. I feasted on his glory stream and leg stump before letting him rest in peace.

Being a secluded area I hid the Has-Beans – BroadBean in the undergrowth, Chain-and-Stiks in a nearby drain and BeanPole in a disused train wagon. By varying the storage locations I was hopeful that one or two would remain undiscovered until my return. Once again I determined to return at intervals until they were ready to take their first baby steps in eternal life.

I was pleased to return to find that two had indeed remained undiscovered – Chain-and-Stiks in the drain and BeanPole in the train wagon. I had high hopes for Chain-and-Stiks thinking there was something hell-ish about her intensity. I later suspected that a telephonic communication device might have played a part in locating BroadBean in the undergrowth as I heard its electronic knell-sound while TrainTracks and I departed the area. (Though I am pleased to say we located BroadBean quite by chance much later at a nearby field of rest. More of which later.)

Thus it was that making friends became relatively straightforward. Of course, even though (like BroadBean) there can be a period of separation, Muters eventually find each other. I was pleased to find DogSmells where I had left her and soon TrainTracks and her became inseparable. But there are also surprises along the way. Shortly after my excitement with BeanPole, BroadBean and Chain-and-Stiks, I was due to pay a visit to the rooftop that was home to Rooftop's ColourSplash. I took TrainTracks and DogSmells along as part of their learning development to instil within them the habit to look for their own bites and niblings.

In fact, it was on the third occasion that Rooftop and I had visited the rooftop in question that we made a welcome discovery. Rooftop, Tracks, Smells and I sat patiently for a significant part of the dark cycle enjoying the coolness of the metropolis air when a familiar aroma rose from the corner of the roof between the chimneys. It was indeed the compacted ColourSplash finally exhaling. The breath of a Muter has the delicate softness of death to it.

Rooftop rose from his seat on the parapet and took a few steps towards his creation still curled up in the shadows of the chimney crevice. Slowly she stirred of her own accord. First a hand stretched out of the shadows, then a knee fell out from the darkness, then a lower leg emerged from the abyss. Slowly ColourSplash emerged a fresh-born Muter, her blouse splashed in deep, crimson patterns. There is always something remarkable about watching the emergence from rest to the state of eternal peace – a state free from fear, worry, anger, sadness. So there, finally, ColourSplash stood before her creator, her gateway. Muters do not need to communicate in the way a Bean might try (and often fail) on such occasions. It is all understood.

The moment complete, Tracks, Smells and I rose from our position and joined Rooftop's side. It was pleasing. I looked to Tracks then looked to Smells. They understood. They too would soon need to take their own first step. But I would be there with them. All the way.

It was a first for everyone: Splash's first steps, Rooftop's first creation, Tracks' and Smells' first opportunity to bear witness. Satisfied that Splash was ready to depart the rooftop, we all turned and stepped towards the darkness.

It was only then, however, something caught my eye – the light from the sky's cool orb caught a flash of movement low to my right coming from the shadowy crevice between the chimneys from where ColourSplash had emerged. My initial alarm was countered by the certainty that I had not detected the aroma of any nearby Bean. Within moments the answer became apparent.

There, standing by the chimney in a dirty white dress was the blond, curly-haired, chubby-cheeked Beanling. The gentle soft aroma drifting to my nostrils was Muter, not Bean. She too had been risen. By all appearances she was intact. Perhaps the bite of my arm and my own nip of hers had done the business.

She, ChubbyCheeks, stood looking at me. She was not the fearful Beanling of a handful of light-darks before. She was perfect. I could not throw her off the roof now, what would be the point? I suppose I ought to let her roam. The Beans would find her and recycle her body. I could be of no use to her. So, with that I turned away and with RooftopSuicide, ColourSplash, TrainTracks and DogSmells, walked off towards the west. Two dozen steps taken, I heard the tiny pitter-patter of feet behind us. I turned. ChubbyCheeks was now six yards away from us. She was following us. I understood. There was a degree of responsibility. She had not been a target of mine, nor an attacker, but the least I could do was escort her off the rooftop and let her find her own way through the metropolis. I could not be of any help to her. She would not survive long. It was unlikely a Muterling of seven Bean summers could ever fight, feast and bite her way to eternity.

How wrong was I to be. How very, very wrong.

8. House Parties

Making friends is not all about open spaces, rooftops, railway lines, parks. And it is not always the case that friends come to me. Sometimes a Muter needs to just go and make friends with the undead. However, with limited Muter numbers (themselves with limited – or rather, 'developing' – skill sets), one has to be careful. Cloth-Head Beans were plentiful. Dressed in black with their cloth headwear, they were charged with monitoring the behaviour of the Beans according to the customs. Though clearly not the most gifted example of a Bean, they could still prove to be a nuisance.

In these early lunar cycles I was sensitive to the development of my niblings and our survival. In this early period there emerged three components required for a Muter's survival in a Bean-infested metropolis; they were: the need for a secure base, a developed sense of protection from Bean threats, and finally, opportunities for feeding, biting, kissing or 'necking'.

Firstly, the secure base. Up until this point I had had a fairly nomadic lifestyle. Moving from place to place is doable if one is working alone, but it could be o'clock-consuming and was becoming further complicated by the rise in the numbers of my Muter colleagues. Not that we would all explore the metropolis together, but it would be convenient to be able to return to a select number of appropriate shelters. At this time I had with me: RooftopSuicide, ColourSplash, TrainTracks, DogSmells, ChubbyCheeks, Chain-and-Stiks, BeanPole (now with an artificial lower leg) along with a few other stragglers. Having a home base would also help us manage the threats, which brings me to my second factor: protection from threats.

As the lunar cycle turned into another lunar cycle and then another, we needed to give a little more thought to the attention we were receiving – managing threats. The more colleagues we numbered, the larger the number of Bean-feasts we enjoyed. But Beans talk and I could detect in the air the incremental rise of the stench of fear during these lunar cycles. This rising fear led in turn to a developing interest from the Cloth-Head Beans, some of whom carried firing devices of different descriptions. My group of Muter colleagues was not the only team in town. There were other groups and pockets of single traders operating all over the metropolis. My colleagues and I would often come across other Muters in twos and threes, but I suspected my group was the most organised. That was, in part, because of my clear intention to nurture the early stages of a newborn. The cool orb of the dark cycle is the time when Beans retreat to their own bases, but for us, Death rests most comfortably in the bosom of the dark cycle.

Although not quite a threat, it was evident that Muters could work during the light cycle, but working during the dark cycle was more comfortable. Harsh light on decaying tissue could be uncomfortable. Similarly, harsh light on the eyes was also undesirable. Pupil-function is not as effective in the Muter as it is in the Bean. The dark cycle was preferred for operation, but it was not a requirement. As Beans tended to operate during the light cycle, so the threat to Muters diminished in the dark cycle. Beans have yet to understand the cool of the blackness. Muters do not hold the light cycle in such high regard, but we do not dismiss it. Far from it. Light forms part of the food chain allowing Beans to survive and reproduce in great numbers which blesses the world with sustenance. The great orb in the sky has allowed the development of massive Bean marsh farms like the metropolis.

No, the great orb is an ally, but like all allies, it is a relationship that needs management.

Finally, finding opportunities to kiss and relieve a Bean of their existence often took time in the early light-darks. With low skill sets, Muters needed to be selective and choose the moment carefully. In this respect, bites do not come to you, you have to go out looking for them. Whether it was for the purposes of feasting or Muter generation (or a bit of both), secure opportunities on the open street were limited, even during the dark cycle.

All three of these challenges could be addressed by adopting an organised approach to a base. This was greatly enabled by the identification and acquisition of the properties of targeted Beans. By acquiring a residence, a Muter could not only return to a specific location (where colleagues could also return), but it was a place free from immediate threats whilst (initially at least) being a source of nourishment. Therefore, in time, I would regularly seek out lone Beans and their homesteads and encouraged my colleagues to do the same. CatNaps is an early (and fine) example which confirmed the merits of property-based bite acquisition.

I had been working my way over rooftops and jumping between balconies of residences of a certain smart area. CatNaps had not been a target of mine. I had detected a small dinner party happening behind a wispy, willowy lace curtain. A half-dozen well-fed and flesh-happy Beans were most appealing, but as I swung and jumped down the balconies I found myself on a balcony just above a large open window. Sleeping peacefully on the window seat lay curled up the young lady Bean with a furry cat curled up in her arms. The woman most probably had no Bean-beanies of her own and furry animals sometimes acted as a substitute for beanie-less Beans. Judging by the aromas, the woman obviously loved the creature much. Too much, it turned out. I found myself observing the furry flesh all curled up in an attractive bundle in the lady Bean's arms. Perhaps a desert, I thought, once I had dined upstairs? But just as I was thinking of such a thing the cat stirred, snuggling in the grasp of the young sleeping Bean.

As it snuggled, I saw its nose twitch, then twitch again. Then one eye slowly opened. Cats are discerning creatures as well and, on seeing my dark sockets looking down at it, it exploded out of the arms of the sleeping Bean and darted out of the window leaping for the adjacent balconies. Immediately the lady Bean awoke and instinctively fell after her charge. The split second act of trying to hold on to the bolting creature (perhaps coupled with the shock of opening her eyes to see me gazing down at her lovingly) meant the frizzy-haired Bean toppled out of the window. She bounced off one balcony before tumbling down through the cooling summer night air, landing clean on the metal-spiked railing below.

To this day, it is the finest and cleanest impaling of a Bean I have seen. I had intended to head onwards to the dinner party, but hearing the wheezing of the immobile Bean and thinking of all that soft breath being pushed out only to be lost to the dark cycle, I wavered. It was only when I smelt the warm juice trickling out of her abdomen and down the railings that I realised it would be an unforgivable waste. I skipped down the side of the building and locked my mouth to her lips and inhaled the high. The gentle rocking of her body punctured more internal organs allowing the juices to flow freely. As she growled in her dying throes I drank from her wounds. After a few moments, I lifted the Has-Bean from the railing and carried her up the side of the buildings and rested her on the roof. I could not resist a few more tasty morsels before I left her. She would ripen in the next few light-darks and would most probably not be missed. There was no disturbance in her flat. As I disappeared over the parapet, I made a mental note to return to her and help her adjust to her eternity. Once she had risen, her residence became a base from which CatNaps herself could operate. Myself, ChubbyCheeks, TrainTracks, BeanPole and others were regular visitors. I suspected that the flat had seen more use in death that it had when occupied by a Bean. With the regular use of CatNaps' apartment as a base for a significant number of light-darks the idea of acquiring a number of similar bases was becoming attractive. There was the odd interruption from CatNaps' relative-Beans and the odd Cloth-Head, but these were managed away. Her neighbours presumably had paid (and continued to pay) little attention to her – a trait common in the metropolis – which was convenient. Indeed, it was a peculiar Bean trait – that is the instinct to gather in groups only to build walls and lock doors between each other. Beans regarded places like the metropolis as 'advanced' and 'civilised', bringing together citizens in civil society. Yet they lock all their doors.

It should also be noted that CatNaps tasted different again. She did not have the sparkle of the lover-Beans, nor the sourness of the aggression fighter-Bean. She had the tang of the Lonesome Bean – full of liquid grape and misgiving. This, she knew, and, in time, she might have sought enlightenment through self-action, much like Rooftop responding to the deep impulse calling one to realise their destiny. Needless to say, CatNaps flourished as a Muter, and I was pleased to later learn that her taste was common in the metropolis (in fact, to some degree, the whole metropolis edifice was built upon it).

My thinking on this matter evolved as I worked my way around the streets. Events would inform my reflection on Beans' way of thinking, which was largely based on paradox and contradiction. The opposite of CatNaps were those Beans who did have the company of other Beans, but, again, there was not a Bean activity to which a contradiction did not apply. Bean 'Love' being an example.

I don't see how something that is so transitory could be so effective at hoodwinking the Bean. I understand 'Love's' immediate purpose – it leads to sexual relations that leads, in turn, to the fertilisation of the lady Bean which, in turn, leads to the creation of Bean-beanies who develop into Beanlings, then Beanteens, then fully-fleshed Beans who subsequently generate the stable marsh farming conditions (a metropolis) that enable the creation of yet more Beans…and so continues the cycle. It is a mechanism for which us Muters are truly grateful. We understand the 'how' of the mechanism, but I still struggle to comprehend 'why' the Beans surrender to it so completely? Why endure the needlessness, the hopelessness of the mechanism's protocols? For what gain? What do Beans achieve from the total surrender to the Love protocol? Or was it all part of nature's plan? A grand design by a grand designer? But who or what could be more grand than death?

Yet, I do marvel at the double-backed beasting act. Not only is it a form of feasting (an example of the Bean developing a death skill, I suppose), but when Beans are bereft of clothing it can make easy work for those of us already blessed with enlightenment.

On one occasion I was loitering on the rooftops (again) and was unsure whether I wanted a male Bean or a lady Bean. (A balanced diet is required.) Watching the streets below I searched for movement. Sometimes the warm ground generated a warm swirl of air that lifted perfume to the roof-level. On this occasion different spices mingled in the air. There was a seventy-summered lady Bean walking with her dog. There was a thirty-something-summered lady Bean walking alone after an evening spent imbibing fermented grape juice. Like CatNaps, I could not detect a trace of a lover-Bean in her make-up, but nor could I detect a creature (canine; feline) in her life onto which she visited her lover-Bean needs. She was, in other words, unhappy and lonesome. (Or was it lonesome and unhappy?) What's more, I suspected happiness would not be forthcoming. She was approaching the number of summers at which reproduction would not be effective. Her body was giving up. I could smell it, literally. The chemicals surging around her fleshy structures were unmistakable. I took pity on her and, at any other time, she might well be the sensible, even ideal, target for refurbishment by death – she was reasonably able-bodied (albeit carrying more fat on her frame to make her truly effective immediately, but that could change). She had probably a reasonable skill set and, although she would not know it, her life as a Bean would not now develop any further. The 'dreams' she might have had as a Beanteen were as they had always been, wisps of light and shadow in the fleshy, grey matter in her head, nothing more. She would find her destiny soon enough where resentment would melt away and all would make sense.

I concluded that she would soon be released from the prison of the Bean fallacy of expectation. Thus I decided to leave her alone on that particular dark cycle.

No, on this particular occasion I wanted a bit of spice and there it came walking around the corner. A similar (perhaps even more-summered lady Bean) walking along, her arms wrapped around the waist of a male Bean. They had eaten well, drunk well and were presumably heading back to a property together. This would indeed be a feast – gently-roasted insides, a mixture of juices and sauces to tease and caress my palate. Yes, tonight was our night.

I followed them along the rooftops of one street, then another and then saw them turn into the property. The excitement between the two was palpable and it rubbed off on me. I worked my way along the rooftops to the roof of their own residence and sat and waited. I observed the illumination inside the property rising, then dimming and so charting their move from the ground floor to an upper floor. I took the opening of an upstairs window in the property almost as an invitation.

I sat and waited.

Aromas soon escaped the property: hot breathy moist air mixed with the sweet vapour from perspiring flesh lifted in an unseen column from the window through the chill of the night to my welcoming dark nasal cavities.

I let the Beans cook and curdle the juices on which I was soon to feast and, after a short period, I slipped down the outside wall of the house and through the open window. I was immediately overwhelmed by the warm breathy odours filling the whole property. Hearing intimate whispers of the Beans in the bedroom as they squirmed and devoured each other, I crept up to their door. As I was about to enter, the whispering stopped and was replaced by the smacking of lips, the heaving of breath and the groans of Bean pleasure. I paused on the landing and found myself staring back at myself in a full-length vanity facilitator. Devices that reflect a lie and deny a destiny. Having a moment to spare, I looked at how I had been transformed in the lunar cycles since my own light-dark of revelation.

I was leaner. Toned muscle was much more visible – quite literally. My skin was – if not a little pallid – pink, purple and green. Touches of black were also coming through nicely. My smile was not apparent, but that is the point of enlightenment – it is understood, there is no real need to express or communicate it. Beans seek reassurance in the faces of others. Muters don't. They are complete. Beans don't like their existence, they complicate it – they hide the reality and dress it up with powder and wear 'pretty garments' to cover the one truth – flesh. The closest they come to tasting flesh was going on in the next room, but even then they complicate it with laws, ethics, contracts and 'love'. They spend over seventy summers trying to avoid a destiny, living a contradiction: if a Bean doesn't like another Bean, he gifts him or her their destiny; if they *do* like a fellow Bean they do everything in their power to thwart realisation of that destiny.

The time had come. I stepped around the corner and pushed open the door of their room. The brightness from the landing spilled into the space illuminating the interiors and the two Beans on the bed. The male Bean was lying on top of the female Bean just as I had expected. They were lying in naked truth. For a moment I just savoured the sight of the perspiring flesh and drank in the warm aromas recently exhaled from their luscious confines. The Beans did not see me initially. They were too busy with their business. When they did, they stopped their writhing. The woman gasped.

'Oh my God. Honey, I can explain,' she said breathlessly.

This momentarily confused me. There was no need to explain. (And why was I being called 'honey'?)

I remained motionless in the illumination of the doorway.

'I thought...you were in Brussels. I never meant...,' she continued.

By which time I was lost. And bored.

I stepped forward into the room. The male Bean clambered off his piece of meat and stumbled back a few paces looking for something, clothing perhaps. I admired the flesh of both. Their physical activities had been pushing juice and spice all around their bodies so their flesh was pumped flush with delights. To make the most of their state (and before the juice subsided) I had to move in.

'Jack?' the female Bean said as I moved forward.

I didn't know who Jack was. Even if Jack was expected, I had no desire to wait for another body and let these two Beans get cold.

'Oh my God,' she exclaimed.

I detected panic. I wanted prime beef so jumped on to the bed and took a sample from her breast, then the other. The male Bean had the same idea and jumped on the bed which saved me the trouble of dealing with him should he try to interfere. I felt his warm naked body cling hard to mine, his hips pressed firmly into my buttocks. For a moment I was in a sandwich of Bean heaven. He didn't bite me but slung his arm around my neck allowing me to bite hard through his forearm. It obviously caused him some discomfort and he clambered off with screams allowing me to commune with his lady Bean and drink fully as her juices flowed. This Bean was very, very tasty. It hadn't occurred to me to feast on Beans who were themselves feasting on each other, albeit primitively. The juices and flesh were so ripe and full of pulsating riches and goodness. Oh, how grateful I was I had not settled for that sad, poor thing wandering home through the streets earlier. Patience does pay. Such pleasure. I must, must do this again, I thought as I gave my being, my cadaver to her as she was giving her body to me.

I sensed the male Bean was panicking and I thought he might join us on the bed again with his fine young thing, but I heard him shuffle, perhaps dress, panicked and head towards the bedroom door. I let him go. I was too engrossed. But then I sensed him stop. The brightness in the room was changing. At first I thought it was the Bean reaching the doorway to the landing, but I was unsure. With great reluctance I pulled my head away from my pleasure and turned to see the male Bean stationary, his eyes locked on another figure standing illuminated in the doorway just as I had been, not moments before. The figure stepped forward. Was it 'Jack'? No, for I then recognised the profile, the odour and shadows of the exposed cheekbones of TrainTracks. She had followed me.

Tracks needed no introduction to her options, it was standing semi-naked in front of her. The Bean rushed my colleague, but Tracks was learning her strength, picked him up and threw him back on the double bed beside me. Jumping on the bed herself, Tracks ripped off his trousers and got stuck in.

So there we were, the four of us in complete harmony. The old and the new. The past and the future. A family at table, feasting together in the quietness of the dark cycle. I was becoming more proud by the day. Did we need 'love' to sit and feast that dark cycle? No. It played no part. It would not make sense to play a part. Love – it epitomised the non-sense of Beankind.

9. Spread the Love

'Making with a Bean' is not always planned. Oftentimes embraces are purely accidental – brought about by the wind of good fortune that blows across this heavenly kingdom. So it was with Diesel. A stalwart of my niblings. From nothing comes greatness.

I had not faulted Tracks for gate-crashing my menage-a-trois. Although it was relatively early light-darks for her and she could certainly hunt on her own, she felt safer if she was accompanied. Similarly, Chubby. Chubby was very passably 'Bean' – with golden-blonde hair, pale soft skin, large eyes – she could move around the streets without difficulty, but she too needed guidance in those early light-darks. I was happy to oblige and so it was that Tracks, Chubby and I would walk the streets of the metropolis like a small family of Beans. Disguised in a selection of 'hooded' tops, hats and long coats, Tracks and I would walk along in the cool, early dark cycle swinging Chubby between us. It was the best of light-darks. Strangely, and much to my pleasure, this arrangement opened doors and solicited many welcome opportunities.

Just as planning cannot be relied upon, the violence and misgivings that a Bean will show another Bean can be relied upon. Even when there appears to be no reason for violence, a Bean will find a way. I am often surprised at the harm Beans do to each other. Perhaps the need is buried deep, innate – another indication of a Bean's impulse to realise their destiny (if not their own, then the destiny of another).

As an undead, Diesel had been a 'street entertainer'. To many, including myself, he still was – his skills had carried over into his enlightenment. All Beans fill their o'clock with juggling and shuffling, but some do it better than others: some juggle Bean-beanies, others shuffle paper, some juggle numbers, but Diesel topped them all, he juggled plastic. Bare-and-barrel-chested, with dread-locked hair and a fine mixed-heritage, he was a type who attracted small crowds – crowds of Beans who themselves had nothing better to do than watch a fellow Bean juggle plastic things, over, and over and over again. Exhibiting the typical Bean instinct for inanity (or – to the Bean – 'creativity'), Diesel not only juggled everyday plastic items, he swallowed swords (which did him no harm) and breathed fire. Juggling in all its forms is indicative of the Bean-condition.

To keep the crowd engaged and give his act an 'edge', Diesel would increase the number of bottle-shaped items, perhaps even three, or four and occasionally, when the dark cycle began, he would introduce fire.

I would watch him for long periods 'perform' his gift, share his philosophy, in shopping areas in light-cycles...and eateries and bar areas in dark cycles. I always took him to be a Bean who understood the pointlessness of his existence. He knew his destiny. He was biding his o'clock. So it was that he found himself on my 'to do' list.

It was a balmy dark cycle. It always is. For me. I watched Diesel-elect from a rooftop not far away from a dark street where he was performing. I was on the look-out for Beans heading home after hours of drinking and indulging in those dating rituals. Chubby and Tracks were loitering in the alleyways below hoping to come across some Beans themselves. Between us, we hoped to attract some aggressive Bean who might be of use.

Diesel-elect was, on this particular occasion, juggling sticks of fire which was, in hindsight, a spectacular precursor to the journey on which he was soon to make. I had no intention of feasting on him to such a degree that would limit his mobility. His skills and attitude (a wholesome disinterest in Bean existence) would transfer well to his functionality as a Muter.

It was in the mid-dark-cycle when I heard a number of hushed, urgent voices of Beanteens walking down the alley street below me. They were hooded and stank of nervous anticipation. Sensing something was about to happen I slipped down the edge of the building and into the darkness of the alley and followed them to the main street where the last dregs of the Beans were heading home. The Beanteens nervously waited for a lull in the foot-traffic before crossing the street straight towards the juggling Diesel-elect. Realising he still had an audience, Diesel continued to throw the flaming torches and blow fire.

It all happened quite quickly.

One of the Beanteens pulled a can of flammable liquid from his coat and threw its contents over Diesel-elect just as he was blowing flames. One moment he was a pretty articulation of the meaningless of Bean, the next he had disappeared in a sphere of golden flames, much like the great orb of the light cycle. It was indeed a peculiar sight seeing a burning star hovering halfway down the main street; it was certainly impressive. It impressed the Beanteens too, because no sooner had the ball of fire died down, the same Beanteen, to the whoops of amazement of his fellows, swung the can of liquid into the dying flames. One could almost see the figure of a swirling man in the swirling yellow and orange flame (as if still trying to juggle) before it disappeared again in the form of a spherical galactic furnace.

I had watched this from across the road in the alleyway from which the young Beans had approached the now soon-to-be Has-Bean, Diesel, twitching on the ground outside the parade of shops. Presuming it 'mission accomplished' the four Beanteens raced back across the road towards the safety of the dark alleyway – my alley.

It was, I suppose, ironic. Presumably having had their eyes blasted by the flash of the fireball, they did not see me waiting with open arms when they ran into the cool darkness of the alleyway. It was, to be honest, a somewhat bizarre sensation. Usually Beans are usually running away from me or at the very least backing away, so to have two Beans run headlong into my arms (like the Beanling to its parent returning from a light-dark of shuffling paper) was moving, even tender.

My bites were quick and sure and I dropped them in time to accept another two Beans who came running and cheering towards their destiny. Pumped full of adrenaline and good cheer the Beanteens were as ripe as any I have tasted. ChubbyCheeks and Tracks were immediately on the scene and devoured the Beanteens mostly beyond recognition or function. I could see the gratitude in their eyes and knew that working in teams had to be considered – not only in the execution of plans, but also in the grasping of opportunities that fly into one's arms.

I sauntered across Main Street to the smouldering ruin of the Has-Bean juggler. The small crowd that had gathered (sadly larger than any who had stopped to watch him work before) swiftly dispersed when I arrived. I picked him up and transported him to a place high and safe to let him rest and recover. A small bite and imbibing of his cooling juice would be enough to send him on his way. Joined by Chubby and Tracks they understood that, although nicely cooked, there was a need to resist a full feasting. We wanted Diesel in fine working order.

It had worked out well. I could see the potential in Diesel. He would be a useful addition to any 'team'. He would be another strong player and bring serious death skills to our work and provide options for colleagues. The family-routine with Tracks and Chubby worked well, but I was keen to build other combinations. Rooftop and ColourSplash were a solid pair and spent a lot of o'clock together and had proved to be very effective. Each looking out for the other. But many of my niblings were solo bites and did not yet have working relationships. And as our numbers grew and the more attention we received from Cloth-Heads, the more we needed to organise ourselves. That included the recruitment of a bit more Muter beef. We were approaching a corner in death's journey. To turn it successfully and advance our cause, we needed to spread the love.

10. Cloth-Heads and the Second Bean Paradox (Ownership and Control)

It was still the early period of the enlightenment. We were growing in numbers, but at this point Muters were seen more as a nuisance than a threat. In the very beginning there might have been some fear, but matters settled down as the lunar cycles trickled on and the Beans became complacent. I think if a Muter wasn't checking out a glory stream of a Bean's family member, we were perceived as an irritant to most, an intriguing anomaly to others. It was coupled with the fact that we were not terribly well-organised in these early lunar cycles. Besides, the leader-Beans wanted to play the matter down. But this is not to say we did not receive attention from the Cloth-Heads (and later, the Rubber Beans). I could report at length the encounters and little tussles we had with Cloth-Heads but, as with all things Bean, they are ultimately of no relevance and would bore you to death. In contrast, the acquisition and development of Muterdom is of significant noteworthiness. Nevertheless, there are a few relevant points of interest about the behaviour of the Cloth-Heads and I shall refer to them in limited style at intervals in these pages. Furthermore, if I am to describe the workings and nature of the Cloth-Heads, now is also an opportune moment to introduce the concept of the Bean Paradox.

The Bean is the epitome of Paradox. There are many paradoxes in Beankind, but I have identified three that warrant a mention. The first (and most pervasive paradox) I shall come to later, but the Second Bean Paradox has relevance to the Cloth-Heads and their origins, so I shall address it here.

Beans have an innate desire to 'possess' (stuff, each other, everything), but if Bean existence is so transitory, how can they 'possess' anything? Everything is on loan. Whether it be the acquisition of the abstract (knowledge, understanding, rights, status) or the physical (objects, property, creatures), it is of no use. Beans even think they 'own' their bodies. (It is no accident that they talk of their 'own bodies'.) What does this mean? Even death does not make a claim on the body. The Bean's body is like air, it moves through space as it decays, yet the Beans imbue their bodies with rights (which they themselves administer).

Beans build their societies around the 'possession' of both the abstract and the physical. They delegate the policing of this possession to 'policing authorities', but, being Bean constructs, such authorities or agencies are inherently flawed. They all fail. The Bean society is itself a monument to failure.

That said, the policing authorities, their agents and their tactics cannot be ignored. In the early light-darks there were fewer Muters and little organisation, understandably. A Muter who found himself in the metropolis and unversed in (and therefore baffled by) the contradictions and preoccupations of Beans, would soon find himself surrounded by Beans dressed in black with cloth hats of various shapes. Sometimes Muters were treated the same as Beans and processed through their systems as everyBeanbody discussed 'rights' and what to do in the allotted time. Later, Muters were treated differently – they (we) were regarded as having transgressed (or likely to transgress) Bean rights or property (corporeal, inanimate or abstract).

As our Muter numbers increased the Beans tried to organise themselves. They became reluctant to engage with us because of the number of Cloth-Heads being inducted into Muterdom and picking up (then both running with and handing on) the baton of death. Once our numbers reached a certain point, specialist Cloth-Heads were introduced. They were also dressed in black, but the cloth had gone and was replaced by rubber. The black Rubber Beans would usually run towards us Muters with a view to apprehending the deceased. Cloth-Heads would still be seen on the streets, but they remained confused, ineffective creatures and confined themselves to policing Bean business.

The Rubber Beans were solely focused on controlling what they believed they owned. Muters would usually run from the Rubber Beans in those early light-darks of learning. It is this marriage of the need to 'possess' and the Bean instruments used to 'control and protect' that are at the heart of the Second Bean Paradox. Beankind cannot possess 'it' if you don't control and protect 'it'. The control is attempted through the agency of the Cloth-Heads and (later) Rubber Beans. And what exactly is the Bean possessing? Put death against any abstract or physical thing and it all falls apart. This is compounded by the very nature of the Bean – confusion and ineffectiveness. Just a handful of stories can illustrate this.

It was another moist night in the warm lunar cycles. I had been resting after a rather fetching feast – a young couple walking their new-born (starter, main, dessert). I was alerted to the gentle but distinct odour of Cloth-Heads. I followed my nasal cavities to a street where something was going on. Looking back now, I realise I was a little bit foolish. My wits weren't quite with me, I was still relatively fresh.

I soon found myself standing in the middle of a long residential street with no exits. A gentle wind wafted the scent of Cloth down the street. I heard some windows around me close, presumably Beans panicking. I detected Muters close by and soon spotted them loitering at one end of the street. Suddenly, a shot rang out and the glass of an automobilic vehicle parked to my left exploded. The heavy sound of approaching Bean boots on tarmac followed. Then, another crack, more glass. I turned and ran down the street weaving through the parked cars away from the Cloth-

Heads towards the Muters. I passed a series of steaming open corpses leaking juice (leftovers of a street party moments earlier, I concluded). Being well-fed myself I was not tempted to stop and sample the warm tenderloins and kept on running towards the end of the street where I found myself at a fork in the road.

A strong scent of Muter wafted towards me from the left fork. Judging by the strength of the odour I guessed about half-a-dozen colleagues were hiding at the end of the dark street (which I suspected was a dead-end of garages and storage facilities). Thinking it best to lead the Cloth-Heads away from the Muters by taking the right fork, I swerved to the right. Suddenly, a powerfully-built Muter appeared on my right hand side. As I leant to the right, he countered my movement exactly leaning leftwards into me. With a nod of his head to the left into the darkness and to the hidden crowds of Muters, we both swerved back to the left and took the left fork. With a hand pressed in the small of my back he indicated he wanted me to keep on running. We stopped a hundred yards down the road at the dead-end. He nodded to me in acknowledgement and we turned and faced the fork in the road.

I was still unsure quite what was going on. No sooner had we turned when eight Cloth-Heads appeared at the end of the road in silhouette one hundred yards away and started to jog forward towards us. My colleague and I did not move. I thought that perhaps the Muters we had passed might be able to make their escape assuming the Cloth-Heads did not see them. After thirty yards of walking into the darkness the Beans started to duck behind the cars taking up positions with their firing devices. I remained still, waiting for his lead.

Three things then happened almost simultaneously. A shot rang out and a piece of brickwork turned to dust behind me. My large Muter friend disappeared from my side into the darkness as quickly as he had arrived. I was alone again. And finally, the tableaux at the end of the road in front of me came to life. What had been a dark road, with silhouetted vehicles and a handful of Beans walking towards me, was suddenly thrown into a whirl of activity and flailing limbs as perhaps ten Muters suddenly appeared out of the shadows and launched themselves into the Cloth-Heads.

Such was the intensity, it was almost personal. But in death, nothing is personal.

There were no other explosions from firing devices. A quietness and stillness settled upon the street but for the squelching as the Beans' organs exploded in the jaws of the vigorous Muters and the cracking of bones as skulls were impacted on any available hard surface. No one would ever know the exchange of ideas and cultures in that forgotten part of town. I watched as the ten or so Muters carved up the Cloth-Heads with an intensity that I speculated had been inspired by their unfinished business. Some of the Cloth-Heads were dragged away for composting while others would no doubt form part of the Muter contingent.

It was not the last I saw of the lead Muter, RubberBeanRunner. In the following lunar cycles, I would first smell the Rubber Bean then see the RubberBeanRunner (or one or two of his team) pursued by the Rubber Beans only to be ambushed again and again. I admired the organisation and the teamwork. They were devoted to their particular target. So, I did wonder if the Rubber Bean Runners had a pre-history with Beans in uniformed authority.

I recount this example because Cloth-Heads and Rubber Beans, being confused and ineffectual, would never be able to protect Beankind from death even if their existence was infinite. Additionally, such is the distrust Beans have for one another (as is clear from the multitude of procedures, laws, conventions about behaviour and ownership) that Bean 'society' inevitably collapses in on itself. (Ironically all these procedures require other Beans (Cloth-Heads) to enforce them but, such is the distrust of the

Cloth-Heads themselves, that there are yet *more* laws and conventions to protect the everyday Bean *from* the Cloth-Head. Framing ownership and possession in these convoluted ways is at the heart of the Second Bean Paradox. And, of course, all this leads to misery and confusion, which, in turn, leads to the First Bean Paradox (more of which, later).

The second example, in case you weren't convinced:

I have lost count of the times colleagues have been fleeing from the Cloth-Heads (and later, Rubbers) in residential areas. We have often been met by the symbol of Beans' fear of other Beans – a locked door. In such circumstances we had the strength and guile to gain entry through windows, skylights, however, Cloth-Heads (ironically charged with the responsibility of protecting the property) needed 'permission' from the owner Bean to enter a residence. How confused is that? No Muter would lock its doors. Everything is open. EveryMuterbody shares everything.

Nevertheless, as our activities developed, Muters began identifying 'safe houses' located along different escape routes where Beans had difficulties policing – parks, schools and educational campuses. Irony of ironies, on one occasion I had a studious Bean-Stew attempt to deny me entry to just such a place claiming it had been designated a 'safe-space' by not only her and her friends but by the campus authorities. At a loss to understand how death was denied entry to anywhere, I did what only I knew how and dispatched the bewildered Bean-Stew to a place where she could discuss the trials and tribulations of Beanhood with her previous (deceased) generations. Again, why try and control what you cannot possess – be it space or light-darks? Fittingly, the Bean-Stew in question became a follower of Chain-and-Stiks from which no space was safe.

All this served as a clear indicator of one of the paradoxes of Beanhood. However, as I was learning, not all Beans are on the same page when it comes to Bean possession practices and acquiescence of surrendering control to the Cloth-Heads. There were some Beans who were in conflict with the Cloth-Heads and had a 'disrespect' for some of the possession protocols. These Beans are not exempt from criticism (they are of Bean, after all), however, what I was to later learn was that the skills acquired in their Bean existence transferred well to death. These 'death skills' would be invaluable in aiding the development of our enlightenment practices. The 'death skills' of, for instance, the former Bean-Stew had been of no real consequence, so we tended to avoid the recruitment of Bean-Stews if at all possible; however, two fine examples of Cloth-Head-baiting Beans who brought many skills to the table were to become GlassCutter and DoorStop.

David O. Zeus

11. Stolen Kisses: GlassCutter & DoorStop

There were periods when I had to retire to the rooftops to avoid
engagement from the Cloth-Heads. It was fitting therefore that I
would encounter, kiss and nurture two of my finest Muters from
the ranks of Beans who were also adversaries of the Cloth-Heads.
One dark cycle I was minding my own business, loitering on the
rooftops of a residential area in a reasonably smart part of town. It
was nice and safe with great views and a place to drink in the
aroma of Beans. I don't know why I was drawn to such places. I
am unsure if I loitered on rooftops as a Bean. Who knows, it might
be because I *didn't* do such things (when I was an undead) that I
do them now. Perhaps I had a fear of heights as a Bean? Perhaps
my reluctance to travel the rooftops stemmed from the belief that I
should engage in Bean-lawful behaviour? Maybe my memories
will come back to me in time, but, whatever the reason, I was
aware of the tradition or habit that Beans were not supposed to
loiter on the 'properties' (strange word) 'belonging' (another
strange word) to other Beans. Ownership and possession are
important to a Bean (as described in the Second Bean Paradox).

It was the middle of the dark cycle. Occasionally I caught the
silhouette of other Muters loitering in the streets browsing the
talent around them. I doubted many of the Beans knew who was
passing them in the street or sitting, huddled under blankets in
doorways. For me, I preferred the view from on high. Also, with
my nasal cavities high in the sky, I was able to perceive the
potential of Bean snacks courtesy of the rising warm air and
accumulate information on Bean behaviour – watching them being

70

picked up and dropped off in automobilic vehicles, studying their behaviour in and around eating houses and public houses – to use for my own benefit at a later date.

On this particular occasion I was sitting minding my own business when my eye fell upon a nervous Bean working in the doorways and alleyways near a few shops. He seemed to take a particular interest in what appeared to be a high-end technology accessories shop. He reeked of anxiety. His beating heart and increased respiratory rate was pumping out the perfume at regular beats. This Bean was fresh, not up to any good and, I suspected, most probably working alone. The good thing about Beans who are up to no good is that they don't want their fellow Beans to know where they are, which means that I had a little more o'clock with them than is usual; they were possibly not missed for a few light-darks giving me (and them) the opportunity to rest and rise at our own pace.

I watched him slip into a side alleyway beside the shop. He was a good size and of reasonable strength, so he too would make a good addition to the team. Realising that he was to be my bite for the dark cycle I slipped down from the roof onto the street below, skipped across the quiet road and quickly scaled the drainpipe of a property above the alleyway where he was quietly working away. It appeared that he was cutting out a pane of glass from a window after which he used a suction device to lift the glass pane out altogether, placing it in the alleyway before disappearing inside the building.

Ingenious, I thought. Such skills and ingenuity would translate well in death (provided I got the timing right). Using drainpipes, I slipped down the side of the building and, skipping between the window ledges of the adjoining building, I followed him through his nicely-cut hole into the back of the premises. I found myself in the rear storeroom of the shop.

A few snipped wires appeared to have taken care of the electronic sound siren device; this Bean was a professional. Following the sound of gentle rustling, I stepped forwards towards the door leading into the shop itself. The glass-cutter intruder was undoing the locks of the front door before returning to his business of cutting through the glass cabinets housing a variety of electrical goods and their accessories – o'clockpieces, music storage and playback pieces, telephonic communication devices and other carefully crafted, glittery items abounded.

He smelt good, but I was curious and I had o'clock. It is always good to study one's prey and learn their ways. I needed to reach a point where I could predict their behaviour. Besides, I might learn how they could contribute to our team. Why was the Bean opening the shop entrance (which led on to an open street illuminated by lamplight) when there was a perfectly safe exit through the back? He was an intruder and this was the dark cycle, he wasn't the vendor seeking to do business.

The glass-cutter intruder got busy emptying cabinets of shiny objects throwing them into a never-ending supply of strong, black bags. Having completed his job in the front of the shop he turned and walked towards the shadowy corner of the shop from where I was observing him. I could bite him now, I thought, but I just wanted a little more time to study, so I slipped into another shadowy corner. He stopped in the doorway where I had previously been stationed. His nose twitched. He looked around.

Thinking he was now going to work in the rear storeroom I stepped towards the centre of the store. My attempt to remove myself from view made me more visible from the street which was, on reflection, unwise, because the second Bean (who had now entered the store through the now-unlocked front door) assumed the figure standing motionless amongst the cabinet displays (me) was his Bean colleague.

The Bean at the door called to me. I instinctively turned and the street illumination must have alerted him to his mistake and my true nature. The glass-cutter appeared at the back of the shop.

'Fuck,' he gasped, seeing me for the first time. 'Thought I smelt some shit.'

'Fuck,' said the Bean at the door.

'What do we do?' mumbled the glass-cutter.

'Move slowly. They're as thick as pigshit. Don't let it sneeze on you.'

'Holy fuck,' muttered the glass-cutter in disbelief.

'You've got the shit?' the Bean at the door said, nodding at the bags on the floor. 'Let's not hang around.'

'There's more shit back here,' said the glass-cutter nodding towards the storeroom at the back of the premises.

'Yeah, but there might be more shits like this around,' the door Bean said nodding towards me. By now the glass-cutter had joined us in the shop proper and there we stood: me between two Beans nodding repeatedly and 'talking shit'.

The bags of shiny things littered the floor around us.

That's curious, I thought, they are not panicking.

I did nothing. It is good to play dumb in these situations. Let the Beans make the mistake.

'Fuck, they're ugly,' said the glass-cutter.

'Let's go,' replied the Bean at the door, firmly.

'I have two bags in the back,' the glass-cutter said, moving towards the rear of the shop.

'It might block you in,' muttered the door Bean in hushed tones.

'Don't worry, I'll be fine,' said the glass-cutter, pulling a baseball bat from his rucksack before disappearing into the back of the shop leaving DoorStop-elect and me standing in awkward silence. He was a big Bean, but not the brightest. I suspected he had been brought along to provide muscle – that he did and I began to involve him in my plans.

He cautiously shuffled forward and grabbed two bags from the floor in front of me before edging back towards the door. I watched him pondering the next move. I was puzzled that they would put themselves in danger for glittery things. He never took his eyes off me as he moved.

'Dumb fuck,' he muttered under his breath, no doubt a bit more confident.

I was aware he was intending to insult me. Insults are burps of unhappiness. An unhappy Bean is a burping Bean. He shouldn't worry, he would soon bleed to death whereupon he would emit a whole host of delicious odours, so I felt no compulsion to make disparaging remarks in return. You don't insult a tender steak, do you?

I observed the veins in his neck, drinking in the perfume of perspiration running down the small of his back and imagining the warm juice flowing about his firm, fair body. I was beginning to understand the confusion in freshly-risen Muters when encountering Beans for the first time. Truly, the behaviour and attitude of the average Bean is bewildering. Perhaps the difficulty of comprehension is compounded by the ghostly memories of summers as a Bean. Just as the vanity, ambition and social standing of the earthworm is bewildering to the Bean, so it is for us. How my bewilderment manifested itself in my expressions I could not say.

GlassCutter-elect returned carrying two heaving bags. I had not engaged DoorStop-elect because there was a chance GlassCutter would escape through the back of the shop. I needed them both within kissing distance. I stepped towards GlassCutter-elect as he walked past me to drop the bags by the front door knowing they would both return to pick up the bags around my feet.

'Move, you fucking piece of shit,' GlassCutter-elect said.

I remained expressionless.

He spat in disgust, frustration and unhappiness and returned to his rucksack and retrieved the baseball bat.

'I said, move it you stinking piece of shit,' he said with the bat raised above his head.

'Don't freak it out,' whispered DoorStop-elect urgently. 'They can be dangerous. Let's just go.'

Alas, there would be no such luck for the Beans. GlassCutter-elect swung the bat to my head. I caught the bat in my left hand and held it firmly in place aloft. Glass tried to remove it, but suddenly became concerned at my unholy strength.

'Fuck,' said DoorStop-elect, but I sensed he wasn't going to try and defend his colleague immediately. He reeked of fear and panic which got me steaming.

I decided not to waste o'clock. With the bat held secure and high in my left hand, I thrust out my right hand to GlassCutter-elect's neck. My fingers closed around his windpipe digging deep into his fleshy unprotected neck and pulled. The windpipe snapped away from his neck as easy as scooping ice-cream from a bowl with a warm spoon. But bowls of ice-cream don't gurgle. I spun around and swung the gurgling Bean over his heels and into a glass cabinet. The fractured glass cut his peachy skin to threads. He began to ooze juice. Oh my.

I felt DoorStop-elect take a step forward, then a step back and then another step back. GlassCutter-elect writhed on the floor clutching his throat wheezing. It was painful for sure, but an eternity of bliss awaited.

I followed the retreating DoorStop-elect to the shop's entrance. He had pulled the door half open before I pulled him back and span him around and gazed upon his Beanling-like expression of surprise – the facial features of a Bean at their moment of reckoning surprises and enthralls me still. In fact, it is one of my favourite moments.

I bit and chewed and he passed.

I did not want to rush these Has-Beans so I dragged them both up to a nearby rooftop and laid them out under the stars. There they could rest for a few light-darks and, when they awoke, they wouldn't be disturbed. Again, any odours generated over the coming light-darks would rise harmlessly up into the sky.

I kissed them both goodnight and shimmied down a drainpipe and was about to skip away into the darkness when I heard the familiar rustle of the black bags in the shop once more. Curious, I padded through the shadows to the back of the shop and there silhouetted in the warmth of the streetlamps falling into the room were *two* more figures. One was rustling through the black bag, the other was rifling through display cabinets for the portable music devices and other electronical playthings.

What was it with these Beans? I stepped quietly into the room and almost reached the middle before I stopped. I watched and waited as they gurgled with glee at their glittery find. Suddenly they both stopped, nothing twitching except their noses no doubt, inhaling the flower of destiny. It was vigorous but quick. They too tried to exit the building and return to their existence, but within minutes found themselves resting, waiting for better things to come, alongside GlassCutter and DoorStop. Feeling the evening was not quite over, I hung around a shop until the great orb appeared over the horizon bringing Beans out of their homes to shuffle paper, stack boxes, stare at glass screens upon which hieroglyphs did a meaningless dance for their waking hours.

By the time I left the area, a total of nine Has-Beans were quietly minding their own business on the roof. It had been a peculiar and spectacular night. I had stepped out that dark cycle to acquire one, perhaps two, muscled team members but ended up sharing the love with a whole new family.

My one final act was bagging up four bags of the objects that had proved so fascinating to the Beans. I had a new theory – one that I wanted to test in the Beanfield.

12. A Developing Palate

A few lunar cycles in, I was learning there were different-flavoured Beans. From where the flavours came from (and how they originated within the Bean), I was still unsure. Initially I thought it was the result of a concoction of Bean afflictions (love, joy, fear, sadness), but I was beginning to appreciate that the Bean's diet (its own nutrition) itself was also an important factor. What the Bean ate or drank the light-dark cycle before I dined with them could make or break a feast. Get the right sauce in the right amount and the Bean juice would give a hit on a Muter's palate to die for.

That is not to say I was not always after one taste, one sensation. No, no, something different was also welcome – something saucy, something sour. All was good. A balanced diet. To get the Bean's insides cooking nicely at just the right temperature was every Muter's desire. This could usually be achieved by getting the Bean to work up a sweat – this could be done by just introducing oneself, but sometimes allowing the Bean to race away would provide a wallop to the palate (hence you might often see a Muter running slower than a Bean – timing is all); alternatively, if a different taste was desired, the Muter could introduce itself while the Bean was at rest. The sudden injection of 'panic' could add a real zip to the dining experience. It was exhausting – not only learning the huge variety of tastes on offer but also how to finely manipulate the variables of the edibles.

In this context I walked the streets and, in time, found myself gravitating to an area in the comfortable part of town; a place where I could sample a variety of culinary delights. Always keen to learn more about how the Bean diet influenced my own dining experience, I entered on a period of research in those early lunar cycles. Selecting a few streets on which were located various upmarket Bean eatery establishments, I started to follow pedestrians returning to local flats in the middle of the dark cycle. It was still relatively safe to roam the rooftops and it was an ideal way to catch a Bean within the optimal hour of their eating. At the beginning it was trial and error, but in time I learnt to distinguish the odours knitted to their breath, oozing from their pores or expelled from their undersides to ascertain what they had consumed. I would then cross-reference this with my own experience of feasting on their organs. I built up a picture of what was desirable. I would even break into the eatery at night and study the menu, then watch what the Beans would order and target them, or not, depending on my desires on any given dark cycle. Of course, I was working in the metropolis. I knew many colleagues who were based in the green, open spaces preferred other diets. I had explored the green open space at one time, but often the livestock could smell us coming which made it difficult to operate effectively. Being based in the metropolis (a place that smelled bad even to the Bean), our odours were disguised and it was easier to move around.

As my understanding developed so did my awareness that a Bean's psychological state also had an impact on the feast itself. A rich meal of marinated meats could be tempered by any one of their afflictions. The short-term psychological state of the Bean was further complicated by their longer-term psychological state – their so-called 'life-philosophy' (if they had one – many didn't) which could render a piece of flesh relatively plain in taste.

As discussed, the taste of a lover-Bean was by and large the most delicious. To catch a lover-Bean, a loved-up-Bean, Love-Cutsey-Pie-Bean was a delight. To catch a hurl of love juice as it hits your mouth, soaks the insides of your throat before cascading down into one's very being, is a thrill all Muters would kill for. I had christened it 'the glory stream'. Catch a glory-stream with a twist of adrenalin and it would give you a kick to last a half-dozen light-darks.

But it is not all about the love affliction. There are other Bean flavours that can weaken a Muter, one flavour being – ambition. Arguably a poor cousin to love, ambition still gives a very respectable kick. It is a form of self-love. Self-aspirational love. As my research continued I was keen to try and find a serving of Ambitious-Bean (ideally mixed with a splash of youth) who dined in one of my previously-identified Bean eatery-establishments. In time, I thought I identified the perfect type of Bean, the 'Stooge-Bean' and on one summer's dark cycle I ended up treating myself to three such Beans.

Lover-Beans are to be found mostly in pairs, but Stooge-Beans tend to move in minimum of threes, often more. I spotted these three particular Beans in a drinking bar and was thinking of following one of them home. I let them eat and I noted that they imbibed a few spirits which would give the juice a nice edge. I couldn't choose between the three. They were Moe, Larry, and Curly. I also considered listening to their conversation before moving on so I might learn where they lived and their plans for other light-darks because, depending on which one I chose, I could follow up with the others later in the lunar-cycle. But just as I was settling in for a period of listening in the corner of the bar garden in earshot of the Stooge-Beans, I found suddenly by my side GlassCutter, DoorStop and Chain-and-Stiks. Knowing where the Beans' future plans was not necessary – there would be enough Stooge-Beans to go around.

Bean-banter is mostly nonsense, but Stooge-Bean banter (usually slurred) has its own nonsense scale. I shall try and convey the gist of it here:

Moe to Curly: 'Derivatives are the past, mate; you need to sink the green into new synthetic CDOs. It's the dog's bollocks. Go for Credit Suisse – with a quarter of its trust in EFG International, it performed a seven per-center last quarter when the libor rate was tanking at the fourth because of the shit euro exchange bollocks and Singapore being scared by the shit going down in Jeddah and the oil markets. It's a cinch-up, fanny-licking opportunity that you won't find this side of the swanny's dog and duck, fuck, mate.'

'Seriously?' Curly slurred in reply. 'Makes sense to me. Game on.'

Larry to Curly and Moe: ''Sense', mate? Sense sucks, mate. What you want is sucks-cess.'

The three bumped fists and downed the liquid (which could not itself be held responsible for the nonsense pouring forth). However, inanity aside, I suspected these Stooge-Beans were still going to be tasty because of the juice pumping about them as they contemplated their 'success'. It was not lost on me that their 'success' was a phantasm, but my success was actual, physical. Yet, I should not despair at their spectral success because it manifested itself on my palate. Which got me wondering, was there a universal Bean definition of 'success', or did it differ within the Bean-experience? And if so, should I (as a Muter seeking the ultimate gastronomic experience), need to be aware of the other 'Bean' definitions of 'success'? Did it vary in different parts of the metropolis? Vary according to the number of summers a Bean had seen? Could it be discerned by garments, appearance, behaviour, choice of abode?

If gastronomic-success were to be informed, even determined, by the acquisition of material goods, then it seemed sensible for me and my colleagues to gravitate to the part of the metropolis that attracted the kind who saw merit in 'things' or 'stuff'.

I also wondered about how the type of company a Bean might keep would impact or inform the quality of the glory stream. Was there a golden combination? Where was the best bite? All this fed into my learning of my developing palate.

But I soon realised that my palate was not the only consideration. I needed to think about which Has-Beans would graduate to be an effective Muters. Early indications were (and later experiments demonstrated) that the death skills of Stooge-Beans were very limited. They became unimaginative, simple dullard Muters who often walked into traps set by the Cloth-Heads. Was a Stooge-Bean's pursuit of 'success' rendering them inconsequential in the greater scheme of things? In fact, at the time of writing, I don't think I have ever seen a Stooge-originated-Muter stake out a Bean.

These thoughts were playing on my mind, so as the three Stooges were leaving the eating establishment, DoorStop, GlassCutter and Chain-and-Stiks turned to me and indicated their wish to sample the Stooge-Beans, but I intimated to my colleagues that I did not want the kiss straightaway. I wanted to conduct an experiment.

We waited until each Stooge had climbed into separate black automobilic vehicles and had driven off in different directions. Within 200 yards my colleagues stopped the three automobiles and extracted Moe, Larry and Curly and dragged them up to a predetermined place on the rooftops near the apartment of a young couple who had entertained us a few nights before (and were resting themselves before rising).

I had instructed my colleagues not to bite the Stooges. I wanted them fresh.

We strung up the three Stooges in a row upside down. What surprised me was their fear. They whimpered and wailed and cried like Beanlings. It was unreal. Not an hour before, they had been full of the bravado of Bean ignorance and committed to their place in the universe. In fact, they had even alluded to themselves as masters of that universe. What I had not banked on was their universe or galaxy was so very small and primitive. They were not fighters, nor lovers. Even seven-summered ChubbyCheeks showed more composure when facing her moment of enlightenment. I soon began to think that the fear-toxin now running through their bodies might limit the kick of the 'success-tang' in their juice – the prospect of which had been so appealing to me.

What is it with Beans? Why the panic? They have had enough summers to prepare for their destiny. What have they been doing in all their summers? They knew I (Death) was coming, so why couldn't they be ready? What was the point or merit in their seeking 'success' if it did not prepare them for death? So, as I looked at Moe, Larry and Curly hanging upside down, wriggling and weeping, I wondered whether their pursuit of 'success' was in direct conflict with their preparation for destiny and was this pitiful reaction particular to Stooge-Beans?

Aware that the weeping toxins might be harming our feasting experience, we tucked in and drank deeply from them all. My fears were confirmed. 'Success' (as Stooge-Beans experienced it) was not conducive to a recommended gastronomic experience. I also concluded that Bean-success failed to prepare the Bean for destiny and therefore the term 'success' was, in every sense, a misnomer.

Having feasted, we let the three Has-Beans hang there and I left it to Chain-and-Stiks to return and oversee their first few steps. I would monitor their skills development in the lunar cycles to come but, I confess, I was not optimistic.

The matter was brought home to me later when I was watching another Bean eatery. It was a smart place; it was a cheap fuel-stop for Beans in a rush. Its furniture was plastic and colourful, the illumination harsh – designed to pull in the Beans (and then push them out, no doubt). It was a place where the Beans collected the food themselves and cleared the tables themselves. It was not a place that would obviously generate an especially enjoyable gastronomic experience for Muters, but (and it is an important 'but') there were signs all over the eating establishment referring to a 'Happy Meal' which got me thinking – what makes a 'happy meal'? After much reflection and soul-searching I concluded it was true – a happy Bean was a happy meal. In other words, a happy Bean was death-ready.

But soon the death-ready Bean was not my only line of investigation. Watching the establishment work late into the dark cycle and feeding many Beans quickly and efficiently, I realised that, as our numbers were growing, we Muters too should scale up and become organised and efficient in feasting. Not only could I share my thoughts with up-and-coming Muters during shared feasts, but some organisation between ourselves would not go amiss particularly as there was an increasing Bean threat. Until the Bean threat subsided (which would be achieved by assimilating or enlightening all Beans), I thought more consideration should be given to Muter organisation, community development and the sharing of best practice.

So it was that, with this in mind, I returned to an alleyway to study the Happy Meal establishment. I had brought with me BeanPole, DoorStop, Diesel and GlassCutter as I thought I might need a bit of extra help clearing the premises. ChubbyCheeks attached herself to us and, although the target venue was possibly a tricky endeavour (centrally-located with a likelihood of Cloth-Heads and Rubber-Beans in the vicinity), it was always a pleasure to have her along. Once it became clear that the eatery's business was winding down late in the dark cycle, I slipped around the back of the building and waited. When an employee was exiting the back of the establishment with bags of rubbish, I introduced myself to him quietly. I was more interested in the manager of the establishment, but had to go through a number of employees to reach him in the kitchen. All were obliging.

I was momentarily disconcerted when I learnt that there was an upstairs eating area that I had not anticipated. Having brought my team along, it seemed silly not to indulge. We couldn't take them all with us, but after a short while I kissed the manager (FastFeast-elect) and moved him and a couple of his own colleagues off the premises. We had to move them to a rooftop some distance away from the food establishment to allow them to rest and rise in peace. I did wonder what the Cloth-Heads would have made of the establishment the following morning – I know Beans are fixated with what they call 'food standards' and 'Health and Safety' – we did not leave it in the best of condition. Nevertheless, it was a job well done. I was pleased to secure the services of the food manager (FastFeast-elect) and I hoped that his death skills would do much to help us manage the transition to a more organised way of feasting. In fact, as our project expanded, FastFeast became a crucial part of our nutrition regime and our culinary development.

I also noted that many of those Foodie-Beans were very tasty – in fact much more so than the Three Stooges. I suspected that the existence of the Foodie-Beans would not mark high on the 'success' scale of the Three Stooges, yet, many of the Foodies were culinary delights. It was an intriguing thought. The more I learned, the more complicated it became and the more I realised it would be more difficult to pass my knowledge on to my colleagues who were less discerning, so, I mentored my new colleagues to keep it simple. In summary: A happy-Bean is a Happy Meal; but a 'successful' Bean does not a happy Bean make.

13. A Developing Skill Set: Location, Location, Location

My quest continued. Could a happy meal be found anywhere? Or were happy meals to be found (at least in greater numbers) in particular parts of the metropolis? Regarding it as a central skill, I set out to collect a random sample from around the metropolis. I wanted to learn – Death never stands still, we're always on the move.

In the middle of one dark cycle, I found myself in a small circular park area (of which there were many in the centre of the metropolis) bordered by metal fencing and trees and surrounded by grand terraced residences. Other Muters tended to loiter in large residential areas of those Beans with low net worth; those Beans would spend o'clock outside commuting to and from one part of the metropolis to another, or cycling in circles, or smoking on corners – routines easily understood and learned by my colleagues. In contrast, high net worth individuals do not leave the house at the beginning of the light-dark and return at a regular o'clock. They are leisure-Beans. Their o'clock is their own, therefore it is difficult for a Muter to learn their routine. So, although pickings could be slim in the high net worth areas in which I was hunting, richness could be found in the streets if one were patient.

Having identified a suitable hiding place in the shadows of the trees bordering the park I planned to leap over the railings of the locked park and glide up behind a lone walker to surprise the Bean with their destiny. Slipping a hand over its mouth, I would lift it off its feet and carry it up to the park in anticipation of a little quiet time together in the secluded grounds.

Fully-grown Beans led very controlled lives especially when interacting with other Beans. This helped greatly because it meant a similarly stifled reaction when meeting me. The subsequent shock meant they made little noise, presumably in a rather quaint way of not wanting to disturb the local residents. Hauling them over the railings often resulted in tears to their clothing and flesh which kept them distracted in those early moments. If I dallied, the sweet smell of their juices emerging from their pricked flesh would ping into the cool night air and spur me on to move more quickly.

On one particular occasion, as I was waiting patiently, I detected the sweet aroma of flesh in the air and spotted two walkers enter the square. I considered my options. As a rule, when hunting alone I prefer the lone walkers. If there are pairs of walkers, I can sometimes take advantage of one Bean while the shock hangs in the air, but there is always the danger the other Bean will run off to seek help from a Cloth-Head Bean which, in turn, meant that I was rushed and could not feast at leisure. For some reason Cloth-Heads tend to respond quicker in the areas where rich Beans congregate. For this reason, I let the pair go.

I did not have to wait long before a lone lady Bean entered the square. I watched as she tottered along on her heels. It was an invitation not to be missed. Again I found myself wondering about the choice of footwear. Why do Beans look for ways to move with difficulty, especially when there are threats all around them? I waited until the fleshpot was approaching the middle of the square and an area of shadows before I began to make my move when all of a sudden I saw small movement through the trees on the other side of the railings. It was peculiar because I hadn't smelt another Muter. I assumed I had had the square and park to myself, but there you go, things change. As our numbers increased, so did our colleagues learn. I had no intention of competing with him for a kiss and stepped back to hang around for the next arrival.

I heard a muffled scream and saw the shadowy attacker drag the lady Bean into the park through an open gate I too had intended to use. Not that I was interested in watching him going about his business, but he was making a meal of it – the lady Bean was struggling for far too long. Perhaps the Muter was a newbie and still honing the basics – immobilise the target, draw juice from a main artery (sending them into shock) before drinking deeply. If the shock didn't quiet the Bean down, the loss of juice would.

Then it clicked. It was Bean-on-Bean. Yes, I had a hazy memory. Beans attack each other for a variety of reasons. It was most probably a male-female attack. I slowly made my way over to the writhing couple of fresh bodies. Indeed, I was correct. That's all it was – just like in the lover-Bean party the previous lunar cycle that TrainTracks had gatecrashed. I stopped ten yards away from them and watched. He was pinning her down with one hand over her mouth and while he tried to hitch up her skirt revealing, I have to say, much peachy flesh. His own trousers were pulled down displaying his pale fleshy buttocks which were throbbing in a manner to make any Muter weak at the knees.

As I stood there watching (and to allow time for the Beans' love juices to start pumping) I concluded the act looked completely ridiculous for so many reasons. It was such a laborious process of reproduction. If successful, it took a further nine lunar cycles. After nine cycles it was a further fifteen summers before the product became independently functional.

(An important note: I do not wish to be dismissive of Muterlings, but at this stage I was yet to learn of their effectiveness in the field. I speak, of course, of ChubbyCheeks. More of which later.)

Again, contradictions abounded. Bean reproduction required two Beans of different (conflicting) persuasions unless two persuasions were not required (as Beans were endeavouring to do by adjusting their behaviour and developing technologies). Secondly, reproduction involved compliance unless it didn't require compliance. Neither contradiction applied to the Muter. We create from nothing and have a fully functional Muter within a matter of light-darks. We never find ourselves in conflict with each other. Once we have risen, we live in harmony. But Beans are different. They build, then destroy. They need to work together, but they fight.

As I observed this mismatch of missions, I was reminded that I cared not for the Bean, but I cared for the enlightenment of a Bean. Looking at the Bean's struggles to reproduce, I felt disgust at the inefficiencies. I would create two Muters in a matter of light-darks and both would be grateful. I didn't dally. Just as this attacker Bean had felt compelled to explore the flesh of another creature, so did I – as I thrust my hand inside him.

I pulled TreeShadow-elect off TottyHeals-elect and lifted him high above my head like an errant child before dropping his mouth to mine allowing me to inhale his sweet breath before I drank from the fount of Bean.

14. TarmacTired

Bean-on-Bean aggression might be undesirable for Bean, but I suspect it springs from the underlying urge to free one and all from Beanhood. In fact, there are a number of Muters who have excelled once they have been relieved of their burden. Consequently, 'violence' can be an enormously creative force. In the early lunar cycles Bean-on-Bean violence brought to us a fair number of the most accomplished Muters. One of the finest being, TarmacTired.

Although the central parks and squares were agreeable hunting grounds, one has to be careful. Repeated feasting in one specific area can be problematic. One can overhunt. The hunting grounds have to be managed; the Beans are learning creatures (albeit primitive). They can learn to avoid an area. Besides, I had selected a handful of park squares for a series of dark cycle experiments which, if successful, I hoped to roll out across the metropolis. It was an experiment that needed a team of experienced colleagues. Recruitment was ongoing.

As our presence in the central dump grew, so did the Cloth-Heads and Rubber Beans press back. I was obliged to take opportunities to escape the metropolis and head for the fields for rest. I had made such excursions since my endeavour to rescue BroadBean from his resting place and it was on just such an excursion that I met and kissed Plot. She was to become a keen colleague of mine and would prove crucial at the end (or rather, 'the beginning'). It is a story worth telling, but I shall leave it for another occasion.) Yet it would be in similar circumstances – when

I was resting away from my usual hunting grounds, on the wasteland of a rather run-down area of the metropolis – that I met and kissed another rather special Muter-to-be.

On a piece of rough ground (surrounded at a distance on all sides by run-down structures), I was quietly minding my own business with Diesel, Rooftop, ColourSplash, CatNaps and BeanPole when I caught a whiff of perspiring flesh on the wind. It was coming from all angles, which confused me. However, the repetitive sound of an automobilic vehicle nearby led me to conclude the aromas were emanating from a wheeled machine circling the wasteland. Presumably the windows had been wound down and the rapid movement of the machine sucked the aromas from its interior prompting them to drift across the wasteland to me and my colleagues. Although Beans were known to approach us, they had always done so on foot (Chain-and-Stiks; BeanPole; BroadBean). The use of an automobilic vehicle was possibly a new challenge. I rose to my feet and scoured the roads on the circumference of the land a hundred yards away. My colleagues rose to their feet also aware of a possible threat. Cloth-Heads do not attack and the perfume did not have the artificial aroma of one of those early Rubber-Bean raids.

At the meeting of the cycle's light with the dark, I spotted a large black automobilic vehicle racing then slowing and then racing again on the road on the perimeter of the wasteland. Were they looking for something? We decided to make ourselves visible, so we stepped out of the vegetation cover and advanced slowly towards a patch of broken tarmac that formed part of a road leading to the middle of the wasteland. Diesel, DoorStop, Glass, ColourSplash, Rooftop and others fanned out in a large circle. Suddenly the black automobilic vehicle mounted the curb, crossed the pavement and turned onto the wasteland and raced towards us. I detected fear rather than aggression in the air emanating from the wheeled machine, so I did not conclude an attack was imminent.

Amidst the aromas I detected a weak Bean oozing sadness and a profound resignation normally associated with a weak, dispirited Bean on the verge of enlightenment.

The automobilic vehicle raced towards us bouncing over the uneven ground before it swung in a crescent movement on the tarmac. Stopping briefly, a rear door flew open and a lady Bean was seemingly pushed out onto the tarmac. The automobile's door slammed shut which pushed yet more fumes towards me from the Beans seated in the moving machine's interiors. I drank in the perfume of youthful male Beans as the automobilic vehicle (and the sweet sound of laughter) retreated to the safety of the perimeter road before it turned away into the darkness of the metropolis. The vehicle was not a threat, nor was the slumped broken figure of a lady Bean lying in a heap on the tarmac.

RooftopSuicide, ColourSplash and my other colleagues all looked at me expectantly, but I was distracted by the receding car and the action of the Beans sacrificing one of their own. I detected no lover or fighter amongst them. Was this a new kind of Bean? A new behaviour? Most of my interactions with Beans usually involved them working as a unit against us. This 'surrender', for want of a better word, was unusual. The automobilic vehicle might have departed, but the keenness of the perfumes of the male Beans had reached my nasal cavities and sunk deep within me. I would know their smell and I knew that I would smell it again, but not so fleetingly.

I approached the small heap of Bean unmoving on the tarmac. She was not enlightened, she was not a Has-Bean, she was not asleep. Her whole being reeked of a Bean tiredness – a physical tiredness, emotional, spiritual, and psychological exhaustion. The smell of resignation I had detected coming from the vehicle earlier had been hers.

We surrounded and looked at the pile of pitiful Bean. She sensed our presence; it was not fear, but an acceptance. A state of

Bean maturity, perhaps. We lifted the tired Bean from the tarmac and retreated back to the seclusion of the vegetation and darkness. She did not have the strength to resist. It was her time. Perhaps she did indeed accept. Perhaps she wanted it. Perhaps she had passed caring for an existence as a Bean.

As I kissed her neck and drank from the fountain of Bean, I could taste her weakness, her tiredness, her surrender. As her breast heaved with the last breath of a short, failed existence as one of the undead, I wondered whether she could foresee the strength, understanding, perspective and clarity with which she would soon be blessed. In the total absence of her own strength I wondered whether her risen strength and power would be unhindered. She might possess a resolve to do anything she so pleased. I wondered what that might be. I thought I knew.

I had seen a degree of resolve in Rooftop in his pursuit of ColourSplash. I had witnessed a strength return to TrainTracks and confidence surge in Diesel. I detected that TarmacTired-elect would be a Muter of note.

Stepping back to allow my colleagues to taste (ahead of an excursion later that night) I resolved to help her. Keen to keep her relatively intact, we soon left her to rest. Those automobilic vehicular Beans had smelt so appetising. Perhaps TarmacTired and I could feast together. As she lay there, a Has-Bean, she was blissfully ignorant of the eternity lying ahead of her. She was saved. Once she was ready we would sit and feast together with old friends.

So it was that I took a particular interest in Tarmac. She would be a case-study – another one. Was she hated, rejected by the Beans? If so, how would her rejection inform her development as a Muter? I was fast coming to the conclusion that a number of factors were present in becoming an effective Muter. It was not all about the brawn of the likes of DoorStop, GlassCutter and Diesel, or the intensity of Chain-and-Stiks. There were other skills worth developing. One should not make assumptions as a Bean is inclined to do. ChubbyCheeks' work was impressing me and challenging my assumptions. It was also a case of imagination and guile. Male Beans such as TreeShadow, (and later CrackleNeck) were not terribly impressive. The ThreeStooges were pedestrian. Their Bean skills were non-existent and their perspective had been so narrow that they were shells of potential. Molly-cuddled by ignorance and ambition. If there was one thing I was learning, Muters were certainly the manifestation of a meritocracy. Although all things are equal in death – it is the greatest of levellers – the death skills can be limited by too much exposure to Bean-priorities. That said, many Muters can turn the limitations into effectiveness, as the ParkSparkle twins were later to show.

15. ChubbyCheeks and FatLegs

At times I think I have seen it all, then I am surprised by those closest to me. As I have said, I confess that I had dismissed Beanlings. I thought they needed to put on weight, build strength and acquire skills transferable to death. However, one of the most impressive Bean-enlighteners is a former Beanling of not more than seven summers (before she was freed from the Beanfold). Her story has changed the way I look at Beanlings and the effectiveness of their enlightenment as Muterlings.

ChubbyCheeks was one of my early bites, but I confess I did not invest too much time in her development. For that I can credit CatNaps and TrainTracks. Even without Naps and Tracks, Chubby is a self-starter and largely self-taught. I don't think Naps quite understood what creature she was mentoring. Naps has bitten a fair number of Beans, but nothing like Chubby. In fact, so impressed have Naps and Tracks been with Chubby that they now make a point of seeking out and biting Beanlings not only as companions for Chubby, but because Muterlings can be so effective as hunter-killers. Of course, the most effective biter of Beanlings is ChubbyCheeks herself.

Chubby could work alone, in pairs or be the central player in a team whilst wholly devoid of self-interest and vanity. I witnessed one of her early solo bites in one of Chubby's favourite hunting grounds – a Beanling playground. It was a master class in approach and execution. With her big, blue eyes and perfectly round, porcelain pale face, her scraggly blonde, wavy hair falling about her cherubic features (including, of course, those chubby cheeks acting as soft, plump cushions for those 'What, me?' eyes), she is a killer who can move about the playground with ease. Not only does she put the Bean parents at ease, but she comes across as being not the slightest threat to the other Beanlings toddling about.

On this particular occasion Chubby started her light cycle on a swing in the corner of the playground. Her eyes searched the playplace for death. I sat hooded on a nearby bench to step in and assist as necessary. It was clear which Beanling had caught her attention – a five-summered creature who was being attended to by his doting mother. Having tied his laces the mother teased and tickled her off-spring lovingly.

'Who's got...fat legs?' the mother-Bean would say gently pinching his podgy pale thigh making him giggle and squirm.

It was perhaps an unwise thing to do in earshot of the killer of killers, Chubby. I knew it would do nothing but put ideas into Chubby's head. The Beanling toddled off from his mother to explore the rides in the padded enclosure. Finding a brightly coloured rocking rabbit on a large spring, the Beanling climbed on and started rocking. A few moments later, Chubby had slipped off her swing and casually made her way towards the rocking Beanling. Up close a fully-grown Bean would possibly know there was something not quite right with ChubbyCheeks. The paleness, the fierceness that could flash in those big eyes, the bloodied gums, but to another Beanling, such things would be lost. So when Chubby gently helped the Beanling to rock on his rabbit, he would have noticed nothing and the mother would only smile from a distance whilst wholly unaware of the imminent and violent enlightenment of her precious Beanling.

After rocking the rabbit for a short while, Chubby sank to her knees on the side of the rocking rabbit away from the mother and pinched the Beanling's thigh just as his mother had done, making him squeal with laughter. After a few more playful prods and having selected the plumpest part of the thigh, Chubby sank her little teeth into the Beanling's thigh.

The sudden change from shrieks of playfulness to shrieks of fear and pain roused the mother-Bean from her bench. Racing to her son's aid to find pieces of his thigh hanging out of the Chubby's mouth, the mother stopped her in her tracks. The playful laughter of Chubby must not have played well with the mother either because the lady Bean immediately grabbed her Beanling with both hands lifting him off the Rocking Rabbit itself now dripping with juice.

The mother looked on in horror as Chubby Cheeks was not going to let such fine nutritious juice go to waste and started licking the toy rabbit ride clean. Stepping back to run might have been the mother's next thought, but it was never really going to happen. Holding her de-juicing Beanling in her arms, the mother did not see Chubby jump up and run straight at the mother Bean's thigh. Sinking her teeth into the exposed pale flesh, the mother Bean staggered back and fell to the ground. There were no delays with Chubby. Within moments she was at the Bean's neck, then back at the thighs of FatLegs-elect. I had not done a thing, yet Chubby had executed two bite manoeuvres in less o'clock that it took to drain one inverted Stooge.

My respect for her mastery of the situation was only broken when I realised Chubby was looking over to me. She needed help. Automobilic vehicles and voices were to be heard on the perimeter of the park. I rose and joined them in the play area.

Bundling the mother over my shoulder to ensure no early alarms and picking up the pale, lifeless Has-Beanling, Chubby and I exited the playplace and left the area altogether (and beyond any Cloth-Head organised search zone). I placed the mother on the roof of a garage and her off-spring on an adjacent roof. I left Chubby sitting with them. I knew she would wait until they rose.

There is something innocent and accepting about Beanlings, even with regard to their destiny. Beanhood clouds the clarity. Beanlings express a truth about their purpose and struggle to comprehend the complexities that full-Beans layer upon their existence. I was beginning to think that Beanlings might be the answer; they don't infuse their existence with 'meaning'. Chubby was blazing a trail and if others were similar, the world might be a very different place as our project progressed. Anyway, in the meantime, she had made a new friend and team member. What a team they would prove to be.

16. Lite-Bites

Watching Chubby work illumined my eye sockets. I was beginning to understand (or rather appreciate) the role of different types of Muters. I had always been aware of the different skills that could be brought to bear upon the injustice and confusion generated by Beankind, but the number of ChubbyCheeks' summers ran counter to my (previous) thesis. I wondered why and how it could be that she was so effective, intuitive, inspired. I considered the possibility that it was the manner in which Chubby had been conceived. I had never bitten or feasted upon her. She had bitten me and I had just nipped her arm in return. She had passed through to enlightenment having been trapped behind ColourSplash in a chimney space. Yet here she was using guile and intuition beyond her summers. FatLegs was just one example. Often I would meet up with ChubbyCheeks after a handful of light-darks to hear that Chubby herself had been exploring the metropolis (often accompanied by TrainTracks, ColourSplash, Diesel) and been responsible for recruiting Bean and Beanling alike. So it was that I wondered whether my lite-bite on her forearm (and her nip on mine) had exchanged just the right amount of 'understanding'. I also noted that, having not been blessed with being the host of a full-blown feasting herself, Chubby could move throughout the metropolis unhindered, her appearance relatively unaltered to the eye of an ignorant Bean.

With this playing on my mind, I continued my travels around the metropolis and decided to conduct some research. Early in one dark cycle I was skipping over the fences of back gardens to avoid the crowds. The great orb had sunk beneath the horizon but the air was still pleasantly warm. Having feasted during the previous dark cycle, I had no interest in hunting, however, having jumped over my tenth fence I caught something in the wind. I sighed and shook my head in disbelief. My desires are not my own. I am indeed a slave to a nature and instinct beyond (and greater than) myself – Death.

I double-backed and loitered in the trees and bushes at the bottom of the garden and there she was lying flat out on her patio sun-lounger under the emerging stars. The illumination from her home was bathing her figure in a delightful hue; a sight to behold – like a piece of roast pork framed by the light of an oven window. A glass of white wine in her hand suggested she was nicely juiced.

What could I do? I was lost. I slowly crept up the length of the garden and stood at the foot of the sun-lounger gazing at her. Her eyes closed, with wires leading to her ears, she was in a world of her own. Normally I would kiss the neck and glug, but as she appeared to be asleep I had options. She was wearing a thin cotton dress that almost covered her thighs. She had seen perhaps fifty summers, but the pale flesh of her calves were plump and fresh and clean of fur giving them a yumminess normally associated with fewer summers.

I could almost see the juice running around her flesh feeding her limbs with energy. Her whole body oozed, almost crying out, 'come-get-me, Nigel'. Once I had seen the calves I could restrain myself no longer, I knelt down and lowered my mouth and tongue to one perfectly formed calf. The skin oozed firmness and freshness. I thought that if I bit too hard the whole of her lower leg would explode in a rainbow of juice, so plump and juicy was the Bean limb. So, for a few moments I ran my tongue (and what was left of my lips) up and down the inside of her calf drinking in the odour of a recent scented bath and imbibing the glistening moisture of sweat generated in that warm dark cycle; as I did so, she moaned a little in acknowledgement. Not wanting to disturb or wake her I applied a little bit of pressure with my teeth in the hope I might generate the smallest of punctures on the smooth, pale packaging through which I could gently suck an aperitif of juice.

Whether I did puncture her skin I could not be sure. I think I did. What I did know was the weight of a thwack on the back of my head that stunned me out of my reverie. I stood up to find myself confronted by a similarly-summered man standing on the patio with a gardening implement. He swung again and shouted something. The package on the sun lounger herself suddenly jumped up and screamed. The thought of taking them both crossed my mind but, what with the noise and my earlier satisfaction, I turned and ran back down the garden as the two Beans shuffled back into the house.

'Did it bite you?' I heard him ask the package.

'I don't, I don't know,' she whimpered. 'I thought it was the cat.'

And with that the French doors were slammed shut, locked and the curtains drawn. Shame, I thought to myself at the time and continued on my way.

I could not shake the thought of those plump calves over the following light-darks and was haunted by my nibble and wondered whether I had indeed punctured the skin. If so, would there be anything like ChubbyCheeks about the Bean? The calf-package (PlumpCalf-elect) was a grown Bean of many summers, so the deliverable was indeterminate. But, in the interests of research, I decided to return to her premises to, at least, close the deal.

I headed back to the house late in the dark cycle a handful of light-darks later. The patio doors were locked and the house quiet. I sat and waited for most of the dark cycle looking for a sign of movement. Having seen none, I was inclined to call it a dark cycle, but before doing so I skipped, danced and crawled myself up onto the roof. Finding the skylight to the attic room unfastened, I crept into the house and quietly made my way down the stairs until I reached what appeared to be the bedroom, partly illuminated by a light further within. I entered quietly preparing myself for engagement with the two Beans. I found a very large bed strewn with ruffled bedclothes and pillows. The bedside cabinet was littered with drinks and pills. SomeBean was clearly at home. The light was coming from an en suite bathroom and a slightest of quirky odours was reaching my cavities. I had not quite come across it before. As I took a step towards the door, it opened. And there she was, PlumpCalf, standing in her nightdress. She was just as plump and firm and ready as I had seen her the handful of light-darks earlier. She stood looking at me as I did at her. She did not move. She did not scream. She was at peace. The opening of the door had inundated the bedroom with the fullness of odour and it dawned on me. She had risen. But she looked just like a Bean. Pale, perhaps, but essentially a Bean.

PlumpCalf did not seem entirely lost either, she had a learned look in her eye. Over the coming weeks as I watched her develop I would be convinced that lite-bites were the way to go. A worthy addition to our ranks.

As we stood looking at each other I became aware of lights and movements outside. There was an odour of both Cloth-Heads and Rubber-Beans. Suddenly there were knocks, then banging at the front door below us. Alert to the inconvenience of a possible threat, I slipped out of the room and skipped down the stairs. PlumpCalf followed me. We reached the first floor (above the ground floor) on which there was a reception room. The banging on the front door below now became much louder. In fact, it sounded as if the Rubber-Beans were trying to break their way into the building.

Why were they here? It soon became clear – PlumpCalf's male partner lay motionless on an armchair. A Has-Bean, he had been resting for a few cycles, but might indeed rise in a light-dark or so. With o'clock against us, I realised I could not carry him clear of the premises, but in a flash of inspiration grabbed and carried him back up the stairs closely followed by PlumpCalf just as the Rubber Beans broke through on the ground floor. Their methodological search of the first floor gave us time to reach the skylight and the roof. I closed the skylight altogether to give the impression to any Rubber that the house was empty. I stuffed the resting body of PlumpCalf's partner into a chimney alcove and, with PlumpCalf in hand, skipped across the rooftops into the night.

So it was that I was forming a view on the different types of Muter just as I was forming an opinion on different types (and tastes) of Beans. My learning was rounded. But with the hopes and plans I had for the summers to come, I needed to pay particular heed to the recruitment to our growing teams. Of course, there would be Beans on which one would fully-feast, but their effectiveness as soldiers or advocates for destiny might be impaired. There were Beans who had limited transferable skills to eternity (for instance, the ThreeStooges) who were also average performers in death; but then there were the emerging lite-bites who could be enormously effective when engaging with the 'world' of the Bean. Chubby was one example; PlumpCalf, another.

For this reason, I embarked on a mission to generate a generation of lite-bites and encouraged my colleagues to do so. Often the Bean might not know what was happening to them – they had had a close encounter with a Muter, but had survived it. In my hazy recollections, I half-wondered whether this had happened to me (but more of that later). To those Beans reading this, a warning: if you feel a little lite throbbing in the calf, forearm or elsewhere, it means 'game on'. Welcome. It is known as the 'death itch'. You are soon to join the club. Contrary to the popular mythology of Muter encounters, not every Bean is a bite, a feast, a piece of meat. Sometimes all it takes is the smallest of nicks, the lightest of licks.

17. Down at the Pub

Sometimes it all got a bit much, so I headed down the pub.

Whether it is hunting and biting or training and mentoring, death as a Muter means one always has to be 'on'. But there were times when I did not want to bite, release, fight. I just wanted 'time-out'. Besides, sometimes just the aroma is enough – I just want to sit, relish the peace of the dark cycle and take it all in – get high on the idea and aroma of Bean.

I studied PlumpCalf in the weeks after her rise. It was a revelation, a marvel. Other than perhaps Chubby, no Muter (up until that point) had been able to move so freely amongst the Beans. PlumpCalf could go anywhere, do anything, yet she had the bite or feast-instinct of a fully-formed Muter.

That said, I was also curious about my own summers as a Bean. I had witnessed the transferable skills of Beans to Muters and realised I took my own skills for granted. I felt I ought to connect with my summers as a Bean, largely so I could learn, become more self-aware. Additionally, I suspected TarmacTired needed to address some of her outstanding issues of her Bean existence (much like Rooftop had clearly done) and I was ready to help. But how could I help her connect with her previous existence if I struggled to connect with my own? My own Bean summers felt so distant. Therefore, it seemed sensible to take time out and just hang with the Beans. Hence, the pub.

I perched myself on a balcony of a small residence overlooking the enclosed beer garden of the public house. I tucked myself away behind some plants. Beans – yet more contradictions

– they seek an existence away from the country and farms, only to bring the country and farms to their concrete metropolis. They even called the pub 'The Turf' hidden away between concrete walls yet there was no proper turf of which to speak within a Bean's sprint. I had dispatched the owner of the residence, in which I was sitting, the previous dark cycle. I would be there for him when he rose. In the meantime, he sat propped-up in the corner of the bedroom where he fell and gasped his last.

Tucked behind the balcony's greenery, I wallowed in the hum of voices rising from the beer garden below. It was a busy night and the cocktail of perfume was delicious. The voices had the energy of the young Bean – full of hope and imagination for their summers ahead. They had not yet reached the stage of their existence to know that any remaining summers would be full of disappointments and anguish. Yet, it warmed me to know that, even though they existed in the bliss of ignorance, they would eventually reach an eternal bliss.

For how long I sat there, I do not know. It was a very soothing environment, wrapped up warm and lost in the babble of Bean and the hiss and crackle of fifty feasts as their insides slowly cooked. All that warm flesh. A less-evolved Muter would not resist it and would be down in the beer garden in a flash picking apart the juicy peaches and squeezing glory out of them as fast you could whimper 'please don't, I want to live'.

As the dark cycle ran on, the sound and scent of two Beans in particular rose from the crowd. One Bean male was talking about his existence on which he was despairing. The other was a listener.

Again, listening to them, I was at a loss – the energy that is invested (and expended) in forming and meeting social expectations, ambitions, legal and ethical frameworks, all come to nothing. In my more generous moments I took it to be the Beans' desperate attempts to fill their summers as they ripened. But what never failed to puzzle me was, why didn't the Beans realise these embarrassing weaknesses for what they were? Each Beanling grows to accept the (their) 'world' as it is. Were it not for death (and its facilitators, like me) would there ever be a point at which the truth was revealed to them? Or was that moment of truth now coming for the whole of Beankind? A time to which I would be privileged enough to bear witness myself?

My ear returned to the two thirty-something-summered friends.

Despite his grumblings, the grumpy, beardy Bean smelled sweet and, having the edge on his companion, I selected him for glory by the end of the dark cycle. Only then perhaps would he understand what his contribution to the world would be. What was noteworthy of his grumblings was how typical they were of a Bean. It centred on 'dilemmas' (usually of a transient nature and framed, by the Bean, in 'past, present, future') and the pitiful significance Beans placed on them.

'You know, if I had my life again,' Beardy Bean said gazing into his glass of brown sauce.

'You're only 37,' his friend, Tubby Bean, interrupted.

'If it had my life again,' Beardy repeated, ignoring his friend across the table, 'I would have married the Brazilian.'

'So, why didn't you do it the first time round?'

'I'd have had to stay in Brazil. I would have struggled to make a living.'

'Wasn't she engaged?' asked Tubby.

Beardy paused and screwed his features up in one of those pretty 'thinking faces' that you never see on a Muter. I love it when Beans think, it gives them what they would call 'solemnity' or gravity'. And it's all for nothing.

'Yes,' Beardy muttered, 'but I would have made a play and I think she would have responded. What is the point of avoiding, denying truth when it stares you in the face.'

'It all comes to nothing, Jack, so why worry,' replied Tubby. 'It's in the past. Just forget about it. It has no bearing on the future.'

'I'm just saying. If I had known what I know now, I wouldn't be in this miserable mess,' Beardy rambled. 'I wouldn't have a relationship about to implode and I wouldn't be about to be fired from a job I care little about, but need. And to top it all, I might get arrested.'

'You don't know what is going to happen.'

'You're telling me Amy is going to stick around?'

'No, your relationship will spectacularly explode in a million different ugly pieces which the world's greatest jigsaw puzzler would not be able to put together, but that could be a good thing. Life is not a jigsaw.'

Profound. Profound nonsense, I thought, shaking my head in despair at the whinging Beans.

'After a period of indifferent existence,' continued Tubby Bean, 'you could find yourself re-born with a new sense of purpose.'

(Perhaps I spoke too soon. It might be the Bean's instinct coming through.)

'Criminal prosecution isn't a certainty, much less criminal conviction and incarceration. These things are botched by the police on a daily basis,' Tubby said to the morose Beardy Bean sitting across the table and staring into his glass of brown liquid. 'You have no idea how crap the police are. They have laws to mask their ineptitude. Besides, you're not a main player.'

'I would never be here if I had pursued Chiara,' said Beardy, massaging his head. 'I took this job really to meet the requirements in Amy's advert for a "solvent, good-looking male" as required by a "young, professional woman" and now here I am.'

'Do you love her?'

'Who?'

Tubby did not reply. Beardy sat motionless in a Bean-like reflective manner as if it would help.

'I love Amy as a person who has contributed to my life and is the mother of my daughter....', Beardy paused before continuing, 'but, I think there was always the prospect that I would end up sleeping with another woman.'

'Other women.'

'Other women,' Beardy repeated with a sigh. 'But, with Chiara, I couldn't imagine sleeping with other women. The impulse would not be there. She was everything I could ever want. She was the woman my twelve year old self would want, my seventeen year old self, my twenty three year old, thirty year old, fifty year old and sixty four year old selves would want.'

'The grass is always greener....'

'It's fucking luscious, mate. Fresh, dewy, healthy, Alpine grass – a deep racing green, not a tired, yellowing patchy grass on the dusty ground of a suburban football pitch. And, yes, I want to roll around in that Alpine grass,' Beardy whispered. 'I know I would have been faithful to Chiara. The treasures were so great. The long, silky, dark hair. The firm, olive skin cooked to a peachy tone. Her pores oozed glistening pearls of the sweetest nature. Her breath would hang in the air enveloping you in a cloud of desire. The flesh of her lower limbs would ripple as she walked; her upper limbs would swing in a come-get-me way. I could lick, love and eat every inch of her. She was my future. The past (as I had known it) did not exist. All time existed in the moments I spent with her.'

(At this point I was slightly taken aback. Was this a Muter talking? Had I stumbled upon a new type of Muter? No, of course not, but was it Beardy's inner Muter talking, reaching out?)

'Do we live with what happened or what might or should have happened?' said Tubby interrupting the moment between Beardy and me. 'Or do we live in the here-and-now? What you are talking about is now fiction. A non-lived past is fiction.'

There was silence between the two Beans as they sat staring into their drinks glasses. I did not learn the circumstances of Tubby Bean, but there was certainly little levity in his odour. Had Beardy brought Tubby's spirits down or was Tubby 'suffering' himself? His words to his friend Beardy might not have suggested he was 'on the level', but just as Beans universally deny their destiny, so do Beans engage in micro-denials. The micro-denials all add up over time to the universal denial of destiny. It trains the denial-muscles of the destiny-deniers.

'Or perhaps you should look up Chiara once you are through this,' said Tubby.

'I'm such a failure,' moaned Beardy. 'I would not appeal to her now.'

'Well, if you really want to take the bull by the horns, just jump on a plane. Get it sorted. You'll have an answer by Sunday evening.'

'So, you are suggesting life is just a series of failures compounded by regret?' asked Beardy.

'In a word, yes.'

I wondered if I should jump in and break up the conversation particularly after the way Beardy had poetically articulated his appreciation for the Brazilian Bean. I was conflicted. If I were to indulge in Beardy, then by all likelihood, he would not have the chance to indulge in the Brazilian Bean and so, having become recently aware of the effectiveness of lite-bites, I concluded that Beardy might be an excellent contender for a lite-bite. We all might have the best of both worlds.

Their conversation was drawing to a close, which a relief, not that I had been gripped but I was becoming bored. I came away feeling there was much work to do. I needed to accelerate the work rate, spread the word. My team was growing, interns were flooding in and our understanding of the Bean was developing. Death must not stand still. We needed to develop techniques, seek team-working opportunities and work on strategies for expansion. The Beans were a mess. With all this in mind, I did indeed refrain from feasting on Beardy opting for a lite-bite in the hope he would make a trip to Brazil and, once rested on arrival, seek out and commune with (even feast on) the Brazilian Bean, Chiara. As for Tubby – his words of 'Bean-sense' had had their day. I gave him an opportunity to reflect on his thoughts from the ultimate and eternal perspective.

I suspected that the light-bites would become the most feared amongst the Beans. PlumpCalf's former partner, ChimneyBlack, had risen and joined the team; he had broadly similar skills though was not as sharp, because, I concluded, his encounter with death had been once removed from my Muter-lite-bite of PlumpCalf. I concluded that he had been blessed with a close encounter with PlumpCalf at some point during the light-darks that had followed by first visit. Nevertheless, we welcome all to the fold, turning none away.

18. A Walk and Picnic in the Park

At last I returned to the business of the research project I had been putting off for a while. I had selected the location – the same park square where I had encountered TreeShadow and TottyHeels. Both Muters were now ready for a staged feast and so were in attendance. TarmacTired was functional and I brought her along in the capacity of an observer. I also brought along a few seasoned professionals: Diesel, DoorStop, GlassCutter, TrainTracks and Rooftop. As ever, ChubbyCheeks was not far behind, but she was looking after (and training up) FatLegs along with Fluffykins and KittenFluff (two new six-summered Muterling twins).

I collected the bags of glittery electronic gadgets, trinkets and accessories (acquired from the birthday party of DoorStop and GlassCutter) from their rooftop hiding place and returned to the park square. The location was an attractive starting place for the research project for a variety of reasons: it was known to TreeShadow and TottyHeels so it was a place in which they would feel comfortable. Secondly, being a residential part of the metropolis with eateries and bars in the vicinity, the area attracted a reasonable amount of foot-traffic especially in the middle of the dark cycle. The park itself, oval in shape perhaps three hundred yards long at its longest point, was secluded and surrounded by trees and vegetation and bordered by a fence. It had four entrance gates that were usually locked during the dark cycle, but two were broken (thanks to my careful planning). The centre of the small park was open grass with the odd large tree under which local residents used to shelter from the great orb in the warmer light cycles. The trees bordering the park were high enough to largely obscure what was going on inside and limit the streetlamp illumination spilling into the hunting ground.

It was perfect. To be fair, it wasn't really a hunting ground. No 'hunting' was required. One does not hunt for food when it is presented to one. No, it was a feasting ground. A picnic area.

DoorStop, GlassCutter, RooftopSuicide and TrainTracks brought a few of their own interns to whom I had not been fully introduced. Arriving at the picnic area, I poured out the bags' collection of goodies noting GlassCutter's and DoorStop's vague recognition of the items. They looked at me quizzically as the ghost of the memory drifted across their minds. I smiled as best I could with my absent lip flesh. We then carefully placed a few of the sparkly items near the entrance gates of the park in such a way that they were visible to passers-Bean-by on the road. DoorStop also cleverly placed a few items hanging in the bushes inside the park (though at a distance from an entrance) that were again visible through the railings to passers-Bean-by. We also placed a handful of glittery things on the ground leading from the entrances into the dark interiors of the picnic area. We retreated to the shadows and waited. Standing motionless in the darkness, our broken features (broken further by the illumination seeping through the swaying tree branches) were invisible to the Bean.

We didn't have to wait long. First to arrive were two lady Beans. We observed their forms (one fat, one thin) walk around the park on the other side dipping in an out of view gaily chatting away. Then, as planned, the footsteps slowed and the chatting quietened. The fat Bean and the thin Bean had found something to their liking by the park gate near DoorStop and his two interns. The Beans disappeared from view for a few moments before their figures were seen fifty yards away tentatively entering the park grounds. Every few moments one of the Beans would point at something on the ground before taking a few steps forward, leaning down and picking it up and stuffing it in their handbag. They tried to suppress giggles of delight as they discovered glittery item after glittery item, all the while moving further away from the road and towards the deep, black shadow of a tree where I knew DoorStop and the interns were waiting.

I was pleased to observe my fellow Muters did not burst out of the shadows at the first smell of the two-legged feasts, no, they remained quiet and patient until the Beans were fully enveloped in the blackness. The only indication that they had transfigured into Has-Beans, was the onset of quietness. There were no screams, no urgent chatter, no exclamations of surprise. It made me proud. I had brought these Muters – both seasoned and fresh – to this place, organised the circumstances of the picnic and they had done it. I knew I would always carry with me the memory of that evening and the induction of ParkSparkleFat and ParkSparkleThin.

We did not have to wait long before, through another entrance, came a well-dressed lone male Bean, athletic and strong. Immediately I thought he would look fine and operate efficiently in Death. He had something about the destiny in him. He too followed the sparkly items but more cautiously than the ParkSparkle twins. I liked that. He followed the accessories to the edge of the large tree shadow, but then paused and looked deep into the darkness. I could see he was half-minded to leave. Perhaps he had detected a whiff of danger or perhaps Tarmac, but I was soon pleased to see him succumb to the Bean weakness for all things glittery. He disappeared into the land of the shadow of tree never to return. My old friend Rooftop and Glass would have made quick work of him, ParkDazzle-elect.

The dark-cycle continued with more visits. In fact, it was an embarrassment of riches. The feasting was only broken by the need to replenish the array of gadgets and glitter in the bushes, on the railings and across the park grounds. One accessory which appeared to be attractive to the undead was the telephonic communication device. A relatively recent invention that allowed Beans to communicate without being face-to-face. Additionally, these telephonic communication devices (which could be carried around on the person of the Bean) had additional features and technology. The device appealed to all types of Bean – many-summered, Beanteen, male and female. I made a mental note to further explore the possibilities of making the most of the Bean's longing for the telephonic communication device. It struck me as a useful tool.

Although the activity was encouraging and provided many answers, it also raised some questions, one in particular. Had I been instinctively inclined to target a Bean that was up to no good? Or a vanity Bean? Did it speak to something deeper in me or was it coincidental and all Beans were, in essence, no-gooders, corrupt, vain and self-interested? Would I be less inclined to target a well-behaving Bean? If so, is this because of some residual behaviour from my own summers as a Bean?

This in turn led me to ponder other questions. What did Muters respect about Beans? If anything? Were there occasions when a Muter would refrain from kissing a Bean?

By the time the great orb broke over the horizon, my colleagues and I had acquired over twenty Has-Beans. I had brought the elements of the game (sparkly stuff; location) to the picnic and my colleagues had knocked it out of the park. It had worked. We had found a new tool to spread the love, judging by the results of the dark cycle and the Has-Beans resting in the vicinity, it was a fail-safe modus operandi. It was not lost on me that we had devised a procedure that could be rolled out across the metropolis and adopted by all Muters born of me or not. Good ideas, even in Death, are hard to keep a lid on. Things were indeed changing. We were becoming organised.

19. TarmacTired Blows Away the Cobwebs

TarmacTired seemed distracted. Every time a large, black automobilic vehicle passed, she would look into its insides and, on occasion, follow it until it was indicated to her that she was chasing the wrong four wheels – a different automobilic vehicle from the one that had dropped her broken body at our feet that light-dark on the wasteland. Nevertheless, it suggested that she was responding to a profound need deep within her. Just as I was drawn to rooftops and o'clock alone, so it appeared that she was drawn to this particular type of vehicle. I decided the time was right to spend a bit of time with TarmacTired and took her to the rooftops in the area of the metropolis in which she had been gifted to us. Thus we spent many light-darks drifting under the stars and sharing.

It was difficult and easy in equal measure. To loiter high in the sky amidst the clouds of sweet moisture generated by the congregation of perspiring peachy flesh was, as ever, heavenly, but it masked a difficulty – to find the sweet scents of those black automobilic vehicular Beans.

The pleasures of the farmyard fumes did not distract us enough to fail. We did eventually identify the wheeled machine and its usual stationary location. Within a lunar cycle of Tarmac's rising she and I stood high above a street on which the black machine was parked. The scents of the three Beans that had dripped into the vehicle's interiors now escaped and rose lightly through the darkness to our nasal cavities.

Thinking it wise to learn more about the challenge that lay within the building (associated with the machine) before Tarmac entered, I dispatched DoorStop, GlassCutter, Diesel and a handful of their interns to scout the premises and clear a path to the three Machine Beans in which we were interested.

The team of hooded Muters approached the building from different directions. Converging on the building they were met at the entrance by suited Beans. No matter, our colleagues made short work of them. One Bean did manage to pull a mechanical firing device from his attire and fire at one of the DoorStop's interns at point blank range, but firing a small piece of lead at flesh which had already reached its eternal state had little effect.

My colleagues breached the entrance and, even from the rooftop above, I could feel the blast of the familiar Bean freshness rise through the night air as the doors opened and juice flowed. The time had come. TarmacTired and I scampered down the outside of the building ignoring the warm fresh Bean breath escaping from the opening windows of the residences before slipping across the road into the target building's interiors. I found the interns feasting on yet more fresh Bean in the corridors. It is always pleasing to see interns turning in a performance. Following the aromas further down into a basement, I joined Diesel and DoorStop and Glass who were pausing before a corner around which two Beans guarded a closed door. The rank nervousness of the Beans guards was apparent.

Waiting out of view, the sudden blast of electronic chatter on devices in the hands of the Bean guards suggested that they knew something was not right. Our fleshy feet and our Muter form did not announce our proximity in the way a laboured approach by a Bean would. Nevertheless, the guards knew danger lurked just out of sight beyond the corner, their sudden and rampant perfumes made that perfectly clear.

David O. Zeus

I suspected my treasure lay beyond the heavy door at the end of the corridor and they were the last line of defence before our full Bean roast. I signalled to my Muters to wait. These were the *hors d'oeuvres*, let them come to us. I was in no hurry. There was no point in having mobility and function threatened by flying pieces of lead.

TreeShadow had the answer. Although relatively fresh, he was instinctively alert to illumination and shade. He cleverly decommissioned the corridor's illumination devices above us bathing the corridor and stairwell in a cooling darkness. This unsettled the Beans around the corner. Moments later heavy breathing signalled the approach of two of the Bean guards.

With a small handheld illuminating device in one hand and a firing device in the other the first guard unknowingly crept forwards and reached the corner. Why Beans hold ahead of them exposed flesh when approaching their enemy, I do not know. Both the snatching and biting of his forearm (no doubt coupled with the sight of a corridor full of green, black, red and pale flesh) rendered him ineffective. He was dispatched quickly.

His fellow Bean guard a dozen steps behind him paused for a moment to pant nervously pushing perfumes around the corner. One of my colleagues quickly succumbed to the temptation and, carrying the first guard (now a Has-Bean) as a distraction and lead-absorber, raced around the corner and overcame the second guard.

The corridor was now clear and we approached the door and reflected upon our options. It was likely that the Beans in the room had firing devices. This time, with a combination of illumination control, the guards' own firing devices and the carrying of the building's Has-Beans ahead of us, we entered the room. Making noise, as Beans are wont to do, they lost several seconds as they absorbed the sight of juice-dripping and disembowelled Has-Beans floating towards them. The lead pellets hit the Has-Beans protecting the musculature of DoorStop, TreeShadow and others before the Has-Beans fell on three Beans. My colleagues swarmed into the room and quickly secured the space.

Entering myself, I immediately identified the perfume of the three Beans who had been in the automobilic vehicle earlier in the lunar cycle before intimating to my colleagues to leave them be. There was enough flesh to go around.

The three Beans crawled to the back of the room. I doubt they had experienced the feelings they usually engendered in their own Beankind. The freshness of their panic was overwhelming. The experience of their own panic panicked them further. It was a luscious cycle. But they were not mine to bite. And we all knew it. Muter colleagues pushed the Beans up against the wall and, using drapery and accessories, tied them spread-eagled from the ceiling. Perhaps they thought they might be spared. I stepped up to each and tore back the cotton packaging to reveal the heaving flesh of their chests. I envied the Muter who would break such fine meat. But I was there only to prepare the feast for the guest of honour.

The Muters stood back and to attention as TarmacTired entered the room. If you had not eyes on the door you would not have seen her enter, such was her quietness on foot. She had been coy since her rising and, though had feasted on Bean, had not kissed or bitten herself. Perhaps these fresh and perspiring and panicking Beans would help her complete her training. It would be apt. It would complete the circle and she could give thanks to the three Beans for opening her eyes to eternal life.

She stood in front of them, delightfully pale, drained of juice herself, her hair matted and wet and coated in a film of earthiness which gave her an air of innocence. She looked at the three Beans we had prepared for her. She seemed confused, bewildered. She looked at them, at me, at them again. She inhaled and inhaled again. Yes, I thought, it is returning. It is the odours that she recognised.

'Fuck,' a Bean on the end of the row said. 'It's that fucking bitch.'

'Fuck,' said the Bean on the other end.

The middle Bean was quiet but for the rapidity of his panting which served only to push more sweetness into the basement room.

Then there were the sounds produced by the Beans. They vocalised more at a higher pitch. They were excited, which excited us but we were waiting for TarmacTired to work at her own pace. I wasn't interested in their last moments, I was waiting for her first moment, her moment of realisation. And then it came – a wave of recognition breaking across the fallen face of TarmacTired. Yes, she remembered now, I could see it in her eyes. What exactly she recalled I did not know, that was between her and the three Beans strung up by their arms in that basement.

Tarmac smiled at the first Bean who was very excited. No doubt if his limbs were free he would have tried to engage with TarmacTired in a playful wrestle of hope for more Bean summers, but he just came across as a wriggling riot of warm flesh. She ran a finger down his chest, smiled and moved on. She looked at the middle Bean who now hung silent and finally walked over to the third Bean. She looked closely at him for a time inhaling his fumes. She understood. She ran her face close up his glowing moist abdomen, but again did not touch. She was savouring this moment of revelation. She knew this was a rite of passage. She returned to the middle-hanging Bean. He was quiet on the outside, but I could tell, a raging, quivering weakness on the inside. She smiled and, if I could hear her thoughts, I think she would have been thanking him. As he had helped her, now it was her turn to help him. To bless him with eternal life.

She did not embrace the neck as one might expect, as that is where any hope of the glory stream is to be found and she did not press her hands together and dive into the flesh of the chest breaking open the rib cage to reveal the basket of fleshy, fruit contained therein – a treasure trove of ripe organ pumped full of juice. No, she slowly sunk to her knees and undid the buttons at his waist and pulled down the remaining garments down to the ground and in so doing revealed the organs which, when biting are not usually full of the richness of juice – no, they are the tender delicacies of a Bean feast. But to TarmacTired they appeared to hold a particular fascination. Cupping the organs in her hand she inhaled the odours of the flesh smiling in warm recognition. The degree of her reticence at seeing the restrained Beans was now reflected in the degree of ferocity into which she thrust her head at the delights she held in her hands. Such a violence of devotion and revelation is seldom seen in fresh Muters. The squeals of the Beans and pumping out of panic merely heightened all our desires, but we restrained ourselves until TarmacTired had feasted on each in just the same way. Only then could we share in her moment, her delight and the rest of the hanging flesh as they ebbed, then flowed, from Bean to Has-Bean.

Each Muter finds his or her own way into the bliss of eternity. Watching Tarmac answer her calling intrigued me and I started to think about my bites and my early behaviour. I had no distinct memory of a visit to a Bean known to me. But had I? Perhaps I had made a visit but had not realised it. Perhaps I had been instinctively drawn to a Bean or an environment but had not been aware of it? I could recognise it in Muters because I had witnessed their last moments and I was there to nurture them when they rose. Rooftop had shared with me his thoughts on ColourSplash. He was now a seasoned pro with armies of his own. I knew DoorStop and GlassCutter never shied away from mixing it up with Cloth-Heads. I was even aware they were planning something big and had put me on standby. So, maybe an early bite of mine had had significance? Or had I already acted on some deep, blissfully 'dark' desire to hunt out a type of Bean? To the best of my knowledge, all my kills had 'equality' stamped all over them. Or would I, in due course, be drawn to them or to their environment?

I left my fellow Beans to finish up in the basement room and slipped out into the night. The cool freshness of the dark cycle and my reflections wetted my curiosity. I needed a bit of space to be alone, so scaling the crumbling buildings I sat under the stars and inhaled the fumes of the meaningless millions all around me. They would join us in due course, but like an errant Beanling, they didn't understand – they were simultaneously irritatingly and endearingly obstinate.

By the time the great orb of the sky was breaching the horizon and announcing the beginning of the light cycle, I had come to the conclusion that my early bites were not relevant. They had been spontaneous. It was a shame that, being a Muter in one of the early waves, I had been alone with no Muter to guide me. Now I was one of the old guard.

That said, I was open to the idea that there was something that needed to be fulfilled deep inside me. Beanhood was a collection of weaknesses ('desires, hopes, needs') which were accompanied by the bruises that Beans inflicted on each other. Weakness and bruises lead to all manner of unresolved stuff in the meaninglessness of a Bean's existence. In fact, a Bean's summers could be defined by these inadequacies – all propped up by the vacuity of their reflections. No sooner have some of their Philosopher Beans acknowledged the meaninglessness of their existence, the Bean tries to layer it (the meaninglessness itself) with meaning! Presumably in the misplaced belief that the act of acknowledgement (of meaninglessness) will somehow imbue it (the meaninglessness) with meaning? If ever one wanted evidence of the compounding idiocy of the Bean, this was it. No, the true philosophers are those who are spurred to act and move the Bean into its eternal state.

So, yes, I am saying that the D-word (deathstiny) is the ultimate and eternal philosophy and we, the Muters, the consummate philosophers.

20. The Calling – PearlLavaliere

My thoughts on the gut instincts of those freshly released from
Beanhood continued to play upon my mind, particularly regarding
my own circumstances. My summers as a Bean would come back
to me, I was sure, I just needed to be alert to it. So, in the following
light-darks I continued to do what came naturally to me – drifting
across rooftops. It was now second nature and, as a result of my
mentoring, had become second nature for my Muter colleagues
too. But reflecting back to the time when it had been me alone
(resulting in my meeting with RooftopSuicide), I wondered
whether this early behaviour – seeking the high ground on rooftops
– was a clue to my unresolved Bean existence. What was it about
the environment that drew me there in the first place? Muters were
not instinctively drawn to the rooftops. So what was it about me?

Again I reflected on my early bites on rooftops. I could not
recall any looks or reactions from the Beans that suggested they
had known me as a Bean. No Bean had identified themselves to
me as I moved in to release them from their hell. No Bean had
addressed me by my Bean name.

I decided to let it play out. Although I was drawn to different
places on rooftops I noticed there were two common elements to
my regular perches. One was high above a residential area looking
north across the dark metropolis. The other was south of the Black
Road looking northwest. But where in the two vistas lay the
answer?

As I tried to put my deliberations out of my mind in the hope
my instinct would emerge, I sat in one of my regular perches in the

residential area waiting for a scent to take my fancy. I soon found myself gazing across the twinkling rooftops in the northerly direction. My attention kept being drawn to little glass enclosures and gardens on rooftops dotted about me. Before I knew it my eye socket fell upon one illuminated glass box and garden in particular directly ahead of me a handful of streets away – a glass box that had always been in the centre of my line of sight, but lost amidst the battery of others. I moved a street closer, sat and watched it. There was a vague familiarity about it, but that was surely because this was one of my regular perches? Yet, it was holding my attention like no other. I moved closer still. It held my attention.

My curiosity piqued, I rose to my feet and skipped across rooftops, up and down the sides of other buildings, each one pumping out perfumes, towards the property with the illuminated glass box atop. Moments later, I found myself on a roof terrace outside the glass box. I stood in the shadows by the edge of the roof wall looking at a seating area populated by potted plants, a table, a couple of comfy chairs partially overhung by a retractable awning. Subdued lighting from artificial lights nestled in the plants and flowerbeds threw light and shadow off at all angles. The glass box's sliding glass doors opened into another sitting area.

I remained hidden amidst the greenery and broken shadows thrown about the rooftop garden. A gentle, sweet aroma lingered over the garden and I detected its source as coming from under a blanket on a lounger by a table in the rooftop garden. I watched. All of a sudden the blanket stirred, crumpled and from its insides rose a slim thirty-summers-something young lady Bean, gently adorned with a selection of delicate accessories – carved stones, metals and other pieces hewn and fashioned from the natural world. I thought of her succumbing to our work in the park square. Although twinkly, such trinkets add nothing to the palate. She rose, stretched, yawned, sending a wave of scent towards me standing in the shadows. Was there something familiar about the scent? She moved to the glass sliding doors and entered the box.

I watched her move within the illuminated interior swaying to unheard music, wine glass in hand. I would let her finish the glass, perhaps have another one. It would add just a certain *je ne sais quoi* to the draining of her juice. I relaxed. The sight was warming. Homely. Soothing. Death does not have to be dramatic.

Just as I was becoming intoxicated by the sight, a male Bean, coming from stairs within the building, stepped into the glass box's room. Perhaps her mate. I was thoughtful, I didn't know why. He seemed like an impostor. My mind did not speculate on his torso or to him as a preferred feast, which was unusual. I moved towards the glass box through the chest-high plants and with each step possibly becoming more visible to the Beans inside.

I was happy to watch, to take my time. It was not as if they were getting cold or their flesh would go off.

The two Beans communicated animatedly. At times they looked out casually through the large windows towards the roof terrace, but they did not see my pale, misshapen features floating amidst the green vegetation. Perhaps they will move outside and we could snack there, I thought. As I moved closer I could smell her flesh through her attempts to smother her delightful aroma by yet more artificial Bean products. What is it with Beans? They always seek to complicate things.

I don't know if I lost track of time, but there was suddenly a moment when I heard a muffled scream. Both Beans were looking at me. I suppose the sight of a Muter was still relatively unusual and the sight of one staring at them from their own roof terrace must have been startling. It shook me out of my reverie.

I didn't want the feasts to escape back down inside the building, or rather, as I realised, there was really only one feast in which I was keen to indulge. I saw the male Bean look towards the door leading from the interior of the glass box to a stairwell. He reached out his hand to pull the female Bean towards the staircase exit but she was transfixed. A clock was ticking, so I moved forward and slid the glass door to the side. I was hit by a wave of warm, moist Bean perfume. My action startled them. Perhaps they thought they were safe behind a glass wall. The female remained transfixed, the male began to panic and stepped towards the staircase exit. She didn't move. A curious look passed over her face.

'Get the phone,' he rasped.

She looked around herself. Her eyes (and my sockets) were locked on each other. She was shaking her head and muttering "no, no," to herself.

'Where's your phone?' he spat. 'We won't have time to both get out of the house if it decides to attack.'

'It's in my bag on the patio,' she said shaking, almost in tears.

'Okay,' he said, heaving perfume in my direction. It wasn't that I was absorbing the odour through the nasal cavities it was almost as if his fumes were being sucked into my being through my own pores and sores. He couldn't dose me in more arousing aromas even if he tried. The sweetness of ignorance.

I stood looking at him. I savoured his innocence. Emboldened perhaps by my lack of moves, he stepped to one side and picked up a wooden pole-like baton and stepped towards me in a threatening manner ready to swing.

What I was really interested in was the woman in the white dress all nicely adorned. Not only her fine shape, but, again, her accessories kept playing upon my mind.

'When I whack him, go and get the phone and call those fucking zombie police,' the male Bean whispered.

I felt I ought to thank him for alerting me to his plan. Realising that we may be joined not only by Rubber Beans but other local Beans, I was inclined to bring matters to a close. I stepped back once, then twice. The Bean stepped forward. Perhaps he thought he was going to mate with the female Bean that night as a result of his prowess. How little he knew. He would be resting as a Has-Bean within forty ticks of the clock.

I stepped back through the open glass doors into the rooftop garden.

'That's it, you fucking piece of shit, fuck off out of here,' he spat.

His language surprised me somewhat. Can fear ever be eloquent, I wondered? Beans took pride in showing compassion, empathy to others including those who had passed on 'to the other side'. They thought it set them apart from (and above) other creatures, but get a Bean alone with a creature who has indeed travelled to the other side and they become remarkably aggressive.

'That's it you fucking fuck, fuck off,' the Bean snarled.

Not poetry, but it had a certain ring to it – the Bean ring of fright.

'Get the phone, Emily. It's going.'

Emily. Did I know that name?

'I'll beat it's head in when it's off the terrace. Don't want to get splatter on the *chaise longue.*

But I was ahead of my male Bean friend. As I stepped back onto the terrace, I adjusted my direction so that I backed into the chair on which sat the lady Bean's bag in which the telephonic communication device was contained. As I stepped back further and around it, I dragged the chair back towards the darkness as an obstacle between myself and the male Bean.

'It's taking the chair. My phone's in the bag,' the lady Bean screamed.

The male Bean fell for my 'defensive' move and, thinking he had the upper hand, took a few steps towards me. I matched his advance with a retreat until we were on the edge of the dark terrace garden. As I hoped, he took a few strides forward swinging the bat towards my temple with a loud expulsion of syrupy air of

'Arrgghh' which, truth be told, almost knocked me out such was the delicacy of the scent.

I threw the chair away to one side and, stepping towards the assailant, I caught the bat and held it fast in my left hand. Then looking deep into his eyes and seeing only fear and confusion, I decided to make it quick and set him on his journey. I grabbed him firmly with my right hand under his jaw and lifted him high off his feet before lowering him for a moment to kiss his neck. Then stepping back a few paces into the darkness, I threw him high and far into the black abyss much like I had done to Rooftop. His cries were lost to the darkness as he fell, the pitiful sounds accompanied only by the snapping and cracking to his bones that echoed about the buildings during his descent and landing. He would rise in time and should we meet, he probably would not have the memory of our embrace on the rooftop.

I was tired of playing now. I stepped back on to the terrace and strode straight towards the figure of the lady Bean frozen in shock, fear, I cared not. She need not have worried.

'It's me – Emily,' she whispered, falteringly.

A nice nick-name for a Bean, but so weak. What did it mean? Why give a name that does not reflect an element of their existence?

She seemed to be showing compassion. There was one thing about her that made her special, familiar – she wore about her neck a band of white balls. Pearls. That was the accessory that had my attention. I knew it had significance. I recalled being mesmerised by the pearls worn by ColourSplash about her neck when she first opened the door to Rooftop.

'Nigel?' she whispered. 'It's me. Do you remember? Anything?'

I remained still. I suppose Beans try to reach out to the dead and want them, in some way, to return and acknowledge the Bean summers. Why-oh-why don't Beans realise that no traveller returns from this fine and fair land.

'Do you remember this?' the lady Bean whispered, touching the white balls on the ornament about her neck.

I stepped towards her softly and touched the pearl ornament.

'It is a pearl lavaliere, a necklace,' she said.

I had no reason to doubt her, but her aroma was now overwhelming.

I gently took her face in my hands. She looked expectantly, trustingly into my eye sockets. I leaned forward and kissed her tenderly on the neck. Sweet. Fine. Glory.

I knew I had found an ally in Pearl. I ensured she was placed in a safe environment – a house of glass and green in a gardening plot not far away. She would lie there undisturbed (this I knew because I had enlightened its proprietor, Parsnip, a lunar cycle earlier). Of course, there would be the period of acclimatisation for PearlLavaliere, but I entrusted some of her early learning to Tarmac, Tracks, Plot and Chubby. I entrusted CrackleNeck (PearlLavaliere's companion in meaningless times) to Chain-and-Stiks. There is no specific reason for entrusting the early lunar cycles of enlightenment to a Muter of the same Bean gender, but the acquisition of death skills is expedited if the body type is broadly similar.

And so, that dark cycle, I took another step in my own learning. PearlLavaliere and I might well have had a history. In time, I might recall some details, but details matter not in eternity. Nevertheless, there was some sensation inside me – gladness, perhaps. One thing for which I am forever grateful is the ability of sharing my gift. Truly, Death is the gift that keeps on giving.

21. On the Prowl

I have already described the different types of Bean and the skills development of Muters. Some differences in Beanhood do carry over to Muterdom although they tend to dissolve as lunar cycles pass and the eternal state imposes order.

Muters are unencumbered by weaknesses of the mind (such as 'doubt') that afflict the Bean. In fact, Muters have no psychological flaws that hinder motivation or limit effectiveness. Nor is a Muter's energy expended in quite the same way after rising. For these reasons, Muters who were 'female' Beans are not (unless in extreme situations) at a significant physical disadvantage to 'male' Muters when it comes to confrontation with the Bean. What a Bean might describe as 'aggression' is more accurately described in the eternal kingdom as 'resolve' – a quality borne in the clarity of death. Thus, a formerly female-Bean Muter has the advantage over the average 'male' Bean. Furthermore, Muters do not sustain injuries in the way the simple, primitive Bean body does. With this in mind, any Beanhood behaviour, physical trait or stature should never be regarded as limiting the effectiveness (or not) of the Muter. Two fine examples, TarmacTired and ChubbyCheeks.

After her encounter with the automobilic vehicle Beans, TarmacTired hit the ground running. Something had clicked and any outstanding (Bean-related) issues had been resolved. She quickly adopted techniques from her training by TrainTracks, ColourSplash and Diesel, but she also brought in new ways of working that developed not only her own effectiveness, but helped us Muters develop as a collective.

Tarmac had one particular successful technique that she passed on to us (though largely to her sisters). Late at night she would loiter in the shadows of dark alleys, street corners and industrial parks in particular parts of town swinging a handbag and shuffling on the spot. Without too much delay an automobilic vehicle (often very self-aggrandising) would draw up by the kerb beside her. She would remain in the shadows teasing the occupant with glimpses of her right (and less) disintegrated profile. The car door would open and she would quickly stride towards the car and slip into the passenger seat. Sometimes the car would drive around the corner and park in a secluded street. At other times, it would remain kerbside. The (usually male) Bean would be in a state of flushed nervous excitement and would even, by all accounts, remove his lower garments revealing to Tarmac the delicacies nestling between his legs. Tarmac had already expressed a preference for the soft parts as a starter (rather than as dessert). It was a source of amusement for me – of all the things to reveal to a Muter, it makes me wonder. Why, oh why would a Bean offer the delicacies so willingly? I did not know. Anyway, it is of no consequence, Tarmac was the most grateful and would oblige most enthusiastically.

After a period of a few minutes of feasting in the vehicle, Tarmac would emerge unruffled, well-fed, and she would find another spot on another street where the same sequence of events would unfold.

After a lunar cycle or two, Cloth-Heads (then later Rubber Beans) would loiter in the area and it became difficult to travel on particular streets. Furthermore, it was at a time when I thought it prudent to acquire more colleagues, so Tarmac, with a few interns, identified (then staked out) properties in residential areas in which there was a constant stream of male Beans knocking on the entrance doors at all hours. Once a satisfactory residence had been identified, my Muter colleagues would slip into the premises, feast on the (usually lady) Beans inside then take up residence in the property themselves. Lo and behold, Beans, Beans and more Beans would turn up at the entrance to the establishment, knock on the door, gain entry and were then willingly escorted to a room for de-Beaning.

Bizarrely, it would seem that the Beans would not alert their family and Bean friends to their whereabouts (often turning off the telephonic communication devices), so these small residences would often become small Muter-factories turning out twenty to thirty Muters every light-dark cycle. The Has-Beans would be dragged out through an upstairs window to be placed on rooftops or in parklands in the vicinity to mature and rise. It became an enormously effective system providing an endless supply of flesh recruits. Such establishments could operate undisturbed for many lunar cycles. We were rarely troubled by Cloth-Heads or Rubber Beans. I say 'rarely', there were of course visits by the occasional Rubber Bean and Cloth-Head Bean, but it did not appear to be part of a larger operation. In fact, Tarmac's activity was the most effective way of swelling our ranks with Rubber Beans. (Cloth-Head were largely ineffective as Muters, so were disregarded in this respect.)

I wondered what Tarmac's secret was. Could she identify those who were fed up with Bean-life? Her niblings were not acquired in the same way as I had done atop buildings (Rooftop), in wasteland beside railways (TrainTracks) or in dreary conditions surrounded by the detritus of Beanhood (wine glasses, tissues) like CatNaps. Nor were they street philosophers like ParkBench (of whom I will speak later). I had to look for my Beans or stumbled across them by accident, but Tarmac...all she did was find a flat and wait for them to come knocking.

If, as I had guessed, TarmacTired had not flourished in her Beanhood (and was even disregarded by those in the Beanfold), her skills and brilliance were enormously effective in eternity. When it came to her mind, soul and body – she owned it in death. She could work alone or as a team member. She had so much to give yet was so very accomplished at taking. She was as full-rounded a Muter as there ever was. Give me a TarmacTired ahead of Moe, Larry, or Curly any day.

Chubby was also entranced by Tarmac's work and tried to copy them with some success. However, it was when she experimented with her own tactics that she came into her own. In lunar cycles, she became effective at attracting not just Bean males, but Beans of all types, shapes, sizes and summers. In time, she surpassed Tarmac to become, I would argue, the most effective machine of enlightenment I have witnessed. She was creative on an industrial scale and arguably the most prolific generator of Muters in the metropolis. She could work alone, in pairs or in groups.

Beanlings approached her in parks and playgrounds, lady beans in parks, playgrounds and, of course, male Beans in parks and playgrounds and from parked cars. On meeting her they all wanted to be friends with her and take her home. She entertained and gorged on them all.

I have been fortunate to have been able to observe how each Muter develops their skill set to fully realise their own potential. It is not always a question of 'teaching' skills but understanding how 'skills' acquired in Beanhood can be realised in death. But, I grant you, these things can take time.

In the early light-darks, Chubby, quite understandably, began her journey by following me around and watching me work from a safe distance. On one occasion I had accosted a jogger on a secluded towpath. Chubby had stood back thirty yards to watch from behind a fence overgrown by vegetation. The few screams of the jogger had alerted a nearby Bean couple. Spotting what they thought was a young, blond and wavy-haired, chubby-cheeked Beanling transfixed by the sight of me feasting on the jogger, the lady Bean of the couple crept up, grabbed Chubby's hand and started to drag the Muterling away to 'safety'. The lady-Bean should not be to blame, for, other than her pale complexion, Chubby's features gave no indication of her state of enlightenment. Meanwhile, the male Bean grabbed a piece of wood with the intention of confronting me. Rather than alert me to imminent danger, Chubby had played along allowing the separation of the two Beans. She knew I could take care of myself.

I was only alerted to the situation when I heard the screams of the good lady Bean. Looking up I saw the male-Bean above me in half-swing ready to hit me, but he too had been alerted to the screams and dashed back to his partner. I followed.

We arrived to find Chubby tucking into the lady-Bean. Immediately, the male Bean found himself between me and Chubby who, to be fair, had made a far greater mess of her feast than I had done of the jogger. He departed at speed, his allegiance to his 'life-partner' being just that – for life.

In that and other similar moments, Chubby began to understand that the skills she had acquired as a Beanling were in fact preparation for death. Her lack of summers was her angle – she had the ability to solicit help from Beans. They would give it freely, they could not help it. There were moments when I almost pitied the Bean – they didn't have a chance and they didn't know it.

As Chubby became more accomplished we began to plan moves around her. One favourite trick in the metropolis marsh farm involved Chubby identifying vehicles full of panting flesh moving slowly through a residential area. She would run after the vehicle waving her hands appearing 'distressed'. On her instruction a handful of us (often myself, Diesel, BeanPole,

DogSmells and PearlLavaliere) would then 'chase' after Chubby. There was no need to cry for help, but her waving arms, straggly, blond hair and those chubby cheeks would be seen by the Beans in the reflective devices positioned in and around the automobilic vehicle as it moved on its way. In no time at all, the automobile would slow further (note, not stop altogether), a door would open and a Bean would encourage Chubby to run faster. Reaching the open door, a Bean would pull the Muterling into the automobilic interior and to safety. The door would slam shut and the wheeled machine would speed away.

Diesel, Stiks, PearlLavaliere, BeanPole, DogSmells and I would slow to a jog and watch. Within a hundred yards the vehicle would begin to swerve before crashing into other cars or street furniture and stop. Moments later a beaming Chubby would emerge drenched in juice and we would be invited to share the spoils.

To mix it up Chubby would be joined by FatLegs, KittenFluff (and her twin Fluffykins), DogCuddles and we would expand the chasing group with DoorStop, TreeShadow and other interns. We could target larger automobilic vehicles, sometimes seating 16. On one occasion, as Chubby targeted a vehicle (in which perhaps a dozen Beans were travelling), a large fifty-seater machine swung into view. She immediately changed tack and improvised, running after the long automobilic machine which went thundering past. I thought the Bean mastering the vehicle would not see a little 'Beanling' racing after it in the failing light. I was mistaken. The machine came to a loud screeching stop and a door opened with a breathy wheeze. Chubby, FatLegs and KittenFluff, DogCuddles all climbed on. The door closed and the vehicle gave an almighty groan as it accelerated away. We lost sight of the machine as it turned a corner, but we kept chasing.

I, for my sins, wondered whether Chubby had bitten off more than she could chew, but I soon felt foolish for doubting her.

Before you could squeeze the breath from a Beanteen, we heard an almighty crash. Aware the sound would attract attention, we raced to find the long automobilic machine had spun around and was hanging halfway off a bridge over the metropolis's Black Road. The insides of the windows were dripping with juice. Chubby and friends had made quick work of the Beanlings and a few fully-grown Beans inside. Chubby and Co. emerged from the vehicle like angels in red, beaming with the joy only death can bring. As KittenFluff jumped off the vehicle, it rocked, slid, wobbled, over-balanced and fell into the black liquid road below. We all raced to the edge of the bridge and watched as the machine bobbed in the blackness and floated down under the bridge. GlassCutter, DoorStop and Stiks had joined us and, sensing a Bean feast and numerous Has-Beans going to waste, jumped down off the bridge onto the vessel now floating away under the bridge. I am happy to report we managed to rescue many fine Muters-to-be from that incident. Others were retrieved at a later date – many by Stiks whose knowledge and understanding of the Black Road was unparalleled.

Chubby's same audacious plan worked once more with an automobilic vehicle full of travelling Beans from faraway lands who tasted quite different, but, however much Chubby tried in subsequent light-darks, no wheeled machine would stop for her. The Beans had caught on. And so we learned to accept that some of these ideas, tricks, moves and techniques had a shelf-life. We had to keep being creative. Which was no problem at all – Death's ways to wrench the Bean from their misery are infinite.

Despite being a victim of our own success, I was always grateful for any activity that increased our numbers and thus effectiveness. With each victory we became more of a presence in the metropolis and could therefore be bolder in our actions. Rather than focusing on individual Beans on streets, parks and in domestic structures, we began to consider ways to exploit the effectiveness of our teamwork as had been made clearly evident in Chubby's pioneering work. I began to think of grander schemes of collaboration. Attacks (like Chubby's on the vehicles) gave me the idea of how we might coordinate our efforts more and target Beans in other enclosed vessels. And so it was that one little nibling, ChubbyCheeks, inspired her mentor – me, Nigel.

So, in summary, the skills of a (formerly-lady-Bean) Muter should never be underestimated, for when they chose to go on the prowl they have an uncanny knack of attracting flesh. All skills and experience acquired during Beanhood were an excellent preparation for death. DoorStop, GlassCutter, Diesel tried to copy Tarmac's and Chubby's tactics on the street, but failed. They could not compete. With Tarmac's and Chubby's work, our numbers would grow exponentially, yet neither could rest on their laurels and neither would ever be satisfied with waiting for Beans to come to them.

22. Hunting Grounds: Going Underground

Even with our increasing numbers (and when I was not mentoring), I tended to work alone. However, there were situations when I gladly found myself in a group. On such occasions, I never failed to note that we achieved more than the sum of our parts. As a group we could do more than anything a Muter working alone could do. Not only that, as different collectives grew, collaboration became more common.

I embraced this evolution. Sometimes it is good and right and pleasant to feast alone. At other times, when riches are laid out on the table, a shared experience is just as enjoyable. Sometimes one goes looking for a banquet, other times the banquet is wheeled in.

As a Nigel-Bean I would spend many solar cycles travelling along tunnels in tubular tin cans under the metropolis. The number of light-darks I (and other Beans) spent in these tin cans travelling around the metropolis, presumably in pursuit of a 'meaningful' existence, were countless. In my early light-darks as a Muter I dismissed the Bean practice as a waste of existence, but now, strangely, in my more enlightened state, I understand that Beans (including me, I confess) were instinctively, unknowingly preparing themselves for being harvested as 'tinned Beans'. How excellent!

In truth, hunting underground is a moveable feast. Our numbers were such that we could not breach the main entrances above ground directly thus finding our way to the underground waiting areas where Beans boarded the tins. The best way to approach those tubular tins was when they were stationary in the dark tunnels, but tinned Beans were rarely stationary in the tunnels. Timing and coordination was required. It also required the keen skills of CentralLine who apparently, according to DoorStop, had his own unfinished business to address.

With CentralLine's skills and growing knowledge of the tunnel network, I felt confident that we, as a group, could take advantage of the sweaty feasts moving below us. Besides, I was fast learning that hunting underground had its own delights. The heat generated by the machinery, the ripe Bean bodies and the lack of ventilation all conspired to create a moist garnish on the ripe firm flesh. It is also important to say that it was not all about planning. Chance played its part.

In the early light-darks (before the 'Great Change' – see Chapter 36) a little commotion at the metropolis ground level (a Rubber Bean security operation, I understand) had driven many of my colleagues underground during a succession of dark cycles. In fact, many Muters used the tunnel network as their way to move about the metropolis. Some, like CentralLine, made it their business to learn where, when and how the tins moved and where they stopped.

As we sat huddled in the darkness, a sudden rush of warm air announced the imminent arrival of a tubular tin of Beanstuff. We did our best to find alcoves at places where we hoped the tins would stop. Often they did not stop, of course, but that did not mean we did not see the distorted, fearful faces of the undead Beans stuffed into their little tins as they whizzed passed. In fact, this worked well. The result of catching sight of our features (illuminated by the interiors by the passing tins) upset the Beans, increasing the rate of their juice pumping around limbs and torsos. Sometimes we would get lucky and occasionally the tin would stop within striking distance. But on one particular occasion, we hit gold.

Rooftop, Splash and I were loitering in a tunnel in the centre of the metropolis. Suddenly, the air moved. The aromas became stronger. The winds of desire ran through me. I could see Rooftop was almost knocked off his feet in anticipation of the approaching feast. It pleased me. I was encouraged that I had brought him to this place not only in a physical sense, but in a spiritual sense, yet I had a slight twinge of disappointment as I knew these carriages usually flew past. To a new Muter this can seem like torture, but on this occasion just as the carriage passed, it slowed then stopped. What was especially exciting was that the tube was tightly packed with heaving, moist flesh.

Aware it might start to roll off again, we rapidly approached the tins. Seven of us emerged from the darkness. The odours suggested the feast contained within was simmering at just the right temperature. We reached the end of the long tin can to see Beans standing and sitting inside. On first glance it looked like the simple-headed generation of Bean – Beanteens. Although physically ripe, it would have been nice to have a little more ripening. However, we hoped we might get lucky and find some treasures tucked deep inside. In fact, if memory serves me, the simple-headed Beans would give up the seats for the ripe Beans (attributable to some sort of deference protocol).

I hadn't really considered how to breach the tubular tin. There were more than enough Beans for all of us and I soon caught the whiff of a few more Muters further down the tunnel heading our way. I looked at Rooftop to find that he and others (BeanPole, TottyHeels, TreeShadow, ParkSparkleFat and Diesel) were looking at me for guidance. We were soon joined by a few interns whom I hadn't birthed. Though I am often loath to assume a leadership role I instinctively waved two colleagues down one side of the tin and three down the other side while I climbed up to the door at the end. I continued to surprise myself with my strength. As a Bean I would never have been able to open such a door, but here I prised open the door with ease and jumped up to find myself flesh-and-bone-to-face with what I took to be the train supervisor – a middle-aged lady Bean with heavy rolls of flesh.

I realised the uniform would require her to act in some sort of defensive capacity. Echoes from my Bean memory suggested such Beans were formidable in attitude but in poor physical shape. She would have been a tasty bite, but there were others also in need of my attention. Her Bean brain was still trying to process what was standing in front of her when I tucked into the rolls of flesh in her neck while simultaneously breaking the vertebrate to quicken the clinch. I normally do enjoy a slight wrestle but o'clock was pressing. Feeling her go limp, and having glugged some fine juice, I moved to the door and the main course. My opening of the door did not turn many heads, most Beans were helping the figures who had been opening the doors (from the outside) to get in. Those heads that did turn in my direction vocalised little as their mouths dropped open expelling a slow breath of sweet inner air which reached my nasal cavities just as the other Beans saw that those whom they had been helping gain entrance were in fact colleagues of mine. There was a brief moment, a still-existence, if you like, that would have made a worthy image-hanging on a wall, entitled 'Tinned Meet'.

The still-existence didn't last long and soon began to move. Normally the screams and shouts would mean I would be aware there was an o'clock limit on my feasting, but I was aware we were all hundreds of feet below ground and far from Bean help and firing devices. Such was the occasion of celebration of sharing between Muter and Bean that it would have been insulting not to feast to the full. The first Bean that I took in my arms was a young Bean-Stew dressed in lycra. Beautifully succulent, her warm, firm flesh was one of many delightful appetizers. Some of the other male Beans apparently thought so too, because I soon found their arms wrapped around me trying to separate me from the warm creature whose energy slowly ebbed away as I celebrated my appreciation of the work she had done maintaining her fleshy firmness. The male Beans began hitting me trying to convince me through the argument of 'pain'. What they failed to appreciate was that pain is an invitation to death. Once there, it serves no purpose, so falls by the wayside. So the strikes to my head, punches to the body and kicks to my legs had no effect on me whatsoever. Attempts at strangulation did nothing. If anything, the proximity of the warmth flesh acted as an aphrodisiac, massaging my expectation.

My pity for them soon tired, so, feeling the young female Bean drop, I turned to the two handlers and dispatched any ideas they had of resolving the situation to their satisfaction. They also dropped to the floor and, dripping with juice and with the soothing liquid running down the exposed sinews of my arms and legs I surveyed the tubular tin. Too much, too much, I thought. Some of the Beans were trying to fight with my Muter friends, others were frozen still in their seats wide-eyed and clasping their belongings close to their chests, little knowing that within moments the belongings would mean more to the rats in the tunnel than to them.

Other Beans were vainly trying to communicate with the outside world using their telephonic communication devices. Some Beans had managed to open the doors and had started running down the tunnel into the darkness but, judging by the screams and the gentle wafting of Muter odour, I realised that this tin of goodies was not going to stay secret for long. The warmth of the air and the rushing winds was pushing the secrets of the open tin around the local network of tunnels.

I pressed on and brought a fair number of Beans on to our side. I made a point of returning to my first bite of the evening, LycraStew-elect, and making her my own. The organs of a fit, nicely-balanced, twenty-summered-something Bean are truly a delight.

I am pleased to say that these moments do not go unappreciated. I will forever remember that underground feast as one of the most remarkable. As we exhausted the peaches of the carriage we moved forward through the doors to the adjoining tin, we found more Muter friends feasting and play-fighting with Beans. It was a momentous event for us all and the thought even crossed my mind that perhaps the Beans did have a point celebrating events on a solar-cycle basis. It would normally be anathema to a Muter to indulge in such traditions but, for a moment, I understood. Perhaps we should consider marking this event on a cyclical basis, I thought. A celebration. Beans and Muters together. Up to that point the greatest feasting event I had witnessed. Little did I know I was speaking too early.

At times I felt the tins judder forward, then stop, then move forwards again. I didn't know how long it was, but eventually the tunnels opened up and grew brighter. We were pulling into a waiting room for additional supplies, I could only assume.

The doors opened. Beans with their heads down, wires in their ears and a dead look in their eyes, stepped on board the tinned meat express. Some Beans standing in the waiting areas could obviously see the feast through the carriage windows and what awaited them. Judging by the shouting and screaming, the sight alarmed or excited them. Many Beans who had climbed into the tubular tin to join us on this special occasion did try to disembark, but my colleagues and I encouraged them to stay. Moments later the doors closed and we were rolling off again into the darkness, re-supplied.

Perhaps this was our destiny – to travel the underground tunnels and gather the tastiest of fresh meat and juice that the metropolis farm could produce. As we journeyed onwards we were joined by more Muters. Word had got around. As the party wound down Muters started to depart, taking morsels and Has-Beans off with them to nurture new beginnings. Muters, myself included, alighted our first tin can and went looking for others. We found many and we feasted. The whole dark cycle passed in a blur of indulgence and re-birth. Never have I felt so privileged and indulged.

How did it happen? Why? These tubular tins packed full of ready-meal-Beans were racing around below us going nowhere. Was it something deep inside a Bean's flesh telling them their destiny was to be found underground? Or was it perhaps our destiny as much as theirs? Whichever, one thing is for sure – destiny is to be found in the underworld. My invisible palace.

23. The First Bean Paradox
(The Destiny Impulse)

Now, let me explain the first Bean-Paradox. If there is anything that dissolves when a Has-Bean moves from its beleaguered state to its enlightened state, it is the affliction of emotion or 'feelings'. You never see a corpse emote. Why? Why, indeed. What would be the point?

Muters cannot fathom the affliction. We become accustomed to seeing it, but becoming accustomed to a weakness is like rain falling in fog – as meaningless as the Bean. Beans like to jostle with other Beans, form relationships, put down roots and gather moss. They don't realise that roots rot and moss dies. The trick of a good death is to keep moving – like that rolling stone – keep clean of nonsense. Beans seek what they call 'closure' yet shy away from the ultimate form of closure. What could be better than having closure for eternity? Sadly, the Beans cannot get their puffy brains around it.

One evening I found myself accompanying PearlLavaliere on a light-touch mentoring excursion. Hoping she would find her feet, I was keeping a low-profile. Before long, she found herself in a small community centre late at night. It must have been one of those affliction groups which led me to suspect that Pearl had attended affliction group meetings herself in her unenlightened state.

Pearl appeared to know the premises and, rather than enter the hall itself, slipped off up the stairs to a gallery overlooking the hall space. I joined her. We could sit in relative darkness and watch the goings-on below. There were perhaps a dozen Beans sitting in a circle. Our vantage point probably meant our perfumes would not alert them to our presence. However, it did mean their own perfumes drifted up to our seats in the darkened gallery. The hall space did not smell like a happy place. For sure, there was a sourness in the air. It was a gathering of unhappy Beans of all summers, shapes, fat and sizes.

We had arrived halfway through a report by a lady Bean who was obviously distressed about her existence. She felt there was no respect in modern Bean society for her endurance of motherhood (something she had really wanted to do, apparently).

'Parenthood is taken for granted. Wealth and status are the currency in this success-driven world, not happiness,' she whined. 'How do I achieve happiness if I feel so worthless? How can I achieve happiness if my contribution, my very existence, is not recognised?'

I was curious. Was happiness an achievement? Why so? It was temporary. Why was something so transitory regarded an 'achievement'? Was the Bean's expectation really that low? Why not strive for permanence? An eternity of contentment, self-realisation, acceptance – destiny?

One Bean replied to the mother-Bean that happiness was a by-product of existence. I didn't jump in, but if I had, I would have asked: if happiness is a by-product, what is the (main) product of a Bean's existence?

'I do not have the funds to relieve my misery, like James,' the mother-Bean continued, nodding at a male Bean sitting in the circle.

'My money doesn't really *relieve* my misery, it just means, as they say, I can be miserable in comfort,' the James-Bean muttered.

'Not only that,' the mother-Bean continued, 'the prospects of returning to the kind of job I want is becoming more unlikely by the month.'

It sounded as if the lady Bean wanted it all – a family, a job, money – which when all mixed up and baked together resulted in a Happiness Cake. Did such cake have a sweeter taste? If everything was sweet, nothing was sweet, surely? Sourness reflects the sweetness. Bitterness is a key ingredient to the sweet life. I could tell you this having feasted on sweet and sour Beans alike for many lunar cycles. Bitter experience had shown that I could not live on sweets alone. The mix made for a healthy diet for the Muter. As in all things, balance was all.

But what did I care? The sweetness or sourness of a Bean did not correspond to the effectiveness of a Muter. Life skills could be helpful, but as affliction is washed away in death, sourness did not have an impact.

What mother-Bean didn't know was that she would get everything in due course. Yet it raised an important point and I felt conflicted. How long should a Bean have to wait to learn the simple lesson?

'But life is a miracle…being alive everyday is a miracle,' said the chair of the session in a quiet voice.

I nodded.

'It is all about being in the present. Being mindful…,' the female chair continued.

It was true again, Beans worry so much about the future and blame so much on the past. My advice to any Bean is two fold: firstly, if you are fixated on a problem, don't worry, because anything unresolved at death will be resolved *in* death and *at* death; not that it matters, because it is all meaningless anyway. It is a double non-jeopardy.

Beans refer to 'sadness'. Is sadness a word which refers to the absence of something? (Happiness, perhaps?) Or is 'sadness' a real and tangible substance? If one is 'filled with sadness' or 'consumed with sadness' does that suggest a presence? Or a *lack* of a presence in the Bean?

Pearl and I listened as we heard the group talk about 'coping mechanisms' as if Bean existence was a disappointment and could be corrected (with mindfulness), yet the Beans couldn't see that it *was* corrected – always and flawlessly – by death. The average Bean seemed to be aware of a better place, a happier existence (and felt such a place was their destiny 'out there' waiting to be realised) yet not only could they not see it staring them in the face, but they even sought to deny it. Deep within every Bean there is the pull towards destiny. A Bean might resist and pull back, but the pull is greater. Like an elastic band, the more the Bean pulled away, the stronger the pull to realise their destiny.

Many times I have entered flats and found people weeping or on the verge of weeping. Yet when they are diagnosed with a terminal illness, they weep too. They fear death – the unalterable state in which the burden of 'coping with life' is alleviated.

Truth be told, this was not the first group meeting. I had been to a fair number. It was easy pickings. If I fancied a sour-grape-bite I was never disappointed. Often the attendees lived on their own which allowed for a convenient base for a short period (and I did not have to pull the Has-Bean to a rooftop). If they didn't live alone, then their partner Bean was likely to relish the additional space and assume the partner Bean was taking time out. Talking groups were win-win as far as I was concerned.

There was a male-Bean in the group. He explained that he had had a breakdown because his 'career was going pear-shaped'.

'I gambled my life on a dream and it hasn't paid off,' he moaned. 'The money, the choices I've made have all come to nought. I was happy, or rather prepared, to endure hardship in my youth, my twenties, but it was on the understanding that something would work. Something would deliver. But it hasn't. So here I am with seven thousand pounds in a savings account, no career to speak of and no home. I can't stay up at night too long because I just get headaches the following day. I struggle to raise the spirit to attend (let alone enjoy) any social event – not through fear or lack of confidence, but as a result of having to endure the despair. I am now approaching my late-forties. More opportunities have passed me by than lie ahead of me. I either passed up the opportunities as they arrived or didn't have the ruthlessness to exploit them when they did. I feel like I am turning into a raincoat that is soaked through. Not only that, I have an increasing sense of mortality. Acquaintances are dying and those who are twenty years older than me don't seem that old. If I could summon up the strength to invite a woman out on a date, I'd be arrested for fucking harassment. I fear people are starting to treat me as, literally, a dirty, old raincoat – a position and apparel that I never signed up for.

'If I'm twenty years older than the attractive woman, I say - "so what?" They say, "fuck off". Ten years ago they laughed and smiled, now they reach for their mace. Where does one go from here?'

(Bored, I looked at Pearl. She was similarly bored, but we continued listening.)

'For years I wanted to live by the sea, maybe overseas, but, no, I took a filler-job here in London to pay bills while I worked to save money, develop skills, but the filler-job morphed into a full-time role, for which I also never applied, not with my heart. The skills I had will not support an existence by the sea. The debts and financial commitments I have cannot be met by carving out an existence by the sea. I might as well have gone and lived by the sea twenty-five years ago. I'd have made something work and now I'd be living by the sea. Now I just have no options and fear that keeps me living in a place I never wanted to live, with miserable people like you for company, which, ironically, is better than those things that kept me company 20 years ago – dreams and ambitions. Now they just hang over me. Happiness is all bloody fiction.'

The man paused, out of breath. I think he had shared all he wanted to.

'Okaaay' said the chair, slowly. 'Thank you, Roger. I'm glad you shared,' she continued before turning to the group. 'It is all about being Mindful. How do we engage the mind to be happy? Happiness is a state-of mind. If you are unhappy, change your mind....'.

What baffled me was that he, Roger-Bean (Raincoat-elect), could not see the potential he had. He was in his prime and beautifully adjusted. His speech could have been written by his Destiny-impulse, his inner Muter. In death all his concerns would melt away. He had come to the meeting with an agenda based around working to a timetable. But who tabled time? On whose agenda were more summers? Not mine. Time is but a countdown. In eternity, there is no time o'clock.

Then things got better. Someone else piped up: 'How do we know we are *supposed* to be happy?'

Silence descended upon the room as if a great evil had been spoken. The lady-Bean continued.

'Regardless of whether it is a "human right" to be happy. How do we know happiness is the purpose of our existence? Sometimes, when I am alone and reflecting, I think maybe we have got it all wrong...because the struggle to 'be happy' feels wrong. Perhaps happiness is an illusion. Might we have another purpose? Something that we serve. Something that comes after us?'

The other attendees looked confused.

'Maybe we are the worker bees. The honey comes later. Somewhere. Somehow.'

I concluded that she might also have been responding to the urge inside her – another manifestation of the destiny impulse.

'Are you talking about heaven?' the chairperson asked.

'A form of heaven on earth,' the lady Bean replied, quietly.

'Or maybe something after death,' muttered another. 'I too struggle so. I wonder at it all. It just doesn't make sense sometimes. Being...alive.'

I reflected that there were corners of the land where similar discussions were taking place. Discussions about the confusion, lack of fulfilment. They were all waiting for something.

Often I learnt that what brought these Beans together was an interest in what they called a 'vice'. Alcohol, sex, violence, shopping and other drugs. Some groups seemed to be targeting vices for discussion. Why do the Beans feel bad about vice? Why do they get together and talk about such things? Does it make them feel better? Vice is enrichment – essentially pleasure. If a 'vice' were self-destructive, wasn't that the point? Perhaps a 'vice' was a tool of the destiny impulse? It was both a distraction from the Bean-existence while simultaneously hastening enlightenment. Vice was the one saving grace for the unhappy Bean.

Still sitting in the gallery above the hall, Pearl was getting seriously bored. One can only sit and listen to Beans whining about their transitory state for so long. She rose from her seat and slipped down the stairs to the entrance hall. I followed discreetly behind her to allow her space. If indeed this was a form of unfinished business, then it was for her to lead. I could only act in support. She paused outside the swing doors to the entrance hall of the hall-proper, before slipping quietly inside. She stood quietly at the back beside a table on which a collection of beverages was arranged.

I intended to wait outside the hall to embrace any escapees. I could smell the downbeat nature of the flesh in the room. There was the danger the concentrated sourness would damage a perfectly good feast, therefore it was incumbent on a Muter to enlighten these Beans. But, Pearl might like the tang that came with self-obsessed whingers.

The swing doors leading into the hall had small windows at eye level allowing me sight of the Beans at the far end. Pearl remained still for a while, watching. I was about to slip in and hurry things along when I saw a Bean rise from her chair and shuffle down the hall towards Pearl. I stepped away from the door and heard the Bean address Pearl (whose own features remained deep in shadow).

'It's okay love, why don't you join us?' the lady-Bean asked Pearl.

I had expected Pearl to engage, but, no, she stayed quiet. The early bites are always the most tentative; there is a period of adjustment.

'Take your time,' said the woman before exiting the hall right beside me. I stepped back to observe her cross the corridor and enter a little kitchen to boil liquid in a device. Normally I would introduce myself, but again, this was Pearl's call. The Bean exited the kitchenette with a couple of steaming mugs and pushed open the door with her foot.

Through the gap of the swinging door I saw her hand one mug to Pearl.

'There you go. See if that warms you up. Come and join us if you like. When you're ready.'

Pearl instinctively took the offered drink and the sour Bean shuffled back down the hall and took her seat.

I waited. For a third time I felt an impulse to move in, but I was beaten to it. The tea-lady Bean had obviously mentioned the young visitor (Pearl) standing in the dark near the door. After a few minutes of muttering, another lady-Bean rose from her seat and walked quietly towards the gloom whispering friendly words as she approached Pearl (who was now ready). It was quick and silent. Within seconds Pearl, without any prompting from me, left her bite on the floor and shuffled quietly forward, mug in hand, towards the group.

It must have made a peculiar sight for the gathered Beans. There were warm Bean smiles as PearlLavaliere approached them from the gloom. They were followed by furrowed brows of confusion at the sight of a creature in a white dress drenched in burgundy juice, herself looking slightly confused.

The Beans' reactions were not simultaneous. Phrases like, 'she doesn't look well, poor child,' and 'Looks like you've had a tough time. You've come to the right place,' rose from the group. It was when the flow of juice (from their Bean friend still twitching away on the floor) caught up with Pearl's feet that one, then two and finally all group members jumped up and began a period of incessant screaming. My apprentice did not dally, she got stuck in. That's my Pearl, I thought.

She made short work of mother-Bean and the chair of the group, but 'James-Bean' managed to make it all the way to the exit where I met him. I was curious, had he forgotten his 'unhappiness'. He certainly wasn't pumping out the sour fumes of his recent past. Similarly bizarre, he did seem inclined to resist the transition from his pitiful state to a state of Has-Bean. His urge was obviously not strong enough to carry him all the way without my help. The destiny impulse can take you to the liquid road, but it cannot make you drink – that is left to the best of us.

Of the others – I did not need to head into action, the action headed to me. Some Beans lost quickly to Pearl, other Beans tried to help the Has-Beans. One lady-Bean ran into my arms and grabbed me firmly by the biceps in a firm embrace.

'Help us,' she gasped, 'it's one of those terrible zombie things,' before stepping back in shock (only to gasp her last). I tucked into the three or four who had headed my way only to look up and see at the end of the hall, in a second beautifully illuminated tableaux, my PearlLavaliere moving between the half-dozen or so feasts sampling the delights of her first bites. This is right, I thought. This is the nature of things. Destiny, eternity is a beautiful thing indeed.

Later that dark cycle, I took time to quietly reflect on recent events. Perched high on the rooftops I gazed out at the nothingness of the dark sky. Beans strive for 'destiny', because, on achieving it, they feel it would make them happy. And happiness is a product or, in some ways, a manifestation of 'destiny'. Somewhere deep inside them Beans believe destiny is a 'thing' or a 'something'. But it is not. It is nothing. Destiny is not *something* but *nothing*. The Beans' denial of the true nature of their destiny was the problem. In fact, the root cause of their unhappiness was the denial of destiny. The striving for happiness – the striving to reach the 'destiny' – resulted in misery. This is the first Bean Paradox and can be described as the 'destiny impulse'. Beans seek their destiny yet deny it, resist it. The more they deny it, the greater the impulse to reach it grows. It is a form of madness – only in a Bean's world.

24. Fizzing on the Streets – ParkBench, FallenCyclist, Papers (Cut and Fold)

*"Life is shit, man. Shit is life. Living shit. Dead shit
is alive. It shits on you so much that you drown. Then
it devours you and you turn to shit, which is then
shitted out, man. You got that? What is the point of
life if it is to be total shit? Hey? You tell me that."*
(ParkBench-elect.)

I have spoken of how both the long-term 'existence philosophy'
and the immediate state-of-mind of a Bean (at the point of
enlightenment) has an impact (or not) on gastronomic success (i.e.
a happy Bean was a happy meal), however, Pearl's adventures
supported the thesis that an unhappy Bean did not necessarily
make an *unhappy* meal. In fact, unhappy Beans can be perfectly
palatable and, in some quarters, are seen as a delicacy because they
have an understanding of the fruitlessness of their existence. So I
accept that, although I prefer the embrace of the reluctant (by
implication 'happy') Bean, sour Beans can be splendid in their
own right. Moreover, sour Beans can be wedded to the *idea* of
enlightenment without directly taking action to improve their lot.

The ways to enlightenment are numerous. Some Beans are
coerced (like Tarmac), some are random (like LampPost – found
tied bare-naked to a lamppost one chilly dark cycle), but,
occasionally, we would be approached directly by sour Beans who
not only shared with us their experience of their miserable
existence (see ParkBench-elect's words above), but even

volunteered to be inducted. These Beans had thought long and hard about their options and actively sought out Muters. There were an increasing number of meetings with these street philosophers. They were, in some respects, a volunteer army. They understood Bean existence was not for them and we were happy to oblige. ParkBench was typical.

I could not tell you for how long we stood listening to the poorly dressed, hairy Bean's musings. We had not been hunting him or his ilk. I suspect it was on one of our park square exercises in a dark cycle. As a rule, while we waited for Beans to totter by and be dazzled by sparkly things, we would clear the park location to avoid trouble. We must have missed ParkBench-elect on the first pass thinking he was a heap of garments lying on a park bench. His perfume was more Muter than Bean. So when he did stir late in the dark cycle we were taken by surprise.

He immediately started sharing his observations and possibly disarmed us all with his charm and insight. I forget who was there, perhaps DoorStop, Plot, TreeShadow, CentralLine, the ParkSparkle twins, Pearl, Chubby, Rooftop, Splash and others, but before you knew it, we were all standing around him transfixed. Such was the clarity of his thinking, I suppose we did not see him as a Bean. He was a convert. It even crossed my mind that he could in due course be a leader, our representative in the Bean world. Perhaps he could be sent out to wander the streets and explain to the Beans the error of their ways. With time and patience he could stand atop podiums and proclaim the foolishness, the corruption and conspiracies, the falsehoods and decrepitude of Beanhood to our audience. But as the darkness started to bleed away over the horizon I realised Beans would not listen or follow him. Beans selected their own leaders. Their system was set up to allow them to choose leaders who deceived them in the ways they wanted to be deceived. I don't know what brought ParkBench to his senses nor how long he had existed in his semi-enlightened state. Perhaps something happened in his dreary existence that triggered reflection, but it left me in a quandary. Do I leave ParkBench to suffer a pitiful existence even though he had seen the light? Or should I bring him over and reward him for his insight? After his presentation, we agreed to think about it. TreeShadow would monitor him in the meantime. Perhaps ParkBench could come in useful at a later date in his current pitiful state.

Not all Beans are so clear in their thinking. Many are contradictory. There are groups of Beans who gather on particular light-darks of the lunar cycle to share their enthusiasm for eternal life and insist they are preparing themselves for it. They write books, share their musings, also stand on podiums and announce that destiny is coming and how glorious it will be when it finally does. Yet when I, or any of my colleagues, try to expedite the process, they run a mile screaming like all the other Beans who believe their existence is everything. Why do Beans, who like the idea of eternal life, baulk at the invitation? Is that another Bean-paradox? Idea – good; reality – bad.

Shortly after my encounter with ParkBench I found myself on the fringes of a social event in a rooftop garden amidst the greenery of artificial vegetation into which was woven a line of illumination bulbs. Beans often meet to stand around and imbibe before their (and our) mealtimes. There is much ritual around such activities and in the warm months many of these gatherings take place on rooftops gardens. Such events are a particular favourite of mine because they provide opportunities to assess potential – feasts, fighters, lite-bites or other.

As my colleague, PlumpCalf, and I loitered in the darkness behind some trellis fencing (selecting Beans whom we would later induct in the Hall of Muter) I found myself transported back in time. I watched as a young male Bean was talking quietly with a few lady Beans when he was joined by an older male Bean. They greeted each other with respect, but it was clear they did not know each other. After a handful of meaningless pleasantries, the older Bean uttered the words that resonated with me:

'So, what do you do?'

I thought for a moment. It was indeed something I had been asked as a Bean. Repeatedly. At the time (as a Bean) I had not really given it much thought. I suppose it was part of the background noise of a meaningless existence. As far as I could recall, I don't think I had ever had a satisfactory answer for my enquirer, though I played along and said something perfunctory and fatuous. On this occasion, the younger Bean (standing on the other side of the trellis fencing) seemed to do something similar, yet, superficially at least, it appeared acceptable to those in attendance. I speculated that the young male Bean had convinced himself of the veracity of his answer to the older Bean, yet it struck me that it was the sort of question that might have acted as the trigger for ParkBench prompting a violent outburst. Had just such a question been the spark of his insight and led him to the bench? Had ParkBench been at such a soiree and had a Bean uttered the words 'what do you do?' to him resulting in ParkBench being tipped over the edge – out of the boat of smug complacency into the lake of understanding? A lake through whose dark liquid he swam to the banks of wisdom from which he hauled himself onto the Park Bench of truth – a place, a pew from which prayers for enlightenment were offered to me and my colleagues?

Don't get me wrong, I don't despise Beans. I feel no anger towards them. They are innocent and unknowing, pitiful and woeful. But we help them master their destiny. Even their gods know where they are headed and make no bones about it in their scriptures: "for you shall enter the kingdom of heaven"; "behold, the time is near". Their gods announce it without anger, but with compassion. So it is with us. I am not angry. For anger, you need to look at the Beans themselves. If the Bean thinks Muters' actions are based on anger, I would argue they are projecting their own frustrations and failures onto us. I am constantly surprised at how needlessly aggressive they are. I can taste their anger whether it is exhibited or not. Anger and aggression is everywhere in the metropolis. It is a perpetual state of the metropolitan Bean. Take FallenCyclist-elect, for instance.

In the dark cycle of a cold lunar cycle I was walking the streets in the capital minding my own business. Having feasted I was feeling satisfied and not in need of further nourishment. The swirl of illumination from passing vehicles and the slight drizzle in the air meant I could walk along unhindered. With a scarf wrapped around my features and my head covered, I was on the way to meet DoorStop and GlassCutter to deliberate about an upcoming visit to a Bean home for angry people.

I was aware of the Bean conventions when navigating roadways and walking ways and, when wishing to move undisturbed (and uninjured) through the metropolis dump, I abided by them. On the dark cycle in question a cyclist was racing up the road towards me as I was approaching a junction (off which ran a darker street). I stepped out to cross the junction as the cyclist veered across the road in front of two automobilic vehicles. The cycle-Bean did not appear to be abiding by road-user conventions himself. Whether the cyclist had clipped the vehicles I could not say, but he partially lost control of the bicycle and careered towards me. I did not make any deliberate effort to move out of the way and there was a mild collision, his front wheel ran into my leg and he fell off. I continued walking, but, thinking the matter was coming to the attention of others, I turned down the side street and headed towards the darkness. I left behind the drivers of the vehicles leaning out of their windows shouting angrily at the cyclist and anyone else who was interested in listening (there were none). The cyclist shouted back towards the drivers before shouting a few words at me as I retreated down the dark street.

'You could have fucking killed me, you fucking moron,' he shouted.

I continued moving down the street looking ahead of me, my features turned away wrapped up and away from his gaze. I wondered whether he would have such courage to shout directly into the face of death when his eschewal of death was apparent from his words. I continued to move on, intent on meeting DoorStop. That said, I noticed that the electric street illumination faltered further down the street; it might provide us with a quiet moment together should his interest in me persist.

More shouting followed.

He was clearly not at peace with his existence, his cycling, his Beanhood, and even, presumably, his future (Bean) prospects (if that is not an oxymoron) so, who was I to delay the inevitable? There are unforeseen opportunities in death after all. Within a half-dozen steps I concluded that this was his opportunity to shed himself of all the anger, frustrations, disappointments, anxieties and restlessness.

As I turned these thoughts over in my mind I became aware that FallenCyclist-elect seemed to be disappointed that I was not reacting to his exhibition of self-importance. His vitriol carried in the wet night air as I walked away. By ignoring him I assume it upset him further, because his cries and curse words, rather than recede as I retreated, grew louder. He was following me. Why do angry Beans crave attention? Anyway, aware that his destiny might be upon him, I pressed on down the street towards the darkness under the faulty lamplight.

'Did you fucking well hear me? You could have fucking killed me, you fucking moron,' he shouted in my ear as he placed a hand on my upper arm.

Feeling safe in the relative darkness I turned to face him. As I did so, my scarf fell away from my features and the faulty lamplight flickered into life.

I will always be surprised at the speed Bean anger can fall away so completely to be replaced by the sudden realisation of their place in the world. Their puffy, fleshy features can be so expressive, evidence of the imperfect evolution of the Bean – the attempt to communicate 'meaning'. Muters have no need for 'expressive features' because everything is understood. Every Muter shares the same priorities. We are not lumbered with possessions, ambition, 'manners'; there is no need to express emotion. To be afflicted with 'emotion' is an annoyance and irrelevance that the modern Bean has tried to turn into an asset. How emotion makes a Bean more effective is beyond me. Emotion is one of the Bean conditions that one can shake off in death. And so it is that flesh can fall away and deteriorate without any detriment to a Muter's effectiveness.

I suppose FallenCyclist-elect might have wanted to shout again, even call for help, but I suspect the drivers of the nearby vehicles would not be inclined to help. Who would want to help such an angry Bean? Besides, with my firm grip on his larynx and my squeezing of his airways, he could not call out. As he struggled, in the desperate ways that Beans do, I wondered whether, when he set out that light cycle (or any previous light cycle), it had occurred to him that he would literally look death in face that light-dark? And at the hands of a creature who saw value only in his death. You cannot impose your own sense of value (as an angry cyclist) on those who only wish you your Bean-demise. The shouts and swearing came to nothing. There was no value in this cyclist's existence.

I was his release. Like a pressure valve, I could set him free. Yet I did not see gratitude in his eyes as he breathed his last. It was almost as if he did not understand. In a spontaneous act of charity and to clarify my intentions, I bit into those plumps cheeks of his. Although already fully feasted that evening, I was impressed by the tang, his delicacy. Before I knew it I was drinking in the red glory that had been pulsing through his body moments before. I was impressed. Anger does have an energy and gives the Bean a fizz, a kick. With this in mind, I was keen to catch up with DoorStop and GlassCutter to explore their plans for the home for the angry. With any luck many of them would be frustrated cyclists. Nevertheless, keen to see how FallenCyclist-elect would rise and what his first instincts would be on rising, I slung him over my shoulder and carried him up to the rooftops to rest. Aware his acrylic cyclist attire would sweat during his birthing period and generate an odour which might draw attention, I placed him on the end-of-terrace roof.

My curiosity had been pricked again and I subsequently made a point of picking up cyclists in busy parts of town. I know Chain-and-Stiks, Tracks, DogSmells also had developed a taste for angry cyclists. Beans think they own the roadways even when using the flimsiest of contraptions.

As described, there is a somewhat fizzy taste to the angry Bean, but one does not always know until the bite that the Bean is angry. It is not just the expression of anger that sets the juice fizzing, the juice can fizz unseen to the unknowing eye. I marvel at a Bean's restraint and the hiding of their afflictions. If Beans are wont to have 'emotion', why conceal it? Are they ashamed? (Of course, they should be, but they are not enlightened to know that they should be.)

I have often found myself at a loose end as I meander the streets and rooftops. Most Beans are indoors, others move swiftly along streets in groups, so unless one is with colleagues, it can be tricky intervening. However, there are times when Beans can be found in ones, twos (sometimes threes) in little commercial establishments where they sit quietly imbibing warm liquids. If they sit in company, they talk (often about the emotions they are enduring).

There were two similar (but separate) incidents that occurred shortly after my encounter with FallenCyclist, but all within the space of seven light-darks of each other. One was with a male Bean, the other was with a lady Bean.

Resting on a rooftop above a main street of shops I happened to glance down to see a middle-summered-Bean male sitting outside an establishment drinking a warm, milky liquid and reading a paper-of-news of the Bean world. (Not Beans talking about their lives, but *writing* about Bean lives. I kid you not.) Realising he had nothing better to do with his existence, I took a slight detour and pulled him away into a quiet alley and had my way with him. What was curious was that he had the same fizzy tang to his juice as FallenCyclist had had. Yet, PaperFold-elect had not been shouting, cycling, in a confrontation with any other Bean, yet his juice was zinging. At the time I dismissed it as an anomaly, but a handful of light-darks later I was passing a similar establishment and, seeing a middle-summered lady Bean also studying a paper-of-news of the Bean world, I indulged myself. Again, zinging juice. The only common element in the glory stream of PaperFold and PaperCut was the paper-of-news. I could only think that it injected the Bean with anger, much like the cyclist; yet it was curious the anger had not been apparent in the demeanour or body language. It was controlled. Why? Another Bean convention? And it could be generated by hieroglyphs on paper alone?

Nevertheless, it led me onto another experiment that, in turn, led to the study of fizz-zing-juice. If ever I felt the calling for something different, I would look for a middle-summered Bean studying a paper-of-news. Younger Beans could return some zing, but it was diluted; many, many summered Beans could, on occasion, deliver a zing, but it was hit-or-miss. It was the middle-summered-Bean that would hit the mark every time.

Occasionally, I would take Pearl, Tracks, Tarmac, Plot and Diesel on the hunt for the fizz-zing. Cyclists were few and far between and usually confined to certain (central) parts of the metropolis, but head to any part of the metropolis dump, find a Bean with a paper-of-news and no Muter would be disappointed.

Chubby would sometimes come along, but she never really appreciated the hit of the zing. When she did join us she was always helpful when there were groups of angry (paper-reading) Beans. She would split them up by tempting them out of the establishment altogether or to a quieter place within the establishment (the kitchen for example, where a feast could be prepared). Similarly, PaperFold and PaperCut themselves (and lite-bites like PlumpCalf) would approach and join Beans at nearby tables. The Beans would be surrounded and efficiently spirited away (by the likes of Diesel or Tarmac) whilst the Papers (Cut and Fold) would handle any unexpected nonsense. I was unsure quite how the Papers became so proficient at the exercise, but there was a very real talent at sitting there and concealing anger like a Bean. The unfinished business of both PaperFold and PaperCut was also interesting, but that's another story.

25. Buried Talents

I was curious about the development of PlumpCalf and other lite-bites. I suspected there was room to grow. Reflecting on her origins I guessed that Plump must have taken to her bed, had an illness, passed over and risen on the other side. The arrival of the Cloth-Heads had not been as a result of my own ingress into the house. I was confident I had not been seen. Perhaps Plump's Bean friends had been worried and followed up with the Cloth-Heads or, perhaps, Plump and Chimney had passed on the good news that they had been kissed prompting the visit after a few light-darks of inaction. That said, I wanted to experiment more and used a method that I often did – which was visiting Beans who were known to be 'unwell'. Any non-appearance at a place of work was therefore explained away and bought us a few more light-darks. You might think the 'unwell' are easy pickings. You would be right.

Many dark cycles I have spent sitting at the end of a Bean's bed waiting for them to stir. As I have described, when the body is in a relaxed state but suddenly zapped by a shot of adrenalin (as the Bean opens their eyes), it gives the juice a nice ping. Similarly, visiting those who are unwell, the body is relaxed, the adrenalin kick does not overwhelm a rather sour taste. Besides, I feel the illness is a teaser of where the future lies; the desire of enlightenment can be detected on the palate.

So, with Plump (and later Chubby) in attendance, we worked our way around part of the town looking for potential house-bound sickies. Penthouses lent themselves to this activity in some respects. We could monitor the Beans contained therein and select with care.

Even penthouse Beans, once re-born, leave all their possessions behind and never show signs of wishing to return to the 'trappings' of Bean existence. In this respect death is a vindication of the irrelevance of possessions and I feel duty-bound to demonstrate it when and where I can especially to those residing in 'quality residences'. Strangely, the palate-quality of the Bean residing in quality residences is not so great. Arguably the quality of the kiss and glory stream of a Bean is in direct inverse correlation to the quality of the residence in which they reside. Although the Bean might feed well, the flesh is often poor and any happy-tang is not present in the same quantities as one might expect. I suspect time spent on (or near) street level would do much to boost some of these qualities.

So, with PlumpCalf (and one or two others) we spent a number of light-darks skipping across the rooftops and waiting patiently on balconies, slipping into penthouses and nibbling gently at the lower legs. We would return on dark cycles to follow to monitor the progress of our lite-bites. I would take DoorStop along in case we were disturbed, but would not let him into the premises himself as the temptation might prove too great for him.

On one occasion we miscalculated. We arrived at a very lavish penthouse, full of paintings, vases, over-elaborate seating and a large grand piano at its centre. Lots of gold and trinkets and hangings adorned the furniture and walls. (I made a mental note to alert the ParkSparkle twins to strip the property of its goods for use in the park-square exercises.) On entering the premises we found a seventy-summered man in a dressing gown preparing for bed. He looked familiar. I realised that his likeness adorned the sides of buildings and were often found in the properties of many of my bites. To keep the story brief, he saw me and panicked, shuffled back to the corner of the bedroom and curled into a ball and whimpered words like 'please' and 'no' and 'not me'. It was distressing and disappointing for both of us.

There was no fight in him. It was not like ParkBench – not wanting to put up a fight because of a philosophical position reached. No, it was as if this piano-owning Bean was not fighting because he associated himself too much with his belongings which he knew deep down were not worth fighting for. If he were to be removed from his penthouse might he put up a fight, I wondered? I had a degree of respect for the Beans who made the effort of fighting.

'I'll give you anything,' the Bean whimpered. 'Take anything you want.'

When that didn't work, he tried something else.

'I can make you famous,' he whispered, brushing away his tears. 'I can give you the world. I can change the way people look at you. I could write a song about you. I can put your name in lights. In fact, what is your name? Let's give you a name.'

I took a step forward which seemed to increase his panic.

'You look unhappy. Perhaps you had an unhappy life?' he gasped. 'That's why you are here. I'm glad you are here. I want to share my wealth with you. We can be friends.'

It was at times like this that I marvel at the Bean brain. They just don't get it. As best I could, I repeated his line.

'I want to share my wealth with you,' I whispered hoarsely.

'Yes, yes,' he suddenly gasped, all excited. Perhaps he thought he had got through to me. 'That's right, I want to share my wealth with you,' he said, pointing to himself then pointing at me.

But the piano man could not comprehend what I meant. I was trying to explain to him that I wanted to share *my* wealth with *him*. So I repeated his line trying to explain that: I want to share my wealth (I said, pointing at myself) with you, I said pointing at him.

'No, no, you've got it all wrong' he responded, nervously laughing, pointing at himself (as the 'bestower') then at me as the one on whom the gift was 'bestowed'.

'No, no,' I said, and repeated the line, again pointing at myself as the bestower, then at him as the bestowed.

He didn't understand and for a short while we went back and forth trying to communicate, but it was all in vain. At least I had tried but I was getting bored. What bemused me was that he took his own lack of understanding as my fault – an arrogance that would irritate a Bean but, as you would expect, was lost on me.

'I have so much left to give. So much more to achieve,' he whimpered as I picked him up. 'I have another three albums in me.'

I bit into his neck. The taste was poor to average. There was no point in making a lite-bite out of him. Any transference of skills or experience would be of no use as a Muter. He wouldn't flourish in eternity because he had been so limited in the Bean existence. He would be a middling soldier. I believe I gave him a name, but it escapes me now.

So, although this Bean, known to many other Beans, was an ideal candidate (being isolated) for a lite-bite, his possession-status and his self-regard had trained him to the point that he was ineffectual. I believe he was lost early on the great battle of the metropolis not seven lunar cycles later. Penthouses or no penthouses, those who possessed them never returned. Death is eternal richness itself.

26. Hunting Grounds Aplenty

During these lunar cycles, Muter hunting practices developed; it was not linear, but more of a simultaneous blooming of practices. This confused the Beans, I'm sure, but Muters are fast learners and excellent sharers. Speaking for myself, I gravitated to rooftops as a hunting ground, finding ways to access apartments with ease. It probably helped me in the early light-darks because it kept me off the streets. I shared my skills with my niblings (i.e. using rooftops to move around and monitor Bean feasts). My niblings flourished. Not only did they master my techniques, they added skills of their own and, of course, shared them with their own niblings and colleagues. Muters became a learning entity.

PearlLavaliere worked moaning groups, TarmacTired worked the streets (or from identified premises), the ParkSparkle Twins and TreeShadow worked park spaces, DoorStop and GlassCutter worked homes for the angry (of which, more later), CentralLine and Jubilee worked the tunnels, Plot and BroadBean worked the fields of rest and, of course, Chubby worked anywhere and everywhere else. We all brought something to the table and feasted well. Our numbers grew. My niblings had niblings of their own and I found myself joining hunts and learning new skills aplenty. There soon came a time when there was not a place in the metropolis we did not reach. We were like a disease (but the good kind – incurable and terminal).

But it was not all about skill sets. Sometimes the hunting grounds themselves informed the development of our practices up to the time of the Great Change (in Bean Behaviour – see Chapter

36). Later, I recalled those light-darks of innocence in the metropolis with great fondness. I never tire at the memory of them – the times when Beans would gather together and lay on a feast for us. Sometimes Bean gatherings were planned with many family members in attendance (for instance, in places of worship when Bean couples committed to be together until death), other times feasts were random – parklands full of exposed flesh lying under the great orb of the sky, inviting us to have our fill. I often found myself stumbling across opportunities arising from spontaneous street parties. Unlike the underground tunnel banquets, no planning was required with regard to many of these feasts. They could not be predicted and would just open up like a ribcage on a spit.

The twenty-something summered Beans are different in many ways (not all twenty-summered Beans had had their brains cooked during three solar cycles like the average Bean-Stew). Like their elders they were confused and sad, but they also possessed a profound ignorance and sought solace in groups (much like Pearl's groups). They would intoxicate themselves with chemicals to 'get out of their heads' (in order, I suppose, to 'feel something' in the barren desert of Beanhood). The chemicals masked their struggle with the destiny impulse. 'Feel empty and lost within? Then imbibe liquids or ingest pills and feel alive!' Often the hunting grounds for these kinds of Beans are underground or hidden away from other Bean activity. However, it inevitably spills out onto the street, especially during the warm lunar cycles. The presence of the scantily clad lady Beans was instrumental in facilitating such events by bringing out the male Bean. (Note: scantily clad lady Beans can be found tottering around in the cold, darker lunar months, but the temperature-stress on the Bean meat was apparent on the palate.)

On one occasion I was making my way over the rooftops to check up on the work of the ParkSparkle twins when a gust of wind lifted the sweetest of aromas to my nasal cavities from the streets below. Making a slight detour, I soon found myself looking down on a small, tight road full of late-night eating and drinking establishments and awash with perspiring flesh. I wasn't the first there. Looking around I could see the silhouettes of dozens of other Muters (many of whom I knew) all looking down from the rooftops at the same thing. Sometimes the prospect of death is just like that, it pulls you in. Not since the underground feast a few lunar cycles earlier had I such a banquet laid out before me.

We Muters waited until the establishments emptied its delights on to the streets, which soon buzzed with jollity. Watching the spectacle I first thought that a couple of Muters had slipped down to ground level and joined in the festivities, but looking closer I realised that it was in fact a number of Beans who were clutching each other and biting each other's necks. I suppose the need is buried deep in the Bean form. Such an act – the act of clutching and hunt for the glory stream – is only fully realised with the evolution into Muter. The Beans play on the outskirts of revelation, which is both endearing and pitiful.

The moment came. Perhaps my colleagues were waiting for me, I don't know, but the Beans were ripe for the picking. I shimmied down the edge of the buildings and slipped into the shadows. I could see other Muters doing the same. There was no fuss, no drama as we all slipped into the celebrations. Such was the chemically-induced distraction of the Beans that Muters could dip into the throng, clutch a Bean and drag them lovingly into the shadows and share that eternal kiss.

At a distance I spotted a lady Bean drifting through the crowd towards me. At first, truth be told, her gait was more like an averagely functioning Muter. Perhaps she was unconsciously trying to attract a Muter, or her body was reaching out to destiny. Her puppy-flesh exposed, she stumbled towards me with a slight vacant look in her eyes, her incoherent mumbling could not hide her true identity. The scent was rampant (albeit heavily disguised)

– she was Bean. She tottered this way, then that, like an exotic bird on the branch of an exotic tree deep in an exotic jungle.

I moved towards her through the swaying crowd passing Chain-and-Stiks, Plot, BeanPole, Rooftop and Diesel, all hugging and kissing Beans like there was no forthcoming light-dark; each one guiding their unsuspecting Bean to the literal shadows and the metaphorical light.

I reached FleshPuppy-elect and slipped my arm around her waist and gently guided her. She sang a modern, popular song destined to disappear for an eternity. She laughed and pouted aromas, which clung to me like dew from a morning fog before tickling my nasal cavities and throat before slipping down into my cadaver. The chemicals imbibed earlier in the dark cycle helped push the happy tang around her body making it lush on my palate. It was a banquet for all seasons.

But, as I have said, sometimes Muters specialised in particular hunting grounds and I studied and reflected on what I could learn from their success. Having witnessed the effectiveness of Tarmac's work in taking over a specific residence, I began to think about 'feasting grounds' rather than hunting grounds – that is feasting opportunities which were predictable. A 'hunting ground' implies there is movement, a 'search', but what if there was no searching as such? We didn't have to hunt, we just feasted? One of PearlLavaliere's niblings delivered just the thing.

Freshly-risen Muters take o'clock to fully develop defensive awareness. There is always the danger that when a fresh Muter meets a lively Bean, it can get messy, so I always recommend a mentor keeps a close eye on their niblings for the first few lunar cycles, especially if the fresh Muter was inclined (even unwittingly) to engage with any unfinished business. Although Pearl was an effective mentor during her niblings' early light-darks, she indicated that she wished me to join her monitoring one particular Muter. I agreed and as DoorStop and Diesel were at a loose end, I brought them along, which was no bad thing.

Pearl's love-bite was a male Bean of twenty-something summers. Quite slight in stature, Pearl had christened him 'Peas' which was apparently what he kept saying as she was having her way with him. We followed Pearl and Peas at a respectable distance monitoring their progress. Peas did seem to have something in mind, but he would not have fully understood even if he did. The fresh Muter led us to a large block of apartment flats in what the Beans would describe as an 'upcoming part of town'. How marvel and awe can be attributed to marsh farm outbuildings, I do not know.

For some reason Peas perched himself on a rooftop across from the main entrance to the apartment block. What was he waiting for? (He would not have known – he was still fresh.) Was it the echo of foolishness a Bean feels for another Bean? Was it a blood relative related to some unfinished business? We waited and watched for the exiting of Beans that might prompt Peas to move. It was only when a black vehicle arrived late in the night and four occupants alighted, did Peas rise to his feet, take a deep intake of the perfumes rising from the group of burly Beans on the street below and follow them into the building after a short period.

Pearl was by his side, so I was confident she would manage any immediate interaction with the Beans, but I was pleased to have brought along Diesel and DoorStop. If the four Beans were in fact the items of interest to Peas, there might be a confrontation. After all, this was an induction of sorts, so the matter had to play itself out and Peas would be the more effective Muter for it.

What became clear was that Peas was familiar with the building. He found the stairwells with ease and was confident turning corners. He made his way to the third floor of the building and walked a short corridor to the source of a number of threatening Bean voices. Pearl followed closely behind him.

Diesel, DoorStop and I hung back deep in the shadows ready to make our presence known if required.

As I suspected, after a shocked moment of introduction, the Bean-boss recognised Peas.

'Hey, Jonny, look at you. What are you doing here?'

Obviously Peas was struggling to comprehend the situation and his own reason for being there. Pea's inability to understand his role and his relationship with the Bean-boss led to a failure to assert ownership over the situation. Whatever relationship had existed between Peas and the Bean-boss had fundamentally changed (although Bean-boss did not know it). In fact, the Bean was clearly resorting to the same relationship behaviour he had exhibited prior to Peas' enlightenment.

The Bean continued to talk dismissively to Peas and began to slap his face in a patronising manner. This did not move me. I am indifferent to the power-play between Beans, however, it would become a matter for me if Peas was not able to follow through on his learning processes.

The slapping and mocking talk was escalating and being enjoyed by the three other Bean-sheep, one of whom joined in. Suddenly Peas tried to step up and bite the Bean-boss. It was an inexpert and confused attempt. The Bean smacked him down and became more aggressive, whereupon Pearl stepped forward announcing her presence.

'Oh, look, he's brought his fucking girlfriend,' said a Bean-sheep stepping towards Pearl and removing a firing device from his garment.

Diesel is probably the most striking looking of those present, so his features emerging from the shadows of the corridor closely followed by the imposing DoorStop shook the levity from the scene. Keen to re-establish the balance of power (so important in relations with Beans), DoorStop grabbed the Bean-sheep holding the firing device and slammed him hard against the wall, removing the device from his grasp, biting the neck hard and drinking the glory stream before letting him slip to the floor. Simultaneously, Diesel grabbed the Bean-sheep who had been manhandling Peas and threw him hard against the wall holding him by his neck.

I emerged calmly and lastly from the darkness and walked straight towards Bean-boss feeling that I ought to let Peas do the honours.

'We can do a deal. Hey, look, ugly fuck, you can have all the people in this apartment block,' the Bean-boss said striking a different and chastened tone. 'I can give you access to all of them. I have keys. I look after this apartment block, you see. There must be hundreds here. All juicy meals for you and your friends.'

I stopped. Intrigued. He took it as an invitation to continue.

'We'd be doing each other a favour. You can clear all these people out and then go on your way. We don't need them here. We can charge much better rates than we are getting at the moment. People like Jonny here,' he said nodding towards Peas, 'were just giving us a hard time. You guys, you're cool. You're almost above the law.'

'What the fuck are you doing, Guv.?,' said the Bean-sheep held against the wall by Diesel. 'They're fucking scum-of-the-earth zombies.'

Irritated by the noise, I gave the nod to Diesel who swiftly dispatched the whining Bean-sheep amidst a moment of pitiful gurgling. (Again, why the struggle against destiny?)

Returning my attention to the lead Bean I stood looking at him processing the offer. I could see that he thought he had a different destiny to everybody else, but it was an interesting offer in the short term. It might allow Peas and a few of his contemporaries to develop their craft in relative safety while simultaneously acquiring more Muters to the fold.

I took a pace towards him to take in his perfume. He took a step back.

'Look, I can go and get the keys for all the apartments in this block from my office. If you wait here I can come back and hand them over.'

'They're in the briefcase, Guv.,' his one remaining Bean-sheep whispered.

I turned to Diesel who picked up the briefcase, broke it open and handed it to me. Opening the case I found numerous sets of keys.

'Fuck, they can speak English,' gasped the Bean-sheep.

'Of course, they can, you fuck,' Bean-boss spat back at his colleague, before turning back to me.

'Look, why don't I go and get more keys to other apartment blocks I look after? We could go into business together – you and I. We both have needs. I recognise yours. You just recognise mine. You'll just have to vacate the property once you have had your fill.'

I studied his features. He was pumping out fear perfumes. I could feel my own team was swooning.

'So we can restock it,' he added hopefully, his breath sweeping over us. Perhaps my uncertainty became apparent, because he persisted.

'But, as I said, we have other properties around London which we could help you with. You'll never go hungry, I promise.'

I leant in and drank in his perfume.

'Why's he doing that?' the Bean-sheep said.

'Remember,' I muttered into the Bean boss's ear and smiled (as best I could).

'You can't trust him, Guv...he's a fucking ....'

A nod to Diesel and Pearl and the last Bean-sheep didn't have a chance to finish his sentence. It had the effect of focusing the Bean-boss's mind (especially now that he was on his own) and he repeated his offer.

Peas, not quite understanding the arrangement stepped forward. I think he thought it was now his turn to bite. It was after all his induction, but I motioned to him that the time was not right. His time would come. And with that, we let the Bean depart.

We did indeed satisfy our needs in the apartment block. In fact, we needed to enrol the assistance of Chain-and-Stiks, Plot, CatNaps, BeanPole, ColourSplash, DogSmells, TarmacTired, the ParkSparkle Twins, PlumpCalf, ChimneyBlack, CentralLine, Jubilee, LycraStew and many, many more.

There were a handful of flats that did hold out with some tenants barricading themselves in. It was then that we had to call on the services of Chubby, FatLegs, KittenFluff and DogCuddles. Once again I was taken by the effectiveness of their techniques. Not only is Chubby the first line of assault, she can also act as the final line of annihilation. A truly remarkable machine and such a simple, pure delight to watch.

Of course, I was keen that the Bean-boss honoured his pledge. We did not see him for a few light-darks, but Peas and I tracked him down to a part of town not so far away. Peas watched him for a week until we felt that a new apartment block would be welcome whereupon we surprised him in an alleyway not far from his home. He was indeed surprised, even nervous, but handed over the keys to another apartment block and promised more. However, he was slow at coming back to us and, with my patience running low, Peas and I paid him a visit at his own apartment high in the sky. His subsequent business propositions bored me and so I was pleased to let the now-experienced Peas finish his unfinished business. Such was Peas' delight that at his bite (and feast) that he pretty much wiped out the effectiveness of Bean-boss as a Muter especially when Peas picked up the bloody mess and threw it out of the apartment block window. Falling fifteen storeys ensured a relatively immobile Has-Bean and easy pickings for the Rubber Beans. So, what skill set does the property agent Bean offer to the future? To be honest, I couldn't tell you, which, for someone with my experience, is saying something.

However, the principle had been established and we did, at intervals, seek to identify individuals and organisations that might be able to supply easy access to Beans stocked high (one upon another) in the metropolis's battery farms.

27. A Cake Walk

I was looking for occasions that would allow my niblings to shine; such opportunities are often to be found in the environments they feel most comfortable. Again, this is also related (in some degree) to any 'unfinished business'. ParkSparkleFat and ParkSparkleThin had acquired their own niblings, but we were coming up against the problem of saturation: the park squares hunting grounds (limited in size) were unable to accommodate the large numbers generated by the Twins. So the Twins invited colleagues to a soiree one evening. Arriving at the venue we decided to use the rear entrance in the interests of discretion. It would allow the event's guests to arrive unhindered at the main entrance.

DoorStop and GlassCutter would secure the entrances at the front of the venue and Pearl, Diesel, Rooftop and Tracks would secure all others. Once the evening had started we made our entrance at the rear with relative ease. There were a few security personnel who needed subduing (in fact a number of them would later prove to be useful additions to our group). We appeared in a backstage area where many Beans were mulling about. There were no threats. The male Beans were slight in build and far from aggressive. The female Beans were just slight in build and nature. As always the Beans were too consumed with their own activities to notice our arrival. The loud indeterminate noise from electronic boxes also drowned out any early protests from the backstage Beans. But it was what the ParkSparkle twins were doing that caught my attention.

Although they had feasted on some of those present, they threw various garments over themselves and headed for the entrance to the main hall. I feared they might be getting ahead of themselves because Pearl, Diesel, Rooftop, myself and others had not secured the outer (larger hall) room. Furthermore, the ParkSparkle twins were themselves dripping with juice – garments stained from the feast. Even throwing a garment over their heads and wrapping it with sparkly accessories did little to disguise their true nature.

I was concerned the Beans in the inner room would overwhelm the ParkSparkle twins. I should not have worried. In fact, I was rather pleased and encouraged. They disappeared through the doorway only for applause to echo from the hall. Flashes of light also seemed to herald a welcome to my young protégés. Curious as to what lay within (and seeing that Pearl and others had everything under control), I followed the twins into the inner room that was bordered by hanging black drapes. I was hit by the luscious aroma from banks and banks of seated Beans. In truth, much of the aroma was contaminated by artificial odours. Spotting a gap in the drapes I slipped into the darkness and made my way around the perimeter to the room and poked by head out from behind a bench of Beans. Fortunately the clouds of artificial perfumes masked my arrival to the groups of applauding Beans about me.

I was met by pure spectacle. ParkSparkleFat and ParkSparkleThin were walking back and forth along a stage gangway down the middle of the room around which were gathered enraptured Beans taking photographs and applauding. I watched as the ParkSparkles stopped, turned, adjusted their attire (soaked in Bean juice) before walking in another direction. The Beans felt under no threat. I was intrigued. Just when I thought the Beans might understand their imminent transfiguration, PearlLavaliere appeared from behind the curtain walking along the gangway to even greater applause. Not only was she literally dripping with the juices of a dozen (now former) Beans from backstage, but she was carrying the severed head of one of the Beans themselves. Had the Beans finally come to their senses? Was this a collection of truly enlightened Beans? The 'elite', perhaps, of Bean society? The pioneers, trailblazers and philosophers who understood what the future really held for them?

Once again, just when I would expect the conventional Bean reaction from somewhere in the hall, I saw a surviving Bean (an almost Has-Bean with juices oozing from her body in the most wasteful manner) crawl onto the stage. Using her broken arms and looking (in Bean terms) 'a total mess' she dragged herself along the stage gangway. She appeared to be muttering something (perhaps a cry for help), but anything she said was drowned out by the electronic noise and the applause. I thought there might be some realisation in the room and hoped my colleagues would not be too far away. Once again I should not have worried for Diesel appeared in all his powerful glory at the end of the walkway. To gasps from the gathered, he strode purposefully forward towards the broken body of the almost Has-Bean on the floor in front of him, picked her up by one ankle and dragged her the length of the walkway joining ParkSparkle. The room erupted in applause. Never have I seen my kind so appreciated by the Beans. They were coming round to the idea of their future. Our future.

Diesel picked up the Bean off the floor and held her high over his head in a show of celebration of how we can all work together. The lady Bean struggled a bit but was weakening, so Diesel dropped her to his waist and with a sleight of hand twisted and broke her neck exposing the soft lusciousness of her flesh, he bit into it and tore his mouth away ripping the neck flesh as he did so. The ParkSparkle twins were splashed with the cascading juice as were the front rows of the gathered Beans. The vision was compelling to such an extent that the applause stopped and there was silence (but for the dull thump of the noise coming over the electronic speaker system).

Silence. (Electronic noise.) And stillness.

And then a shake of the head from somewhere, followed by a gasp somewhere else, which was, in turn, followed by a solitary clap from one Bean, then another, then another until the whole space was full of thunderous applause, shouting and cheering. To this day it was probably the most moving encounter I have experienced between Bean and Muter. A light-dark and a place that will be forever (quite literally) in my memory.

My other colleagues (including DoorStop and GlassCutter) soon entered, but I believe some Beans took exception to their musings and before long the gathering descended into its usual disagreements and struggles. That said, it was a very productive dark cycle and we came away with a lot – not only the feasting, but, with the wealth of talent on show, there were numerous lite-bites that would bear fruit in the lunar cycle to follow.

That occasion filled the ParkSparkle twins with such confidence and *joie de vivre* that they could almost operate on their own at similar events often taking along their own niblings. It reassured me that all Muters have a role to play and can perform at the very highest level – giving meaning where meaning is in pitifully poor supply.

I reflected. Existence is all about articulating a universal truth. Death is that universal truth. Therefore my advice to any Bean is: prepare yourself. Why train and prepare for an existence that is just a few seconds of glory stream away from oblivion? No, prepare yourself for me. Call me Death. I'll be with you soon.

28. Tough Times and Mentoring

Sometimes it is difficult. After the street parties (and the success of many other operations) there were increased numbers of Cloth-Heads and now, Rubber Beans. It was therefore prudent to keep to certain parts of town. ChubbyCheeks had also been busy and was attracting a lot of attention. The papers-of-news included hazy images of Chubby and FatLegs playing and enlightening full-size Beans in the parks in full light cycle sight. The papers-of-news even suggested the Cloth-Heads and Rubber Beans were keeping a specific look out for her and her team (FatLegs, Fluffykins, DogCuddles, KittenFluff among others). So it was that, with our success and expansion across the metropolis, some tough times came calling. We had to re-group, reflect. Our needs and practices needed to evolve. We needed to work together, harder.

It occurred to me that we (or rather I) needed to think about finding a proper base, perhaps in an area of the metropolis farm that was a bit safer, more secluded. We could also use this time to develop the skills of our new contingent. Our numbers were growing exponentially and it was becoming increasingly important to manage skills development. Again, this seemed to fall to me.

Though a veteran of death, I still struggled to understand Beanhood. It was no secret that fresh Muters struggled to comprehend their new environment and therefore it was perhaps understandable that a Bean would misread a freshly-risen Muter's manner on first meeting. The ignorant Bean would usually dismiss the Muter as no-threat, irrelevant to their safety, even imbecilic – with the Muter derided as a figure of ridicule. Often this perception results in abuse of the Muter. Even though the Muter's purpose is singular – to release the Bean from its torment – that does not warrant the abuse. Arguably the abuse stems from fear and, of course, I understand that fear generates aggression, but language such as 'you stupid motherfucker, fuck off you ugly piece of shit' and, 'go fuck yourself you stupid, moronic zombie' are wholly uncalled for.

Late one dark cycle I led a few fresh-risers into a relatively safe feasting area (populated by Beanteens) for hunting practice. The Beanteen is a fresh Bean, a fresh Bean is a dim Bean. It was, by Bean standards, a small run-down area of the metropolis that even the finest Bean poet would lose the will to describe – concrete pathways, stairwells smelling of Bean waste, a parade of shops selling stuff other Beans had thrown out. It was a place where Beans came to die and a place where male Beanteens thrive. Hence they are useful starter-grounds for Muters because the Beans do not necessarily run away. It is the early, corrupt manifestation of the First Bean Paradox – they are simultaneously excited by, and yet fear, the imminent prospect of death. They almost resent the Bean-breath they exhale. You could smell that they are constantly on the cusp of enlightenment. For this reason Beenteens are useful starter kits for Muters.

I also have a tenderness for these sorts of places because I think the squalor, the emptiness reminds me of my first bites such as the one in that small park area. (I had yet to meet that Bean who got away. Note to self: I must find him; his odour will never leave me.)

So, I led the four fresh-Muters (SwapShop, SugarRush, SimplyFine and TyreTreads) to the edge of the estate. I also brought along CatNaps, Diesel, Plot and Pearl for support. Away from the artificial street illumination, we Muters stood in a circle for a few moments to compose ourselves. The four newbies looked at me. Like most fresh-risers they looked unsure. Perhaps they were waiting for me to take the lead, but I was clear in my own mind that they needed to find their own way now.

I slowly raised my head and drew in air through my nasal cavities. They mimicked my action. Nothing. They looked blank. I did it again. Again they mimicked it. First SwapShop and then SugarRush smelt it – fresh Bean. They both turned and looked down towards the illuminated walkways of concrete. Their gaze was followed by the others – SimplyFine and TyreTreads. I nodded my approval and slowly the four newbies sloped off into the night. I scaled the sides of the building to the roof. CatNaps, Diesel, Plot and Pearl disappeared into the darkness.

I scampered across the rooftops following the progress of the trainees. I thought it important that they experience a ground-level approach to the target. Once they had learnt the basics of ground-level approaches, then one could introduce them to altitude. I had a bird's eye view as they made their slow progress towards the brightly illuminated parade of shops at the far end of which eight Beanteens loitered. The Beans smoked, they drank, they laughed and kicked and spat at each other in acts of mutual endearment. Ah, the emptiness of existence. My Muters did not try to disguise their approach using shadows and variations in speed. Their approach was direct and methodical. They were spotted by the Beanteens at fifty paces. At first the Beanteens expressed concern to each other, but as the Muters reached a distance of thirty yards a couple of them shouted abuse. The Muters did not break their shuffle. Perceiving my colleagues as harmless the Beanteens continued to heckle. Answering to a wholly different value system the Muters did not react. Vanity is the preserve of the Bean.

The Muters found themselves in front of the Beans, but being new, they had yet to develop the true instinct. They had not bitten yet. I watched as the Beans' disrespect grew.

'Fucking fuckers, look at them.'

'So fucking pug-ugly.'

'Fuck, look at her,' one Bean said nodding towards SimplyFine. 'She might have been all right once upon a fucking time.'

'I'd have fucked her.'

'You can fuck her now if you want,' another said, laughing. A couple of the Beanteens then pushed their friend towards SimplyFine. I suppose in her Bean existence SimplyFine would have been an attractive mate – twenty-something summers, slim, with long blonde frizzy hair.

So, when the Beans mocked Simply to her face she was confused. She did not react. I could imagine her thoughts – what were these strange smells, these rich odours? Why was this feast talking to me? She was in a period of adjustment. Give her a lunar cycle and she would be snapping the Beanteens' windpipes within moments.

'Look at him. Shit. What the fuck happened to you mate?' said one Bean to TyreTreads who had been hanging back.

TyreTreads had been an after-thought of mine. He had come staggering towards me one dark cycle and asked me for 'a light'. As he came closer, he obviously realised that I had other talents. He turned and stumbled away as best he could. Feeling that I should not let volunteers go unrewarded, I jogged after him. He sped up. We reached a four-lane road. In his efforts to remain in existence he found himself under the wheels of a very large, multi-wheeled, dirty automobilic vehicle. Having rolled over (and crushed) him, the automobilic vehicle stopped a short distance away and its driver dismounted his cab. However, on seeing me standing over the crumpled mess of a Has-Bean, the driver jumped back into his large vehicle and drove off. Realising that further hits to the body by other vehicles might limit his mobility for an eternity, I picked up the Has-Bean and carried him to a place of safety. Nestled in a quiet roof top garden for a handful of light-darks, he rose to meet his Maker and I was proud to make his acquaintance. Which led us to here, a training bite.

Sensing that my colleagues might be feeling a little overwhelmed (or lost) confronted with the company and the (literal) verbal diarrhea of eight Beenteens, I concluded that I ought to intervene. I slipped down a few floor levels to balconies overlooking the concrete area. Diesel had reached a similar conclusion and had sauntered up to the group from the darkness without making any threatening plays. Nevertheless, he had a startled look about him on account of his enlightenment injuries, but on this occasion the look was more of a startled glare.

'Fuck. Now he is scary,' said a Beanteen pointing to the approaching Diesel. Indeed Diesel's appearance was striking. His garments were melted onto his skin which itself had melted into itself. He was skin in garment form.

That was not to say TyreTreads was not a striking sight – the manner of his passing was clearly emblazoned across his front – not only the treads across his clothing but also the crushed skull and bones (which clicked and cracked as he moved). If I had been a Bean, I might have felt somewhat jealous of the first impression TyreTreads and Diesel would make. My own 'looks' were somewhat average. There was no discernible trauma of which to speak, just a receding fleshline.

I half-expected TyreTreads, SugarRush and SimplyFine to become part of the same team. They were inducted at the same time and could have complementary skill sets. TyreTracks had in fact rested (and risen) in the garden of SimplyFine. I had been looking for a suitable resting place and, having not expected to encounter Treads, did not have a designated resting place near where he fell. I improvised and, having located a block of flats near the road, slipped Treads amidst some rooftop greenery. 'Simply Fine' (the tattoo on her hip) had been sunbathing on her roof in a bikini with wires running to her ears. Much like Muters, I suppose the fleshy display of limbs and toned torsos inspires desire in a Bean. I had already feasted that light cycle, but to come across flesh laid out on display on the rooftop was too tempting. I decided to keep her relatively intact, the preservation of her organs and body might prove useful. She had been more of a lite-bite therefore.

With Beans liking each other less and less, many, thankfully, exist on their own. With Bean communities on the decline, it all helped to secure resting places for Has-Beans.

Returning a handful of light-darks later, I checked on the two Has-Beans resting on the roof, their odours being carried away on the wind. I sat swinging on a suspended bench on the roof listening to the throng of activity on the streets outside when all at once I heard a key in the door to the flat at the bottom of the stairs. Who else existed in the premises? A male partner? A female housemate? (Would it be a tussle with muscle or an exquisite liqueur? Either was agreeable.)

I remained seated on the swinging bench under an awning, flicking through magazines charting the fall and fall of the Bean.

'Don't mind me,' a chirpy female voice called up to the roof from the flat below.

I stayed silent and heard the Bean totter into the kitchen apparently all in a rush.

'Need some sugar, love,' the Bean voice sung.

Go ahead, I thought to myself. I was going to ignore the Bean, but it wasn't long before her sweet breath started to float up the staircase to the roof.

'Can I take some coffee, sweety?' the voice called again.

'Are you there? Are you upstairs, Gorgeous?'

The lady Bean rummaged in the kitchen.

'How much sugar can I take?' she squeaked. I heard footsteps around the flat below. Was she searching for her friend? I didn't want her to discover the Has-Beans and raise the alarm; it could complicate matters.

'I think I am going to take it all,' her voice came from the kitchen. 'No, I'll leave you enough for four teaspoons full just in case you bring back a nice man tonight.'

I would have moved downstairs to greet the guest, but I was detecting the stirrings of both TyreTreads and SimplyFine.

Moments later the lady Bean appeared at the entrance to the roof. A buxom twenty-summered, painted blonde Bean in an orange singlet stood standing her eyes fixed on the two fresh Muters opposite her returning her gaze quizzically. TyreTreads was quite a sight. Even standing still the smallest of movements caused some of his broken bones to crack and grind. SimplyFine stood beside him, virtually unmarked. It was probably this that threw SugarRush into confusion. Were it not for Treads, then Simply might just be taken for a Bean, albeit a little pale. Unable to scream as a result of her hyperventilating panic attack (and realising neither Treads nor Simply had control of the situation), I stepped in and released SugarRush-elect from her despair. So, before you know it, I had three new-borns in a flat.

I was accumulating them thick and fast. In the metropolis farm one could not move for Beans. They needed nurturing, some fast-track training, hence our rendezvous with the eight Beanteens in the neglected part of town.

We were the victims of our own success? Those four Muters – SimplyFine, SugarRush, TyreTreads and SwapShop (himself born when trying to swap a knife device for paper-green in a local shop) – swiftly dispatched those eight Beenteens on their first outing. Sure, Diesel and Pearl had to lend a hand and catch two escaping Beans, but it was a far cry from my own first feast. It was clear to me that our mentoring programmes were working. I could relax – death would get us through these tough times. The world was changing and the Beans knew it. They were getting nervous. After all, why else would they be watching me?

29. Am I Being Watched?

During this period of intensive mentoring I made a point of spending some o'clock alone. It is always good to take time to reflect on eternity. I also felt it was important that those in my charge had o'clock to themselves too. They needed to go out and do their thing.

Just as learning and developing skills is good for Muters, so I grudgingly admit that learning is a good thing for Beans, but learning (and skills development) takes time. So I knew I had to be patient. Although I admire the exemplary work of ChubbyCheeks and her crowd of Muterlings, the skills that Beanlings bring to death are limited or, rather, they are 'specific'. Spectacular, yes, but specific – Muterling-specific – which requires intensive mentoring in the early lunar cycles. Chubby could not wrestle one Rubber Bean to the ground let alone several, but she does not need to. No, she uses guile to approach and withdraw from danger yet is wholly fearless when sharing death. But, for most of the other Muterlings, it would appear, initially at least, that in order to live death to the full, a simple understanding of (albeit a distaste for) Bean priorities and skills are useful to manage an encounter with a Bean. Furthermore, a prolonged period on the marsh farm allows Beans to fatten up their organs and acquire a few death skills. This Muter patience and restraint (often lacking in a Muterling) means Beans have the opportunity to restock the farm.

But how long does one give? In order to restock, the Beans engage in courtship rituals, the rules for which neither Bean sex understands. They are unable to read the game of the other. Their needs are straightforward – a line from A to B – yet Beans somehow find ways to keep going in circles.

So it is – Death being patient, Beans wasting o'clock.

I was mulling this over as I stood leaning against a pillar in the shadows of a street watching a male Bean and a lady Bean stand opposite each other going in merry circles. Their existence is limited to eighty summers at best (and the first and last of those twenty summers are of no use to anyBean), yet they waste so many summers in the middle doing a dance of delay. As a proud Muter I have an eternity yet I don't procrastinate.

I watched, becoming evermore contemptuous. I was only waiting because I was conducting more research. I planned to feast on him after their bodily communion. I would let the lady Bean exist after giving her the very lightest of nips. It would not be enough to enlighten her but it might, just might, enlighten the subsequent Bean-beenie. That would be a coup – to catch and convert. To have a MuterBeanie. Would that make the ultimate Muter? Anyway, that was my research project. Unfortunately, it was interrupted by some rather pressing concerns. I soon learnt that, as I was conducting fieldwork on Beans, the Beans were apparently conducting fieldwork on me.

I watched the male Bean, shuffling from foot to foot, laughing and sharing a few thoughts with the lady Bean. Again, I shook my head in disgust at the delay. Beans pride themselves on communication and even creating devices to enhance communication, but, what does it lead to? Prevarication and procrastination.

I've often wondered why the advent of Muters and death had not happened before to the degree that it was now happening in the metropolis. I know deep down that it had been attempted, but that those past endeavours (in their various forms) had not been communicated during the Beanteen schooling. It does not matter. History is the past. The past is written by the 'living'; the future, by the dead. I suppose this is what I am doing now. You don't need books where you're going, but there is no harm in having one reference manual to which both the undead and dead can refer in this handover period.

'I love you,' the lady Bean whispered to her Bean. 'I want you.'

'And I want you,' I had to stop myself from mumbling in reply.

The softest of breezes meant that I could taste his breath. Standing twenty yards away in the shadows I took a moment to imbibe the mixing of their breaths – a cocktail of juices being pumped around and readied in their soft, warm bodies. How could any Muter resist? The Beans are a factory that just keeps on giving. Many Beans might think we loiter in the shadows as forlorn and unhappy creatures, but really what we're doing is just soaking up the delights, bathing in the milk of anticipation.

That was why this particular street was a favourite of mine. I had come here often. It had a hot liquid establishment at each end. Wafts of warm bread lingered in the street especially on warm dark cycles. One side of the street was littered with eateries – owned by Beans who spoke in peculiar tongues. A cold cream parlour, a drinking house, a grape bar and a warm liquid shop lined the other side. Around the corner were more feasting places. It brought a wide variety of Beans to the area. They would linger and talk, laugh and giggle – activities that encouraged the swirl of juice, so I shouldn't complain.

Anyway, on this occasion, I got bored and stepped forward out of the shadows. The male Bean immediately ran off, so I tucked into the lady Bean. (Research would have to wait.) It was as she whimpered 'Help me,' that I detected a sudden rush of aromas hurtling down the street towards me. I suspected the source (Beans) was perhaps fifty paces away moving through the darkness, but it was clearly a disturbance in the air. The fear, anticipation and adrenaline both enhanced and contained in their tight wrapping of black rubber suits was unmistakable. They were moving swiftly towards me, but not discharging firing devices – most probably, I concluded, because of the Bean in my arms.

I dragged the limp Bean into the shadows of the rear entrance of a nearby building. Knowing the area well, I wouldn't have a problem finding my way out of the street, but as I reached the shadows something nagged me. It was a very slight additional aroma to the usual Rubber Bean – like a herb or spice – clearly discernible, but slight. And it was not a type of Bean or a Bean in a particular type of situation. It was a Bean not encased in rubber. I had detected traces of the very same aroma at intervals in the preceding few lunar cycles, but thought nothing of it. But now it was intermingled with the approaching Rubber Beans.

A thought suddenly occurred to me. Was I being followed? Was someBean watching me? Far be it for me to fall into the habit of Bean-narcissism, but it did make me wonder. Had I missed something? Was I becoming so active that I had attracted the attention of a particular squad of Rubber Beans (or one specific Bean working with Rubber Beans)? I knew ChubbyCheeks was attracting a lot of unwelcome attention, was it now my turn? Was I becoming too successful?

The spice wonder was clearly at the rear of the crowd meaning he (for it was a male) was in the position of some authority. A leader. Not a leader in the historical sense when leaders 'led', but a more recent-history leader (political leader) where they 'led' from the rear. He must be an individual of some influence. So, why was he watching or following me?

Thinking it might be good to hang around and explore further, I delayed my exit from the scene.

Dragging the weakening lover-Bean back into the shadows I managed to find some railing onto which I impaled her to prevent an easy escape. It was frustrating as some of LoveHurts-elect's juice would be lost, but I hoped to address the Bean incursion and return. I scaled the side of the building and from the roof of the two-storey building watched as the Rubber Beans shuffled down the street. I then noted the other end of the street had been secured by a roadblock of Rubber Beans.

Drifting perfumes suggested the aromas of yet more (Rubber) Beans were being pumped out on nearby rooftops. This was indeed a cunning plan. Fortunately, DoorStop, Diesel and Pearl were not so far away and were soon introducing themselves to the Beans in question.

I skipped across a few rooftops passing TarmacTired and TreeShadow (both quietly feasting) to a place almost directly above the leader-Bean. This was indeed a level of coordination yet unseen by the Beans, which was only confirmed when I heard him utter a command to his soldiers over the radio.

'Do not kill him,' the Bean leader said. 'Er, rather, do not destroy him.'

I lowered myself to the shadows of the building's ground level. Now behind the crowd I could hear his panicky team members report over the radio that a number of 'fucking zombies' were now present and 'how the fuck are we supposed to know who is the fucking leader'.

Reassured that my colleagues were keeping the Rubber Beans engaged, I walked through the shadows until I was a handful of paces behind the Bean leader and his Rubber Bean escort (who I considered to be the Rubber Bean commander).

When the commander halted to speak into his radio, his companion (the spicy-perfumed 'leader') continued a few steps. I took my opportunity. I wasn't interested in the commander and dispatched him quickly. The leader was unaware for a moment until the radio dropped out of the commander's hand smashing on the pavement. When the leader did turn to face me, I was but a pace away from him.

At such a distance I have an effect on Beans. They know that if they survive (which they never do) they will never come as close to death. There is normally a moment when their will to exist collapses and the realisation that everything they had ever wished for and worked for has come to nothing. In that moment they know that they have been living a lie. It is a profound moment to witness. I do not resent them. I am supportive and, in their words, loving. However, there was a slight difference in the reaction of this leader-Bean. I detected an interest (albeit partnered with an absolute terror). Perhaps I gave something away in my expression, but my expression would not be discernible by a Bean, surely? I was inclined to be patient and not release him. I wanted to hear a little more from him and hoped he would be forthcoming – he was (albeit after a little encouragement).

I grabbed him and swung him into the shadows and held him off his feet firmly against a wall.

'Stop! Wait!' the leader-Bean cried. 'I know who you are. Your name is Nigel.'

I did indeed stop. I was curious.

'Do you remember? Of course you do,' the Bean leader panted, before pausing. Aware that o'clock might not be on my side, I moved in close. It helped.

'I know you have suffered in your life,' he continued. 'I know you have experienced loss, frustrations with the systems that we have. You had a relationship with...,' he said, before pausing in fear. 'But she is now part of your...community. She is one of your "colleagues". You call her Pearl.'

I paused, in part because the information was useful and I wanted to communicate that to him.

'I know more. I would like to talk,' he said quickly. 'Perhaps I can help you find what you are looking for.'

My eye sockets studied the pitiful, yet knowledgeable, Bean.

'My name is Josh,' he continued. 'Call me Josh. I am here to help. In fact, I need your help too. Nigel.'

I was aware that behind us the Rubber Bean incursion on the street was failing – no doubt in part because of the sudden absence of instructions from the commander.

'Will you help me? Please?' asked Call-Me-Josh-Bean. 'We can help each other.'

Indeed, perhaps Call-Me-Josh could help me find out a few details of myself. There were gaps in my understanding. Perhaps he could be of use.

Leaning in and drinking in one last pull of his aroma and using my tongue to taste his soft moisture, I took my leave.

The Rubber Beans were indeed in full retreat and had left a few of their own in the street in the panic. The girl's lover had also fallen foul to the wild shooting by the Beans. Back on the rooftops I rejoined my friends and departed the area.

It was a curious encounter. At a moment when I was thinking about the lunar cycles available to consider further skills development, Muter expansion, the replenishment of farm stock and research in general, the indications were that there were other factors (Beans consulting their own research projects) that might have a bearing on our plans and o'clockframes. The Beans were on the move. If the Beans were getting nervous now, it was about to get a whole lot worse for them. After a whole lunar cycle of planning, DoorStop's and GlassCutter's scheme was soon to bear lots of juicy fruit.

30. Bean-Boxers: Dunky & Smashy

With our increased success we received increased attention. It was to be expected. In addition to the attention from Call-Me-Josh there were the dark box Beans. It was a concern.

The dark box-carrying Beans ('Bean-Boxers') usually worked in groups. One would hold the dark box on his shoulder, another would talk into it with earnestness or self-importance. (I was unsure which. Perhaps both. I was unsure about my vocabulary – did they mean the same thing?) Many Beans lavished an importance on the power of the dark box and its 'art'. Why? I have no idea. It was an extension of the telephonic communication device and allowed for the sharing of communications (albeit communications from a redundant perspective – Bean). Then there were the lone Bean-Boxers who carried smaller dark boxes and lifted them to the eye in the act of recording a moment in Bean existence. These Bean-Boxers moved around the metropolis dump of their own volition like rats around the sewers – sniffing about for something in the sewage.

I had first become aware of the lone Bean-Boxers who might be following me a lunar cycle beforehand. Though I was conflicted, I did not react like a Bean (i.e. thinking that their interest in me was evidence of my inherent 'value'), no, I assumed it was because my image could be of use to them. Beans like Call-Me-Josh might be interested in what I had to say or think; the lone Bean-Boxers were different. They were hardcore shallow and, thus, distilled Bean.

It's a curious thing. Beans place value on how they are perceived by other Beans. The degree of value could be described by the number of images captured of them using the dark box technology. It is therefore useful to see Bean-Boxers following Beans whom they see (in Bean terms) 'important'. These Beans of import could be leader-Beans – Beans who have successfully sought roles with control over other Beans (becoming the living embodiment of the Second Bean Paradox). Consequently, there is the assumption that those Beans *not* followed by Bean-Boxers are of less import. Many Beans have a sense of diminished self-worth if images of their decaying nature is limited in circulation, yet, I understand, there is also a 'feeling' that those who do have images in circulation are also imbued with a sense of worthlessness. Is there no end to the inanity? Surely, it is evidence of their own understanding of their inherent worthlessness? Bean-technology has accelerated and exacerbated this absurdity, but it has most probably hastened our journey to mutual discovery of each other. So, on reflection, it is something for which we Muters can be (literally) eternally grateful.

The majesty and significance of the Black Road was lost on the Bean: the road dividing the metropolis was both alive and dead; ever stationary, yet ever in motion; gentle but powerful; merciful and unforgiving; solitary yet welcoming to all. It is both of its moment and o'clockless, a slippery creature sliding across the landscape minding its own business and forever replenished by itself in different forms. It was a model for our own evolution. Perhaps our Muter form could also be described in similar words – the Bean form would be a tributary in the story of homo evolution. In time the Muter form would echo the great cool orb of the sky – o'clockless, illuminating, reassuring.

Thus was I caught in a moment of reflection sitting by the Black Road one dark cycle, lost, alone, at peace. All of a sudden there was a change in the direction of the breeze – the wind was wanting my attention. Rather than whisper into my ear, the breeze wafted the gentle perfume of a Bean – perhaps a ten second dash away from me – to my nasal cavities. I thought I was alone, far from Bean; I wasn't quite. Fortunately, it was a time when we did not venture into the metropolis without a few colleagues within reasonable distance. Both Diesel and DoorStop were in the vicinity. They too had detected the aroma and left their perches to investigate.

I joined Diesel and DoorStop under one end of a bridge arching over the Black Road and cornered the two equipment-laden Bean-Boxers. We carried the two Beans down a handful of steps to the liquid's edge where we could sit and reflect together under the bridge and away from prying eyes. The Bean-Boxers were carrying a number of the portable dark boxes each.

The Bean-Boxers' business summed up another contradiction of the Bean. The average Bean valued privacy and security, but adopted practices that allowed other Beans to violate privacy and security. The privacy of the individual is violated, but the action is protected. The Bean sought 'respect' yet permitted (even celebrated) its violation.

It had me thinking that the Bean-Boxers who stood with a foot in each of these two competing camps should himself be conflicted by the clash of opposing ideas? But no. Of the two, the quivering indeterminate-summered, podgy Bean-Boxer smelt of no conflict, so I decided to conduct an experiment. I picked up his friend (a pencil-like Bean-Boxer) and held him upside down over the black liquid letting his head sink below its surface. The pencil-Bean-Boxer flailed around struggling for breath before I lifted him out. (This was a trick I had learnt quite by accident. It helps get the juice and spice racing around the Bean body in quick time.)

I watched the other podgy Bean-Boxer quake as he saw his friend submerged into the liquid. After a period I would lift the pencil-Bean-Boxer out of the blackness allowing him to gasp before dunking him again. After a few such actions the other Bean (guarded by Diesel and DoorStop) swung the dark box up to his eye and pressed a button. There followed flashes and nervous smiles. After a number of dunkings the podgy Bean-Boxer was bold enough to direct me when to lift and when to dunk. What was curious was that the Dunking Bean also became aware of what his friend was doing and became distressed. The sight of his fellow Bean-Boxer using the dark box to record his distress appeared to trouble him. Not only was this an excellent way to zip that juice (evident through the aromas being pumped out), but it was curious to see that the two Bean-Boxers who had been working as colleagues were now at odds with one another. This, I can safely say, would never, ever happen between Muters. In death all is understood. Perhaps that was why Beans invented 'ethics' (as discussed later), because they lack an elemental code.

Anyway, to prove the point, once the Dunking Bean had been dunked enough we swapped them over. This time we smashed the head of the other podgy Bean-Boxer (Smashing Bean) against the stone surface of the bridge. The Dunking Bean, having recovered from his spluttering, picked up his own dark box, held it to his eye and pressed the capture button. Like his friend, Dunking Bean began to give me direction on how and what to do. Whatever one might say, I concluded that Beans (based on this research of the Bean-Boxers) were consistent in their contradictions.

We continued for a time until Dunking Bean seemed satisfied with the images he had captured on his box. By which time I had become familiar with the image-box itself so decided to try it for myself. DoorStop took over Dunking Bean and Diesel took over Smashing Bean.

Once Dunky-elect and Smashy-elect had slipped into a state of restfulness, we placed them neatly in an alcove under one of the bridge arches hiding them behind their belongings with the plan to return a few light-darks later.

This would be the end of the story, but imagine my surprise when, a few light-darks later, I was tucking into a paper-of-news-reading Bean to see images (printed within the paper-of-news) of Dunky and Smashy with me, Diesel and DoorStop. I could only assume the redundant images were automatically dispatched to the organisations responsible for producing the paper-of-news. Contradiction and inanity were now automated. Amazing.

Anyway, it struck me at the time that a small, discreet moment captured on the dark boxes could become a fixation for the Beans. In the following light-darks (leading up to the attack of the Merry Beans) I noted that Beans were particularly keen to collect redundant images if they were present in the image itself. Very occasionally, as I was recognised in the street, some Beans approached to capture my image with them. I was happy to oblige to make them actors in their own dramas and grant them a last wish.

31. A Box of Errant Beans

Colleagues were feeling the pressure. The Rubber Beans were pressing hard. EveryMuterbody wanted to contribute and I was pleased to acknowledge that the skill sets of many of my niblings were as complete as one could wish. Furthermore, they had established their own teams in different parts of the metropolis each ploughing their own fields.

One such field was being readied to be farmed by DoorStop and GlassCutter. If successful, its yield of Muters would be unparalleled. In one dark cycle it was estimated that many hundreds, if not thousands, of Beans could be enlightened and all by a relatively low number of Muters. It would be my colleagues' own project, no doubt becoming their speciality and their distinguished contribution to the new kingdom. If the ParkSparkle twins could have their moments and specialty, why couldn't DoorStop and GlassCutter? If successful, it could be rolled out across the metropolis farm. In hindsight I think their project marked a sea change; it was a moment in the battle when the Beans lost an advantage. I am the first to give credit to DoorStop and Glass. In fact, I should have seen it coming.

Like us all, it stemmed from DoorStop's and GlassCutter's unfinished business. They did their homework and, in truth, I, Diesel, Pearl, ColourSplash, Plot, Rooftop (in fact, most of my crowd and many of their niblings) went along for the ride. We were more than happy to help and free the oppressed Beans from their miserable existence.

The target was a large building dedicated to the control of angry, unhappy, troublesome Beans. These Beans who did not conform to the idea of control. So it was that these large buildings were erected to house the Errant Beans. In the distant past (many hundred solar cycles ago) the leader-Beans would arrange to free the Errant Beans from their misery, sending them to a land (our land) from which they would not return. But Bean-thinking had become confused in more recent solar cycles and now the Errant Beans were locked behind metal doors confined to small spaces, unable to roam.

As I have said, it was DoorStop's and GlassCutter's show. I stepped back and let them allocate Muter colleagues to observation posts around the complex allowing me to sit back and watch the drama unfold. Not everyMuterbody would be required inside the building, the locked doors helped, but a handful of alert Beans needed to be on the outside to deal with any foreseen difficulties (Rubber Beans riding to the rescue).

Normally such a large event would be conducted in the dark cycle, but it was DoorStop's thinking that because the establishment was self-contained, it did not really matter whether the great orb was high in the sky or the cool orb was hanging low in the darkness. In fact, more Beans would be on the premises if the operation were conducted during the light cycle.

So, as the great orb rose above us, I watched DoorStop scale the walls and climb onto the building's roof and head towards previously identified access points – apparently, he knew the layout of the building from his Beanhood. DoorStop, Glass and a few others disappeared into the building. After a short o'clock, we received the all-clear signal and we could enter. Myself and possibly thirty colleagues – niblings and niblings once and twice removed – all descended onto the building grounds, crossed the courtyards and entered at different points.

It was a theatre of dreams. Entering the main building there were rows upon rows upon rows of Beans stacked up above one another. It was true, all the Beans were held secure behind doors and DoorStop and GlassCutter had secured the opening devices for each door. We could feast, bite and swoon at leisure. One never really knew what to find behind each door. Not only was there a ready-meal waiting, there was usually a bit of a tussle as well to work up the juice and the appetite. Opening every door was just a pleasure upon a treasure. It was as if the Beans had known what we were thinking, or instinctively (like the First Bean Paradox) they were preparing for this light-dark – this was what the farm was for. I was unsure whether the apartment blocks (administered by the likes of Bean-boss) were modelled on this building, or vice versa? And whom should a Muter thank? Was it the leader-Beans? Engineers? The conforming or non-conforming Bean? Or possibly, even, the so-called ethical Bean (see the Third Bean Paradox) who had done much to fashion the thinking for the disintegration of Bean society and who had worked stoically to make things easier for us all?

I'm unsure how many light-darks we spent in those premises. Of course, we had to stay long enough to allow the Has-Beans to rest then rise. It was an endless supply of nibbles. In fact, so plentiful was the flesh that we were unable to feast that much, so we left many hundreds of lite-bites. Rubber Beans did turn up in force and there were a few half-hearted attempts to gain entry, but before long the smell of rank fear permeated the whole area and movements slowed. Besides, DoorStop and Glass had prepared well – they had organised a small contingent of RubberMuters to cause mischief among the Rubber Beans as they wallowed in a prolonged period of indecision. What with our other operations going on around the metropolis their resources were no doubt stretched; it became clear that they would not join us inside the box.

At the appointed o'clock a team led by Diesel was dispatched to acquire the underground tin can station situated a short panicked-Bean-run away from the box of Errant Beans. Diesel and colleagues slipped through a weak perimeter of Rubber Beans with ease; nothing was able to confine our gloriously expanded army. Who knows, perhaps the Rubber Beans and other leader-Beans were happy for their errant cousins to realise their destiny, but they were not to know the impact our project would have on the metropolis.

Such was the success of that light cycle that DoorStop and GlassCutter followed up at other similar establishments. Our numbers rocketed. A number of these targeted establishments were so well protected and suited to our needs that the newly-risen never really left – they were schooled and mentored behind secure walls. Such establishments became large bases from which to operate. No more single apartments or apartment blocks. We had campuses.

This development got me thinking about the home base issue that had been preoccupying me for a while. It was important to seize the light-dark and establish a series of, not only mid-sized satellite homes, but ghettos. The Beans had tried to confine us to certain parts of the metropolis, now it was time to embrace it. A home base brings security, peace and comfort. If empty venues were not available, then we would take over occupied space. It would not be long before our numbers would challenge the number of Beans.

It was ironic that those Errant Beans the authorities had been trying to lock away from the 'community' became a great source of inspiration. Those former Errant Beans reintegrated into the Bean community literally cutting through the niceties like a hot knife through milk. In some respects the metropolis became, for a time, a playpen. On reflection, the whole Muter project never looked back after those light-darks. The death skills the enlightened Errant Beans brought over were invaluable. For that, my gratitude would know no bounds.

32. The Third Bean Paradox (Ethics)

One way Beans (especially those new to Beanhood) seek validation in their meaningless existence is through 'ethics'. You cannot see it, smell it, touch it, taste it, so what would be its point, you might ask? Is it something to fill the meaningless solar cycles before destiny is realised? Perhaps. After all, ethics is accompanied by marching in the street and shouting things about a Bean's personal experience of existence or aspects of the existence of *other* identities of Bean (often based in faraway lands). In this respect I marvel at the lengths Beans go to keep themselves busy. Correction – it is not so much a 'length' but a circle. No sooner have you thought a Bean has come to the end of its 'length' than the Bean starts again and repeats, covering the same ground. And it is this circle of self-absorption and procrastination that lays the groundwork for ethics. 'Ethics' is largely based around the need of the Bean to influence behaviour or to justify actions already taken or yet to be undertaken. Needless to say, most fly in the face of the destiny impulse. Any code of ethics is full of contradictions: Bean ethics are predicated on the value or preservation of (Bean) 'life', but if the fallacy of preservation is removed then what place is there for ethics? There are no ethics in eternity, so, one might argue, there is no such thing as 'ethics'. It is the folly of a misguided imagination. The Ethical Bean is a desperate Bean. Ethics – arguably the Third Bean Paradox – the attempt to attribute worth to worthlessness.

However much I try to engage with the Bean, the Ethical Bean is never far away. It is only at the moment of enlightenment that the Ethical Bean may (I stress 'may') reconsider the foolishness and irrelevance of their ways.

Reflecting on Beankind's habit of seeking worth and potential in meaninglessness reminded me of an encounter I had had with a Bean-Stew a lunar cycle earlier. (The typical Bean-Stew often presents as an Ethical Bean.) It is an encounter worth reporting here as it also made me aware of debates going on in the Bean communities.

On the occasion in question, myself, ChubbyCheeks, Pearl, DoorStop, Tarmac, GlassCutter and Diesel were checking out a new part of the metropolis to establish contact with other Muters and explore hunting grounds and opportunities. (Besides, I welcome the opportunity to spend o'clock with my own niblings.) However, parts of the metropolis were becoming more and more deserted at particular times of the light cycle. Beans were either moving out of the area or locking themselves behind their doors if they were not in the workplace – all presumably in an attempt to escape their destiny. This Bean-flight from neighbourhoods was to be expected. So what was *un*expected on this particular light-dark was to suddenly round a corner under a railway arch to be met by seven Bean-Stews. They were accompanied by a handful of forty-summered Beans also ethical in nature (i.e. Beans whose brains never really developed).

The breeze must have been blowing in the wrong direction because we had not detected them before we encountered them. Having been surprised so suddenly, we halted. The curious thing was that these Beans did not turn away from us in fear, they did not run. (That said, I could detect the nervousness being both pumped out of their pretty, sweet mouths and contained within the odours oozing through the pores of their peachy flesh.) So, there we were – seven Muters standing opposite seven Bean-Stews (and their many-summered companions). We were transfixed, in shock. It had never happened before. For a split moment I thought they might be Rubber Beans in disguise and on a mission. Perhaps Call-Me-Josh was in the vicinity giving orders, making observations. But a moment later I determined they were not black-clad Rubber Beans for their attire was different and unusual, comprising bizarre, abstract colours and patterns. Their hair was longer than the regular Bean and also unconventionally coloured. Some were very lean (but not athletic), others too fat. For a few moments we expected them to turn and run – something we would encourage them to do, in fact. Making attempts at escape gets the Bean juice pumping and induces a tenderness to the kiss. But I was not to know that they were supreme, perfect examples of the Ethical Bean.

I noted there was one Bean-Stew for each of us, but I indicated to my colleagues to wait which, in truth, they were inclined to do, being just as bewildered as I was. Suddenly one Bean-Stew took a step towards us. Then another nervously followed. The first, in a most bizarre fashion, took a deep breath, took another step forward and addressed us.

I marvel at the Bean's thought processes – at times they are so sensible, yet often (and ironically), the good sense comes from a place of stupidity. By 'sensible' I mean those who embrace and submit to their destiny as a result of suffering the dispiriting Bean experience, in contrast to the majority who try to deny their destiny and try to delay it. What I find truly unfathomable is the Bean who does not admit to a destiny (even *denies* the destiny), yet somehow thinks I am interested in the ways and wherefores of the Bean existence and how they apply to *me*. It is like a worm trying to convince me that burrowing underground at a snail's pace is superior to my farming, hunting and spreading of the good news across a metropolis farm. At first I half thought that the approach by the Bean-Stew was a self-defence technique (it appeared to be working on a number of my colleagues demonstrated by the fact that we all remained completely still, through astonishment).

'Come with us, come,' the lady Bean-Stew said. 'We know what to do. We can help.'

I was transfixed. To what were they referring?

'You have rights,' the lady Bean-Stew continued. 'We can learn to live together in peace. We know that you are afraid. You have nothing to be afraid of if you come with us.'

I turned to DoorStop, Chubby, Pearl, GlassCutter, Tarmac and Diesel. They turned to look at me. Through the folds of their pale and rotted faces, I could discern that they were as confused as I was.

'You have just as much right to be here as anyone else. As much as anyone living.'

The lady Bean paused.

'I mean that with all my heart,' she said opening her coat, exposing some flesh and tapping her heart.

(That's a mistake, I thought.)

'We will stand up for your rights,' the lady Bean-Stew (Right-to-Life-elect) continued. 'There are many of us. After all, we know we will be like you one day.'

I nodded, as did DoorStop and Diesel. However, I suspect Right-to-Life-elect, mistook our nods as understanding and a form of encouragement. The lady Bean-Stew continued.

'We have lawyers who can fight your case in the courts. There are people in the media (even national television news) who are helping us push our agenda. Brilliantly bright, clever people.'

I was unsure about the reference to clever, bright Beans especially those who worked 'in the media'. As I have previously reported, it was really the diet of the Bean that influenced a Muter's choice of target combined with their state of mind. Any so-called (and self-determined) 'cleverness level' on a 'cleverness gauge' was irrelevant. After all, these 'clever' Beans could have poor diets and be found at the 'despair end' of the Bean self-worth spectrum.

We stood opposite each other in silence. There was a stillness to the energies within. The perfumery was pleasant – the simmering, controlled excitement from the Bean-Stew was topped off with lashings of spicy self-righteousness. Right-to-Life-elect, perhaps feeling embarrassed (or empowered?), then stepped forward and solemnly declared to those present:

'I just want to state for the record that you, and your friends here,' she said looking at my colleagues, 'you do not offend me. You do not offend my sensibilities, my belief system, my existence. My rights are your rights. And I will defend that to….' she struggled for a moment, 'to my dying day.'

(Not long then.)

She had not finished, adding, 'If I can say that without offending you.'

It didn't. Offence is a Bean concept, of course. It does not exist in death and, like most things Bean, is entirely meaningless.

The mention of death stirred Chubby first. Such is Chubby's brilliance, her following actions were a masterstroke. She held out her hand to another lady Bean-Stew opposite. The Beans broke into a wave of pleasure, applause and self-regard that pushed the juices around their bodies resulting in an exhalation of sweet breath into our faces. I was surprised Diesel, Glass and DoorStop managed to hold their place and resist the feasts pulsating in front of them. But, like us all, we knew Chubby was the master and had a play in mind. This was her call.

'You see, it's easy. Come with us, we can protect you and give you the life you deserve,' the lady-Bean said. 'You are no different to us. We can show people the truth and show up the ignorant, stupid fascists who believe you are a danger and a threat to us – the living.'

By now Chubby's target had taken eternity's greatest serial Bean-killer's little hand in her own and turned and walked away towards an illuminated side street. Pearl similarly offered her hand to a Bean and so did Tarmac. Their hands were taken by the Bean-Stews and they followed Chubby (and her bite-elect) down the street.

Diesel, DoorStop, GlassCutter and I left with the remaining few Bean-Stews. Now confident, the Bean opposite Diesel held out his hand. Diesel's gaze dropped down to the exposed soft pale flesh of the exposed forearm. He gently took the offered hand and raised it slowly upwards examining it in close detail to giggles from its owner and the other Beans present.

Then ever so slowly he lifted the forearm to his lips, ran his nostrils along its length.

And sunk his teeth into their softness.

I don't think the Bean quite knew what was happening. It was only when he saw his own blood ooze out of the periphery of Diesel's mouth (still clamped on to his arm) that his face registered that he had possibly twenty Bean breaths left.

DoorStop held off as long as he could to allow for the sudden surge of juices around the warm body of the Bean opposite him in a flash of panic evident from the rapid exhalation of breath right into DoorStop's face. My colleague picked up the male Bean and, lifting its neck to his lips, DoorStop bit into the softness dousing himself in a glory stream of such splendid magnitude before munching on the juicy piece of neck-flesh. The Bean opposite me (Right-to-Life-elect) turned to face me. There was both a mixture of horror in her face and confusion. Confusion perhaps that the prospects of being 'understood' by Beans and 'protected by Beans' did not appeal to us. I grabbed her by the neck and paused only to let her pant her breath into my facial cavities. I drank it in.

'You can't kill me. I have rights. I have the right to life,' she said breathing all over me.

Oh dear, I forgot, I thought to myself. What have I been thinking? What have I been doing these last lunar cycles?

Violating a Bean's right to life? I wanted to explain, but she would understand soon enough anyway.

For a moment I think she really believed she made some sense to the twisted face in front of her – as if her opinion counted, meant something, anything. Her opinion on her life and 'rights' only counted if it mattered to me, which, reader, if you haven't guessed already, didn't. What is it with Beans? The road to me is paved with self-pity and self-interest.

How could she measure her worth? Yet again, what is with the Bean obsession with 'measuring'? And 'legitimacy' and 'rights'? When it comes down to it what matters comes down to need. Beans suppress need, try to measure it and applaud their own restraint. Muters acknowledge, accept and embrace need, because we accept it as destiny. Perhaps that is why there is a failure of communication and understanding. A shared understanding of need cannot be agreed. As if the opinion of a twenty-something summered Bean could stand up to the scrutiny of eternity. Death had built this planet and she thought her 'right to life', weighed against my eternity, was a contest? Anyway, she soon didn't. In fact, such was her conversion Right-to-Life was soon running a very fine ghetto in the north of the metropolis. Whether she had unfinished business in that part of the metropolis, I could not say. What I could say was that the ghetto provided a very important resource for the independent Muter and generated a great deal of local interest from the Rubber Beans, which is always a sign of success. She should be proud.

Right-to-Life-elect's screaming alerted some of the Beans who had escorted my colleagues away. Chubby's Bean let go of Chubby's hand and raced back to me in a vain hope of helping, but on seeing Diesel and DoorStop feasting away, the lady-BeanStew panicked and ran back to Chubby. A nice trick of Chubby's was to raise two arms up to the returning Bean-Stew. Do they ever learn? The Bean picked up Chubby and ran off puffing and panting towards the illuminated street. They disappeared around the corner. I wondered how long Chubby would hold out for – long enough to get the juices pumping and spicy? I counted the running steps of the Bean after they disappeared from view – only six, before they faltered and stopped.

As for Right-to-Life-elect herself? She looked at me one last time. I slipped both hands into her mouth and pulled – upwards and downwards. Her neck and jaw cracked with the movement. By opening her throat up in this way I had access to the heart of the Bean-Stew. The literal heart. I reached down her throat into her chest and pulled. A moment later I watched as her heart spasmed a few times in my hand. Timing is all. I bit into the juicy muscle, grateful that I could taste the essence of Bean as it twitched its last.

And so it was. What is to be, soon comes to be. Even if Beans think there is an alternative ending, it always ends with me and learning that ethics play no part. I knew that they would all learn in due course and that was something that gave me great satisfaction.

33. World Piece

Our numbers were climbing exponentially and soon to reach a critical mass. We were no longer sole traders. Successful recruitment drives at apartment blocks, residences and standalone events (underground tin cans, parks, rag parades, street parties) had solidified our presence in the metropolis.

These larger numbers of Muters were creating ever larger numbers of Muters, most of whom needed assistance. Tarmac, Rooftop, Chain-and-Stiks, Pearl, Diesel, TreeShadow, Plot, the ParkSparkle twins, Central Line, Jubilee were all creating armies of niblings themselves. The more recent acquisitions (PuppyFlesh, TyreTreads, SimplyFine, Peas) were also well on the way to creating battalions of niblings. Not to mention the granddaddy of them all – ChubbyCheeks and her own legions. DoorStop's and Glass's new initiative for taking over the homes for the angry, Errant Beans both posed a question and answered it.

But still my Muter colleagues turned to me for guidance. Being one of the founding fathers, I suppose I felt I could not step away from the responsibility. It was my duty to step up. I knew deep within me that there would be other leaders who would come and join me – a brotherhood, if you like – who would lead us into eternity, but in the meantime I was happy to play my part alone.

It was true the Beans were pushing us to parts of the metropolis where they could monitor (even try to contain) us. I could understand their logic on one level, but how do you banish destiny to a part of town? For how long? To do what? Deliberate? Assess? Consider options? But why ponder, discuss, panic about the inevitable? (These are rhetorical questions, I honestly don't know the answer. Ask a Bean.)

I pondered the need for more established accommodation. Places that were secure, safe. Rooftops were becoming clogged with Has-Beans. We needed a place to store them in bulk and a base from which any Muter could operate with a degree of safety. Additionally, the Rubber Beans' methods were evolving. I was detecting new foreign odours. Matters were pressing, so, with DoorStop's and GlassCutter's work in mind, I began to think big, by which I mean, establish a home base. A place of rest. A piece of our world in their world. Of course, I would still use the rooftops, apartments, bridges and other places, but we needed to call somewhere home. I considered options.

We looked at a large house where Beans did not live but kept their wares. A large, unused block of a building with large open-plan floors on which were littered disregarded machinery. It would prove ideal. Spread over six or seven floors it was a maze of stairwells, corridors, ramps, pits and dead-ends. There were a few dozen Muters already in the building, but it could accommodate many thousands more. It had a few layers of dark basement that could accommodate an army. Muters are not typically drawn to each other in a social sense. We are not that insecure. In the circumstances, however, it was a more practical development, one borne of necessity. Beans operate in gangs therefore lone Muters were vulnerable. So, we learned. We evolved. Quickly.

Another option we looked at was a half-completed building intended as an office block. Large and similar in layout to the house of wares, it had open spaces and closed spaces. The exterior walls had numerous openings to the air. It could house many tens of hundreds of Muters safely.

The question was: which one suited our needs best? The answer came quickly – both. Our numbers demanded it. And so it was that word was passed around inviting Muters to a piece of our world in the metropolis. Beans had done similar in their past – put pieces of land aside for those who had evolved. Usually they were on the outskirts of the metropolis. Now we had fields that not only housed the enlightened below ground, we had floors and floors rising high into the sky.

There was one issue relating to the establishment of World Piece I and World Piece II – they did attract the attention of the Beans. Fences and barriers were erected around the World Pieces, but they were not sufficiently guarded to limit our movements. We were reaching a time when the smell of Bean-fear lingered over the metropolis and even oozed from the pores of the Rubber Beans patrolling nearby.

Our numbers continued to grow and we were soon outstripping our home bases. World Piece I was already at capacity. We needed more open-plan environments that we could own during light cycle or dark cycle. Furthermore, we needed more organised opportunities for the training of newbies. I felt there was a milestone approaching. We were always on the back foot. We were tiptoeing around. It did not feel right that eternity was tiptoeing around the transitory. Furthermore the Rubber Beans (dressed in black) were now being accompanied by Green Rubber Beans who were more aggressive.

I was still drawn to vistas over the city even though I had had one unanswered question answered (Pearl). Was this my rooftop wanderings a habit or was there something else still lingering in me – another question? Some more unfinished business?

One dark cycle I sat pondering the need for space high above the empty streets. How could we take the management of our accommodation to the next level? I gazed out over the metropolis at the sight of hundreds of large buildings – structures in which Beans spent all their light cycles. The buildings were similar in structure to World Piece I and II, but were occupied. Then it struck me. Of course, why was I looking at empty buildings for our needs? Why not kill two birds with one stone?

Tarmac, Chubby and Peas had demonstrated that the principle of acquiring 'lived-in' Bean space could be done, albeit on a small scale – domestic or vehicular. DoorStop and GlassCutter had taken it to the next level by acquiring homes for Errant Beans. If we could take over some of these buildings used in the light cycles, then our numbers would grow yet again. There was no point in mounting an attack in the dark cycle, it would have to be done when the 'office' buildings were brimming with juicy fruit. There's no point raiding an empty larder. I realised I would have to lead this project myself because much of my Beanhood had been spent in such places. I had died a hundred deaths in those buildings during my solar cycles as Nigel-Bean. It would be a challenge, but we had reasonable numbers and, in all likelihood we would find many, many enthusiastic takers within those high-rises.

The decision made, I realised I ought to do some reconnaissance.

I skipped over rooftops, analysed the Bean flow in and out of massive structures containing thousands and thousands of Beans. I assessed the access and control routes that could be used by Rubber Beans should they respond to our arrival. I watched and waited. Before long I detected the wafts of an angry Bean. Not one, but two. A female and a male. Inevitably this piqued my interest (teasing my palate) and I slipped into the structure. I made my way down a stairwell to a suite of offices on the upper floors. Taking care of a few Beans sitting outside the office in which the Bean feast was simmering, I found a partially open door through which I watched and listened to the hullabaloo all the while trying to restrain myself from bursting in and having my fill. After all, this was a reconnaissance mission.

'I didn't sign up for this,' the young lady Bean cried.

'Yes, you did. Here in your fucking contract,' the much older male Bean said waving a bit of paper in her face.

'I didn't know what I was signing'

'You can fucking read can't you? They taught you that at school, didn't they? Or are you one of those who had to wait until university to pick up the basics of the English language,' he spat.

'Your attitude offends me,' the lady Bean whimpered indignantly.

'Offends you?' he asked, incredulous. 'How about this: 'fuck off back to nursery school.''

'I will sue you,' the young lady Bean cried through her tears, determined not to give up.

I admired her persistence in spite of its wholesale ignorance. I wondered whether the ignorance developed as the Bean progressed through their years or whether it was always present and just manifested itself in different ways as solar cycles progressed.

'Go right ahead,' the manager Bean replied with a wave of his hand. 'I'll rip your fucking little self-righteous whinginess out of you and throw your sorry carcass out of the court to survive in the dog-eat-dog world called life.'

At times like this I wondered why Beans attributed a beauty to their existence.

'Why do you always have to swear? Grow up. You're supposed to be a grown man,' the lady Bean whimpered.

'I swear because I *am* a grown-up. And I'm angry having to deal with whingers like you.'

'I'm not whingeing, I'm just standing up for my rights. My generation cannot afford a house, have a nice car, go on overseas holidays, have children especially when my partner is trying to find time to write a book and I want to do a Masters degree. It can't be done on what you are paying me. I have been here a lifetime – three years. I am making a stand for the rights of my generation.'

I did think of stepping in, but the male manager Bean looked as if he might kill the young lady Bean himself. With his intent almost clear, for a fleeting moment I did question myself and wondered whether he could possibly be a Muter. But no sooner had the thought occurred to me, I dismissed it. He didn't smell that way and the anger of a Muter is non-existent. Balance is restored in death, but perhaps it was another stage of the evolution of Muter of which I was unaware? An articulate upgrade?

'You are twenty-fucking-seven. Your generation has no fucking idea what previous generations had to endure – the world owes you fuck all. Life is work; work is shit. If you get used to it, the only thing you have to show for it after a handful of miserable decades is a miserable death. That's if you are lucky. So, get used to it before you die.'

'Your generation is supposed to pave the way for our generation,' the lady Bean protested in response. 'To make things easier for the upcoming generation. You don't realise how hard it is for my generation. There is so much pressure to realise our dreams and ambitions.'

'Fuck you. Fuck all of you and your whole fucking generation. You little bunch of whining fucking snowflakes. You're fired. Now fuck off out of here and back to your cot, you fucking piece of fucking crybaby pigshit.'

The young lady Bean gasped. At what, I could not be sure, his message was clear, he seemed to be making sense.

With the workplace conversation completed the lady Bean turned and left the room in tears.

I was stoked, the aromas coming from the room pretty much flattened me, but I was in a quandary – which one I should approach? The older male manager Bean or the younger female Bean? Both would have a zing to their juice. In terms of death, neither would be much of a triumph. He had presumably worked in an office for most of his existence and, as I understood it at the time, many solar cycles in an office provided no useful death skills at all. She had had many fewer summers, so would have fewer skills still. And if the manager Bean was correct about her and her generation, her skills were further in question. So, on a skills basis, it was even-stevens. However, I wondered whether his unfinished business might be more impressive. I suspected he would develop a taste for early-office Beans. This in some ways might be his death skill. In fact, he would be able to work his way around office buildings enlightening and recruiting the Beans including early career Beans who, it might be argued, were physically stronger (but with a skills vacuum). He could prove to be a real boon especially as I was considering how to expand into real estate. So, on balance, by enlightening the manager Bean I might be recruiting (by a much larger factor) many, many dozens, even hundreds of early-career Beans. For this reason GenerationManager-elect won.

As he collapsed into my arms, the juice zing was of yet another I had never quite tasted. I even speculated he might have been reading a paper-of-news before his meeting with the younger lady Bean. GenerationManager-elect sighed the sigh of a hundred Beans as he passed into the state of Has-Bean. Never have I experienced such peace come upon a piece of meat. The peace had a tangible physicality to it and was something quite beautiful to behold.

I was always surprised by the efficiency and effectiveness of death. After only a few light-darks GenerationManager rested and rose a different creature. As I escorted him across the rooftops and across the metropolis he uttered not one grunt. Not that I would expect him to communicate, but he was in a state of zen-like peace. His whole corpse was adjusting to the brave new world.

I introduced him to some acts of feasting and also ensured he spent time with others including Pearl and Diesel. He was a reasonable learner and he gravitated to spending some time with

DoorStop and GlassCutter. (It appeared GenerationManager had some unfinished business with the Bean authorities. It is remarkable quite how many seemingly middle-class affluent Beans have had some sort of trouble with authority and/or Cloth-Heads.)

Once GenerationManager had learnt the basics I sought his assistance on a variety of excursions to establishments to see if there were any other latent skills hidden beneath his decaying exterior. Broadly speaking Muters had operated in the dark cycle, feasting on the Beans who wandered the streets late. As our numbers grew and our level of coordination developed we encroached more during the light cycles raiding automobilic vehicles (often coordinated by Chubby) or tubular tins moving underground. As we became more effective the average Bean became ever more careful. I was always painfully aware that many, many Beans spent their light cycles sitting in buildings staring at flickering screens of illumination. Our early visits to such places made clear to us that Beans were not happy in the environments, therefore, given the choice, we preferred to engage most Beans in the dark cycles when they were away from the office blocks. However, having spent o'clock with FallenCyclist and the Papers (Cut and Fold) and others, I had acquired a taste for something else so, to mix it up, I decided to pay a few visits to the stacked farm building while simultaneously establishing a World Piece III. Feast, recruit, World Piece. Three in one.

The more I thought about it, the more excited I became. The benefits were numerous. Such a target would be, to put it bluntly, a new killing field. Bean-feasts caught in a structure (of their own making) with limited to no exits. Introducing this new tactic (assuming it was successful) would also mean adding to the workload of Rubber Beans.

Although my own Bean existence had been in a similar structure, I was curious to see how effective GenerationManager might be. We had identified a new set of targets in a part of the metropolis that would be challenging for Rubber Beans to reach and then access whilst providing us Muters with rooftops extraction options in the case of retreat.

In the end I decided to take GenerationManager back to his own farm building. Though not an ideal location in itself, I concluded the positives outweighed the negatives. That said, I called on the services of all my Muter teams and their niblings to take the matter forward. We would lock down the building. It would take a full light-dark. I would accompany and mentor GenerationManager and a couple of others with similar Beanhood experiences. So, the o'clock chosen (in the middle of the identified light cycle) we attacked from all angles – high and low.

Access was swift and uneventful. Security was limited. A handful of us (including GenerationManager) emerged from the stairwell door into what was the corner of a large open-plan office. Beans stared at glass screens on their desks behind their partitions. The aroma of Bean wafted towards us. Most had only thirty, thirty-five summers to their names. I turned to look at GenerationManager. He had been unaware of where we were taking him, in part because I wanted him to react instinctively. Would he feel comfortable in this environment? Would he develop special skills for entering these types of marsh farm buildings? Would my choice of choosing him (rather than the GenerationMe-elect lady Bean) be vindicated? Would he make me proud?

Muters are not expressive as a rule, but on that occasion the change in his facial muscles (hanging about his face) were clearly discernible. The world had opened up to him. He looked at me, his expression said it all. Thank you. Thank you, Nigel.

And with that he brushed past me and entered the fray. Within moments there was screaming, shouts, all of which pushed Bean breath into the space raising the temperature yet further. Beans panicked, ran and in the centre of it all was GenerationManager. In short, my choice was more than vindicated. It was a stroke of genius. It was almost as if the office-bound Bean had been created for GenerationManager. His savagery and efficiency was far beyond any early-stage Muter that I had seen – tearing the flesh away from the young Bean bodies with his teeth or hands, ripping limbs off their bodies and dousing himself in the juice. Those others of us present stopped our own feasting and marvelled at the sight, assisting him where we could. It was quite simply, sublime. How foolish was I to have thought that expanding into real Bean estate would be a challenge. Whether GenerationManager ever met GenerationMe-elect in person, I could not be sure in the mayhem. There was so much activity, so much fervour, so much splendid death that her enlightenment on that light-dark could not be determined. What I can say is that I never actually met GenerationMe as a Muter.

Witnessing the beauteousness of the colourful beginnings for an untold number of screaming, pleading Beans made me aware that unfinished business and Muter death skills come in all shapes and sizes, yet marry and merge in a profound loveliness in the end.

What had been regarded as a challenge (raiding a battery-farm during a light cycle) rapidly became the staple of our diets and action. Recruiting more Managers from a particular generation worked wonders. It reached a point that our homes were not only warehouses, boxes of Errant Beans, but office farm blocks themselves. Ultimately, we have to thank the Beans themselves for building these battery farms rising high into the sky (like giant tombstones) and stocking them with freshly packed meat. How could it not be an invitation to us, for death? The constructions were the very embodiment of progress. I understood the Beans desire to build bigger and higher. It was a response to their deep-instinct to prepare themselves for death. It was the First Bean Paradox in all its glory. The engineering feats were indeed a testament to evolution.

We stayed on the premises for a number of light-darks. We feasted and recruited. As we were in control of the premises, we let the Has-Beans rest on site. We controlled the lower floors and the upper floors trapping many floors of panicking Beans on the middle floors. When the Has-Beans rose we had a controlled learning environment as the newbies stalked and engaged those Beans trapped on those middle floors. It was a wondrous thing – a school of Muters moving quietly through the remaining floors feasting, recruiting and lite-biting. Of course, numerous Rubber Beans gathered outside what was now World Piece III, but again the Bean indecisiveness, the conflict between their various agencies (no doubt prompted by the destiny impulse) meant that they did not try to spoil the party.

34. Telephonic Devices, Bean-Stews, HappyCampers

The establishment of World Piece III changed things. Such was its success we rolled out the practice across the metropolis, which not only fed into our numbers, but stretched the Rubber Beans (and the increasing number of their Rubber Green Bean friends). We had to work quickly to capitalise on our success for this coincided with the beginning of the 'Great Change' in Bean behaviour. Many office buildings were shutting down or had significantly increased security. Beans limited their travel across the metropolis and many tubular tins stopped running altogether. Those that did continue were populated with black-clad Rubber (and occasionally, Green) Beans.

There was one other factor that became apparent at this time – the use that Muters could make of a technological development of modern Beankind. It might be a reason why death had struggled to get the upper hand in past precessional cycles. But it was clear that we had reached a watershed. We would not have been as successful were it not for Bean technology, more specifically the telephonic communication devices and the associated computerised programmes contained therein. There were early indications of its potential, but it had never been useful on an industrial scale like it was now. Perhaps the Bean's desire to innovate is yet another example of the destiny impulse at work and all part of the First Bean Paradox.

Muters excel at operating alone, but they are also effective in twos and threes, and even much larger groups. The groups within groups were often niblings arising from unfinished business (for example, myself and Pearl; Rooftop and ColourSplash). There were also those Muters who had been enlightened at the same time and had become effective teams (DoorStop and GlassCutter; the ParkSparkle twins; Papers – Fold and Cut). So as our numbers swelled I saw not only merit in Muters having known each other during a shared Beanhood, but also the merit of being enlightened at the same time. Bean technology could assist in this.

I considered options. I regret returning to my own cliché, but there is never a better moment to reflect on options than the middle of the dark cycle on the rooftops of the metropolis. A peace descends upon the fields of battery farms. A form of death, I suppose. Bodies – millions and millions of them – stacked up and resting in peace. The soft warm aromas rise in the cool night air like an offering to the dark, empty sky.

I was acutely aware that hunting Beans, who were walking in pairs, was o'clock consuming. Larger events (tubular tins, cake walks, boxes of the Errant Beans, tombstones in the sky) take planning or are fortuitous and often there was an immediate Rubber Bean backlash. But technology offered an alternative.

As we explored the World Piece III premises during that first light-dark, I lost count of the times the telephonic communication devices began to sound – sometimes in the pockets of Has-Beans, in their bags, in their desks or even in their (severed) hands. It soon dawned on me that there was a fresh, fleshy Bean at the end of every ring. The communication devices not only recorded an owner's location, but it could also track the location of his fellow Beans. Used wisely, the device might have the capability of leading us to numerous feasts and bites and, most interestingly, it might facilitate the addressing of any unfinished business by the risen Muter concerned. Taken all together, this could lay the groundwork for effective teams. All of which was welcome in the face of the increasing Bean threat.

Almost by accident I had employed the use of the telephonic communication device in the early mentoring of Plot, but it had not really occurred to me to use it as a tool in a large-scale Bean-hunt. The success of World Piece III had once again thrust the possibility to the forefront of my mind. Having mulled it over, I decided to use it in a low-key way for individual hunts – as a research project. When the moment presented itself, I would organise a collection of devices at an event and follow-up with its users later.

I was conscious that unfortunately the use of a telephonic communication device could work both ways. The Beans could track their resting friends back to storage units in the World Piece establishments. (This is what in fact happened. It would ultimately lead to the attack of Merry Beans on World Piece I, but in the meantime we were fortunate enough to exploit the device without much trouble.) Although some Muters did suffer for it, we quickly turned it to our advantage.

Chubby had made particularly effective use of the device.

Thankfully many Beanteens (and some Beanlings) carried the communication devices allowing Chubby opportunities to indulge in her predilection for anarchy of flesh. Chubby, often ably assisted by FatLegs and PlumpCalf, would visit open park spaces in the metropolis even during the light cycle. Such locations were tricky to approach for Muters at the best of times, but Chubby and FatLegs could walk right in. Beans would lie about on the grass exposing the flesh allowing aromas to swirl around the park land uncontaminated by automobilic vehicular exhaust fumes. When Beans rest, their heart rate slows and the happy juices flow pleasantly around their lush bodies. It is a gift – bodies and bodies and bodies all lying exposed in readiness for their destiny. Beans even closed their eyes almost in a plea for destiny to come take them. And Beans do this in their free time! NoBeanbody asks them to do it – to lie still in open parkland, eyes closed and submit themselves to the sky. Even if they have fifty summers left there is something deep inside them that compels them to 'assume the position' that they will one day assume for eternity (until they rise again). It is curious that the modern Bean chooses to live in such large metropolises yet, given the chance, they seek out open spaces on which to lie down and rest.

Chubby would secure the attention of a Beanteen or Beanling, draw them away from any Beans (perhaps to a forested, wooded area of the open space) indulge in full feasts or light snacks perhaps in the company of others (including myself). In time, the parents of the Beanteen or Beanling became worried and, using the telephonic devices, tried to track down their offspring.

If Chubby chose not to draw the parent Bean to an appropriate secluded place for enlightenment, she would move the telephonic device to a location of our convenience or use it to pay a visit to the Bean family. This practice allowed us to enlarge our ranks with the particularly effective 'Muter family unit' – another discovery.

If the parent Bean was unsuccessful in locating their precious Beanling immediately, the Has-Beanling would rest for a few light-darks before rising and use the telephonic device to track its parents down. Such family reunions were unlike any other. Violent kisses and hugs of such generosity that make me weep with joy. The subsequent bond is so great that it has forged the most remarkable family units. Whole families could be inducted within a few light-darks. And, as no family member was short on unfinished business with extended family members, it had additional favourable knock-on effects. It meant, as our groups swelled, there was a higher degree of understanding and a common behaviour developed.

Coupled with the fact that Chubby did not have the appetite of a fully-grown Muter (she just liked the chase) ensured that many of the family groups were lite-bites. Chubby could not only approach Beans with stealth, but the Beans often had trouble engaging 'defensively' with her sweet nature. This failure resulted in Chubby being able to litter the metropolis with lite-bite groups. She was truly a wondrous machine of death.

Using the telephonic devices we had acquired, our numbers jumped yet again and we needed to think about establishing yet more safe spaces in which Has-Beans could rest. GenerationManager (and his ilk – similar 'managers') and their niblings found meaning in visiting Bean-Stew accommodation – structures closely packed-and-stacked with meat – in campus establishments where Bean-Stews were trying to 'educate' themselves about their transitory existence. These establishments were easy pickings. Whole corridors of flesh could be stripped and juiced in a handful of ticks of the o'clock. Even those Rubber Beans who turned up stepped back and watched. I was unsure as to why. Perhaps they acknowledged there was no value in preserving the Bean-Stews because deep down they knew such activity, engagement with waste-paper practices had no purpose? I am surprised the Beans don't fully comprehend this. 'Learning' is the first thing that dissolves in death – like drips of juice on a hotplate, it disappears in the brilliance of a eureka moment of enlightenment. As a Bean matures, it dawns on him that his learning will be lost to the soil or to the flame. The Bean body knows this and starts to shake off its learning and the mind returns to a state of infancy. The arrival of death is the eventual lesson. Know death and you know 'life'.

Beanteens on the edge of Beanhood and the Bean-Stew brain is a vacuum of understanding. But nature abhors a vacuum and in their vacuous state, Bean-Stews fill themselves with what they describe as 'hope' and 'ambition' for, don't laugh, their 'future'. It is, of course, not *the* future (their destiny) they are thinking of, they just infer the emptiness of the solar cycles that lay ahead of them as something that can be filled with more learning, ambition, acquiring influence and possession of (usually, material) things. But the emptiness they see in their solar cycles is not emptiness. It is more accurately described as 'meaninglessness'. They might be forgiven for this misreading, after all they are just emerging from the first infancy of mind and moving into the state of Bean ineptitude. But at this cusp of Beanhood they manifest (for a handful of solar cycles) as the finest examples, the embodiment even, of shameful Bean foolishness.

It is the same with all their learning environments. Beans devote rooms and buildings to hold the scribblings of their 'learning' on paper and venerate the bound papers as if they contribute something to knowledge. An athenaeum is but a monument to waste paper. It is no flattering observation that not only do Bean-Stews frequent them, but decaying Beans too. For a while I thought ChubbyCheeks had identified such places of waste paper as hunting grounds, but more recently I have suspected that Chubby is perhaps *seeking* something rather than hunting. She moves from athenaeum to athenaeum, watching, searching. Often she goes alone. She does not take her niblings with her which implies her pull to the place of waste paper is something other than a temptation of an easy bite or the thrill of a glory stream splashing colour on the papers in a place where Beans sit and solemnly study hieroglyphs in silence. She is not seeking 'knowledge' or a primitive form of Bean enlightenment (she has enlightenment in abundance), but I believe she seeks a particular Bean. I have escorted Chubby on a number of occasions. She would just wander the aisles. Perhaps she is wallowing in the sadness and futility of the Bean existence, I thought as I observed her watching the Beans some of whom would draw hieroglyphs on the paper no doubt hoping that their wasted efforts would be added to the piles of other wasted efforts in the place of waste paper. But perhaps it is some of Chubby's unfinished business...perhaps with a Bean who scribes in an athenaeum? I am unsure. I would recount our experiences here but I lose the will. For another time.

But I digress. Back to Chubby's acquisition of family units using telephonic communication devices. The HappyCampers were a family acquired by Chubby in just such a way. No sooner had they risen, Chubby introduced them to hunting, so, with a few others, we followed them on what must have been a regular family outing. The HappyCampers were a mother and father, two female Muterlings (of under ten solar cycles who looked up to Chubby), a former female Beanteen and a former male Beanteen. There was no real planning involved, but the family outing soon arrived at the family attraction in the centre of the metropolis.

I was aware that Beans perceive themselves to be lords of 'their' dominion and not only feasted on the creatures of the land and of the liquid, but kept them in cages for their own amusement. On this occasion the trip was to a collection of clear liquid tanks in which the creatures of the boundless ocean would swim in circles the size of a small room presumably to titillate the taste buds before the Beans indulged themselves devouring swimming creatures in eateries nearby. Normally the liquid tank parks (housed in buildings under artificial light) would only be open to the Bean during a light cycle proving a challenge to Muters even if moving as a family unit. However, on the occasional light-dark the liquid tanks were open late into the dark cycle. So, on one such occasion, the number of families (led by the HappyCampers) paid a visit.

The HappyCampers (themselves accompanied by Chubby) borrowed a handful of tickets from a young Bean family exiting an underground station before approaching the main entrance to the liquid cages building. Owing to our appearance a number of us roving Muters sought entry elsewhere. We slipped in through a skylight and made our way down the back stairs, meeting and greeting a few staff members on the way. As with many Beans, those manning the doors were not altogether together. Beans, when confronted with death, tend to fall apart. They get excited and breathy, pushing out aromas into our faces – which is the last thing you want to do if a meaningless existence still appeals.

A strategy was in place. It was agreed that the family would move through the building until it reached a central tank in which were swimming the large aggressive creatures. Myself, PlumpCalf, Diesel, CatNaps, Pearl, DoorStop, Plot, Stiks and others would then herd whole families of Beans towards the central area whereupon the HappyCampers would kick off the feast. Other Muter families would then enter through the main entrance and help guide yet more Beans to their destiny. Should the HappyCampers and other Muter families be overwhelmed then the Beans could always be tossed into the tanks with the aggressive creatures. Knowing Beans enjoy feasting on swimming creatures it would be an opportunity for the Bean to feast, fattening themselves up before being 'fished out' of the tank to be feasted upon. Alternatively, it would give the swimming creatures the opportunity to feast upon the Bean. It was win-win.

Indeed it was. In no time at all there was panic all around the establishment. Beans were running around in circles either screaming indiscriminately or screaming for their Beanlings from whom they had become separated. Some Beans fought and pushed Muters into the liquid cages, which was no great shakes because apparently the taste of the swimming creatures was no less appealing to the Muters. Other times my colleagues threw Beans, Beanteens and Beanlings into the increasingly pink liquid much to the delight of the creatures splashing about inside. The excitement could not only be watched from up above, but also from below the liquid behind glass walls. There were even dry tunnels running under and through the liquid cages where one could watch all the drama unfold. It was a feast for the eyes more than anything.

We had anticipated that we would be gone by the middle of the dark cycle, but many Beans began crowding into corners where they pulled out their telephonic communication devices. We had seen a slowing of Beans entering the premises, but before long (as a result of the telephonic devices), more Beans started flooding in. You could not make it up. Before long we detected Rubber Beans (Green and Black) outside the establishment, but they seemed reluctant to enter. The Beans continued to panic. I watched as some Beans wavered between the choice of submitting to a HappyCamper or jumping into one of the liquid-filled cages.

Before the end of the dark-cycle we decided to exit and, hiding in the middle of the crowds of remaining Beans, lite-bites and Muter-families we raced from the building towards the waiting crowds of Rubber Beans. There were loud cracks as some Rubber Beans fired their firing devices, but confusion and panic reasserted itself and we were able to slip away into the darkness. Though we left many Has-Beans resting inside the premises we made a point of acquiring the telephonic devices keen to build extended families in the coming lunar cycles.

What had begun as simple rooftop reflections on how to take the next steps, a milestone was reached. The acquisition and use of technology would help take our business to the next level. It would quicken our work and effectiveness, building teams of Muters who had known each other in Beanhood – their unfinished business often binding them together in effective teams. The Rubber Beans were doing their best to ramp up their efforts, but it would soon become a numbers game – there would soon be too many of us for the Rubbers alone...unless, of course, they changed strategy. But if there is one thing you can count on, it was the Beans' ability to find a way of shooting themselves in the foot. And this they did, with a great flourish. It was all part of the lunar cycle-long 'Great Change' in Bean Behaviour.

35. Attack of the Merry Beans

Having acquired many telephonic communication devices allowed us to track down Beans in the surrounding areas of the metropolis. Niblings were able to retrace their steps to former friends and family. However, it also had the reverse effect. In the past the Beans might have left it to the Cloth-Heads (and then later Rubber Beans) to retrieve their friends, but I am guessing both Bean types were developing a reputation for not being effective. For this reason we would receive a visit from the odd civilian Bean or even, on occasion, a visit from a collection of civilian Beans. It brought Beans to our home bases (World Pieces) perhaps in the hope of rescuing Beans (or Has-Beans) acquired by myself or my colleagues. Sometimes these visits were spontaneous, on other occasions there was a degree of organisation involved. Now and then I suspected Call-Me-Josh was in the vicinity, but I had no indication he was doing anything other than observing.

Incursions by groups of Beans were not unknown, but during one particular lunar cycle everything seemed to be coming to a head – the idea of World Piece was breaking out across the metropolis, technologically-assisted Muters were common and the Great Change in Bean behaviour was imminent. One significant incident on the eve of the Great Change occurred on the dark cycle that we were attacked by the Merry Beans. The incident did not actually trigger the Change itself (for that see the following chapter), but it nevertheless marked a sea change in the way Beans and Muters interacted. It had everything – an attack on World Piece I, the use of telephonic communication devices, the First

Bean Paradox, the Second Bean Paradox and even hints of the Third Bean Paradox.

On the dark cycle in question it was business as usual in World Piece I. Things were relatively quiet. The premises were stacked full of many, many hundreds of Muters resting in their quarters, feasting on flesh or enjoying the security, shelter and company of colleagues. I was enjoying a little downtime myself. Many of my niblings were spread across the metropolis at different establishments or were engaged in a little hunting, but there were a decent number present in World Piece I, including Pearl, Diesel, Chubby, PlumpCalf, Plot, BroadBean, Stiks, DogSmells and SimplyFine among others. Rooftop and ColourSplash had also dropped by. TyreTreads and the ParkSparkle twins had just returned (with a number of their niblings) bringing fresh Bean flesh, which they passed to FastFeast for processing, and storage.

Colleagues sat around in a circle catching up on the light-dark's events and followed protocol by placing the telephonic communication devices in the centre of the circle to alert us to any incursions by Beans. As I rested in the cool darkness off to one side, the insides of my nasal cavity ever so slightly began to be washed by fresh, Bean aroma. I did not suspect any Rubber Beans to be associated with the incursion – the mix of aromas was too plentiful and devoid of rubber. Besides, Rubber Beans had yet to be proactive in engaging with us during dark cycles (perhaps being thwarted by those plagued with the Third Bean Paradox). I concluded it must be citizen Beans. So it was not a total surprise when the communication devices started to ping and alert us to the approach of friends of those Has-Beans who were hanging about us on the World Piece premises. (In fact, that very dark cycle we had collected many hundreds from expeditions to office skyrises destined for refurbishment as World Piece V and VI.)

It was then that I noted that the scent was not quite the usual aroma of 'normal' Bean flesh, but the aroma of Merry flesh. I don't know why their perfumes carry so effectively, but I suspect merry aromas are lighter, more ambitious with more punch and thus travel more easily through the air. Judging by the activity on the telephonic devices, the numbers approaching World Piece were considerable – perhaps a hundred or more were descending on our location.

A perimeter fence had been erected around World Piece I by the Bean authorities. It was usually policed by Rubber Beans, but when the telephonic communication devices showed that numerous Beans had breached the fence we knew something usual and dramatic was happening.

Having reached an agreement on a simple plan, my colleagues and I spread out through the premises alerting other colleagues and assuming positions. Rather than repel the visitors the plan was to stage a welcome party. The large number of resting Has-Beans could be used to entice the visiting Merry Beans deeper into the darkness of the World Piece I structure. The visitors were looking for their friends and we would allow them to find the Has-Beans propped up in corners, lining the corridors, stacked up in the basement or hanging from the rafters and stairwells.

Soon aromas announced the arrival of the Beans immediately outside the building. They did indeed smell different. There was an edge. I had come across the perfume before in office buildings and on the streets, but only with individuals or in small groups. It was different to the aroma of the indigenous Bean. These were from a different land – that I could tell. A land that prided itself on being free. A land that aspired to the merriness of the individual Bean. Within the perfume of these Merry Beans there were mixed up aromas of fighter-Beans, lover-Beans, Ethical Beans. It was the merriness that linked them all. Things were changing in the outside world of the Bean perhaps. This was all part of the beginning of the Great Change in Bean behaviour.

Soon the Merry Beans were at the entrance to the building but it became clear that they intended not to enter the World Piece I premises all at once and all together. In fact, it was now clear that there were perhaps two hundred Merry Beans in all. They split into smaller groups and headed for different entrances. It would be a challenge for them to navigate the structure. The numerous rooms, corridors, stairwells all looked the same. Additionally, there were large spaces that ran from the ground level to the highest floor. Loose wiring and scaffolding both aided and restricted movement around the building. There was no interior electrical illumination at all. Some illumination fell through the open window spaces into the building interiors courtesy of the large flood-illuminations placed on cranes and scaffolding around the perimeter by the Bean authorities. It was not only a maze of concrete, but a maze of illumination and shadow – perfect for us Muters, but I imagine a nightmare for the visiting Merry Beans. The open spaces allowed for aromas to drift about the building so it was easy for us to determine the routes the Merry Beans were taking. If they were indeed looking for friends, then we did not want to engage them near the entrances. With this in mind the word was passed around that we should withdraw into the centre of the building with specific teams assigned responsibility for meet-and-greet.

I detected the lady Merry Beans ahead of the males. If I could smell them two floors up, then my fellow Muters would have also noticed their presence on the premises. I jumped down from my hiding place and slipped off into the darkness of the building following the fresh scent of flesh. Knowing colleagues would be looking after other groups, I wanted to observe the lady Merry Beans. The aromas swept around the building including those of Muters moving away from the fighter-Beans thus drawing the visitors deeper into the building. I suspected the Beans did not know what they were walking into.

I kept to the darkness and followed the smell and the chattering of lady voices on the first floor. I also knew that if lady flesh was detected then Bean males wouldn't be far away, so I would not miss any loving embraces with fighter-Beans (usually the male). From a distance I observed the ten or so lady Merry Beans. They appeared to have found a young female Muter and were trying to communicate with her.

'But she's so sweet look at her,' nervously giggled a lady Merry Bean as she crept closer to SimplyFine who was only too aware of her role of drawing in the Beans. SimplyFine remained impassive.

'Oh my god,' another gasped in apparent delight.

Sounds don't usually affect me, but the whispered chatter and gasps of the Merry Beans as they went about their business enthralled me. A welcome soothing sound that spoke of destiny. They became emboldened at SimplyFine's (then SugarRush's and finally TyreTreads') unthreatening demeanours. Within moments the lady Merry Beans were linking arms with my colleagues and posing for image-captures using the telephonic communication devices.

'Let me, let me,' said one Merry, then another as they posed and linked arms with my obliging colleagues.

The Merry Beans became increasingly relaxed pouring warm breathy aromas forth from deep inside their lushness. I knew TyreTreads, SugarRush and Simply would struggle to resist for much longer. When a banquet is smothering you in its warm riches it is difficult to resist licking and kissing. Suddenly a telephonic device rang. A Merry Bean answered it, nodded, muttered a few words saying all was 'okay' and 'yes, they would keep looking'. The conversation over, the lady Merry Bean (WhiteTeeth-elect) turned and held up her telephonic device to SimplyFine showing a picture of a smiling Bean.

'Have you seen this person?'

SimplyFine gazed at the image-capture, then at WhiteTeeth-elect then back to the image-capture. Simply had been operational for a few lunar cycles and she was learning strategy. What she did next, made me proud. In fact, what TyreTreads, SugarRush (now joined by LycraStew) all did, made me proud.

SimplyFine nodded (much to the excitement of the Merry Beans), turned and walked deeper into the building followed by Treads, Sugar and Lycra. I followed at a discreet distance keeping in the shadows. After a tour of corridors and a stairwell which prompted hushed gasps and whispering at the sight of numerous resting Has-Beans, the group came to a stop in front of one Has-Bean suspended from the ceiling on a meat-hook. The Merry Beans gawped in what I knew to be Bean-horror, but to the inexpert eye might have been interpreted as Bean admiration and wonder.

It appeared that the Has-Bean hanging in front of them was indeed the 'this person' they were looking for, but it was evident that the Has-Bean was resting peacefully and should not be disturbed.

The following hushed and urgent discussion was broken by the echo of shouts and screams in other parts of the building followed by the sudden ringing of the telephonic communication devices in the hands of the lady Merry Beans with us. Within moments the air was pumped full of aromas dripping with delicious panic.

'We'd like to go now, thank you,' WhiteTeeth-elect said to Simply who just smiled in response. WhiteTeeth-elect turned towards the direction they had come, but found her way blocked by TyreTreads and SugarRush. The Bean turned to Simply again and repeated her request (in fact, her last ever to be uttered as a Bean). Simply smiled leaned in close (wholly unthreateningly, mind you) and locked her lips onto WhiteTeeth-elect's mouth in a passionate kiss.

To the background of the shouts and running from the corridors above and below and the repeated electronic clamour of the electronic communication devices, the shock of the Bean friends morphed into hyperventilation, which pushed massive amounts of warm, moist breath into the corridor. I could almost see the warm red, oxygenated lungs working at capacity within their firm, fleshy, heaving chests.

The screams that followed merely served to push more moisture into the cramped corridor.

Simply broke away from the kiss pulling the lips of WhiteTeeth-elect away with her. The lady Merry Bean stood in shock, her eyes wide, before trying to feel for the (now missing) flesh around her mouth. All she could find at the end of her fingers was the hard enamel of her gleaming, perfectly white teeth. She looked great, a treat. To meet WhiteTeeth in an alley would leave an unsuspecting Bean in no doubt about her intentions. Her best features were on full display.

Deciding it was time to make my presence felt, I emerged from the darkness. My arrival appeared to clarify the threat for the Merry Beans. Screams and shouts and cries for 'help' merged into meaningless noise. They vainly attempted to make a dash for freedom, but where they were (unknowingly) headed was a place where pert ambition and hope sag into the mute acceptance of deathstiny.

Although my fellow Muters were not all tacticians, a group dynamic does emerge when the need arises. I've observed that the more cognizant Muters (myself included) set the tone or action and then my colleagues follow. When the Merry Beans found one path blocked by Treads and SugarRush and then another route blocked by more of my colleagues answering the call, they took a turn deep into the darkness. Our group's squeals and panic joined others around the building and, as we had planned, they were all

converging on the central space that ran from basement to roof –
an atrium.

We emerged in the spaces bordering the precipice over the
abyss to see groups of Beans fighting off my colleagues, jumping
onto scaffolding or hanging off the wires trying to escape their
destiny.

Fine examples of steaming prime Bean beef burst into the
building atrium from outside which only added to the buzz. Some
Beans growled and shouted and stormed up the gangway from the
ground floor charging Muters with sticks of wood striking them in
the vain hope of stopping them. Some of my colleagues retreated
but only to allow the fighter-Beans deeper into the building.
Emboldened by their apparent success, the Bean-beefs pushed
further into the blackness shouting for their mates.

All the screaming, shouting and panting served only to push
out sweet perfume from their pink insides. Had they a plan? Just
when the atrium space was a cauldron of aromas and sizzle, the
Muters – as one – moved in. Beans flew from the corridors and off
the balconies down into the basement. As other Beans scrambled
across scaffolding my colleagues positioned on lower levels
loosened nuts and grips resulting in the whole scaffolding edifice
collapsing taking dozens of Beans with it.

After shouts of 'It's this way', the remaining Beans
disappeared down the one stairwell open to them (intentionally
open, of course). We followed, unperturbed, knowing where it led
– to the basement that had no windows, no escape routes except a
ramp that had been designed for automobilic vehicles to roll up to
the outside world. Towards the ramp the thirty remaining Beans
raced. But they were not to know that we had been expecting
incursions from Rubber Beans so we had modified a pit that lay at
the bottom of the ramp – flimsy wooden planks and boards
covered the pit. As the Beans desperately raced towards what they
hoped was a continuation of their miserable existence, so did my

colleagues funnel them towards the planks covering the pit. Bean squeals echoed around the basement as the Beans raced ever closer to the trap. I arrived just in time to see them framed in silhouette against the illumination from the dark cycle's great cool orb before they disappeared as the planks gave way and they fell helpless into the pit. Anticipation is a delightful bedfellow.

In beautiful harmony, the sound of the flooring's splintering mixed with the screams as all but one of the peachy fruit plummeted the twenty feet into the pit below. A hard concrete landing was not to be their end for, waiting patiently at the bottom of the pit, were the expectant and broken features of many of my colleagues. The screams were quickly muffled by a vigorous interrogation of the panting prizes.

However, there was one, one Merry Bean who had been taking up the rear of the escaping group (possibly hoping to bathe in the claim as the last Bean to leave the building – such is Bean vanity), but he was now somewhat chastened. Seeing the flesh of his fellow raiders pulled, chewed and gorged on in the pit below had an immediate and sobering effect. I strode towards him slowly trying to smile and calm him. I didn't want him gorged. We had fed plenty that dark cycle. He had a future with us intact. He didn't struggle. He tasted strong, but sweet. I hung him high on a hook to let the blood drain and as a sign to others he was to be left until he rose again when the time was right.

I headed back into the building and surveyed the scene. A tangled mass of Bean flesh wrapped around and impaled on scaffolding poles. Colleagues were feasting or lite-biting those strewn around the atrium. It was an impressive number for an unplanned event and all achieved without lifting a finger.

I found the Has-Bean WhiteTeeth-elect quietly resting amidst the scaffolding. I kissed her myself on her neck and drank deeply. I did not interfere with her cheeks or face. SimplyFine had left her own distinctive mark on WhiteTeeth. The Merry Has-Bean would make a fine addition to our ranks. I pulled her from the tangled rubble and dragged her up a few floors to the same corridor in which her former friend hung. Perhaps they would rise together and become a tight unit. There were no other incursions that dark cycle so we had ample o'clock to stack the Has-Beans in organised groups in anticipation of their rising. It had been an eventful dark cycle, but I had a nagging feeling that we would be seeing more Merry Beans in the future.

The perimeter fence around World Piece I was subsequently doubled in height and density, as it subsequently was at the other World Pieces. A bizarre measure indeed – as if you can contain death. The Cloth-Heads, who had been a common sight parading along the fences, were replaced by large numbers of Green Beans. The average citizen Bean was being kept further back. We were even seeing more Rubber Bean support units being established across the metropolis.

For all its advantages, World Piece I was attracting more attention than any other Muter home base. Bean security measures were more coordinated than ever before. Not that such measures prevented my senior colleagues from escaping into the metropolis whenever it pleased us, but we had to keep an eye on the newbies.

I soon suspected the feasting of the Merry Beans that splendid dark cycle had turned the head of a significant number of the leader-Beans from within the metropolis and beyond. A quick review of the papers-of-news and announcements on the telephonic communication devices confirmed this. Further evidence of the interest was evident from the rising numbers of Bean-Boxers beyond the perimeter fences. It was both an inconvenience and to be expected, but I had dealt with similar bursts of interest before. I could manage.

Nevertheless, it was becoming clearly important for someBeanbody. I was not wrong. One always knows things are going to get worse when leader-Beans are involved. Leader-Beans (closely followed by the Bean-Boxers) promise a better existence, which, if you haven't realised yet, is a highway to….,well, me. That said, I put out the alert to other World Pieces to be alert. A war was coming.

36. Where Did It All Go Right? The Great Change

Many light-darks later (perhaps a few lunar cycles even) in the middle of the 'Great Handover' (a three or four light-dark event in the metropolis that is distinct from the lunar-cycle-long 'Great Change in Bean Behaviour'), I found myself sitting with Pearl and Chubby on top of a tower that formed part of a bridge across the Black Road that ran through the metropolis dump. Below and around us the dump was sinking under a thick cloud of Bean fear. It was a busy time, a wonderful time. Sometimes it is important to take in the view, just sit back and soak up the terror.

I turned and looked at Chubby, her eyes dead with mischief and excitement, she knew it too. Soon all this would be ours. Our own slice of heaven. What were we going to do when all this was over? It would be just us. Us happy few tens of millions. We had recently paid a visit to Call-Me-Josh and inducted him (see following chapter describing our communion). He was resting now, but I was looking forward to meeting him. His name in death, I would grant him later.

As little pockets of fire lit up the metropolis I was grateful I did not end up in a grave with the words 'Rest in peace – loved by a (Bean) mother, (Bean) father and (Bean) offspring. We shall meet again in eternity. Etc. together forever.' I wanted to see this sight laid out in front of me. I did not want to rise *after* all the excitement was over. I wanted to be here, to have a ringside seat at the drama, the handover – the Great Handover – the moment when 'Homo Sapiens' tipped his hat and bid farewell joining, Homo

Erectus, Homo Neanderthalensis in the footnotes of inconsequence. In the words of a dead language, 'Homo Mortem Aeternam' had arrived, as promised, as predicted. Welcome to the next thousand precessional cycles.

I surveyed all the buildings and roadways that made up the metropolis. A place where Beans came together to exist together, to share together, to hate together, fight together and despair together – all in the unfounded belief that existence would be worth it in the end. Perhaps I was being unkind and they did like each other, but so often they didn't taste like it. In my experience, the more Beans congregated, the more they seemed to fight, the more they fretted over laws and regulations that either repressed their instincts or kept them apart. Ironically such practices had helped when the Great Handover beckoned.

As the traces of colour of the great orb sank below the horizon and the Bean-powered illumination flickered into existence across the city I could hear the howls of protest at the dying of the light. That dark cycle the metropolis was changing hands. Everything the Bean did would accelerate the inevitable. Still why couldn't they just accept their destiny? Perhaps that was it. Beans were 'forever' in denial. It was the essence of their existence, in their very make-up. Deny destiny and you have the Bean.

But *where* did it all go so right? *Where* and *when* had the seed of success been sown? A seed that had blossomed into the flower of no return. Had there been a specific moment or incident during the lunar cycle of the Great Change? When did it become inevitable this time? (After all, Muterdom had risen before, but it was too much too soon and so had failed.) So, what was different this time? Could I trace it to a moment in my own experience? I concluded that there had indeed been a moment after which things irreversibly changed. It was a kiss at World Piece I, not long after the Attack of the Merry Beans (many light-darks earlier).

249

The acquisition of (and feasting on) the Merry Beans at World Piece I had attracted much attention. Bean-Boxers were plentiful and massed outside the perimeters of World Piece I. But where Bean-Boxers lurk, others soon follow – leader-Beans. But this term is misleading as it implies an innate leadership quality. No, these hominids seek to lead, not because they are well-suited (though they are invariably cloth-suited), but because they are *ill-*suited to lead.

Following the appearance of Bean-Boxers at World Piece I, automobilic vehicles carrying large numbers of Rubber Beans and Green Beans arrived. Hidden in the middle of the convoy was a black-windowed, automobilic van-vehicle out of which climbed a handful of Ill-Suited Beans. They reeked of self-interest, so all was not lost. It had its advantages for us in World Piece I – for the self-interested Bean is the unwary Bean.

Watching them from high up in the World Piece structure, I concluded that there was one plump-headed Bean among the van-vehicle Beans who must be one of the most ill-suited of the Ill-Suited Beans. It is curious that one Bean is required to give legitimacy to another Bean. Here we had endorsements of their ill-suitedness by the presence of Rubber Beans, Green Beans and the Bean-Boxers. In the absence of accompanying Rubber and Green Beans, the Ill-Suited Beans are as any other – a heartbeat away from resting as a Has-Bean. But, for us Muters, we are grateful for such a hierarchy of ignorance. It enhances the feasting to come.

I watched as the Beans swirled around each other. They grouped at the perimeter fence and surveyed the World Piece structure looming large above them. As they lingered at the fence the wind gently wafted their sweet perfumes up to higher floors of World Piece I itself. Aware that many, many hundreds of Muters would be alerted to the presence of such fresh meat, I realised the visit needed to be managed. I wondered if Call-Me-Josh was near, but I suspected not. I certainly could not detect him in the swirling aromas and it did not seem to be an exercise he would be involved in. That is not to say he was not observing from a distance, no, but it certainly wasn't one of his clandestine operations. This was an exercise in self-validation of the ill-suited ones. Of course, as I have already explained, Bean existence is a constant attempt at self-validation (the irony of self-validation – needing approval of, or attention from, another Bean – was not lost on me). Remove self-validation and all you have is destiny. The reason 'self-validation' is a struggle for the average Bean is because it is not the nature of things. Beans expend great effort in developing technology of self-validation, yet their greatest efforts (and expenditure of metal treasures) are directed to developing technology to control other Beans or, failing that, expediting the journeys of members of their Beankind to my kingdom.

The aromas had something of the 'other' to their nature. I couldn't quite place it until I heard, ever so softly, the gentle sweet hum of the main, Ill-Suited, plump-headed Bean as he addressed the Bean-Boxers. He was from another land where other languages are spoken (but he wasn't a Merry Bean, for sure).

The group of Ill-Suited Beans moved slowly, another bad sign. Beans usually emphasise the importance of their destination (hence their desire to move fast), but if they move slowly (particularly when there are Bean-Boxers in attendance) it suggests they are wallowing in the moment. This can be dangerous. It makes the Rubber Beans nervous, but as I watched, I noted that the Rubber and Green Beans were acting defensively, not hunting with intent. I also detected the presence of Ethical Beans, which lessened the immediate dangers to Muters. Furthermore the presence of the Ill-Suited suggested the threat to us (from the Rubber and Green Beans) was limited especially as they were being accompanied by the Bean-Boxers. We were safe.

The group approached the fence on which were hanging the image-capture representations of some of the Has-Beans thought to be resting (to be exact, they were hanging) inside World Piece I. Words of weakness and self-pity scrawled on pieces of paper littered the fence.

So, with the Rubber Beans and Green Beans not likely to be antagonistic, I concluded that it was therefore reasonably safe to approach the Beans gathered by the perimeter fence as they read the words of pitiful weakness. I dispatched a handful of Muter colleagues to approach them unthreateningly. The dark boxes had been focusing on the van-vehicle Ill-Suited Beans looking at the pitiful paper pleas, but as my colleagues approached the group of visitors, the Bean-Boxers' attention turned to FatLegs, Diesel, DoorStop, Pearl, Tarmac, PlumpCalf, Dunky and Smashy, Colour Splash, Rooftop, Simply Fine, Plot and a dozen others, all led, of course, by the grand-master herself, ChubbyCheeks.

I watched from World Piece fully confident in my team. I was hit by a sudden waft of nervous excitement from the Beans gathered beyond the fence. There was no aggression. I watched as the most Ill-Suited, plump-headed Bean turned and approached the wire fence. Soon there was only an arm's length separating the Bean from my Team, in other words, separating the Past from the Future. The Ill-Suited plump-headed Bean tried to speak to my Muter colleagues, but there was nothing of interest he could say to eternity. Smashy and Dunky, as was expected, took a certain interest in the Bean-Boxers. FatLegs and other Muterlings moved forward.

Then on cue, FatLegs, Fluffykins and KittenFluff pushed through to the fence and reached out to the Ill-Suited Bean. Gentle laughter and applause from Ethical Beans drifted up from the perimeter fence to my ears. Chubby hung back. In a previous lunar-cycle she had been the target of interest from the Rubber Beans. There was no need to provoke their interest at this stage (even though Chubby was always up for a challenge even having taken an recent interest in the Green Beans).

It all happened very quickly and it was difficult to judge from my vantage point what had triggered it. Perhaps it was FatLegs' call to arms. At a moment of his choosing he reached out his hand through the fence in an attempt to touch the Ill-Suited Bean. Further applause and a waft of perfume indicated a lowering of the Bean guard and the rising of their foolishness. After much fervoured discussion amongst the Beans, a slight opening was made in the fencing which allowed FatLegs, Fluffykins (followed by other Muterlings), Pearl, Simply and PlumpCalf to walk through the gap towards the Ill-Suited plump-headed Bean. FatLegs and Fluffykins took the Bean's hands and stroked it gently. Then, to much laughter and murmuring, they turned to lead him back through the fence onto the World Piece premises.

After a few steps and some applause (and much dark box activity) a number of Rubber Beans stepped forward to stop the Ill-Suited Bean from passing through the fence. This prompted excited discussion between all the Beans. Seeing that progress was delayed and getting bored, FatLegs and Fluffykins simultaneously sunk their teeth into his hands. It caught his attention and focused his mind. Chubby's other niblings made the initial bites on his immediate neighbours. Chubby herself emerged from the group of Muterlings and headed straight for the nearest two Green Beans. She was ably backed up by Pearl, Tracks, Tarmac, PlumpCalf (and others) who all threw themselves at the Rubber and Green Beans. A handful of Cloth-Heads in attendance clearly didn't know what was happening and shuffled away.

Meanwhile Diesel, DoorStop, GlassCutter and a handful of others grabbed the main Ill-Suited Bean and a selection of other Ill-Suited Beans and pulled them through the fence and into the compound. The Beans were soon lost in the writhing bodies as other colleagues of mine (some of whom had been approaching from the sides) joined in. Screams and perfumes were being pushed into the atmosphere. I had noted that there were some Green Beans on the nearby rooftops with firing devices, but I had anticipated their wish to engage with us would be limited by the presence of the Ill-Suited Beans and the abundance of Ethical Beans and Bean-Boxers in the crowd. That said, I had BeanPole, Chain-and-Stiks, BroadBean, Peas and ChimneyBlack distract them. Dunky and Smashy took care of the more annoying Bean-Boxers, biting some and dragging them (and their equipment) inside the compound.

The grey-haired, balding, automobilic-van-vehicle, plump-headed Ill-Suited Bean was carried into the World Piece. On meeting him myself he did not look like he would have any death skills of note, but there was no harm in having another body around. It was only right that he was inducted by those who had selected him, however, I did suggest that they did not make too much of a meal of him. It might be useful for Beans to see what leadership looked like in death. (Who knows, it might even encourage their followers to expedite the destinies or other Ill-Suited Beans?)

In the light-darks to follow we did see a massing of Rubber and Green Beans on the perimeter, but they appeared to do more procrastination than preparation. Perhaps they understood their fate. However, as a way of keeping them satisfied, we did release a few of the lite-bites, but kept their main Ill-Suited plump-headed Bean, VanPlumpy, until he was ready to feast for himself. Afterwards there were a handful of snatch squad attempts on me. They would try to identify themselves to me, saying: 'We know all about you. We know you understand. We've been reading your words.' Whether they think my disappearance will change anything, I think not. Once again I wondered whether Call-Me-Josh was involved. I made a mental note to not delay my visit to him.

At the time, the incident clarified for me that Muters' health and safety was always lifted if Bean-Boxers were in proximity. This could work to our advantage. Up to that point I had viewed the Bean-Boxers as possibly the most pitiful of all Beans. This was on the assumption that they accepted that they had no intrinsic value themselves, subsequently deciding to pursue a small degree of *self*-validation by validating (or, more commonly, denigrating) others. If your own story has no merit, seek self-validation in reporting on another Bean's meaninglessness. But, on reflection, I did wonder whether perhaps a Bean-Boxer's meaninglessness itself was a form of unusual death skill.

I encouraged Dunky and Smashy to mentor the Bean-Boxers we had acquired that light cycle so to see if their death skills could work *for* us rather than against us. Both Dunky and Smashy were pleased with the challenge and nurtured their niblings back to health in no time. Before long their niblings would reintroduce themselves to the equipment that had been brought over with them and start broadcasting. Much like our use of the telephonic communication devices, we could now share death to the wider metropolis. One clever thing Dunky did do was *not* to bite one lady Bean-Boxer. She remained untouched and Beanful and I encouraged them to keep her undead as an experiment. Of course, it was an unsettling time for her and she made a few attempts to escape, but once she felt that she was not going to be touched or kissed she tried to communicate with the outside Bean world using Bean-Box technology. This was yet another useful addition and I encouraged Dunky and Smashy to keep her Beanful for as long as possible.

Bean-Boxing aside, it was probably the acquisition of the Ill-Suited Bean, VanPlumpy, that was the moment in the Great Change that triggered the beginning of the final act and led us ultimately to the Great Handover. Although the Rubber Beans remained a presence, they were largely replaced by Green Beans. There was not a street in the metropolis that did not reek of fear. You could smell the onset of destiny. Like the change of a season, it hung in the air. It was quite magnificent to behold. So much was happening. The panic, the panic, the panic. It was this ever-increasing Bean panic for 'life' that was arguably hastening their destiny.

Little had I known when I stepped off that heap of rubbish a dozen lunar cycles earlier quite how the vistas would open up to me and the honour and pleasure I would feel to witness the metropolis turn towards its destiny.

After the attack of the Merry Beans and the visit by the Ill-Suited Beans, matters progressed rapidly. There seemed to be confusion and panic in the ranks of the Beans. We took advantage and acquired more World Pieces. The Beans also appeared to be locking down the dump. As a result we found it easier to move around the metropolis dump and so we explored. We made many new colleagues and allies – not just Beans, but creatures of all descriptions. It was a revelation.

Inspired by DoorStop's and GlassCutter's work (at the Boxes of the Errant Bean) Chubby was keen to visit establishments known to her during her brief and pitiful existence. So it was that we found ourselves at the Box of Creature Delights. It is a descriptive passage for another time, but I can attest that the enlightenment of creatures (kept in cages and enclosures for the Beans' own amusement) was a minor milestone in itself. We moved from cage to cage to enclosure and wrestled the creatures into submission and drank deeply on glory streams both small and monstrous in size. On one occasion I found myself cornered by one of the more formidable creature-beasts and an array of hissing serpents. During our tussle I was impressed with its aggression and strength, yet it eventually succumbed. I drank deeply. Its juice contained a power that I was sure would have helped the creature-beast overcome its dominion but for the Second Bean Paradox. Such was the impression that the creature-beast made upon me that I decided to return to witness its rising. I sensed the beast had potential in the new kingdom. I was not to be disappointed. We became inseparable.

It was apt that my new companion confronted the boss manager of the Box of Creature Delights establishment. The Boss-Bean was not impressed that the creature-beasts had turned against their jailer. "Cursed Be All of You," he exclaimed as my new four-legged companion tore him limb from limb. At the end, Death will rip apart the jailer. The curse personified my new colleague four-legged colleague – a creature-beast representing and protecting *all* creatures. Cursed the creatures had been in existence, but blessed were they all in eternity. The jailed had become the guardian.

In fact, my MuterBeast companion had a tremendous impact on all my business with Beans. I had had no idea the level of fear that would be generated when a Bean came upon a creature blessed with eternal knowing. The MuterBeast's roar was a curse on the very existence of Beankind; a curse of a power unknown to their realm. Its sound alone could rip the spine from anyBean. Moreover, the sight of the Beast would send a Bean into a fit of panic – a pit of fear so deep that their soul and whole being became perpetually trapped in the blackest, thickest tar of terror. Moreover, its close proximity inspired a dread I had not anticipated in Bean. Their language would curdle and twist in acts of monstrous, captivating wizardry. Their very words would surge and ripple through their soft flesh before being expelled in shrieks of desperation. In fact, the Bean's body became an embodiment of the foulest of Bean utterances.

A cornered Bean would shower the creature in breathy, furious agitation as it approached – 'No fucking way! Fuck you, fuck you, fuck all of you, you motherfuckering fuckers,' they would cry before the MuterBeast ripped them to pieces with a ferocity too profound to properly describe here. The MuterBeast encapsulated the predicament of the Bean in the metropolis at that time.

Once again I had to be grateful to ChubbyCheeks for leading me to the Box of Creature Delights and introducing me to my most trusted ally – the MuterBeast and guardian of deathstiny. This loyal companion of mine was both curser and curse and I was pleased to eternally anoint him with this role; in truth, forever would he be manifest so. I named him CurserBe.

37. Let's Talk About Us, Call-Me-Josh

I should, of course, report my visit to Call-Me-Josh. He had been proving increasingly familiar with us. So, with a lull in our engagements with the Rubber Beans of all descriptions, it seemed an opportune time to visit. Besides I had visions of him being a witness and ally of ours at the Great Handover.

I had considered visiting Call-Me-Josh in his floating, private habitation on the Black Road, but he had been spending so little time there. So, with the Beans confused and scattered (as the metropolis was cleansed by fire and falling stone), I made my way to Call-Me-Josh's observation post a few hundred yards from World Piece I. Square, solid, artificial, it was part of a collection of stacked cabins that had been placed there a lunar cycle (or few) earlier by mechanical lifting arms. The cabins were situated behind high fences of cutting metal wire and the compound was illuminated by electrical bulbs atop high poles. It was obviously a place the leader-Beans wished to protect from the Muters. A home to a hundred or so Beans, it had never appealed as a target to me as such. GlassCutter and DoorStop were keen to take it over, but I encouraged them to sit back and focus on the boxes for Errant Beans – something that had become a specialty of theirs. The time to visit Call-Me-Josh and his fellow Beans would come. I knew the compound's security would weaken in time and an opportunity would present itself.

I was still presumably an item of interest for him. I would often pass the compound of stacked cabins aware that I was being watched using telescopic image recording devices on its roof and on nearby poles. I would be out on fieldwork and his aroma would regularly reach my nasal cavities carried by the slightest of winds. Call-Me-Josh's perfume was distinct and I knew that he was ensconced in the fortified structure. There were times when I would return to the venue of a feast, perhaps to pick up a resting Has-Bean, only to find Call-Me-Josh at the location with his Cloth-Heads, Rubber Beans and, more recently, Green Bean friends.

During our brief and fleeting interactions his manner was pure, his attitude inquisitive. He would ooze both fear and excitability that was an intriguing mix. It was unusual to be respected for my work. So many Beans were unwelcoming and difficult, so he was a welcome distraction. I would be only too pleased to make his proper acquaintance. I could add value to his understanding of Muterdom and he also knew about me and my Beanhood. His knowledge of Bean thinking, Rubber Bean practice and his appreciation of what my colleagues and I were trying to do was worthy of note. Maybe there was a bit of destiny impulse mixed in with his behaviour as well. Whatever, our further acquaintance would be mutually beneficial I was sure, so I remained alert to an opportunity for a private audience with him. I suspected our final conversation would be short. He would not want to dally when destiny was standing over him. Besides, I had a sneaking suspicion he was always destined to become a brother-in-arms.

During earlier lunar cycles, I had assigned Chain-and-Stiks (with TreeShadow and LycraStew) to monitor Call-Me-Josh's movements to and from his box-abode (that floated on the Black Road). It was made easy because not only was Stiks herself familiar with the Black Road, but there were suggestions Call-Me-Josh was watching her too. With Stiks' death skills including the ability to move on the liquid itself, his own movements were not unknown to us. Whatever his interest in Stiks, it was important to watch the watchers.

In the run up to (and during) the lunar cycle of the Great Change, it had been a busy time for everybody. So, what with the Merry Beans, the Merry Green Beans and the excitement all over the metropolis, a visit to Call-Me-Josh had not been pressing on my mind. However, with the Beans in disarray I was advised that the security at the compound was degrading, in fact the number of Beans functioning at the compound was greatly diminished. The Bean attempts to raid and dismantle World Piece I had drawn in many of their number – first as an 'attacking' wave of Bean, then as a second wave of Bean trying to recover Has-Beans. Is it a form of arrogance? Whilst wanting to deny their own destiny they see fit to deny the destiny of others? Even when Has-Beans are on the cusp of enlightenment?

In the middle of a dark cycle we approached the compound finding it largely deserted. His Black, Green and Merry Green Bean friends were either busy trying to re-group or tied up at the Greenwitchery base (more of which later) and other sites across the metropolis. As ever, I was not alone. Chubby, Pearl and Tarmac were with me along with a handful others – one of whom might have been a surprise for Call-Me-Josh. I speak, of course, of CurserBe – my loyal MuterBeast in all his glory.

It had not been lost on me that Call-Me-Josh had been reading my musings. I was pleased to share. In fact (and as he probably learnt a little too late), his attention proved really quite helpful. We entered the premises finding most of the cabins had been vacated. The handful of cowering Beans we did come across were swiftly embraced. We followed the recognisable perfume up a few flights of stairs.

Sensing that Call-Me-Josh was going to be important, I wanted my closest colleagues to be with me. His knowledge of the Beans, his sympathy and understanding of Muterdom would make him a welcome addition to our ranks. Furthermore, his death skills would also give perspective and insight as we all moved towards a place of peace and a kingdom of realisation.

I suspect Call-Me-Josh detected our aroma first. He had been crouching over his desk studying the screens of various computing devices some of which were monitoring the events outside. Loud chatter crackled over the airwaves relaying the sound of Bean panic. Sound does not carry the power of Bean perfume, but if it did, that room would be an oceanic cacophony of Bean. The only real world aroma we could detect in the upper floors was Call-Me-Josh's. Had he been completely abandoned? Were the Beans in full retreat?

Careful not to be surprised ourselves, we entered his operations room from different points and having secured the entrances revealed ourselves to our old friend. Looking tired, unshaven, he was dressed in the white robe I had often seen him wear. He was taken aback on seeing me and immediately tried the old trick of trying to establish a rapport.

'Hi, Nigel, it's me, Call-Me-Josh. Remember?' he said, perhaps trying to be oh-so-Bean casual. 'You write about me. I read your blog. What can I say – it's good to see you again. How have you been?'

I didn't feel the need to reply. Monologues in such circumstances are the Beans' subconscious attempts to delay the inevitable. However, as I walked towards him, it seemed to unsettle him and he slowly, but again casually, backed away. It was a large open workspace with many desks and computing devices and papers. Walls and upright stands were covered with maps, diagrams, notes and image captures. Windows with strong transparent glass looked out over the compound and towards World Piece I. Fires burning in the landscape between their home and my home threw dancing shadows on the interiors of Call-Me-

Josh's workspace. So it was from here that he had spent his Bean time examining our endeavours.

'Look, I know death is a destiny, mine, yours, everybody's, but right now?' he said, interrupting my assessment of his environment. 'What's the rush, Nigel? I will be joining you at some stage and I look forward to it, honestly I do, but I need to wrap up a few things here. Don't say it, I know,' he said holding up a finger in an attempt to impede my approach as he moved slowly around a desk, '"what's the point?" but I think that we could learn a bit more about you from the Bean perspective.

'In fact, we could learn to live together. Bean and Muter. Let the Beans learn to live with death. We have lost our way, our understanding, of what it is to be flesh and blood, juice. We only think of Bean-life, when there is so much more. Besides, let them (us Beans) develop death skills so that when we join you, it would make the eternal life that more….tolerable, profitable. Besides, the study of you (which I am calling Muterology) could really change the world, because we (the Beans) would know death is not the end. There really is, er, life after death.'

I never quite know how much my expression is giving away, but I suspect that on this occasion it was relatively accurate. Call-Me-Josh changed tack.

'You should know that the country is now in full and total quarantine. You have done fabulously well. The American military is doing its best to keep you guys at bay, but as you can see,' he said waving at the images on the screens and towards the window, 'they are struggling a bit. I suspect they will pull out altogether soon. I think you have won, certainly the battle of ideas, Nigel. A little bit of conversation would be good at this stage. I can help arrange that. Important people do listen to me. If I can show them there is a third way, they would love to hear it. Trust me. They all have the greatest of respect for you and everything that you have achieved.'

I listened and was in no rush, but I suspect he knew he was not winning me over.

'Truth be told, Nigel, we are all scared,' Call-Me-Josh continued. 'We accept our destiny, we just want to manage it in our own way. It would work to your advantage too. You Muter guys are here to stay. In fact, you need Beans like me...on the other side, as it were. Beans who know and respect everything you are doing. Not an enemy, but a partner.'

Chubby sidled up to him and took his hand, which obviously panicked him.

'Oh shit,' he muttered, looking down at her.

He knew who Chubby was and what she could do. He knew Chubby wasn't interested in his Bean reasoning at all. After all, if Chubby had been a Beanling she would be just as bored by his words, so why, as a Muterling, would she be any more interested? It was just like Chubby to get to the nub of the matter, but unlike an ignorant Bean who might take Chubby's gesture as conciliatory, Call-Me-Josh knew death had spoken and that his experience of existence as he had known it was down to its last few dozen breaths. That did not stop him trying though, such is the ignorant hope of the 'ignorhoper' Bean.

'Hello, Chubby. Do you know who I am? I'm Josh – "Call-Me-Josh". I'm a friend of Nigel's. I've learnt a lot from Nigel and hope to learn a lot more. Your nick-name as a Bean was Ena – shortened from....'

Call-Me-Josh paused, licked his lips. He was panicking. He knew Chubby wasn't interested, nevertheless, he struggled on. 'Did you know that? You were a very good Beanling before you met, um, Nigel. But I know you are a fantastic Muterling now. The best, in fact. You have personally bitten, kissed and feasted on thousands, if not tens of thousands, of us Beans. Respect.'

Nodding, Chubby giggled a giggle I had seen before (before she had feasted).

I took a step closer as did the others. Call-Me-Josh was now surrounded.

'It's a mess out there you know,' he said, turning to me and now sounding a little more panicked. 'There are outbreaks elsewhere around the world. We think the source of the outbreak in Rio was from one of your bites. Everybody is losing touch with everybody else. Countries are falling apart. I think we here in the UK are the first to go down properly. I think we, the Beans, are going to lose this one, Nigel. But you don't mind do you?'

He seemed sad. Resigned. He had seen this too many times. Poor Bean. However, one final idea appeared to occur to him – one final attempt to monologue and reach out. 'Seeking a common humanity' a Bean would call it.

'Do you know who you are Nigel? It is not entirely clear from your writings whether you do know, Nigel. I know a lot about you. You were born in Oxford thirty eight years ago. You moved to London, worked in an office, but hated it. (But you knew that already.) You were in a relationship with Pearl. A very good strong relationship by all accounts. You had a child. Remember? Do you remember, Nigel? I can tell you more if you like. I just need a bit of time to check more records and dig deeper into your background. I can help you find what you are looking for. I have a lot of it here,' he said waving at the office and the boards and papers around him.

'You were engaged to be married, once. To PearlLavaliere,' he continued, pointing to Pearl. 'That necklace that you see there hanging around her neck was in fact your engagement gift to her. Really. Yes, it was.'

Call-Me-Josh paused, perhaps waiting for me to reply, or waiting for me to halt my slow advance towards him.

'You were happy. You liked life, Nigel. Liked living (or rather 'existing' as you say). But things went wrong and you became unhappy. And then you died. You were killed. It was terribly unfortunate. You just got unlucky, Nigel, in those early days. You have been so instructive in taking this virus-outbreak-thing to the next level. I have often thought, if it had not been for you, all this would never have happened, it would never have taken hold. Death would never have come to this city. You are a leader, Nigel. I am asking you to lead, take decisions, now. I know all your colleagues respect and listen to you, Nigel.'

I stopped my advance. I was curious, but perhaps not quite in the way Call-Me-Josh had hoped.

'Please know, I can help you, Nigel. I can answer your questions. Where you came from. What brought you to this point. Tell me how can I help?'

Chubby, Pearl and others slowly moved in. I think Call-Me-Josh knew what was going to happen. He knew my writings better than anyBean.

Chubby gently led Call-Me-Josh to a large, slanted, display table and we invited Call-Me-Josh to lie down. He was a wise Bean and he knew the beginning was upon him. Of course, there was some confusion and bewilderment, even resistance. But that was the Bean in him.

'Some have said all this had been predicted, Nigel. The story has already been told,' he muttered in resignation.

We tied his head, wrists and feet to the table using wires as he continued to mumble.

'So, I suppose my efforts to avert the inevitable were always going to be in vain. I regret that. I thought I had a role though. I didn't have to be master of anything. Just a bit part would do. If I had known my fate (that it was all for nothing), I would have spent more time by the water. Too late for regrets though.'

Chubby looked at me hoping to be the biter. But still sensing that Call-Me-Josh did indeed have a role yet to play, I felt it was important that he be a shared lite-bite. But I could not deny Chubby the first taste. Grabbing a nearby sharp, metal implement, she pierced the side of his abdomen with and drank. Then Pearl, Tarmac, Diesel and I each took the end of each limb and bit, lightly piercing his soft, pale, puffy flesh.

He was rambling now. He was approaching his peace.

'More time on my boat. More time on the sea. More time on the Black Road,' he smiled and sighed. 'But there is no more time. One always answers for one's choices at the end.'

'It is the beginning,' I whispered in return.

He departed peacefully. Normally I would remove the resting Has-Bean to a secure location, but the area was such a war-zone it was unsafe, besides, no one would bother him here for a few light-darks. And there we left him.

The deed done, I looked around the office and indeed found images of me and my colleagues on the wall. Chubby was especially excited to find not only numerous images of herself but dozens and dozens of her niblings. It was almost a complete family album. There were charts and maps of the metropolis shaded in different colours and what even looked like that favourite Bean thing – 'plans'. Plans with words; plans with pictures; plans with diagrams.

What is it with planning and the Bean? Why does one seek to determine the future when there is no future for the Bean other than destiny? It is fiction. But it would not be long before such matters would go the way of the great orb and melt through a hazy horizon into nothingness.

With that, I exited the cabin and surveyed the drama of the battlefield. Not my battlefield, the Beans' battlefield. It was a painting. Colourful, dynamic, dramatic. The Bean collective was retreating into desperation right across the metropolis. Much like an individual Bean at his or her moment of reckoning, it was a scene of panic, of grand drama with a sensuality not to be experienced until the end of times.

With my trusty, four-legged MuterBeast companion by my side, it felt meant to be.

38. The Great Handover: Greenwitchery and the Battle for World Piece

So, there we were, a few light-darks after communing with Call-Me-Josh I found myself sitting atop the two-towered structure spanning the black liquid road with Chubby, Pearl and Plot watching Bean attempts to escape the raging, fiery chaos across the metropolis. I was filled with pride, honour, inspiration. But what remained of my role now that the Great Handover was in full swing? Just continue to spread the love? Perhaps that was my role – to continue as a mentor? But what of leadership? I always felt I was a forerunner of others, a strand in a band of brothers.

Whatever my eternity, I would always embrace new members of the community and help newbies learn the ropes and, where possible, assist them in addressing any unfinished business. As Has-Beans they arose unprepared. They had no idea that their existence rarely prepared them for eternity in the real forever. This was amply demonstrated by their desire to fight and claw their way back to meaninglessness where possible. In those early moments of the Great Handover I knew they would feel intensely threatened. They would throw everything at us – all the 'treasure' that they had weaponised. The folly of Bean. Inanimate rock is mined for inanimate metal. The metal is assigned value on paper, which is in turn processed into data after which the data is traded and its 'value' used to manufacture exploding metal weaponry devices. The result? An inanimate, rocky vista. And the cycle starts over. Quite beautiful in its way, but I marvelled at the misery of the convoluted process to destiny and meaning. The one upside, perhaps – expedited death in many cases. Ironically, any treasure left over from the manufacture of exploding devices was used to develop ways and means to delay their own destiny.

Anyway, all would be clear soon. The war of revelation was upon us. The Great Handover. How many little battles were fought during the Great Handover, I could not say. Thousands upon thousands. Battles in homes, office structures, on street corners and wastelands across the metropolis. Many thousands of starting points, but only one endpoint. There was nowhere to hide. There were now enough Muters to manage the transition brutafully. Within a light-dark or two, when enough of the fighting Green Beans (many of them Merries) had joined our ranks, we could claim a new dawn.

I was jolted out of my musings by the sudden vibrations of the Black Road's twin-towered structure (on which Pearl, Chubby, Plot and I were sitting). Something was stirring below us. Adjusting my position I looked down far below to see Rubber Beans and Green Beans manning the asphalt road (spanning the Black Road) and determined the source of the vibration and noise. The asphalt road running between the two support towers was breaking apart. It was rising. I recalled the nature of this structure from my Beanhood. It was engineered so that vessels could pass between the towers and continue up the Black Road further into the heart of the metropolis. But was this intentional? Were the Rubber Beans trying to cut the north of the metropolis off from the south? Were they attempting to separate one side from the other? In the hope to stem the flow of Muters? Were they trying to isolate settlements and communities? Divide and conquer? Or was it trying to stem the flow of Beans?

In the flickering light of fires and exploding light above, I could see the shape of a large, metal vessel gracefully moving slowly up the Black Road towards us. More Beans? More Green Beans? At a time when Beans appeared to be vacating the metropolis, it was curious to think more Beans were being brought to the fight. The large vessel approached and quietly slipped by underneath us. Perhaps its arrival brought hope to the Bean or even more witchcraft to unleash on the Muters. It was grey and smooth and had, what looked like, large firing devices fixed about its bulk. I watched the vessel glide slowly up through the liquid blackness. They were on the move from the Greenwitchery base. They were organising themselves.

If indeed the vessel was moving Green Beans to the centre of the metropolis, then that might leave the GreenBeanBase exposed. Perhaps it was time to explore options and pay them a visit there?

The GreenBeanBase was a place of witchery. A place where Green Beans (many of whom were Merry) had hoarded, over the previous lunar cycle, their explosive witchery, their heavy, green automobilic machines and even their sky machines. For many light-darks they had collected their tools, their firing devices, machines and camped out vast Green Beans numbers. These Beans and their witchery were brought into the metropolis by way of the Black Road and deposited at the Greenwitchery base on the edge of the road – a place that had a history of Bean warfare. So, early on, it suggested the Beans' intent to organise and escalate.

I turned to Plot. Our sockets met. She understood. She had a mission. I nodded and I sent her off to the place where she had risen. The place we had met. Now she had work to do in that place and other fields. The o'clock had come to raise her armies.

I turned to Chubby. Of course, she was welcome to join me, but I knew she had an errand to run. She wanted to be present for the rising of her recent and most prized bite – one she had found in the place of waste paper.

Finally, I turned to Pearl. Beautiful Pearl. I knew she had a job to do as well. I would join her shortly, but in the meantime I decided to return to World Piece to coordinate a visit to the Greenwitchery base on the Black Road where many GreenBeans

271

seemed to be based. There were countless skirmishes on the way back to World Piece I. By the time I arrived it became clear they did intend to make inroads into our territory and breach World Piece. Automobilic vehicles were placed in the surrounding streets and the aroma of the massing Green Beans was overwhelming. In fact, the Green Beans camped around World Piece I had been rising in number since our acquisition of the Ill-Suited Bean, VanPlumpy. I could write at length of the ensuing battles, but death has pretty much one face. I'll keep it brief. (I'll expand in other passages when I have the o'clock.)

I suppose of all the large scale battles, there were two of note – the GreenwitcheryBase and, of course, the battle for World Piece I itself. The assault on our first (and largest) home base was inevitable and would be a substantial challenge. I suspected the abandonment of the efforts of Call-Me-Josh signaled the end. Knowing that all World Pieces would be attacked, I dispatched CentralLine, FallenCyclist, Jubilee, BroadBean, Rooftop, ColourSplash, DogSmells and CatNaps to the other World Pieces to ensure they were not overrun.

With destiny rushing towards us all I began to think, why should I wait? Perhaps I should rush towards destiny and take the fight to the Bean? Although, during these light-darks, death was everywhere at all times, I could not be in two places at the same moment. I dispatched GlassCutter, DoorStop, Peas, GenerationManager and their own armies of Muters to the Greenwitchery Base on the Black Road. They were all accomplished at raiding fortified boxes. They would understand how to coordinate lines of ingress and knew the workings of Bean defence. The Green Beans had brought machinery and vehicles that were large and heavy. Some machines could travel through the air. Many had firing devices attached to their sides, tops or undersides. But this witchcraft did not worry us. The Beans would often find themselves cornered and immobile, even contained within their automobilic metal machines. They had poured so much o'clock and treasure into developing the contraptions that were almost the physical manifestation of the First Bean Paradox. If Muters could mount an attack from the land, the Beans could be driven into the Black Road. They would sink below its slippery surface only to rise as enlightened a light-dark or two later. We could bring clarity to their confused mission. I concluded that the Muter assault should be conducted before the Beans dispersed themselves too widely over the metropolis. I wished GlassCutter, DoorStop, GenerationManager, Peas, good killing and they departed with teams of many hundreds. Some might not return, but many more would be liberated.

Meanwhile I coordinated the defence of World Piece I with Diesel, Pearl, TarmacTired, the ParkSparkle twins, PlumpCalf, Chain-and-Stiks, Papers (both Cut and Fold), WhiteTeeth and hundreds of the more recent acquisitions. It made sense, after all many were familiar with the World Piece structure and had participated in defences from regular smaller incursions. I kept Dunky and Smashy and the Ill-Suited leader-Bean, VanPlumpy, close, thinking their influence might be of use. Of course, there were two companions with whom I would never part – ChubbyCheeks and CurserBe. FatLegs was never far from Chubby and they had legions of their own. The presence of Muterlings would confuse any approaching Bean, many of whom were acting on instructions from Ethical Beans. There was also an ace up my sleeve – I almost pitied the Green Beans at the World Pieces and the GreenwitcheryBase, for they were unaware of the support that we would soon have from Plot and her armies returning from their lands.

The assault on World Piece I began. The Beans tried everything. First they tried stealth (but how much death can a Bean outwit?) by dropping on ropes from sky machines onto the roof. I would like to say I organised my colleagues promptly, but they made me proud and, having learnt from the attack of the Merry Beans, they adopted a similar strategy – let the visitors enter the building and work their way towards us through the maze of corridors and shadow. We heard their shouts of 'clear' through their masks or over their communication devices as they made their way through the darkened structure. I suspected they were confused by the sheer numbers of Has-Beans hanging around them or resting in piles. The trouble was they would have difficulty discerning a Has-Bean from Muter. So, in time the shouts of 'clear' diminished as my colleagues engaged. There would be bangs, booms, mist, streams of liquid fire, but nothing was a nuisance.

Soon there were similar incursions from the ground entrances on all sides. Again, bangs, fire and mist. I suspect that some of the white mist was intended to limit the effectiveness of our Muter senses, but our senses have matured beyond the Bean. Or perhaps it was an attempt to obscure the sight lines, but again it hampered the Green Beans more than it impeded the Muter defence.

It was an enormously busy time, so I had to refrain from updating these records. It went on for a number of light-darks and I was aware that there were other skirmishes around the metropolis including attacks on World Piece II and III too. The first wave of Green Beans inducted many into enlightenment. We carefully hung (Green) Has-Beans along corridors or piled (or stood) them up in corners thus confusing the second wave of Green Beans whose 'ethics' often required them to leave none of their Beankind behind. With this confusion in mind we made a conscious effort to 'lite-bite' many Green Beans hoping they would return to their ranks and 'spread the love' in the coming light-darks. So, all in all, the trouble for the Beans was that we ended up acquiring numerous (Green) Has-Beans. (It proved to be a rapid expansion of our ranks and would assist in addressing the small pockets of resistance as the Great Handover concluded.)

As the battle continued the Green Beans became more desperate. More sky machines came, but as the Green Beans descended from the machines it was especially pleasing for me to witness newly-risen ClearGreenOne and ClearGreenFive jump on the rope and ascend to the hovering machine. Far be it for me to expect a newbie to know how to operate the sky machinery, but it was not necessary. I can only imagine the surprise of the Beans operating the sky machine when they turned around to see excitable Green Muters behind them. ClearGreenOne and ClearGreenFive did not disappoint. They managed to guide the flying machine down into one of the GreenBean command centres. The subsequent rising ball of yellow-red warmth and the threshing broken metal of the machine carved pretty holes in their plans. Before you could count a Bean's last dozen gasps, we had many freshly cooked ClearGreen colleagues (some of whom could almost be mistaken as twins of Diesel).

Yet it all puzzled me. Why, if a Bean can do it, do they use a machine to do it? What is the point of getting metal to do it? What is the purpose of the Bean if it is to surrender its existence to machinery? Where is the thrill, the toil, the drama in inanimates? If followed to its natural conclusion (advanced mechanised machinery), Beans would be redundant, superfluous. Again, was this evidence of the destiny impulse?

There were other attempts – their motorised two-wheeled vehicles that allowed them to move swiftly around the compound and surrounding streets and in and out of World Piece itself. However, as detritus, cadavers and blocks of the building fell and cluttered the avenues it made it all the more difficult to keep the wheeled vehicles upright.

As the terrain in and around World Piece I became increasingly difficult to manage so the Green Beans tried using larger, four-legged creatures to mount raids into the compound. Sitting high on the creatures' backs, the Green Beans galloped about the streets and in and out of the structures. But the creatures suffered injuries from both the shooting of the Green Beans and attracted the attention of the many fierce MuterBeasts (formerly of the Bean caged establishments). Not only did the MuterBeasts' presence unnerve the four-legged galloping creatures, but it also provided feasting opportunities for our new friends, CurserBe included. Knowing our previous success, we experimented with a few lite-bites. These grand, graceful four-legged creatures rested and rose quickly. Diesel and I and others even mounted the enlightened and fierce creatures and led the charge back to the Bean. Even the sight of us on the creatures' backs moving through the gloom soon made many Merry Green Beans turn and flee screaming for mercy and their gods.

Aware of the pressure we were under, Diesel instructed his trusted niblings to organise Muters from the Errant Bean Boxes to help to engage the Green Beans' supply lines. ParkSparkle, PlumpCalf also worked behind the enemy lines. As we sought to replenish our own numbers, it seemed reasonable to think the Green Beans would try and replenish their own and so they did. Green Beans would come from different parts of the metropolis monitored by my colleagues. Large, green automobilic vehicles were hijacked by my colleagues on route. Just as the vehicles of reinforcements pulled up at the command post behind enemy lines, the canvas would be pulled back to reveal a box full of Has-Beans resting or, failing that, a truck full of eager Muters.

By the end of the second light-dark the Green Beans were defending themselves on all sides. Diesel, keen to get involved with the aid of Green-newbies, led some of his niblings on a snatch raid into the Bean command. I was pleased to meet the Bean Commander whose aroma had been lingering in the area for a lunar cycle. Although, no doubt the Merry BeanCommander thought himself as a prize, regaling me his plans for success and my (alleged) destiny of failure, I got bored and left it to Diesel to dispatch the ignorhoper Bean.

Under other circumstances I would imagine that once the Commander had risen he might bring a lot of skills of use to deal with the predicament we were facing, but I was coming to the conclusion that his skills would not be needed on this occasion. The old kingdom was coming to a close.

With the metropolis soon to be our own it was right that Muters would need to spread the word far beyond metropolis circles and close the tedious conversation of Bean once and for all. There was still juice to be spilt and flesh to be gorged even after the final claiming of the battery farm dump itself. For this reason I encouraged colleagues to not feast relentlessly on the flesh of the fighters and perform numerous lite-bites so that any retreating Green Beans would carry our message forth. However, this actually panicked the Green Beans further. No sooner had we started following up with the lite-bites, their Beans-in-arms would immediately turn their firing devices on the lite-bite Green Beans unleashing the power of the hot lead pellets into the flesh, ironically gifting the lite-bites their destiny. This, in turn, created further tension and confusion amongst the Beans. Some lite-bites ran towards us surrendering themselves altogether to their destiny, other lite-Bites would try to disguise the nature of injury from other Green Beans in the hope they could be treated and 'survive'.

A combination of all these things soon led to a loss of effectiveness of the Bean attacks. Each Green Bean knew that if they were not lost to their destiny in the embrace of a Muter, there was the likelihood another Green Bean would turn their weapon on them. Two ways lay before them, but only one path.

The tide had turned. After a few more skirmishes, the Battle for World Piece was concluded. It seemed to sum up everything about the Bean – desperate, treasure-funded, inevitable, framed by fear and all about control. It neglected the one thing that was all-powerful, unassailable, ever-present – deathstiny. Bizarre. Yet the Bean kept sending hordes to assail it. How? To what end? What does a successfully assailed destiny look like?

It got me wondering – was that another iteration of the First Bean Paradox? Was the journey of Bean to learn just that? The unassailability of destiny? If it was, then I could act as a witness. In Bean words – death will get you in the end.

So it was that the immediate 'threat' passed. Of course, there would continue to be small struggles across the metropolis, but the story was over. Almost. There were a few other items on my 'to do' list, but I was now largely a spectator.

39. The Times They Have a Changed

The tables had turned. There was indeed a change in the air. The Merries were running. In fact, all Beans were running. Before our eye sockets the metropolis was becoming a relic of Bean. A time of revelation and realisation was upon us.

With CurserBe by my side, I headed to the Black Road. Muters swarmed back and forth. The perfumes of running Beans could not be disguised. I wandered over a footbridge towards the temples of Bean – temples to their ambition, temples to their meaninglessness. Occasionally a Bean would come running up to me 'help me, help me' the He-Bean or She-Bean would scream through the darkness as they approached me only to stop in horror. I would help some, others I would leave to the colleagues who had been chasing them down.

I was being drawn to a part of the metropolis and soon found myself standing opposite a large, flat-faced glass building on a relatively narrow street opposite a similarly large flat-faced glass building. A vehicle had damaged the main entrance so access was easy. With CursedBe padding along beside me, I climbed to the fifth floor of the vacated building, opened the door and entered a world I had not seen for nearly four hundred light-darks. It was an open place with furniture and electronic devices in which low emergency illumination cast long green shadows. The aromas of panting Beans running in the streets below were drifting in through the cracked and broken floor-to-ceiling windows.

With each step I took, things were becoming clearer.

It was a place where I had spent five to ten solar cycles. So much Beanhood spent in a place in which I had learnt nothing, for which I had felt nothing. Why do Beans choose to sit away from the sky wind, the liquids, the soil? Why would they rather sit amidst cardboard, chipboard and carpet? I walked through the avenues of seating places in front of computerised boxes designed to exchange hieroglyphs with other Beans sitting beside them or in places far removed. And all in the hope of accumulating treasure that could be exchanged for time 'relaxing' in a handful of light-darks amidst the sky wind, the liquids, the soil. They embrace the boxes of Beanhood, but fear the box of eternity.

I moved to the far end of the working space. I was drawn to a noticeboard pinned full of Bean sadness. Like the pitiful papers on the fences by all World Pieces, it was decorated with messages and image-captures of smiling Beans (no doubt all dying inside).

> *Matthew, aged 27 years, rest in peace, my friend.*
> *Jemima, 24 years, see you on the other side.*
> *Arthur, my man, my buddy, you will be missed.*

And there in the middle of all of them was a picture I recognised from lunar cycles ago.

> *In loving memory of Nigel. Rest in Peace for eternity.*

And even a few pictures of a partial smiling, laughing Nigel-Bean. I say 'partial' because I could detect, within the puppy-flesh features, a soft creep of sadness, disappointment in existence.

Of course, I did not have to walk the floor to know that the Bean had been hiding there ever since I had entered the working space. His perfume filled the place. Like them all, he thought he would remain undiscovered. There was, in his aroma, fear and sadness typical of the environment.

I found him crouched under a desk. He was shaking. He had seen perhaps thirty summers. I looked at him curled up into a defensive ball. Wanting to see more, I pulled up a chair on wheels and watched. Sensing I was not immediately interested in feasting on him, he eased himself into a more comfortable seating position under the desk.

'Are you going to kill me? Eat me?' he muttered under his breath, shaking his head. 'It's come to this. Fuck.'

I remained quiet.

'I know you, don't I? You used to work here?' he continued. 'You're one of the early ones. They talk about you. You won't remember me. I worked upstairs. I saw you occasionally on the stairs before, you know,....you died.'

I watched him. Curious.

'They liked you, I think. You were distracted. You had some difficult times. You were unhappy, apparently. Is that why you are here? Looking for something? Perhaps I can help.'

I remained still, studying his features. My smile was not what it had been.

'Do you understand me? Do you have memories?' he asked. 'I know about your family. But it's none of my business.'

Still, I was quiet.

'I have a family,' he said, filling the silence.

The Bean held out his telephonic communication device. Displayed on its screen was a young lady Bean and a Beanling. I studied the image of the two ripe Beans smiling back. Little did he know – never offer one's communication device to a Muter. All credit to him, the family looked juicy and the youngling would make a fine nibling of Chubby's – a fine addition to her fine army of Muterlings.

'I need more time. I know everybody's time comes,' he whispered, still nervous. 'But I need *more* time. There are things I want to do. I have a family now. And I have almost written a book.'

Perhaps, almost unsure himself, he sighed and looked away, taking his eyes off me for the first time.

'It has to work. It's why I work in this place. This was never me,' he said waving at the sickly-green illuminated space around him.

'So, you see, there is still stuff to do. I feel my lucky break coming.'

A bold statement, I thought.

'I can do this if you let me. Help me. I don't want to die now. It can't all come to this. Surely.'

He was doing what many Beans do, usually late at night with friends. Often as their bodies age and destiny creeps that little bit closer. It is a plea. I have lost count of the times Beans asked for more o'clock. They all want more summers to achieve their ambition. To reach a state of happiness, a state of peace, they cry. They proclaim a hope to live in the moment, yet they seek o'clock to achieve it. I recalled a common obsession of Beans – the maintenance of their body, to fight its decay.

Massive Bean structures and businesses have been built upon denial and 'self-improvement'. Whole existences devoted to realising it. And then what? The body, with all its organs, 'dies'. You cannot guild a liver.

I wanted to explain this to the Bean in front of me, but I knew he wouldn't listen. It would become clear soon enough. Ambition is invention, a fiction. Is it ever realised? No. The only realisation is in death.

And so there he was. A broken Bean sobbing on the floor. The reality of ambition exposed for all (me) to see.

'I just need more time,' he repeated. 'I could have been a contender,' he whispered mournfully. 'I had a plan. I just need more time.'

'For what?' I hissed as best as my rotting voice chords would allow.

He looked up somewhat shocked that Death had spoken to him.

'For what?' I whispered hoarsely.

'For what I... For.... To realise my destiny,' he whispered. 'Get my book out there. Then maybe a film, who knows. I could die a happy man then.'

I smiled. It would all make sense in time.

'You were alive once, Nigel. You must remember, that's why you're here. You should know what life and living is like – having dreams, hopes, ambition?' he pleaded. 'It's hell.'

He paused and sunk his face, head and hope in his hands. I could try and explain it to him, but like so many others he would learn soon enough. Every Bean's ambition should be to know death, only then can he know how to exist.

'What's it like?' he asked, pulling his wet face from his hands. 'I'm curious.'

What could I say? What words could I use?

'Does it hurt?' he asked again.

I reflected on my own Bean-death. I had cried out, but it was more in shock and fear of the unknown. There was some discomfort, but the body soon adjusts.

I shook my head.

'I'd like more time,' he pleaded again, quietly. 'Time for goodbyes.'

He pointed at the telephonic communication device in my hand.

I was in no rush. He was no threat. Perhaps he needed a period of reflection. I would give him his o'clock. I handed the device back to him, rose from the chair and walked back to the large glazed window overlooking the street below. Looking out now I could see the world had changed. The concrete and

283

monuments built to enclose the Bean during all light-darks were empty. Streets were full of smoking automobilic vehicles upturned or parked at awkward angles. Occasionally a running Bean awash with panic could be seen darting between shadows. Even the flickering street illumination suggested a Bean metropolis was in its own twilight moment.

It was all so different from the time I had last stood there looking down at a Bean jungle – complacent and proud in its perceived control of itself. The early Muters had struggled to find their way. They were regarded as occasional pests, not the pioneers they were. Was I indeed the turning point as Call-Me-Josh had suggested? Had I or, at least my generation, brought a degree of organisation? Had that been lacking in the times Muters had tried before? So it was that I reflected on the light-dark I had been born.

40. My Birthday

The first memory of my birthday began with me standing at that very same large, plate-glass window on the fifth floor of the building. Indeed I must have worked there for at least five solar cycles, perhaps ten. I recalled feeling (in a Bean way) comfortable, confident, knowledgeable, yet there was no tangible joy as such in my repetitive light-darkly existence. Bizarrely, on reflection, I associated my existence at that time with a form of death. If I had a 'calling' it was being denied to me, but I knew the world in which I lived. In other words, I knew nothing.

I do recall the reports of a type of, what the Beans called, a 'plague'. The Bean authorities were floundering and, in hindsight, wholly unprepared. The 'inevitable' is a child of hindsight.

It was said that urban office Beans were particularly susceptible to the plague for all the obvious reasons. The initial transmission was through close contact, so those in enclosed spaces were susceptible. When a Muter was spotted, streets and nearby buildings were locked down. Sirens announced the arrival of the Cloth-Heads (at that time Rubber Beans were a twinkle in the eye of the Ill-Suited Beans).

Beans were compliant because they were accepting of the authorities' line on survival and safety. After all, they did not wish to contract the plague, fall ill and rest. (Why embrace destiny when there are hieroglyphs to review and sort?)

I recalled looking down at a commotion in the street below and being grateful for the break from the computer device and its flickering hieroglyphs. The commotion in the street below had been prompted by the arrival of a freshly-risen Muter. The Cloth-Heads, with firing devices at the ready, were closing in on the pioneer – one in the infancy of learning. It was the early light-darks when there was no actual firing of their devices by the Cloth-Heads 'unless absolutely necessary'. Apparently, the Ethical Beans had a hold on Beankind (promulgated by the Bean-Boxers no doubt) and were sailing the high seas of indignation and boarding any incident, raising a flag and claiming it as their own. Pirates of the plague. Thus it was that this was a time of shouting Cloth-Heads and the slow careful acquisition of the Muter in readiness for custody, care or reassignment. Not like now. At that time Muters were unusual enough to attract a crowd rather than create a stampede. In the previous lunar cycles there had been similar incidents in surrounding streets, but this was the first time a Muter had been spotted on our street. An announcement over the building's tannoy asked all employees to remain indoors. It was late afternoon and I had no intention of being stuck in a locked-down building as the great orb sank lower in the great blue. I had Bean plans. Therefore, before all doors were locked, I skipped down the emergency stairwell (never locked owing to Beans' obsession with regulations) and slipped out of the back door into the alley behind the office building.

Emerging from the doorway I learnt that the Cloth-Head operation was far larger than I had anticipated. The fire door clicked shut behind me preventing any retreat back inside the building. There were at least two, possibly three, Muters in the immediate vicinity of the building. The Cloth-Heads in attendance did not have enough Bean-power to manage the situation safely according to their strict protocol. Individual Cloth-Heads were unclear about the rules of engagement – they were facing unarmed Muters stuffed full of Bean rights.

Finding myself halfway down the alley (possibly too tight a space through which to squeeze a vehicle) there was, to my left, a

Muter thirty yards away, with her back to me, being harassed by the Cloth-Heads. To my right my route was blocked forty yards away by another Muter. As I was assessing my options I heard shouts and turned to see the first Muter lumbering towards me with a confused look on her face. Or what I took to be a confused look at the time.

Considering it was the early light-darks, I was relatively sympathetic to the plight of the deceased. I had been raised in a society that had a habit of frowning on its own history of harassing and expelling the sick, disfigured, unbalanced, diseased and dispossessed and here was the perfect embodiment of all such ailments and predicaments stumbling towards me. I too had been suckered into the view that we must not turn them away. Prophets embraced lepers, the least a modern society could do, would be to show some regard for the dead. The irony and my blissful ignorance still strikes me to this light-dark.

As I stood my ground looking at the creature stumbling towards me I tried to read its expression to find that I could not: it had no real expression. Its facial muscles were fallen, grey and green. I searched for the existence she had lived before the bite. Had she been attractive? Desired? Lusted after? Who knew? It was a distant memory lost in the rotting grey matter in the skull matted with blonde hair and a flapping scalp. Even now, in my now lucid state, I remember thinking the filth and dirt was something I was unaccustomed to whilst simultaneously thinking that any such observation was irrelevant. She was a corpse. It was the last time I saw my future from the other side.

The Cloth-Heads shouted, breaking me from my musings. Still believing she was no threat to me I took one or two steps back, but obviously not fast enough for the shouting Cloth-Heads. She stumbled towards me. I instinctively held out my hand to stop her entering my personal space. In that same moment she grabbed my hand, pulled it to her mouth and sunk her teeth into it. A moment later the Muter's head exploded from the short bursts of hot metal pellets from a firing device. I was showered in dust and debris from the mortar exploding from the wall behind me, but more importantly the flesh and grey matter of the target herself entered my mouth, eyes and nose. My ears were pounding, my eyes full of dust and grime and my skin wet from the fluids ejected from the falling corpse. I heard footsteps of the Cloth-Heads racing up to me as I fell back to the ground.

The dark cycle that followed remains hazy. I was taken to a big white building, cleaned up, debriefed and shouted at by the Cloth-Heads.

Discharged in the middle of the dark cycle I found myself exiting the building at a time of another young lady Bean. We exchanged pleasantries and stories of how we had come to be there. She seemed intrigued by my story.

'Wow, actually seeing a plague-infected thing up close, what was it like?'

I shook my head and withheld all the necessary information tantalisingly enough to secure an agreement to go for liquid refreshment whereupon I would share all (possibly to induce desire to make the Bean double-backed beast with her). Go for liquid refreshment we did, but, truth be told, I was feeling slightly odd. Woozy. Tiredness, I thought.

We left the bar and strolled along the dark street into further darkness, which prompted her to cling tightly to my arm. We stopped. The lady Bean looked at me and took a step backwards into a darkened doorway. Understanding the Bean ritual of pre-beasting, I took a step forward. She took another step back and I followed her still. Soon she was deep in the shadow of a shop doorway. I stepped forward to join the lady Bean and as I did so, I saw a flash of light coming towards me. It wasn't her face, it was the broken, pale face of another. Before I could comprehend what was happening, I felt teeth sink into my neck and rip away a mouthful of flesh. My flesh. I swayed and felt myself being pulled into the shadows and felt the lady Bean's body pressed softly against me as it was itself being pushed from behind by another violent alien force. I was pulled forward again as the creature bit harder and deeper into my flesh and face. I felt wetness everywhere and nothing else. My last moments as a breathing Bean was seeing the rotten flesh of a female Muter. I had had my kiss. And there I was conceived – in a dark doorway in a three-way clutch of fresh and rotting bodies. As the weak light of the Bean existence faded I noted that I always knew a female would be the death of me.

After that, I don't know what happened. The next thing I knew was 'coming to' confused, but enlightened, in a pile of Has-Beans in a city dump south of the Black Road running through the larger dump, the metropolis. The rest, as you know, is death.

41. Unfinished Business and the Complete Plot

I left my former Bean workplace leaving the Has-Bean ('TheLastContender') resting. He had struggled a little, but soon realised that he himself did not know what he was struggling for. I pitied him. To relieve him of the pain and anguish was the right thing to do. His pleading was typical. He needed time to make his mark (whatever that means), because existence in the metropolis 'was difficult'.

As for myself, I had one final visit to make. Not too far away.

As I strolled about the metropolis the heated air (generated by the fires found at every turn) swirled around the streets mixing with the breath of panting, fearful Beans racing back and forth. It was a heady mix indeed and made Muters delirious with desire. I had delayed making this visit to my target building partly because it was tricky (centrally located, well-populated) and I was uncertain of my motivation. I eventually concluded that it was related to my own unfinished business. But not just my own business, it was Pearl's too. In fact, Pearl had initiated and pressed for this visit. I suppose in the early light-darks I had not immediately addressed my own unfinished business because there was no one there to guide and mentor me. But now I had an army of my own who was there for me and would help. The location had been secured and made safe for death by many of my closest colleagues.

The walk to the place in question induced memories of the anxious, fractious journey I had taken there as Nigel-Bean. Anxiety borne of fear of change and, funnily enough, fear of death.

And now here I was, walking the same route but wholly liberated. I felt a fool for fearing destiny.

I turned one corner, then another, then another until I reached the large building itself. Its grand entrance once welcomed vehicles with their flashing lights carrying weak Beans. Now, its entrance was broken and open. It was a place built to resist destiny. A place where Beans hide from (and fight against) the loving embrace of the light. A temple to folly. Fortunately, some Beans do triumph and do find the pleasures and treasures that await; treasures once found, are never relinquished. Yet, for their shame, other Beans struggled on in denial.

Although I had scouted this place many times, I was now able to walk in through the front door. I could smell Beans in the building, but they were few in number and were not protected by the Rubber Beans who were engaged elsewhere. This temple was not worth protecting. (Not like the structure housing leader-Beans I had visited the previous light-dark.)

I walked past weak Beans lying gasping for death on beds. I took pity on them and shared the lightest of kisses with many of them. They would soon join us in peace, strength and eternity. At other times I saw the white-robed Beans dispatching the sick Beans with knives, saws and firing devices. The robed Beans had finally understood the futility of their fight. How pleasing.

Beans once thought the planet was the centre of the universe, even the great orb of the sky regularly heaved itself across the great heavens to gaze fondly on their achievements. But now they had slowly learnt of their irrelevance and place in the cosmos; yet even now many still clung to things that gave their existence meaning. Their self-absorption was relentless.

It is only in death that their story is written. It is only in death that their potential is revealed. The stories that would be begun that very dark cycle of the Great Handover would resound for eternity – for far longer than the number of summers of existence endured.

Whether it is a self-pitying existence or a hopeful existence, the story begins at death. One of my early bites, Plot, illustrates this. She achieved meaninglessness in her twenty-something summers even though she was a true Bean ignorhoper. But in death her contribution to the Great Handover would be groundbreaking, quite literally.

I had met and kissed Plot in my early lunar cycles. Acclimatising to my role and receiving a little too much unwanted attention from the Cloth-Heads, I had taken refuge in a parkland area above the metropolis. I could lose myself amidst the quiet fields of the trees, grass and stones away from agitated Beans. These fields were places where I had re-acquired a few Has-Beans of mine (such as BroadBean). Not only could I safely pick-up new-borns from their resting places, but I could also acquire the odd fresh Bean who would visit these gardens and talk to a resting Has-Bean. They would bring flowers and gifts and weep for the buried Bean that cared for them no more. It was a place for me to learn of desperation and futility. I would listen to the grieving Beans as they shared the ignorance of their existence with a pile of rotted flesh deaf to their pleas. If I were being generous I might say the Beans visited such fields of Has-Beans to share and seek guidance from those who were better placed to advise.

As one particular light cycle was coming to a close I came across two lady Beans (of perhaps twenty summers each) sitting on a bench, quietly talking. The lady Beans seemed unhappy. Or rather, one of them did. They were undetermined about their Bean existence. I had wondered whether they might have been ready to opt for a brighter future, like RooftopSuicide. As I was wont to do at that stage, I paused downwind in the shadows and listened, trying to ascertain their readiness as I waited for the parkland to fall into darkness.

'It's too much,' one Bean ('Carey' Bean) had said as she sat down on the bench. 'I'm a fraud.'

'We all feel like a fraud,' her friend ('Freya' Bean) replied, joining her on the bench.

'Why can't it be easy?' Carey-Bean whimpered. 'Sometimes when I walk about London I feel empowered – that I am at the centre of things. This place,' she said waving at the skyline of the city, 'will help me to realise my dream, my potential'.

'And it will,' replied Freya-Bean lovingly.

'But sometimes I feel the opposite, so overwhelmed,' Carey-Bean continued. 'How can I reach, achieve anything in a place that is teeming with so many people? I am a fleck of dust in the scheme of things and even as a fleck of dust I feel I am taking up too much space. If I just lay down here in this cemetery, no one would notice. The world and everybody in it would all just carry on as normal; my whole existence brushed off like dandruff and forgotten.'

'Don't say that. That's an awful thing to say,' Freya-Bean said. 'I would definitely miss you.'

'Yeah, but you would go into the office the next day. You would still be texting Duncan. Who knows, it might bring you two closer together.'

'Don't say that,' replied Freya-Bean, aghast.

'But it is true,' cried Carey-Bean. 'There might be a little part of you that was glad that my not being here somehow did bring you two closer together.'

'Carey!' Freya-Bean protested.

'If I were buried here, would you visit me?'

'Of course, I visit my mother,' Freya-Bean replied, nodding towards a patch of cold earth a dozen yards away. 'Mum bought the grave next to her for me, so that we could lie together side by side forever one day. Anyway, you can't let life get you down. Take it one day at a time.'

'But I just don't see the point. Everything is illogical. Life is illogical. Any hope you have is overwhelmed by everything else. Even if you get what you want, you end up losing it or wanting something else.'

'Carey,' Freya-Bean protested again, warmly.

'But it is true, isn't it?'

'But all you can do is try. Try your best,' said Freya-Bean. 'Try to live a life without regrets.'

Freya-Bean seemed bored with the Bean-friend-Carey's whinging and was keen to move things on.

'Shall we get out of here?' Freya-Bean said. 'It's depressing being around death. Let's go to the Marmaduke.'

'I thought you were meeting Duncan?' asked Carey-Bean unenthusiastically.

'We can both meet him,' said Freya-Bean, keen to get away having paid her respects to her mother. 'You like him, don't you?'

Sad Carey-Bean gave her friend a blank look.

'Okay,' her friend said, presumably reading the facial expression (which was beyond me), 'I'll put him off. We'll go to the Marmaduke. Maybe meet him later.'

With that, the Sad Carey-Bean rose to her feet and walked off into the encroaching darkness while her friend Freya-Bean remained seated on the bench typing furiously away on her telephonic communication device.

I was curious. (And a little peckish.) They both smelt good in their different ways. Would Carey-Bean change her mind and conclude she had a reason to delay her destiny? Or was she, like Rooftop (and later, ParkBench), indeed inclined to answer its call without my intervention? As I watched Carey-Bean retreat into the blackness towards the metropolis illumination and as her perfume, carried on the lightest of breezes, receded, I felt torn between the two.

Freya-Bean was still riveted to her telephonic communication device and oozing the sweeter aromas of the happier Bean. So, in fact, there was no contest. Freya-Bean was not going to meet her love interest, Duncan, in her current form. As I crept up on her from behind she would not have known that she was breathing her last. But do any Beans know when the countdown of their last ten breaths start? I suspect not.

I picked her up and carried her deeper into the darkness of the field of Has-Beans, biting and drinking her juices. I was gentle and considerate and feasted with care. I wanted to preserve her mobility. I placed her remains on the burial plot beside her mother-Has-Bean. Being the relatively early light-darks (and before the excitability of the Bean authorities), I suspected they would follow her wishes and bury her in the adjacent plot. I could return later to be there for her rising.

However, Sad Carey-Bean's misery about her own existence and her hopes for her destiny were not lost on me. I kept Freya-Bean's (that is Plot-elect's) telephonic communication device believing it might help with her unfinished business (perhaps with Sad-Carey-Bean?) at a later date.

I returned to the field on a number of occasions to monitor Plot-elect's progress. Indeed, she had been buried a handful of light-darks after my kiss. After a further handful of light-darks I noted stirring in the earth of her burial plot. As is usual with GroundBreakers, Plot took her time to work her way through the soil, but soon I was able to detect aromas and disturbances. Eventually, first the hand, then another hand, then an elbow, then another, then the head and finally her upper body. She was dressed in an evening gown now deeply soiled from the journey from her buried wooden box. On arrival into the failing light she was, of course, in a state of confusion. I pulled her from the ground and, hearing voices approaching, reorganised the earth to disguise the evidence of her rising.

I escorted Plot to a secluded spot two dozen steps away, under the tree and out of sight. The voices continued to approach. I watched intently as a male Bean and a lady Bean emerged from the darkness and came to a stop by Plot's former resting place. I recognised the Bean aroma of the female – Sad-Carey-Bean. Plot's Bean friend.

The male Bean and Carey-Bean spoke in hushed voices, but moving closer and, courtesy of a kind wind, the words carried to both Plot and me.

'I miss her,' the Sad-Carey-Bean said softly to the male Bean beside her.

'So, do I. It's so weird,' the male Bean replied.

'Life is short. I can't believe the last conversation we had. I was so selfish.'

'You weren't to know, Carey.'

'I still feel bad.'

'Don't worry,' the male Bean said, slipping his arm around her shoulders and pulling Carey-Bean close to his body.

'I'm scared,' she whimpered.

'Me too,' he whispered in reply.

'Do you think this sickness will spread?'

'What do you mean?'

'Someone told me that Freya was taken by a zombie thing,' Sad-Cary-Bean whimpered pathetically.

'No, of course not. It's just a bit of weird flu. It'll pass. '

'Are you sure?'

'Absolutely. These things do.'

'Don't leave me.'

'I'm not going anywhere,' he said.

'I mean it, Duncan.'

'So do I,' he replied, planting a kiss on Sad-Carey-Bean's lips. 'Shall we go?'

'Yes,' she said, turning away from Plot's former resting place. 'To the Marmaduke?'

'Yes,' he said nodding, 'where it's nice and warm.'

And with that they turned and disappeared into the darkness.

I turned and looked at Plot. Her gaze was fixed on her former friend (Sad-Carey-Bean) and Duncan-Bean, her former beau. She looked confused. I was unsure whether this could be attributed to the usual confusion of the newly-risen Muter or over the events she had just witnessed. If so, it could prove useful.

I handed Plot her telephonic communication device thinking it might play a role in her early light-darks as a Muter, allowing her to reconnect with her previous meaningless existence (with Sad-Carey-Bean, among others). Of course, it would have been a pleasure to introduce Sad-Carey-Bean to destiny myself, but I was curious how the light-darks spent in a field of rest impacted a Has-Bean's development and death skills. It might be the case that Plot herself wished to kiss her former friend and her former Bean companion (Duncan-Bean) once she had gathered her Muter senses.

Later, on witnessing Plot's resolve of kissing both Sad-Carey-Bean and Duncan-Bean, I could only assume that they might have formed part of Plot's unfinished business. The male-Duncan-Bean became LiplessMuck. Carey-Bean became FlowerToss and was lost in a street party raided by Rubber Beans in another part of the metropolis a few lunar cycles later.

I reflected on events surrounding Plot's enlightenment as I climbed the stairs through the Temple of Destiny building. Sad-Carey-Bean had vacillated and, as a result, had become less effective in death. Plot had had plans, hopes and expectations of a bright, exciting Bean existence, but had embraced the opportunities afforded by death when it arrived unexpectedly.

One often hears Beans talk of regrets. They then seek to avoid regret by taking action. Yet regret is banished in death, for an eternity, so many of the actions taken during a Bean's existence have no purpose. They are based upon an irrational need. If Beans knew this, there would be no fuss, no debate, no whining.

I reached the top of the stairs and soon reached an eating area that led to a roof garden space overlooking the city. A metropolis in its death throes was a joy to behold. In the ever-changing illumination of the faltering electrical lamps, the multitudinous flames and, of course, sudden bright explosions of light generated by the Merry Green Beans' greenwitchery, the metropolis twinkled and shimmered in a great goodbye. The illumination show was complemented by the symphony of sounds – crackling fires, booms, sharp cracks of firing devices and, of course, the Bean screams as they echoed about the buildings and neighbourhoods. Some parts of the metropolis had grown dark and quiet – no doubt successfully claimed by my colleagues hard at work. In time the darkness would claim the whole of the marsh farm. Muters had no need for artificial illumination. The remaining power units giving juice to the metropolis would soon die.

I waited and looked across the view possibly for the last time. Not only was it a familiar sight to me, but it had been a familiar sight to Nigel-Bean. During my pitiful Bean existence I had spent many, many light-darks on this rooftop. It was beginning to fall into place. I had a buried memory of this rooftop, this view. This was indeed my unfinished business.

This was not my bite. It was Pearl's. She and Chubby and Diesel and others had arrived earlier in the dark cycle. It was understood I would be met on the roof. My place of places.

Moments passed and I heard noises behind me. I turned to see Diesel dragging the Bean target oozing juice over his familiar white robe. Behind him followed Pearl holding Chubby's hand. Others also joined us on the rooftop. There was my first colleague,

RooftopSuicide, who I had met on an entirely different rooftop many lunar cycles earlier. I had been there for him. Now he was here for me. DoorStop, PlumpCalf, ColourSplash and FatLegs (never far away from his beloved Chubby Cheeks). Tarmac joined us, as did BroadBean, Chain-and-Stiks and BeanPole, Diesel and GlassCutter. All the old, decaying faces. In fact, I suppose I had been there for them all, and now they wanted to be here for me.

I looked down at the half-conscious Bean. It was a face I recognised. I lifted him to his feet and held him up by his neck. I wanted him to open his eyes. My features had changed since my death, but there should be enough left for him to recognise me. The rooftop setting probably helped too. After all, I was standing on the spot where he had so often found me as a Bean.

I shook him and slapped him. His eyes opened and he struggled to look at me. He was gurgling on his own juice. Not that I ever doubted myself, but in that moment I thanked the Creator, any Creator, for the invention of death. (Or should I have cursed the Creator for the invention of existence?) Arguably 'Life' was an experiment gone wrong and we should thank the lucky stars it had been kept to such a brief time-span. There is an unrelenting honesty in death. Beanhood is full of deceit, platitudes, self-interest and self-absorption, malice, complacency, delusion and illusion. Death sweeps them all away. All one is left with is honesty, transparency, clarity. All wrapped up in a bow of timelessness. There really is justice in death.

That said. I felt no hate. Just pity. Should he rise, he would have learnt the errors of his ways. In some respects I felt I could punish him. I could let him continue to live as a Bean for many summers. But death is forgiving. I offered him to Pearl. She stepped forward and bit gently into his neck and drank a little, enough for him to open his eyes. They exhibited a pitiful fear, yet I could see the recognition in his eyes and he tried to mouth my name. The Bean name he would have known for me. His body began to quake. I picked him up, walked to the edge of the roof and selected a spot high above a smashed and burning automobilic vehicle. And with a heave I threw the Bean off the roof and watched him fall into the claws of the burning, twisted metal. He would be sliced, but not wholly incinerated; though enough to act as a reminder. These things come full circle. Perhaps I would retrieve him when I exited the building and let his charred remains cool in safety.

It was not the end. It was the beginning. There were many to attend to. So many Muters would be rising in the coming light-darks. They would need to be guided as we worked our way through the remaining Beans. I was not the leader. There would be others who would come. Brothers-in-arms. Perhaps I had met them already. Those more meek than I. They would inherit the earth. My business here was done.

42. The Meaning of Bean

On reflection it all came together so easily. I suppose that is how destiny works in (and at) the end. It's a hidden beast that races towards you while you run to meet it not knowing the beast's form until it finally breaches the horizon, both bathing and crushing you in enlightenment.

How things have changed from my time wandering the rooftops of the metropolis by myself. I have enlightened many who had struggled as Beans – losers who struggled to make sense of their own Beanhood whether it be the restlessness of Chain-and-Stiks, BeanPole, TarmacTired; the listlessness of PlumpCalf, Diesel; the neglect yet potential of DoorStop and GlassCutter. Then, of course, there was the sheer brilliance of ChubbyCheeks wholly overlooked and patronised by her Bean-forebears. If Chubby had continued on her Beanpath she might never have flourished. She might have sought meaning in an existence based around designing the interiors of structures or the cut of rags to dress decaying flesh. And when the emptiness of her existence overwhelmed her spirit and death welcomed her, the absence of death skills would be, in Bean terms, criminal.

I am proud to report that all my niblings have gone on to develop their own specialties utilising their death skills to the full, whether it be focusing on boxes of Errant Beans, farm structures, or the generation of Beanlings and MuterBeasts. Moreover, all had addressed their unfinished business. Together we came shamelessly into our own. There is only community in death; a community where each and every newcomer is truly welcome.

The 'meaning of life' is a contradiction in terms. The Beans try to exclude death from all of their deliberations, it is a mistake. Death is their destiny. Destiny is not transitory. Death is final, eternal. Meaning is found in destiny. The meaning of Bean is death. What Beans experience is 'existence'. Yet what is 'existence'? Nothing but an accumulation of summers, a collection of protocols and the veneration of procedures. It is an anecdote at best. These Bean's frailties create unfinished business, all of which are left to death to resolve.

I had never worried for Beankind, the emptiness would pass for each sufferer – one hopes within two-dozen summers, or thirty, or forty. At worst it would drag on for eighty summers, but an eternity of bliss and enlightenment was always promised.

Beans had always known it was to come. It had been written in the stories and myths of old. Ancient Bean societies had only delayed the inevitable. The modern Bean in his complacency had ignored the signs, ignored the writings, dismissing them as foolish. The story had come in many forms but all had the same ending. Appropriated by writers and artists alike, the story is one and the same. Only the names change. It has been told since the beginning of time. The Great Handover was always going to happen. Deep in the Bean it has always been known, but did the 'modern' Bean heed the message? No.

And so, on this light-dark I open the door to you, reader. Eternity has come. My job is almost done. If there is a Bean crouched somewhere struggling with what has come to pass, think of me, my words. Imagine me standing quietly behind you, whispering sweet nothings in your ear. Whether I kiss you tenderly that moment, that dark cycle, or during one light-dark to come, I do not know. But I shall let you ponder, reflect on the barren nature of your existence as you prepare for my embrace. Do not be fooled by the witterings of your fellow Beans, for they know nothing. When we meet they too will be cleansed of their 'knowledge'. Thank you for reading these words. My name was Nigel.

After the Temple of Folly I wandered the streets of the metropolis with my close colleagues and CurserBe. It was turning into a street party indeed. I had never anticipated the Great Handover would be so momentous. We laughed and smiled and kissed and hugged Beans alike. Yet still many Beans ran up to us requesting assistance. If they did not race into our arms screaming they could be found, shy, cowering in the shadows. It was the first moment we could truly walk the streets freely.

CurserBe feasted on all flesh that moved. If death were a beast it would be my loyal companion. He guarded these lands. No Bean would escape him. Such was the MuterBeast's power and loyalty to death, no Bean could resist. If death had a sound, it was the bellow of the cursed one – CurserBe's roars echoed around the dark metropolis, like a thunderous bell ringing for the end of the o'clock. Of course, there were little skirmishes with Merry Green Beans, but, as the great orb hinted at breaking the hard blackness, the battle took a turn. I had no doubt as to why. Plot had returned, leading the armies of GroundBreakers from the fields of rest. All Beans were overwhelmed at the sight of those whom the Beans had been foolish enough to lay in the earth intact. One cannot blame them for their ignorance, after all, it was meant to be – deep down the Beans knew they were responding to the unspoken need.

We headed to the Black Road. We relished the sights of my colleagues tossing Beans into the fire. Even the Black Road itself had risen to the occasion holding raging fires on its surface. Those Beans who had headed to the Black Road in hopes of escape, found themselves tossed off the walkways into flame.

I stepped onto the bridge crossing the blackness near the Bean's great monuments to leadership and futility. I surveyed broken bridges, broken structures – brick, glass and wheel – and the raging flames on land and liquid. The howls of the remaining despairing Beans grew as Plot's armies marched through them to a triumphant beat. As dawn broke, so had a new eternal age. A kingdom of the ages.

Almost in the quietness of that moment, I saw approach from the other side of the bridge, the familiar hooded figure of Chain-and-Stiks. She was leading a fresh Muter. I recognised him instantly – Call-Me-Josh. With his scraggly facial hair, he was still dressed in his white robe, with the wires that had held him down still about his head. He too had risen and looked fine. Stiks brought him before me and I gazed upon his serenity. He was indeed at peace. I embraced him as my brother. He surveyed the Black Road below him. It was his. He would indeed live for eternity by its liquid blackness. He should be proud, his work had brought us here.

Moments later, I felt Chubby's presence at my side. She touched my hand. I turned. She had brought another freshly risen Muter – a Bean whom she had found in the place of waste paper. He looked wise. For all the sitting and pen-scribing he had done in the athenaeum, it had come to nothing. Only now he understood. I knew that he meant much to Chubby. No doubt an element of unfinished business for her had been addressed that dark cycle. Such a nibling for Chubby was a true colleague of mine. I took him as my brother also.

And there we were. My old colleagues, my trusted companion CurserBe and my new brothers, MasteroftheBlackRoad and AthenaeumScribe. Flanked by Chubby and Pearl, I stood and watched as the metropolis illumination flickered and died, only for the dump to be illumined by the reassuring power of fire on land, on liquid and in sky. For what was to come, was hinted in the brightening blueness – the great orb beast that would rise above the horizon, devour the darkness and bear witness to a new and eternal kingdom – our shared and common Deathstiny.

END

[Nigel: Parts II and III to follow]

Cast of Colleagues
(in order of appearance)

28. SwapShop; SugarRush; SimplyFine; TyreTreads

29. LoveHurts; [Call-Me-Josh]

30. Dunky & Smashy

32. Right-to-Life

33. GenerationManager; GenerationMe

34. HappyCampers

35. WhiteTeeth

36. (Ill-Suited Beans) VanPlumpy; CurserBe (MuterBeasts)

38. ClearGreenOne; ClearGreenFive

39./41. TheLastContender

41. Plot; FlowerToss; LiplessMuck

42. MasteroftheBlackRoad; AtheneumScribe

David O. Zeus

Acknowledgements

Acknowledgements

Many people, including DMAG, AFG and family, PJB for reading. Thanks also to Michael Hensley for allowing me to reproduce the cover illustration here; the illustration itself has been a source of inspiration for Nigel over the solar cycles as this book took shape.

Cover illustration (and on inside page) by Michael Hensley, reproduced here with his kind permission. Illustration Copyright © Michael Hensley. See Michael's websites for details and his other work:

www.michaelhensley.art
www.artistanatomy.com
www.michaelmhensley.com

Cover design by Liliana Resende:
https://lilresende.wixsite.com/work

About the Author

Born in the UK, David O. Zeus was tutored at the Old Granville House School before having a short spell at university, after which he joined the army (11th Hussars) where he saw action at the Battle of the Hornburg. While recuperating from his injuries on the remote island of Nomanisan he began writing. He is married to Donna Mullenger and lives for most of the year in the place of his birth, Little Hintock.

www.davidozeus.uk

Found on Twitter, Facebook & YouTube Channel as 'DavidOZeus'

Available Titles

Collected Stories – Volume I
Collected Stories – Volume II

Upcoming Titles

Collected Stories – Volume III
Collected Stories – Volume IV
Nigel (Parts II and III)

Collected Stories: Volume One

The seven stories enclosed in this first volume are:

The Legend of Muam Tam Say: An encounter with an ancient wonder of the natural world in the shadows of the Himalayas; a short extract from the diaries of a young soldier on the eve of the First World War describes the impact of the 'natural wonder' on the young soldier.

The Dot Matrix: A young man re-evaluates his office-bound existence when he comes across the printout musings of an old dot matrix printer.

Scary Afternoon in the Garden: An eleven year old boy describes his encounter with the 'creatures from the woods' when they visit his garden one really, really, scary afternoon.

The Florin Smile: A meteor shower brings a new chemical compound to earth resulting in a change to some people's smile and changes the way people assess (and assign) value in modern society.

Parked in a Ditch: 'The course of true love ne'er did run smooth for a middle-aged, middle manager stuck in the mire of administration.' The planning (and execution) of Plans 'A' through to 'G' of a office-bound, wannabe romantic.

Fear of Lions: A doting uncle offers advice to his niece on how to confront her fears...and deals with the unhappy aftermath.

The Totty Boat: A grumpy uncle writes a letter to his young nephew offering advice on the stuff that matters.

Collected Stories: Volume Two

The seven stories enclosed in this second volume are:

Foggy Love Bottom – a story of love and loss set in a little village with a peculiar name and history.

In ***Scary Morning in the Woods****,* the garden attack (as described in *Scary Afternoon in the Garden)* leads the townsfolk to nervously take the fight to the creatures in the woods.

In ***I'm Not Matt Damon*** a lone human being, Duncan Sheldrake, is recreated by aliens (after the destruction of planet earth) in their mistaken belief that he was once the great leader of humanity and finest representative of life on earth – Matt Damon.

The Elephant of Marrakech – a man retraces his steps to Marrakech to 'find the elephant' and make the decision he should have done seven years earlier.

Book of Giants: Journal 9 – a survivor's journal written eighteen months after an apocalyptic solar flare led to the disintegration of society and the re-emergence of ancient giants.

Sack Truck – a man loses his job as a result of the perfect storm of a confused memory (of a *Viz* comic character) and the fast-changing social mores of the modern world, all prompted by an innocent reference to a 'sack truck'.

A Life's Work – a 100 year old New York mob-boss is released from prison after 50 years and is given the opportunity to reflect on his life as a gangster.

Printed in Great Britain
by Amazon

23683444R00182